AT PASSION'S TIDE

Also by Pamela Windsor
Rebel's Rapture
Forsaking All Others

AT PASSION'S TIDE

PAMELA WINDSOR

CUTTING EDGE

ISBN-13: 978-1-957868-37-0

Published by
Cutting Edge Books
PO Box 8212
Calabasas, CA 91372
www.cuttingedgebooks.com

AT PASSION'S TIDE

PROLOGUE

I t was a seed time, a time when new concepts, new ideas, and new directions came into being. It was a time of growth, of development, a seminal epoch of culture and conflict, of men and manners, and of vast dynasties founded and lost and made again. It was an epoch of ferment, a climate that has carried to this very day. It was the last half of the nineteenth century.

Not since the renaissance had there been such an explosion of intellectual, creative, and physical energy. In Italy, Marconi was at work finishing his wireless telegraph. Darwin had published his theories of natural selection and the Augustinian monk Gregor Mendel had blueprinted his laws of heredity. Karl Marx, Nietzsche, and Schopenhauer were polishing their plans for a new order of things and on the Left Bank in Paris, Degas, Monet, Seurat, and Renoir were pioneering new techniques in painting. In the world of fashion, the last half of the nineteenth century saw the introduction of synthetic dyes and the beginnings of mass-produced footwear and clothing. The hoop skirt came into vogue for formal and semiformal wear and some said that its cage of flexible metal strips was inspired by the network of iron hoops that the English architect Paxton designed for the famous Crystal Palace in Hyde Park.

Everywhere it was a throbbing, vital time and nowhere was this more true than in the world of commerce. There, vast fortunes and great dynasties were being built by men who were part rugged individualists, part robber-barons, and part gamblers, men who combined great vision with even greater ruthlessness.

Among these were the great shipping merchant families, those dynasties of trade that stretched around the world and were the very lifeline of progress. It was their mighty fleets that opened the doors of nations and many of their names carry to this very day: Furness, Grace, Matson, Cunard, Munson, McCormick.

This was a world that moved from continent to continent, from packets to parlors, from grimy waterfronts to grand mansions. To the great merchant tycoons, speed was the all-important factor in building their empires of trade; in the last half of the nineteenth century, the key to speed was the mighty clipper ship. Competition was fierce, for trade routes, captains, crews. Success or failure literally hung on the wind, the turn of a sail, and the cut of a hull. The choicest of plums was the Atlantic run where the growing, bustling, wakening giant that was America absorbed raw materials and raw people as a sponge absorbs water. On this vast and turbulent highway, the sinews of a new land were carried from shore to shore.

Yet this throbbing era was often self-contradictory. It was a strange admixture, intellectual and material expansion combined with Victorian rigidity. The past held the future tightly within its grasp, as a cocoon imprisons a butterfly. The era made exacting demands on those torn between tomorrow's promises and yesterday's rules. This is the story of a young woman who learned there was but one answer to a new world full of old demands, to seize the floodtide of her feelings. It is the story of inner and outer promises and an era in which today was born.

CHAPTER ONE

Everything's the same, the girl murmured to herself, even the mist rolling in from the water, letting you see only a dozen yards ahead. The surf was a remembered sound, a soft thunder special to the Cornwall shore. And the salt-smelling wind, the milk-white cliffs back from the beach, the great rocks that rose up from the water's edge, all utterly unchanged. The girl felt grateful for that as her horse tossed his head, moved on along the beach. The value of constancy, she pondered, was it only appreciated out of pain?

She drew a deep breath as the tall, gray stallion carried her along the firmly packed sand. It had always been her favorite place, this wild stretch of the Cornish coast, especially now, in the early morning, the beginning time when day crept upon the world. She had said she would never return, but she was back, riding along the beach as she'd done as a little girl. It had been an angry promise bound to shatter. One can't turn away from yesterday any more than from oneself. She had learned that much. Perhaps, she reflected, turning away was always a mistake, just another form of running.

No matter now, Rosaleen Powell told herself. She was here and she reined the stallion to a halt, turned in the saddle to look backward, up to the towering cliffs where Raven's Wing looked out across the coastline, its great Elizabethan turrets and gables stretching skyward, a regal and proud house, stately and warm. Raven's Wing, the girl repeated inwardly, the family home, an inadequate coupling of words for a place that held the secrets of a thousand dreams, tears and fears. Not just a grand mansion, but a seed place that gave shelter, comfort, security, and something more—a sense of oneself. People don't just live in houses, Rosaleen mused as her eyes stayed on the great structure atop the cliffs. It's a kind of exchange, they each take from the other until they come to fit each other. She'd often taken note of how houses were like people. Most were totally undistinguished and some were narrow and drawn-in and mean-looking while others were all surface frippery and still others slab-sided, stiff, and cold. But there were those with dignity and strength, the stuff of character. Raven's Wing had always been such a house, and now it stood like a grand old dowager, full of the richness of memories.

Rosaleen touched reins to the stallion and he moved forward along the beach. She breathed deeply of the bracing air, sat straight-backed in the saddle. She wore a lavender sweater which, though fashioned of heavy wool, did not hide the deep and full swell of her breasts. Those who met Rosaleen for the first time were usually transfixed by her glistening, jet-black hair, cream-white skin, and violet eyes that never completely stopped smoldering, even when they danced with laughter. Only later did they take in the finely edged lips, the thin, straight nose that flared slightly at the nostrils, and the slender, graceful neck. But Rosaleen Powell was no fragile, drawing-room beauty. In her loveliness there was fire and an inner strength that had once been mostly stubbornness. Now it had known the crucible of pain, of tears that deepen the soul as they bind it tight with grief.

As she rode, the mist lifted a little and her eyes swept the stretch of beach, the sandstone cliffs to her left. It was a place of constant beauty, this Cornish coast, sometimes made of flame-red sunset skies and sometimes of unending gray as everything, cliffs, houses, and shorefront, lay under weeping skies or the terrifying beauty of the squalls that swept in from the sea with unexplained battering rage. And always, the ever-present sea birds, the gulls and the gannets, swooping and diving, their cries more mournful than the wail of a lost child.

This place had its own fragrance, the bite of the sea, salt and spray, commingling with the scent of the gorse and the heather, a perfume of openness, no cloying darkness about it. Around the curve of the beach, still shrouded in morning mist, the sandstone cliffs grew into dark-gray basalt, forbidding and awesome, rent with narrow clefts that dropped into hidden wooded glens, sometimes carrying crystal-pure waterfalls with them. Along the base, the shrubbery grew in thick and careless profusion, special, hardy plants that defied the salt of the sea that flung itself into the air to let the wind carry it inland against the cliffs.

Sometimes, Rosaleen remembered, she would come out in the night, hurrying down the road from the moors to the shore, sometimes afoot, sometimes on her mare. On the still nights, the sea was quiet, rippling ashore in small, lace eddies, and a sickle moon hung low. There was an enchantment to the wild shore at those times, and she would stand silently, as if sharing some deep secret with an unknown force.

Rosaleen let a smile touch her lips as she urged the stallion on. Yes, this had been her very special place, this stretch of shore, fit for a young girl to let her wildest imaginings take flight. And she was back now and it felt as if she had never left. The good things are like that, she decided, they don't disappoint or hold back. Rosaleen let her eyes move across the shoreline as the mist lifted further. The stallion's hooves on the sand were a soft rhythm and she watched as the mist continued to shred as the sun took hold of it until it quickly became a huge, tattered scarf hanging in long remnants in the air.

Rosaleen's violet eyes narrowed as she peered ahead. Something was on the beach, half-cloaked in the mist. She rode forward and the mist lifted upward and she saw the dory drawn up on the sand. She frowned. A figure was starting to run from it, a man, making for the base of the cliffs where a line of stunted cedars and a dense growth of lupines hugged the rocks.

She saw the other men suddenly, four of them, running toward the dory. They came from farther up the beach where the mist still lay heavy and they were chasing the lone figure. She saw two try to head him off as he turned to run along the water's edge. He tried to turn and head back again for the cedars, but the other two men were in his path, spreading out to stop him. Rosaleen felt the frown digging into the smoothness of her forehead.

Sometimes the young farm lads came down to the beach to roughhouse and let off energy, especially if they'd spent the night at the taverns in Groat or Bodwin. Still frowning, she saw the fleeing man veer off, gather speed, outdistance the other two as he neared the line of cedars. But the first pair were close, able to cut in sharply, and they caught him just as the others came running up. The mist had lifted and she could see clearly. She heard muffled shouts, saw arms upraised and brought down on the struggling figure in their grasp. Then, in horror, she saw the sheen of a knife blade raised into the air, plunged down. These were no farmhands out to work off their energy.

Rosaleen dug her heels into the stallion's sides and he charged forward at once. "Stop! Stop that!" she cried out, and knew instantly the wind had whipped her voice harmlessly back. The four men, intent on their attack, didn't hear the sound of the stallion's hooves on the wet sand, only looked up as she charged up to them.

"What are you doing there?" she called out. The beaten man lay motionless, face down, and one of the attackers held the red-stained knife in his hand. All four of the men snarled at her out of lined, brutish faces. The nearest one made a guttural sound and leaped forward, seizing the stallion's reins. Rosaleen brought her riding crop around and slashed his knuckles. He let go with a howl of pain. Two of the others started for her and she kicked the stallion forward, saw them sent sprawling like ninepins as the horse bowled into them. She wheeled the stallion around, saw the fourth man, bigger than the others, leap to one side, then dive at her. He brought a heavy hand down on her arm, pulled hard. She felt herself go half off the horse. A club of an arm circled the back of her neck, pulled again, and she came out of the saddle, falling as he staggered back, landing on top of him. She felt his one hand grab her breast and then, the riding crop still in her hands, she brought it up in a short, slashing arc and saw his face spurt crimson as he rolled away with a shout of pain. Two others were coming at her as she lashed out with the crop from one knee. One staggered back, a hand clapped to his forehead, the other twisting away in time to avoid the blow.

Rosaleen leapt onto the stallion, pulled herself into the saddle as the horse wheeled. She started after the fourth man and saw him dive for safety as she thundered by. Reining up, she turned to charge them again but they were running, the big one holding a hand to his face, the hand stained with red. Only their victim lay unmoving on the ground. Rosaleen glanced at the fleeing figures. They had horses around the curve in the beach, no doubt. Her temper raging, she wanted to go after them, run them down, but another glance at the still form on the sand ended the thought. She swung from the saddle, knelt down beside the man, gently turned him over, and felt her lips draw back as she saw the harsh bruises on his face and, more important, the spreading red stain on his shirt. He was a young man, she noted, light-brown hair and even features. She put a hand to his face. He was alive, but unconscious, and badly in need of a doctor.

Rosaleen rose to her feet, brought the stallion closer. She moved behind the young man, got hands under his shoulders and lifted, glad for the strength that was hers. "Easy, boy, easy," she murmured to the stallion as she leaned the unconscious figure against the horse, bent over, got her shoulder under his thighs and lifted. Feeling him go up to fall forward across the horse, she straightened, pushed with her hands until his form was draped across the horse's withers. She swung onto the saddle, wheeled the stallion around, and galloped back along the beach, turning at the road that led, curving, up to the top of the cliffs and Raven's Wing.

The mist was almost completely gone as she reached the house, the sun skipping across the water. The figure draped across the stallion didn't make a sound and Rosaleen, her lips drawing tight, rode the stallion up onto the flagstone terrace, to the tall, oak front door of the house. Yesterdays flashed in her mind again as she leaned down, turned the doorknob, and opened the big door. She'd been fourteen when she'd done this, in a rebellious mood, riding the bay mare, then. She'd ridden the horse into the big living room, thinking her father had already gone for the day. But he'd been in the house and her riding privileges had been taken away for a month. But now she steered the gray stallion into the great room with impunity, reined up beside one of the long sofas still covered with dust-protector white sheets. Rosaleen slid from the saddle, took the stallion's bridle, and turned him until he was against the sofa. She pulled the unconscious form from the horse, lowered it onto the sofa. The white cloth pulled down with the young man's weight, fell to cover his legs as a makeshift blanket.

She made a face as she saw how large the red stain had become. She put her head down near his, and felt the soft warmth of breath on her cheek. He was still alive but he badly needed medical attention. Doc Traynor was ten minutes away, in Bodwin. Rosaleen's eyes softened at the thought of the physician. He was a good man, better than most despite his abrupt, uncompromising ways. She rose, looked down at the silent form, one arm hanging limp, twisted. There was no one to send for Doc Traynor. She'd been alone in the huge house since arriving two days ago, and had rather liked the solitary feel of it, until now. Rosaleen spun on her heel, pulled herself up onto the horse, and sent the stallion moving across the room. She ducked low as he went through the doorway, reached out to catch hold of the edge of the door and send it slamming shut.

The stallion's hooves beat a staccato tattoo on the stones of the terrace as Rosaleen raced from the house. She rode across the field, away from the road to the beach, feeling a surge of pleasure as she took the low, stone wall in one easy leap. It was a sign, and not just of remembered happiness. She galloped down Paddingway Road, thundered past McAlew's farm with its white farmhouse always looking as if it'd just been built. She thought she saw Sarah McAlew behind the long, horizontal window but she kept the horse racing down the road. She thundered into Bodwin, glad that Doc Traynor's office was in the near part of town. Out of the saddle before the stallion halted, she jangled the bell at the door. It opened almost at once, and Freda, doctor's helper for years upon years, stared at her as if she'd returned from the grave. Perhaps she had, after a fashion, Rosaleen thought.

"A man's been badly hurt. Is the doctor here, Freda?" Rosaleen asked. The woman never had a chance to answer, her round face still in shock as the long, narrow-faced figure appeared behind her. He'd grown even thinner, Rosaleen thought. She could see the rush of questions in his eyes but Doc Traynor was a physician first, above all other things.

"Where, Rosaleen?" he asked quietly.

"He's at Raven's Wing. I brought him there from the beach," Rosaleen said.

"Hitch your horse to my rig. I'll get my bag," Doc Traynor said, turning away. Rosaleen stepped back, pulled the stallion to the side of the neat, whitewashed house she had visited at least once a year since a little girl. During daytime hours, Doc Traynor kept his buggy harnessed and ready to go at an instant's notice. A "doctor's wagon," with a large, folding top that gave good protection in any weather, it had forty-eight-inch wheels for high road clearance, a fancy cane-work lower section, and a slat-bottom frame painted with green trim. It was a familiar sight on all the roads of Launcer County at any hour of night or day. She'd just finished tying the horse to the rear of the frame when Doc Traynor appeared, his black hat on, to match his black frock coat and black trousers. He had a way of flapping his arms when he hurried so that he resembled a long-legged crow. She climbed upon the seat of the rig beside him and he sent the horse moving with a quick snap of the reins. Rosaleen sat back silently, deciding to wait. It wasn't a long wait.

"I'd heard someone was at the house," he said.

"Paddy Rowan's delivery boy, of course," Rosaleen said. "He's new and didn't know me when I stopped by for some things."

The long-faced man nodded, gave a quick glance at her. "It's been a long time, Rosaleen," he said. "How many years, now?"

"Enough," Rosaleen said. It hadn't been all that long as some measure time, but to those who count by the heart it had been decades.

"You know that Olivia's near, don't you?" Doc Traynor asked. "She and her new husband have rented Braemore."

Rosaleen's surprise answered him. "I didn't know," she said. Why hadn't Olivia been asked to look after Raven's Wing? The question hung, deserving an answer she couldn't give. *Olivia.* Rosaleen turned her younger sister's name on her lips. There'd never been closeness between them, not even as children. Some said she was jealous of Olivia being her father's favorite. Rosaleen almost snorted aloud. Never jealousy, not in the real meaning of the word. She'd always hated selfishness and manipulativeness and Olivia had always had both. She had her own magic and used it to the fullest. The weak have their own weapons, she had decided in later years. Doc Traynor's voice cut into her leap backward into other days.

"Will you be going to visit Olivia?" he asked.

Rosaleen gave a small shrug of her broad shoulders and her eyes narrowed. "I don't know," she said. "I didn't know she'd married."

"Some six months back, a chap named Anthony Darby," Doc Traynor said. Rosaleen glanced at him. He'd offered the information blandly yet there'd been something in his voice, a controlled evenness.

"You don't care for him," the words slid out.

"I hardly know the man," the answer came. "How long will you be at Raven's Wing, Rosaleen?"

"I don't know that, either," the girl said. Raven's Wing came into view and Doc Traynor's questions took on an impersonal tone of medical inquiry.

"This man, who is he, Rosaleen?" he asked.

"I found him along the beach," Rosaleen said, quickly recounting what had taken place. Doc Traynor was still frowning as the rig drew up to the terrace of the big house. "Thieves? A highwayman's attack?" Rosaleen ventured.

"Rather far from the highway, don't you think?" Doc Traynor countered, fastening a sharp glance at her.

"What then?" Rosaleen asked. "Something personal?"

"Maybe," Doc Traynor said, clambering down from the rig. "Or just about anything. These are troubled times. The French underground is still trying to overthrow the Nationalists. The Turks are preparing for war with the Russians. The Fenians are hard at work stirring up trouble in Ireland. It all washes onto England's shores sooner or later. They all come here looking for support, money, men, ships, or sometimes just to meet somewhere." He shook his head, turned toward the big oaken door. "Well, let's have a look at him, anyway."

Rosaleen untied the stallion, stabled the horse as Doc Traynor went on into Raven's Wing. When she returned to the house, she saw he had the young man's arm in a makeshift splint, the dust sheets torn in strips to hold the splint in place. Working in his shirt-sleeves, Doc Traynor was pulling a wide swath of bandages across the man's chest. She saw the small pile of bloodied clothing on the floor. "He's still unconscious," Rosaleen said.

"Yes, they did a job on him. They were out to finish him."

"Will he live?" Rosaleen asked, looking at the man. "He's quite young."

"That'll help him," the doctor said. "He has a concussion and a nasty chest wound that I've managed to patch for now, plus that broken arm and other assorted wounds and bruises. He ought to be at the hospital at Northcut, but I'd be afraid to move him now."

"I can see to him here, at least till he comes around some," Rosaleen said.

"There's bound to be fever. If it can be kept from rising too high, he'll have a chance. That will mean cold cloths on his head and neck every hour," the doctor said, eying her.

Rosaleen shrugged. "I've really little else to do here for the moment," she said.

Doc Traynor put a small bottle on the table. "Give him a tablespoonful of that every two hours when he comes around. If he comes around," he corrected. "Let me know how he is tomorrow." He took his coat from the chair, slipped it on, and put instruments and jars back into his medicine bag. She walked to the door with him and he paused there, looking down at her solemnly. "It's good to see you at Raven's Wing again, Rosaleen," he said. His voice turned brusque as he added, "It's time you made your peace with the past."

"Let the past make its peace with me," Rosaleen flared at once.

Doc Traynor shook his head. "You're still as headstrong as you are beautiful, Rosaleen Powell," he snapped.

"And you're still as vinegary as you are capable," the young woman returned. She softened her tone to add, "Thanks for coming." Doc Traynor's narrow face seemed to grow narrower. He grunted and strode to his waiting wagon. Rosaleen allowed herself a small smile and returned to the living room. The morning had come and gone, she saw by the tall clock in one corner of the room, a magnificent old piece designed by Vulliamy. She brought a porcelain basin of cold water and cloths from the bath chamber, made compresses and applied them to the young man's bruised face and the back of his neck. He didn't stir, his breathing still a terribly shallow, almost nonexistent thing. She carefully noted the time when she finished, set the basin aside, and decided to pull the dust sheets from the furniture. The great room was transformed at once, no longer a shrouded museum but alive with all its beauty and the strong, echoing furniture that gave character to the walls.

None of the overdelicate, prissy pieces from the studios of the Adams Brothers, she sniffed. Sir Mallory had much preferred the strength and grace of Thomas Sheraton with his dark-toned mahogany inlaid with marquetry of light wood of every sort, and his ingenuity with "harlequin" furniture. Thomas Sheraton's work was one taste she shared with her father, Rosaleen mused. She moved to her favorite piece, a long, deep-toned sideboard which combined grace with solidity, a broad center drawer flanked by two rows of narrower drawers. She reached out, pulled the center drawer open to gaze down at the beautiful serving plates of faïence, a service for twenty-four. They were Rouen dishes, magnificent examples of the *en broderie* manner and entirely worthy of the house of Sir Mallory Powell, founder of the Powell Shipping Lines. Rosaleen ran a finger over the azure edges of the plates, each one an echo of wonderful, festive banquets at the great dining table with her father as gracious host. Sir Mallory never believed in the business of shunting children off by themselves to eat and so, even when little, she and Olivia took part in the lavish dinners, though they were served quickly and excused early. But the moments were taken in, absorbed, lessons in manners, graciousness and taste no course in etiquette could ever match.

Rosaleen closed the drawer and shut off the stream of memories as she heard the sound of the afternoon post outside. She went out to the post box to find two letters, both from Plymouth, applying for the position offered in the *Plymouth Times*. She went back inside, sat down at the writing desk and set up an appointment for each of the applicants, then put the stamped letters back in the post box to be picked up tomorrow. It was time to apply the compresses again, and this time, as she knelt down by the still unconscious figure, she saw the flush on his face, felt the warmth of his forehead. Her lips tightened. The fever had come and she made the compresses as cold as she could. Finished with her nursing, she found wax in the kitchen and began to polish the sideboard, then the other pieces. It was more than an afternoon's work, particularly as it was interrupted each hour to apply the compresses. The fever was higher each time, now, yet he wasn't burning up with it as she had seen some people taken. The compresses were helping. So far, she thought silently.

When the night came to wrap its cold arms around the house, she lighted the fire, a low flame at first so that she could warm some chicken and sauce in a kettle over it. She took a bottle of sherry, an *oscuro* from the Anina district, from the wine cabinet. Sipping it before the fire, she was caressed with warmth from both inside and out. She built the fire higher when she finished, tended to her nursing chores again. He felt feverish, but no more so, and she settled down before the fire, moved to dip into her purse when she heard the movement behind her. She whirled, saw the figure on the sofa stirring, his head turning to the side. She was up in an instant, saw his eyes struggling to open. His lips worked but no sound came from them and he made a futile attempt to sit up. Rosaleen leaned forward and saw his eyes seem to focus. He tried to form words again, his breath coming out in a strangled, gasping sound.

"Tell…tell Coops," she heard him whisper. "Tell Coops…they didn't get it…tell Coops."

The few words were too much and his eyes rolled closed and his chest heaved with each breath. "Your name. Tell me your name," Rosaleen asked, leaning close to him. She put a hand on his arm, moved it gently. "Can you tell me your name?" she tried again.

But he was beyond reaching, eyes closed, but not in the same kind of unconscious coma, she saw. Instead of the shallow half-breaths, he drew deep, full draughts. He was in a deep sleep and she felt his forehead. It had cooled and she rose, fetched a quilt and covered him with it, watched him for a moment. He was sleeping the sleep of the totally exhausted and she turned away, settling down before the fire after putting fresh wood on it. The night wind had come in over the cliffs as always, sweeping against the house in a never-ending contest. She fished into her purse again, brought the letter out and spread it on her lap. She had read it when it came, of course, and acted on it at once. Her father would never have sent it had he not thought it supremely important. Or, she realized, had he any other course. And he knew she would honor it, Rosaleen admitted. He knew her as well as she knew him. The wounds were still there, unchanged by the letter, but Raven's Wing was a love they both shared, rising above all else.

And so she had responded and come back at once, but now she began to read the letter again, this time to let each sentence tear away the years. Words are but the lumber of communication, Rosaleen decided. It is in the unsaid that truth hides. "My dear Rosaleen," he had begun and she'd grown angry at the formality at once, a cutting of its own. But then, she'd realized, a lesser man would have done differently. Sir Mallory would respect the dignity of old angers and she could only accord him grim admiration for that. She let her eyes move to the lines that followed:

> Our lifelong friend and caretaker of Raven's Wing, Patrick Kitchner, has died. That leaves Raven's Wing empty, with no one to see to it at all. There are other

things which events and time dictate I discuss with you
but this unexpected blow is of first importance.

Rosaleen half-smiled, reading the words again, phrases so carefully chosen, saying so much more than the words themselves.
"Time and events" dictated he discuss certain things with her,
the phrase telling her that he was retracting nothing but bowing
to other pressures. She smiled again and read further.

I ask you to go to Raven's Wing, look after the horses
and the house itself, and answer whatever letters may
come in reply to advertisements I have placed. You have
let anger and grief be your life for too long. I trust you
can put them both aside for this.

Rosaleen lifted her eyes from the letter, leaned back against
the solid wing chair. Anger and grief, she mused silently. They
had indeed ruled her for too long, but he had been part of both
and he'd no right to ignore that so easily. The moments flashed
back, shatteringly clear, as if they were only yesterday and she
twenty again. Colin's face came before her at once, the soft, hazel
eyes and the wavy brown hair, a face that always carried a gentle
smile in it, just as it did that first morning she met him along
the beach. He lived down at Gwyneth, the fishing village at Bay's
Head, he told her, and he had come there to write the story of the
Cornish fishermen, that hardy breed who fed most of England
and Wales out of their luggers, the "sailing drifters," as they were
called. Even that first morning he had caught her up in the excitement he had for his work. His book would be the definitive study
of the Cornish fishermen, their lives, their pains and fears, their
work and their humanity, their needs and their fulfillment. And
from that very first morning, she and Colin Todd touched in that
special way that only those meant to touch can know.

How long did it take them to fall in love? Rosaleen asked herself. A month or a moment? A year or an afternoon? It wasn't important now. All that stayed was the fact that she had fallen completely in love with Colin, with his gentle strength, his caring for others, the depth of his compassion. He wasn't well off enough to marry her then. He'd told her that at once. But when his book was finished it would be part of every library in the world, his publishers had assured him. They'd be able to marry then, in comfort and in happiness. It was a wondrous goal to wait for, but it would take time and Rosaleen remembered how her body throbbed in wanting, a wanting that had been set afire that first time he had taken her. It had been in the morning, in the shelter of the Gorannock rock when the sea was soft. She had come to him, all of her, offering the soft eagerness of her young breasts, the smoothness of her legs, and he had been so wonderfully gentle, yet full of sweet fire.

The mornings had been theirs after that. In the evenings he wrote and, many days, he sailed with the boats out of Gwyneth, part of the crew of the sailing drifter *Jenny O.* But those mornings they had together were not enough, not for her, Rosaleen remembered. She had voiced the wanting they both felt.

"I want to share everything with you, Colin, your work, your every moment. I want to be part of your life. I want to live with you, Colin," she had said.

"We can't marry yet. I can't support a wife, you know that," Colin had said.

"I didn't use the words marry or support, my darling," Rosaleen had said. "I'll be able to pay my own way. Mother, before she died, set up a small trust fund for me to allow me to be independent. It's not much, but it'd pay my way."

He had held her tightly. "Your father would cut it off," Colin had said.

"No, no one can do that. It's mine to use as I please," she'd told him. "It's wrong to go on this way, to deny what's meant to be. I'll make father see that."

Colin was a London man and he'd traveled well. Hardly a small-minded provincial, he held no narrow principles and he hungered as much as she and so it was sworn between them to make their world as best they could, wrapped in the kind of loving that was forever. But Rosaleen had been wrong about making her father understand. Sir Mallory had never liked Colin. He cared nothing about dynasties and the amassing of power and wealth and his gentleness was seen as weakness, her love as nothing but headstrong infatuation. She had faced her father, in this same room; that night returned with all its searing force.

"I forbid it," he had raged, his eyes cubes of ice. "I absolutely forbid it."

"I love him, Father, and I'm going to him," Rosaleen said flatly.

"No," he thundered. "You don't know what you're talking about. You don't know anything about love."

"Perhaps it's you who knows nothing about love," Rosaleen snapped, her temper flaring. "We'll marry when the book's finished. Till then, we'll be together."

"My daughter, a Powell, living among the herring fishermen and their grubby little sailing drifters? The daughter of the owner of the finest fleet of clipper ships to sail the seas? No, I won't have it," Sir Mallory shouted.

"That's what really bothers you, is it?" she threw back. "That a Powell should be living among the common people. That's more important than my happiness, isn't it?"

"Happiness comes and goes. A reputation is built out of the years and the hard work in them," Sir Mallory shot back. "You don't know anything about happiness. You're a silly, stupid girl prattling about things beyond your years. You're just intrigued with the idea of living in sin, being a rebel."

"That's not so and it's not fair. The real sin is to turn away from what's meant to be—and I won't do that," Rosaleen countered.

Sir Mallory exploded in quivering rage, his face flushing, his hands trembling. "I'll disown you. I'll never say your name again," he shouted.

"That'll be your choice," Rosaleen said icily.

"And that writer of yours, I'll see that his book never sees print. I've the power and the influence. We'll see how much he cares for you then," Sir Mallory flung out, and Rosaleen felt the cold fear rise inside her. She knew her father. He was capable of it. He had fought and clawed his way to power and he was not above fighting on any level when he felt the need. She knew the depths his fury could go, because she knew how she could hate. She was Sir Mallory Powell's daughter in too many ways, she realized. It was she, not Olivia, who had his determination, his drive. Wasn't this very night proof enough of that!

"You hurt Colin and I'll ruin you," Rosaleen heard herself say. "Somehow, some way, I'll bring everything you have down around your head if you hurt Colin."

His eyes had held hers, flinging fury back and recognizing what he saw in her violet orbs. "You'll be a strumpet and a fool but you'll not be a Powell. You'll not be my daughter any longer," he said.

"I won't want to be and I'll not have a father," Rosaleen flung back. He had stalked from the room then and he was gone to London early the next morning. They had exchanged their last words that night and, later that day, Olivia had tried to argue her into changing her mind. But only because Olivia could never understand giving up so much material comfort for anyone or anything.

So it was done and hand in hand she and Colin had walked from Raven's Wing. He'd held her as she sobbed the rest of the day away, his understanding a rock to lean on, one that would be there again and again. She had not heard another word from her father after that night. She'd gone with Colin to live in the small shack in Gwyneth and became part of that world and his work. Colin lived the life of the Cornish fishermen, sailed with them in calm and in storm, worked beside them, came to know their every secret so that the book would not be a collection of data and statistics but a tribute and a monument to the men of the sailing drifters who fished the wild coastal seas to live.

Rosaleen recalled how she had become part of that world, was accepted and welcomed, even by those who knew her background. With Colin beside her, the trust they'd given him was extended to her. She had always been an excellent small-boat sailor but Colin sailed with the fleets and she wanted desperately to do something to contribute to the book. It was Colin who made the suggestion one evening as they sat entwined before the fire.

"Become a gipper," he said. "They're a damn important part of this industry and this way of life. You could give me their essence in a way I could never get on my own."

The thought had intrigued her at once. The gippers were called by that name after their work. In the colloquial speech, to "gip" was to gut a fish. When the boats unloaded their catch at dockside, the fish were poured into long tubs. The gippers, all women, lined the outside of each tub, scooping up the fish and using a special knife, gutting them with one twist of the blade. As freshness was paramount in marketing the catch, they had to gut the fish at once and so they worked on the dockside in every kind of weather, pitiless downpour, burning summer sun, howling east winds, weathering the very same conditions as the fishermen. Some were young girls, most matronly women, and not a few were long in years, but all were part of the fishing industry, many with sons and husbands aboard the sailing drifters.

Excitedly, Rosaleen joined the ranks of the gippers and learned quickly. But not just the gipper's skill, but the aching pain of back and arm muscles pushed to their limits. As Colin drew out the inner souls of the men of the sailing drifters, she learned the depths of the women whose work was so vital to the marketing of the catch and so little known to the world. She came to know their joys and their pain, their hopes and fears and the special spirit, the camaraderie that was part of their life. She learned, too, about the women who hand-spun and twisted the hemp into the twine that made the nets, each narrow length called a "lint," and how the rotting effects of salt water on the fibers was lessened by tanning the nets in a solution made from the bark of ash trees.

Gipper girls were paid a wage plus so much a barrel of finished, gutted fish. The women who worked on the nets were paid by the piece and an *awlne,* a French measure, was used, equivalent to five feet seven inches. She had seen the wage list and copied it down for Colin, little enough yet sufficient for too many. Spinning, by the pound, was two pence; twisting, one penny; knotting a net for mackerel two "deeping" by the *awlne,* three farthings; knotting a herring net three "deepings" by the *awlne,* one penny. Beating or mending nets paid one shilling a day with "victuals," or one shilling three pennies with breakfast only.

During the busy times, she learned to her surprise, farm laborers came down from their fields to earn extra money. In May, when the mackerel fishing season began, barley sowing was finished and they could leave their fields. In the fall, after the harvest was in the barns, they could work on the boats for herring until November when wheat was ready for sowing. These temporary fishermen had a saying: after plough and mow, it's reef and stow.

This new life fascinated and excited and at night she would transcribe for Colin, in her own words, her understanding of the weariness, the exhaustion of flesh and spirit that was a part of the women of the wharves. She did not neglect to record the dogged spirit of closeness that was theirs, also. The work itself, hard as it was, gave her a new dimension, a new sense of the world and an understanding and compassion she welcomed.

"You're bringing things to the book I could never have gotten hold of this way," Colin told her, and they worked together during the night and she glowed with pride. And above all else, there was Colin, his love and his wanting made of soft fire. None of the excitement wore away. None of the passion and none of the tenderness became routine. Against the warmth of his body on the sweet nights she could only count her blessings.

And it was Colin who watched her closely when holidays and birthdays came around, watching to see if the moments dug at her, ready to help in an instant. But she didn't wait for a word, a letter, a gesture, not from Olivia and not from Sir Mallory.

"There's no point in watching and waiting for something that won't come," she told Colin matter-of-factly.

He had held her close. "You're remarkable, my Rosaleen, or a terribly good actress," he said.

He suspected the latter, she knew, and she didn't deny him that. But there was no acting on her part and Colin never understood, perhaps never wanted to understand, that facet of her, the reverse side of her father's coin. She'd even stopped being angry about Olivia's silence. Olivia would never be one to risk her father's wrath, not in a head-on collision, and so the excommunication was complete. It didn't matter to her. She had Colin and their happiness. It was more than enough, complete of itself.

That was the way of it and Rosaleen looked down at the letter, picked it up as she pulled herself to her feet, poked at the fire, glanced up at the great room. It was full of shadows, the night's and her own. She went to the figure on the sofa, still in the deep sleep. But his forehead was cool to her touch, the fever broken. She moved to the window and peered out into the stygian night, the moon covered, nothing but blackness surrounding the house, as if the world had fallen away into a giant, bottomless pit. Her lips tightened. She knew about the world falling away, being torn away with a wrenching cruelty she could neither fight nor accept. She still remembered that day as clearly as the other turning-point days in her life.

She had stayed at the cottage that day and the afternoon was starting to slip toward dusk when they came from the docksides. The old men came first. She would always remember that, those who'd learned to live with fate and pain. Behind them, the men from the boats and the weavers of the nets and then the gippers, the women whom she'd come to know so well. When she opened the door to see them there, gathered outside the cottage, no words were needed. She had stared at them as if they were ghosts, her violet eyes unblinking, and she heard the words as if they came from behind some thick curtain that muffled their sound. Muffled, but not silenced. The sea had erupted … one of the sudden squalls that sprang out of the sea like a raging panther … seizing the boat, overturning it … plunging all aboard it down into its briny hell. There'd been no survivors and, as it so often happened, it all took place within sight of the shore. But those were only details. The world had stopped and details were superfluous.

Some of the women stayed the night with her as was the custom and she was grateful for that, but the explosion of grief did not come until she was alone the following night. Those first twenty-four hours had been spent beyond stunned shock. They were unable to believe, to embrace a world without Colin. When the reality struck in all its cruel and monstrous horror, she cried until there were no more tears inside her, through days that were but one unmeasured gray shroud. She stayed in the cottage, going out only to buy what little food she needed to sustain herself and the weeks went into months before she could bring herself to face a world that went on as if it hadn't been shattered beyond repair.

Once more, it was Colin who reached out to help her, through the pages of his manuscript. It was so near to completion, and in its pages Colin was still there with her. She turned to the task of finishing the book, of editing and polishing the manuscript. It was a labor of love and she flung herself wholly into the task. Colin had ordered one of the new writing machines by the American, Christopher Sholes, but it hadn't arrived yet and she most probably wouldn't have used it if it had. There were spaces still to be filled and a final chapter needed. She returned to the fishermen and their luggers, to the friends she had made among the gippers, and they helped her set down the finish of the manuscript.

She wept on the day she carried the manuscript to the post office in Bay's Head, surprised to find she could still feel enough to weep. She sent it on to London, her own final good-bye to Colin, and returned to the cottage. It was only later that she realized it had taken her the better part of a year to put the thick manuscript in finished form. But time was meaningless and she existed in a void. She stayed at the cottage, unwilling to leave the place where she had known such total happiness. Some of the women came to her, led by Agnes Walsh. They asked her to come back to the tubs with them and be a gipper again.

"It's exhaustion you need, the work that leaves no time for thinkin' or grievin'," they had told her. They were right, of course, but she turned away from the advice. She preferred to cling to her emptiness, only faintly aware that grief had become a master.

She became almost a recluse, spent the long days recreating happiness, thinking back on little moments of discovery with Colin at her side, such as the time she'd asked Abraham Evans why the nets were always hauled on the starboard side of the boats. His answer had been more than an explanation, affording a glimpse into the faith of the Cornish fishermen.

"Don't you know your Book, lass?" he'd asked quickly. "John 21. Simon Peter complained that they'd toiled all the night and caught nothing and Jesus said to them, 'Cast your net on the *right* side of the ship and ye shall find. They cast therefore and were not able to draw it up for the multitude of fishes.' "

Later that evening, Colin had told her: "On the sea, there is a reason for everything, whether it has its roots in experience, tradition, or faith." They were words that echoed those she had heard her father say when he talked about the problems of running the vast Mallory Shipping Line. But with the memories, she was up every morning at dawn to stand alone on a high place and watch the boats leave the harbor. She'd come to know the tall mizzenmast of the Lowestoft luggers and the sweep of their hulls, and she watched until they cleared the breakwaters, their mainsails shaped like an irregular polygon, billowing out when the sea wind caught them.

The months came, and slid away, piling atop each other, driftwood cords of time, and she knew she was in a trap yet she could not break free. The letter, when it came, was as a sword that cuts a knot. She lifted her hand, looked down at the letter again, and recalled how furious she had been when she first read it. He'd no right to ask anything of her, she'd fumed, not after all the years of silence. But the sword freed her from her own trap and in her anger and fury she realized that there were rights and he was trading on them, rights of flesh and blood, of other yesterdays and other indebtednesses that neither time nor deed nor scathing words could abridge.

So she had packed her things and prepared to leave. But first she'd gone down to Gwyneth to say her good-byes, to all the friends she'd made, to Abraham Evans aboard his drifter, to Agnes Walsh and the other gippers, and especially to Margaret Boynton. Margaret, into her late fifties, had been the first to introduce her into the gipper's life, a woman of independence and compassion who delighted in helping others. "You'll come back to see us, Rosaleen," Margaret said, hugging her. "You're not the kind to forget the friends you've made."

"No, I'll not forget," Rosaleen had said. "Never. How could I?"

Rosaleen folded the letter in her hand, returned it to her purse. She shook her shoulders, casting off memories. The fire had burned low and she put a thick log on it that would simmer through the night. The young man still lay wrapped in sleep and Rosaleen silently left the room, went to her bedroom, and flung off clothes, hiding herself under the warmth of the down quilt that had been in the family for a hundred years. She turned her long, lithe loveliness to the side and slept, one hand cupping her breast, as if Colin were holding her. There was no past, she had learned. The past is only today, a little while gone.

CHAPTER TWO

She'd just finished rashers and eggs and lingered for a moment at the kitchen window, noting that Patrick had kept the Japanese ivy from overrunning the ledge. The sound came to her from the living room, a faint bustling, and she ran in at once. He was awake, making an effort to sit up and gasping in pain. His eyes, light blue, saw her and he fell back on the sofa, breathing heavily.

"It's all right," Rosaleen said, going to him. "You're safe." His eyes studied her as he drew deep breaths and she saw the pain mirrored in his face.

"Where am I?" he asked. She told him of interrupting the attack on the beach and all that had followed and when she finished, his face relaxed some. "Then it's my life I'm thanking you for," he said, drawing breath in deeply with each few words.

Rosaleen shrugged away the gratitude. "I'm glad I was there to help," she said. "I'll make you some tea and some eggs."

"I hurt too fierce to do much eating," he said, but when she brought the food, he managed one egg and a mug of the tea. She helped him sit up against the back of the sofa with the aid of two pillows.

"Now, suppose you tell me who you are," Rosaleen said. "What's your name?" She watched the caution come into his eyes and he didn't answer. "Last night, you mumbled something about someone named Coops," Rosaleen prodded. "Do you want to tell me about it now?"

He shook his head slowly. "I think maybe it's best you don't know anything more," he said.

"Best?" Rosaleen said.

"Best for you. And I can't stay here. It's too dangerous, for you as well," he said. "They'll find out I'm here and come to finish the job."

"You'll not be leaving here for a while," Rosaleen said. "You're in no condition."

"But I must," he said. Trying to sit forward, he gasped in pain, fell back.

Rosaleen tried not to look smug. "I can hide you here in Raven's Wing where they'd never find you. And they'd get nothing out of me. I'm not afraid of a few thieves and ruffians."

His pain-filled eyes gave her a quick glance. Rosaleen stood up, moved the pillows; he fell back to lay on the sofa again. "I'll see Doc Traynor later and get something for the pain. Meanwhile, sleep is what you need," she said.

The young man nodded gratefully, closed his eyes, and was into sleep within moments. Rosaleen watched him for a spell, felt sympathy inside her. He had a sense of responsibility, his concern for her safety proof of that. When he felt better, more assured, he'd confide in her, she felt certain. She left the room, busied herself with the chores, fed the stallion and the two mares and let them out to exercise in the paddock. She gave each a quick dusting with the body brush and then stabled the mares and saddled the stallion. She left him hitched outside while she went into the house, quickly bathed, and changed into a short, dark-red, basque-bodiced riding jacket. She paused in the living room and saw the young man was awake, pulled up on one elbow, his eyes surprisingly clear.

"I'm going to Doc Traynor. He'll be happy to hear you're feeling better," Rosaleen said.

"I can't stay here. I won't risk you more on my account," he said.

"Nonsense," Rosaleen dismissed. "When I come back, if you insist, I'll find a place for you to hide away here in Raven's Wing. Just you relax till I get back."

She felt his eyes follow her as she hurried from the room. She unhitched the stallion and rode into Bodwin at a relaxed canter, the sun warm, the air smelling of new buds and new grass. A soft wind rippled the heather across the flat fields and Bodwin was sleepy and quiet as usual in the afternoon sun. Doc Traynor was out on a call when she arrived and so she tied the stallion to a post and took the opportunity to stroll through the town. It, too, was unchanged. When she walked by the chemist's shop, Mr. Haworth charged out, his pince-nez spectacles quivering on his long, thin nose.

"Rosaleen Powell. It's true, you're back," he called. "I'd heard talk you were back at Raven's Wing but I didn't believe it."

"For the moment. I doubt it'll be for long," Rosaleen smiled. Harold Haworth had been a frequent visitor to Raven's Wing over the years. He and Sir Mallory played cribbage or chess at least once a week. He was one of those she always thought of as cardboard people, a name and a form and nothing else memorable.

"Olivia was just here, not more than an hour ago, buying orris root and lavender buds for that lavender powder of hers. You know Olivia and her powders," Haworth said.

"Yes, I do," Rosaleen said, a lacing of bitterness in her tone. She reprimanded herself for it at once. A meeting with Olivia was bound to happen sooner or later if she stayed for any length of time at Raven's Wing. Rosaleen told herself to be prepared for it.

"It's good to see you, Rosaleen," the man said, intruding on her thoughts. She nodded politely and he disappeared back into his shop. Rosaleen recalled how, as a little girl, she would stare in fascination at the colored liquids inside the large, full-bellied, apothecary jars. She started to move on when she saw Doc Traynor's carriage coming up the street. She stepped out and waved him down, climbed up on the seat beside him, and told him how much better her patient was feeling.

"Maybe he's right about being afraid," the elderly man thought aloud when she finished. "Maybe I ought to try moving him to Northcut. I just don't think he can take the road trip so soon."

"There's no need. Whoever they were, they've fled, I'm sure," Rosaleen said. "He's just on edge. Besides, I'm curious about all of this. I'll get him to tell me more."

The carriage halted in front of his house and he fished into his bag, brought out a small vial of white pills. "Give him these. They'll help the pain. Take one every three hours, tell him. I'll stop up tomorrow and have a look at him," Doc Traynor said.

Rosaleen pushed the vial into her jacket pocket, climbed from the carriage, and pulled herself onto the stallion. She took the most direct route back, cutting through the fields and across the stone ridges that came down stair-step fashion. Reaching Raven's Wing, she hitched the horse outside and hurried in, the vial in her hand. She halted abruptly at the door of the living room. The sofa was empty, the quilt half on the floor. She half-ran to the bathroom but the door was open, the bathroom empty. She called out, knowing there'd be no reply and there was none. He had fled. Tom and bleeding chest, ripped leg muscles, broken arm and all, he'd somehow dragged himself away.

Rosaleen ran outside, cursing the extra time she'd spent in Bodwin. She leapt onto the stallion's back and raced down the road to the beach, reining to a halt when she reached the sand. The dory was still there but he'd not come this way. There wasn't a footprint on the newly washed sand. She turned, rode back to the top of the cliffs, past the house and across the field to where the thick stand of cedars began. She pushed her way through the trees, ducking branches.

"Come back, please," Rosaleen called out. "You're not strong enough." She halted, listened, called again. "Do you hear me?

Come back. You'll be safe," she tried again, but her only answer was the soft rustle of new leaves. She went in deeper and then turned, rode out of the cedars and across the moor, looking for a trail of heather that had been bruised and trodden upon. She halted after an hour, unable to pick up a trail of any kind, realizing that she was hardly adept at this sort of thing. Riding back to the house, her lips were set tightly, her violet eyes dark with concern and anger. It had been a foolish act, an unnecessary gesture, she told herself. It was only later, after she'd stabled the horse and returned to the living room, that she saw that one of her father's two heavy-barreled Lefaucheux pistols was missing from the small wall cabinet. The young man's fears must have indeed been deep, she commented silently, and picked up the quilt, put away the other sheets, and tidied up the sofa.

The evening had slipped over the house then and she changed into a peignoir, pink with tiny, blue irises embroidered on it, one of those that still hung in her room, she had found in surprise. She started a fire, took a book from the library, a biography of Coleridge, and settled herself on the sofa and let the fire reach out its warmth. The night wind came to swirl around the house and she read a while and felt her eyelids growing heavy. She put the book on her lap, leaned back and thought about the youth that had fled, still marveling that he found the strength to do so. Or perhaps fear supplied him with the strength. It was for the best, though, Rosaleen had decided. She faced enough unknowns. She didn't need any involvement with bandits, revolutionaries, or whatever they were. She had just closed the book and decided to go to bed, when the crash of glass shattered the silence of the house.

The wind had blown one of the windows in, she thought, but the thought was swept away as the figure crashed into the room through the broken window, followed by a second. The first one turned to her and she recognized him at once, the biggest of the four men at the beach. His cheek bore the harsh, red line of her riding crop. He started for her as the second man rushed to the front door, yanked it open, and admitted the other two. Rosaleen seized one of the iron pokers from the fireplace stand, swung at the heavy, lined face. The man ducked and cursed, and she swung again. He gave way and out of the corner of her eyes, she caught one of the others coming around from the side. She spun, lashing out with the poker. She heard the biggest one coming at her and tried to bring the poker up, but he was upon her, his hands tearing the weapon from her grip and then one of them crashed heavily against her face. Rosaleen saw flashing purple and yellow lights as another blow snapped her head back. She felt herself thrown against the sofa and then her head cleared enough to see the two others being let in the front door.

The big one with the slash on his heavy face towered over her. She kicked out with one foot but her aim wasn't high enough, the blow catching him along the inside of his thigh. He roared in pain as her heel dug in and twisted away, then she bolted up, trying to duck away. Another pair of arms seized her from the side, flung her back on the sofa. "Hold the bitch," the big man snarled. Rosaleen twisted her head, sunk her teeth into a forearm. The arm was torn away, a cry of pain accompanying the release. She started to pull free when the big man's heavy hand slammed into her face, the sharp pain making her cry out as she fell back. Two more hard slaps made her head snap sideways as she hit the sofa. "Goddamn bitch," she heard his voice fling out.

The slaps stopped and she shook tears of pain and fury from her eyes. She was pinned down, her arms pulled back, one man holding her from the back. The big man, his heavy face contorted in anger, glared down at her. "Now where is he, bitch?" he snarled.

"He's gone," Rosaleen snapped.

"Don't lie to us. He was in no shape to leave," the man shot back.

"I'm not lying. He left. I don't know where he went," Rosaleen said, putting small triumph into the last sentence. Her answer was the heavy hand smashing across her face again and she cried out at the pain of it.

"The truth, God damn you. You took him someplace. Where?" the man snarled.

"No. He just left," Rosaleen spat out between sobs. Her face hurt.

"She needs convincing," one of the others said.

"I guess so," the big one agreed. The slap came at once, then another, snapping her head from side to side until her face seemed on fire and she was crying out in protest and pain.

"I don't know. Please, no more. He left, I tell you," she gasped, and another slap seared her reddened face. "I don't know anything more," she screamed out, then sobbed as the hard slaps rained down on her again. Finally they stopped and she felt her breath coming in short, harsh gasps.

"What'd he tell you?" she heard the voice demand and shook her head, whispered the word, "Nothing."

"You know, I think the bitch is telling the truth," she heard one of the others say. "She wouldn't have the guts to hold back if she'd anything to say."

"Maybe you're right," the heavy-faced one muttered. Rosaleen lifted her hate-filled violet eyes to him. "Then we might as well make the visit worthwhile," she heard him say, his tongue coming out to lick thick lips. He reached out, his heavy hand closing around the top of her peignoir. He yanked and the material ripped away and she felt the rush of cool air against her breasts, saw the desire flare in his eyes. "Let her go," he rasped. "I like a little fight in it."

"I'm next," one of the others called out with new excitement in his voice.

"No. Oh, no," Rosaleen said, trying to shrink back into the sofa, but he fairly leapt onto her. She clawed at his face but got only handfuls of thick greasy hair and then his heavy lips were pressing onto her breasts and she felt his knee pushing between her legs, the rest of the peignoir tearing away. He bit down on her left breast and she screamed in pain and heard his guttural laugh. "No, damn you, no," she cried out, but he was pressing down on her and she could not fight off his strength and weight. She felt naked flesh, hard, pushing against her thigh, seeking as he pulled himself higher onto her. One hand seized her thigh, wrenched it aside, and she screamed as she felt him reach her, start to push into her. The shot drowned out her scream for an instant, sharp and loud as a cannon in the room. She felt her attacker's body shudder, heard the guttural cry of pain from him, and then he was toppling from her, falling from the sofa to the floor. Rosaleen pulled her legs up, pushed, half-rose, saw the others whirl as the heavy-faced man lay on the floor, clutching his shoulder.

She followed their gaze, to the foot of the wide stairs in the front hall. The bandaged figure stood on the bottom step, pistol in hand, taking aim again, and she saw the others scatter for cover. He hadn't fled at all, Rosaleen gasped silently. He'd simply hidden upstairs, where she'd never thought to look. She swore at her own stupidity as the pistol shot rang out again, the bullet smashing into the edge of the fireplace where one of the other men half-rolled, half-dove to safety. But now she saw guns appear in the hands of the other two. They fired back, almost in unison and she saw the young man try to move behind the balustrade. But his movements were slow, his leg dragging, and she screamed as his bandaged figure quivered with the impact of the bullets. He staggered, slowly crumpled to the floor, as if he were a puppet that had had its string cut.

The big man on the floor was holding his shoulder and cursing out orders. "Let's get out of here, goddamn," he snarled. "Christ, my shoulder's all busted up. Give a hand here."

The others went to him, dragged him to his feet, started to the door with him. One cast a look back at Rosaleen. "What about her?" he asked.

"Forget her. He's finished this time. Let's get out of here," the big man barked as they reached the door. Rosaleen watched them disappear into the night and in moments heard the sound of hoofbeats galloping away. She ran to the crumpled figure at the foot of the steps, bent down to him. His eyes flickered open for a second and he tried to form words with his lips but there was not enough life left in his battered body as fresh wounds spread new stains over the bandages. His eyes closed for the last time, and Rosaleen's lips pressed tightly into each other.

He could have stayed hidden, she murmured again. But he hadn't. He'd come down to help her. It was all so clear, now. He knew they'd come back seeking him but he'd thought, perhaps really hoped, they'd leave once they were convinced she knew nothing. But they'd decided to stay and enjoy themselves with her and he'd come down to repay his debt to her. She touched her hand to his young face and felt her throat close with the sob.

"Who were you?" Rosaleen whispered softly. "You came to the beach beneath these cliffs. Why? Were you trying to come to Raven's Wing?"

The rhetorical questions danced in her mind. It could all have been simply a monstrous coincidence, meaningless to her. Yet the possibility could not be entirely dismissed. She would make mention of it when she went to London, Rosaleen decided. But not before. There was no way, now, to judge guilt or innocence, the right or wrong or depth of it. She knew only that it had been a horrible thing, soiling and degrading, and she shivered as she thought of the big man swarming over her, touching her, coming so close to debasing all that had been beautiful. Slowly her thoughts began to crystallize into decisions.

She had to get rid of the young man's lifeless form. Going to the village in the morning would only stir up a hornet's nest of talk and endless speculation. Gossip was a commodity quickly bought. She wanted none of that. It was over, for now, perhaps forever, and she'd keep it that way. She'd take the body out to Sopwith Road, Rosaleen decided. Yes, that was the best place. They were always finding victims of highwaymen along Sopwith Road, and in the morning he'd be found and taken as but one more. She'd leave it to the constabulary to carry on from there, as far as they wished, which, knowing the local sheriff, would not be far indeed. She'd tell Doc Traynor that the youth had run off, just as she'd believed he had, and Doc Traynor would say no more about it. He was one of the few who never carried tales.

Rosaleen stood up and went into the living room, suddenly aware of the cold chilling her body. She glanced down at the peignoir. It hung in tatters and she was all but naked. She went to her room, threw away the shreds of the peignoir, and pulled on a gardening outfit. She pulled her long, gray cape around her shoulders as she hurried past the still form and out to the carriage house. She brushed by the Whitechapel buggy. It was much too shallow and exposed and the same applied to the dropfront phaeton. Her eyes sought the round-bottomed Brett with its expansive brown canopy and deep flooring. She halted before it, nodded in grim satisfaction as she let her eyes make rough measurements.

The stable was the next stop. There, she took the stallion, brought him to the carriage house, and harnessed him to the Brett. He wasn't a carriage horse but he was strong and he'd race if she found need to do so. She drove around to the front of the house, her glance taking in the soft mist rising up into the night. Inside Raven's Wing, she paused before the tall grandfather clock in the foyer, her eyes narrowing in thought, pulling on memory. The overnight stage from Penzance to Bristol raced its way along the fog-shrouded curves of Sopwith Road, but the stage would have passed by now, the clock reading almost midnight. There was no reason to put the task off any longer.

Rosaleen drew her breath in sharply, pulled a sheet from the hall closet, and dropped it over the still figure. She bent low, rolled the man over, and wrapped the sheet tightly around him, folding the ends in at head and foot. When she finished, she took the sheet at the front end and began to pull, dragging her burden to the waiting carriage. She halted, her breath coming in short, harsh gasps. Bending again, using her back and shoulders, she managed to heave the inert weight half into the carriage. She paused to gulp in air, then completed the grisly task. She lay the figure on the floor of the carriage and drew the brown canopy down as far as it would go, stepped back, and peered at the carriage. It seemed entirely empty. She pulled herself up atop the seat and snapped the reins over the stallion. The carriage rolled smoothly forward and Rosaleen turned from the driveway onto the narrow road that led to the shoreline. Sopwith Road paralleled the shore and the night fog had long since rolled in on it as she turned onto its curving bed. She slowed the carriage as the fog pushed a wispy curtain in front of her, brought the horse to a walk.

The trees were wraiths, disembodied arms that reached out from the sides of the road. She pulled the gray cape tighter as the clammy chill of the fog seeped through her flesh. By day, Sopwith Road was well traveled, but people shied away from it at night because of the fog which sometimes made it impassable. Rosaleen frowned as she strained her eyes to make out the outline of the road and watched for the edge of the trees to follow around a curve. She counted the curves, the way she did when she rode the Bristol stage as a little girl, trying to remember how many to a mile. The fog thickened and the carriage seemed to move through a formless, shapeless void. She decided she'd gone far enough, and was about to rein the horse to a halt when the sharp jolt almost pitched her to the ground. She clutched at the small rail of the seat as the carriage leaned to the left, halted, deep into the rut.

"Damn," Rosaleen snapped out as she pulled for the stallion to move forward. She felt the horse strain, the carriage move a few inches, then halt again. After three more tries to pull the wheel free, she climbed down to the ground. The left front wheel of the carriage was deep into a rutted ravine that cut diagonally across the ground. She went to the rear of the wagon, called out to the horse, and put her shoulder against the backboard. The carriage shuddered but nothing more. Rosaleen returned to the front of the carriage to glare at the wheel, her brows knitted together. She was still glaring at it when she heard the sound—slow, cautious hoofbeats. Panic seized her at once and her eyes flashed to the carriage. The sound came closer and Rosaleen peered forward until she saw the shape slowly form itself out of the swirling fog, a lone horseman.

The horseman halted, a ghostly figure in the fog, and Rosaleen felt herself shudder. She reached up, took the whip from its holder alongside the carriage seat. The horseman moved closer, and Rosaleen wondered if he were a highwayman. She took a firmer hold of the whip and the figure took on form and definition, a tall man in a black cape with red trim at the edges. She looked up into a face of high-cheekboned planes and full lips, a strong, handsome face with deep, intense, dark-fire eyes. If he were a highwayman he was indeed a handsome one, Rosaleen found herself thinking, one with a presence and an electricity about him. He moved closer and Rosaleen shot a glance at the carriage. From the ground, it appeared empty. She hoped it would appear the same from horseback. Unhurriedly, he swung from the saddle and his eyes surveyed the wheel.

"You've gotten into a fix," he remarked in a smooth, mellifluous voice.

"I'm afraid so," Rosaleen said, managing a smile, gathering confidence as she dismissed his being a highwayman.

"A bad night for traveling, especially alone," he commented, his eyes holding contained curiosity.

"The fog came up suddenly," Rosaleen said.

"Three hours ago," he remarked blandly, and Rosaleen's lips tightened. The remark had been a correction that contained a question unspoken.

"You're traveling in it, alone," Rosaleen countered. The strong face broke into a sudden smile, faint amusement in it.

"*Touché,*" he said with a mock bow. "The price, unfortunately, for tarrying too long at Muttonhead Tavern." He bent down to the wheel, peered between the spokes. "The axle's all right," he said after a moment, then rose to his feet. "But the rut is deep. The carriage will have to be lightened," he said, and in the deep eyes she saw the waiting again.

She forced herself to stay expressionless. "The carriage is empty," she answered.

"Is it?" he asked, and Rosaleen felt her stomach turn over. His arm reached out to the door of the carriage. Automatically, she started to halt him, then pulled back as the door came open to reveal the sheet-wrapped object on the carriage floor. Suddenly, it seemed as obviously a body as if there was no sheet around it. Rosaleen muttered an oath under her breath as her mind raced frantically for an explanation. The truth, she decided, or at least part of the truth. She let herself look uncomfortable with a touch of deference in her manner.

"I suppose you're wondering," she began. He didn't reply, the answer in his eyes. "I've just been hired on at Raven's Wing. That's the Mallory house up on the cliffs."

"I know," the man said with an edge of impatience. Rosaleen put a touch of Yorkshire servant girl into her speech as she nodded to the sheet.

"I heard this noise at the door and went to it and there he was, lying there and three men riding away. I saw he was dead when I bent down to him," she said. "I didn't know what to do, me being alone there."

"I'd heard that one of Sir Powell's daughters had returned to the house," the man said.

"Yes, but she's in London now," Rosaleen answered quickly. "So, as I said, I didn't know what to do but I knew one thing. I didn't want a lot of questions and the constabulary mucking about when Sir Mallory returned, my being brand new and all that. God knows what he might think. It might mean my job."

The deep eyes didn't soften but his voice had less of an edge to it. "So you decided to get rid of him on Sopwith Road in the night fog," he said.

She let herself look contrite. "I didn't want any trouble. It just seemed the best thing to do. Maybe a gentleman such as yourself wouldn't have done it, but I had to do something. I just didn't want a lot of questions, people wondering and talking."

"You've been hired at the house, you said," the man questioned.

"Yes, sir. General housework."

"You've always been a servant girl?"

"Oh, yes, sir," Rosaleen answered, keeping the speech inflection, proud of the proper note of humility she put into it.

"And you took this stallion from his stall and harnessed him to the carriage, all perfectly done. Very remarkable for a servant girl," the smooth voice commented. Rosaleen kept her face expressionless again though she swore silently inside herself. He had a way of setting small traps and she'd stepped into each.

"My father taught me about harnessing carriages," she offered, and knew it sounded lame and hated herself for it. The faint amusement seemed to touch his dark-fire eyes again but he accepted the answer, turned to the carriage.

"I'll take care of this business, first," he said, reaching in, drawing the shrouded form partly out of the Brett, dipping low to lift the weight onto one shoulder. Rosaleen watched him disappear into the fog and in a few moments her ears caught the dull, thudding sound. She waited, her hands clenched, and the tall figure reappeared, the rolled-up sheet in his hands. He tossed it into the carriage and closed the door.

"Take the horse by the bridle," he said brusquely, and she moved quickly to obey, watching him go to the rear of the carriage, his quiet efficiency a comfort. She saw him put his back to the carriage, brace his feet apart on the ground. "Now," he called out, and Rosaleen pulled at the stallion's bridle. The horse strained, but this time the carriage moved, lifted, the wheel starting to rise out of the rut. She pulled harder at the horse, heard the tall man's straining groan from the rear of the carriage, and with a suddenness that almost sent her toppling, the carriage lifted free. The man was at her side in an instant, taking the bridle from her, slowly wheeling the horse around so that the rear wheels didn't plunge into the rut. She took hold of the other side of the bridle and helped turn the horse, her hand brushing his.

"There, now, that does it," he breathed after a moment. He stepped back, turned the deep, intense eyes on her. Rosaleen kept her deferential, servant-girl tone.

"I'm most grateful to you, sir," she said. "Really most grateful. I don't know what I'd have done if you hadn't happened by."

"My pleasure," he said, turning, and with one easy motion he swung into the saddle of his waiting steed. "You can sleep easy. I won't be telling a soul about our meeting here in the fog."

"Thank you, again," Rosaleen murmured as she climbed into the carriage. She lifted the reins, paused with them held high to look at the strong face, and wondered if she didn't see a quiet amusement in the deep of his eyes. She wondered if he lived near, or was on his way to see someone, a woman, perhaps. Did he come this way often? The questions pushed at her and she fought them down. She snapped the reins and the horse broke into a trot at once. She glanced back to see him sitting quietly atop the horse and then the fog swallowed him up and she snapped the reins again, urging the horse on through the swirling night.

She drove recklessly through the fog, picking out landmarks and finally the road sign that pointed the way to Bodwin and the moors beyond it. She turned off Sopwith Road there and headed back toward Raven's Wing. The knots inside her stomach began to unwind. It was over. The stranger in the night would keep his word about remaining silent. Somehow she was certain of it. She made a face at the thought, being certain about a total stranger. Yet he had given her the certainty. She heard a wry sound escape her lips. Life was indeed made of strange twists and turns. The tall man that had come out of the fog had been the first man to reach her with anything since Colin, to touch her with trust, and he was but a passing stranger she did not dare meet again.

He'd given her more than practical help, Rosaleen reflected. He'd given her the awareness that she could still feel, still respond, and she'd wondered about that. Since Colin's death, she'd been made of emptiness, moving through life like a sleepwalker. But the woman inside her still lived. She had responded to the tall man's strength, his handsomeness. It had been a gift he'd never known he'd given.

The road turned and straightened and she smelled the damp sea air. She'd left the hall light on as well as the living-room light and she peered through the swirling night and suddenly the smeared yellow glow filtered through the fog. Hurrying on, she reached Raven's Wing, the black bulk looming before her. She drove into the carriage shed, unhitched and stabled the horse, then hurried into the house and to her room, pulling off clothes and falling into bed, exhausted. She lay still in the darkness and let her whirling thoughts find a semblance of order. Her purse lay on the chair near the bed, the letter still inside. It had brought her back to Raven's Wing and it still demanded more of her. She'd not put it off any longer, she decided in the darkness. In the morning, she'd feed the horses early and leave for Groat, to catch the stage for London. Tomorrow, the years would come together. Tomorrow, she'd face Sir Mallory Powell for the first time since she'd left Raven's Wing. It seemed a lifetime ago. It was, in its way.

CHAPTER THREE

The tension set in when the coach reached Guildford and worsened as it moved through the "green belt" outside London proper. Like a slow fever, it crept over her until, when the coach started down Kensington Road into Knightsbridge, she had to dry her palms on a handkerchief. Rosaleen felt anger at herself. She'd left Bodwin feeling confident, perhaps even a shade triumphant, and she hadn't been so dressed in a long, long time. She'd chosen the gown of pink tarlatan that still hung in the closet of her room, the effect striking against the jet of her hair. Over it, for the coach ride, she'd worn a small semifitted tippet of deep blue. But as the coach passed behind Buckingham Palace and onto the Strand and then came to halt at Charing Cross, her confidence had waned, even though the three male passengers in the coach still looked at her with that special mixture of awe and desire. Secretly, she was surprised at how good it felt, another thread of self-confirmation returning, a welcome and warm feeling.

She took a hansom cab from Charing Cross to the Powell Line offices on Fleet Street, drew a deep breath as she opened the door to the handsome, dark-wood reception room. It was an act that turned the clock back in one sweeping moment and she found herself remembering all the times she'd come here with her father, as a child, awed and fascinated, then as a young girl full of interest and enthusiasm for the gleaming ship models, and finally as a young woman who sailed her own boat and who'd come to love the sea and ships as Sir Mallory did. Perhaps some kinds of love were in the blood, Rosaleen mused. Perhaps the genes bestowed so much more than we realized upon us.

She halted inside the big reception room and her eyes immediately sought out the beautiful ship models that graced the spacious room. Some were in cases, some not, and slowly she went from one to the other as if greeting old friends too long unseen. The sleek white-hulled clipper, the *Star of Burma*, was first and then, on a shelf close by, the four-masted bark, the *Glencarry Envoy*. She halted before the grayhulled windjammer, the *Empress of Bristol*, went on to the *Ellora Hall* and the *Star of Hereford* and so many others, all queens of the Powell Line, all still in place on their neat mountings and most still sailing the seas. Rosaleen turned from the ship models, surveyed the room where the quietly rich panels of fabric, deep gray with red trim, set off the wood. Nothing had changed here, she thought as she stepped to the heavy wooden desk and ticked the little bell on it.

The first to emerge from his side office was Nicholas Carlson, forty years the office manager. His eyes fastened on her, stared at her as if she were a ghost. A stooped, balding man, always a little mousy in appearance and in character, he was confidant to everything that happened to Sir Mallory and he would of course have known about the past. She saw the thoughts of it move into his face, apprehension pushing aside simple surprise.

Rosaleen almost smiled. "He asked me to come," she said quietly. She saw Carlson's face relax visibly, a deep breath escaping him as he moved toward her, reached out to her, grasped her hands in his.

"Miss Rosaleen... it's been too long, too long," he said, his eyes sweeping up and down her figure. "You're more beautiful than ever. It's wonderful to see you here again." The man paused, dropped his voice a few notches. "You say he... Sir Mallory... asked you to come?" he questioned.

"Yes, he sent me a letter, in point of fact," Rosaleen laughed. "I assure you, I wouldn't be here otherwise."

"Yes, of course. But you know what a temper he has and I wouldn't like to see him get excited, not these days," the little man said. Rosaleen felt the frown dig into her brow, the remark implying more than it said. She was going to ask more but he started to back off with excited little motions. "Let me get the others. They'll be so happy to see you," he said, disappearing into the other offices then emerging in short order, followed by James Higgens, the bookkeeper, and Ezra Watson, the chief clerk, and, moments later, Thomas Alderson, the traffic manager. Watson, a jolly, effusive man, embraced her, and Alderson, usually reticent, surprised her and almost shouted in joy at seeing her.

"I've thought so often about you, Miss Rosaleen," he said. "Thought and worried and wondered. But, of course, there was no asking him." He moved his head to the closed door behind him.

"Of course," Rosaleen said, not in sarcasm. It had been a subject none would dare broach to Sir Mallory. Thomas Alderson, at fifty youngest of them all, still had his flame-red hair, she noted. They were all a little older, a little more worn, but all fixtures of the Powell Line home office. Only Harriet Woodbridge, secretary and second-in-command under Carlson, was missing, away on a week's vacation, she was told. Harriet was also a fixture, with the company almost as long as Carlson. When all the exchanges were finished, Carlson moved his stooped frame toward the tall, closed door to the inner office.

"I'll tell him you're here," he said, and Rosaleen nodded, feeling her stomach suddenly constrict. She watched Carlson rap twice on the door, symbolic in itself, always closed, always austere. He opened it, disappeared behind it for a moment, then came out and beckoned her. Rosaleen straightened her shoulders, drew a deep breath, and swept past Carlson into the office.

Her breath caught as her eyes found the man standing behind the heavy-legged desk across the thickly carpeted office. His eyes were still the same, sharp and imperious, the eyes of an eagle.

But the rest of the man struck her with shock. The once-powerful shoulders were held low, the strong, firm face was lined, sunken. Always clothed in finely tailored garments, his suit hung loosely and the steel-gray hair seemed dull and lifeless. He held himself stiffly, his always ruddy complexion mottled. She'd readied no words and they came of themselves, almost stammered out.

"Hello, Father. You asked me to come," Rosaleen said. The sharp, imperious eyes moved over her. The eagle might be a ravaged one but it was still an eagle, she commented inwardly.

"Yes, so I did," Sir Mallory Powell said, and his voice was still the same, Rosaleen noted, commanding, firm, deep. "You look well. Time hasn't hurt you, Rosaleen. Not on the surface, at least."

"Not on the surface," Rosaleen agreed evenly.

"Sit down, Rosaleen," her father said, and she watched him sink down into the big leather chair. He seemed glad to sit. But his eyes gave no echo of his words. "It's been hard, very hard these past years, especially this last one," he said, then waited for her to comment.

"Isn't the line doing well?" she asked.

"I've had a terrible run of bad luck this year and last. Things that just happened," Sir Mallory said. "It's been hard, taking all my time and energies. I haven't any time left to deal with Raven's Wing or Olivia and her demands or anything else at all."

"So that's why you've sent for me, after all this time," Rosaleen said, unable to keep the ice from her voice. "Need and necessity, nothing else."

The sharp, imperious blue eyes bored into her. "What else should there be?" he questioned.

"Apologies, concessions, perhaps even a touch of sorrow," Rosaleen flung back.

"You were always too quick with your tongue," the man returned sharply and then the hard eyes softened and a sigh escaped him. "But I suppose you've got that directly from me." He sat back in the chair, the lines of his face deepening. "There comes a time when a man realizes the mistakes he's made. That doesn't make talking about them any easier," he said. Rosaleen made no reply, letting the admission stand for itself. "Olivia was another of mine," her father said. "She was always charming and always spoiled, always able to wind me around her finger."

"I know," Rosaleen let drop.

Sir Mallory ignored the remark. "I can't deal with it now. I can't wrestle with her constant demands for money and that new husband of hers with his schemes. I dislike the man intensely," he said, his voice growing hard, angry. He was unaware of the echoes in his words. Rosaleen let them pass. His eyes found her again. "I'm turning to you to take charge of Raven's Wing and all other family affairs so I can concentrate all my energies on the Powell Line affairs."

"What about Olivia?" Rosaleen tossed at him.

"You're the oldest. You're the next in line," he snapped. It was a turn-aside answer she refused.

"That's not enough," she stabbed.

His eyes hardened on her. "All right, you've the steel for it. Olivia could never handle the Powell affairs. It's not in her," he said.

"Maybe it's not in me either after all this time," Rosaleen countered, and he shook his head in disagreement.

"You know better," he said.

"And you expect me to agree, just like that. Really, I find that amazing," Rosaleen flared.

His head rose, the old imperiousness seizing control, and he speared her with a hard stare. "Yes, that's exactly what I expect because it's your place. It's a responsibility you were born to, not one you can choose to honor," he returned. Rosaleen felt the rueful admiration inside. When he had to, he could still thunder out the words to strike deep. He saw the admission in the violet depths of her eyes. "I'll sign power-of-attorney to you today so you'll have control of the family accounts. I'll leave it to you to handle everything from there."

"Especially Olivia," Rosaleen commented. "She should be on a flat allowance out of the trust fund and no more." She watched her father grow uncomfortable.

"An allowance. That might be a bit drastic, don't you think?" he grunted. Rosaleen almost smiled. Olivia's hold was still there, her marks still deep.

"It's overdue," she spat out, and he allowed himself a helpless shrug, an admission of more than he wanted to say. He rose, pressed a buzzer on the desk, and Higgens entered.

"Those personal papers I gave you, bring them to me," he ordered the bookkeeper. Higgens left and Rosaleen caught her father's sideways glance. "You've not seen Olivia since you returned to Raven's Wing, I take it," he said. "She and her husband have rented Braemore."

"I heard. A place ten times too big for them," Rosaleen said.

"That's her husband's doing, putting on airs," Sir Mallory said, defending Olivia again, Rosaleen noted with a stab of anger.

"Olivia was never against that," she commented, sorry at once for sounding bitchy. Higgens returned with a file folder and withdrew. Sir Mallory opened the file, drawing out a half-dozen legal-looking documents. He signed two, pushed all of them at her.

"There's no need for you to read them all now but you're in charge as of this minute of all the family accounts. There's enough for you and Olivia to live modestly without dipping into capital funds, but it's not as much as it once was. I've had to go into capital for the business, much as I hated doing so," he said, his mouth growing tight. "I expect you'll keep me informed of any major decisions you take," he added. "Or of anything important."

"Yes, of course," Rosaleen said, then hesitated a moment before going on. "There was a strange incident, probably meaningless. It began when I was riding along the beach the other morning." She told everything and he listened without comment until she repeated the words the young man had whispered while still in a coma.

"Coops? Tell Coops?" Sir Mallory frowned. "You're sure that's what he said?"

"Yes. Does it mean anything to you?" Rosaleen frowned back.

Sir Mallory's lips pursed. "One of my finest skippers is a man named Captain Coops. He sailed the Pacific run for twenty years until I brought him to the Atlantic crossing."

"Then maybe he was trying to reach Raven's Wing," Rosaleen said. "Perhaps to reach you and through you this Captain Coops."

Sir Mallory half-shrugged. "It's possible. Captain Coops will be in port next week. I'd like you to come back then and tell him about this. He might have questions for you ... or answers."

"Next week? All right. I think I'll have someone to stay at the house by then," Rosaleen said. She put the papers into her purse as Sir Mallory rose, his eyes troubled, full of his own thoughts. Rosaleen paused, suddenly hesitant. She had thought the first moments would be hardest, most awkward, but it was now, the parting, that suddenly lay between them like some invisible and unwelcome presence.

"I'll be leaving now. Good luck with things," she tried, immediately annoyed at not doing better. It had sounded inane, and worse, impersonal, and she didn't feel impersonal at all. "I'm sure you'll turn things around," she said, making a better start.

"I'm concentrating on the Atlantic run. That's everything today," her father said, almost abstractly. A name rose from the past at her.

"Is Frank Shields still the main competition?" she asked.

"More than ever. He's had as much good luck as I've had bad," Sir Mallory bit out, paused, brightened for a moment. "You take care of family matters and I'll be able to concentrate on things here. I'll fight back."

Rosaleen exchanged glances, which were better than words, she decided. Carlson held the door for her and she went outside. She recognized the well-dressed man in the black frock coat and small diamond stickpin, a small man with a somewhat pompous air but with sharp, quick eyes in a round face. Dr. Winston Matthews, Sir Mallory's London physician, was a skilled and well-known practitioner who did not hide his high regard for himself. Rosaleen, like most others, forgave him that because it was deserved.

"Miss Rosaleen. It's been a long time," he said with a courtly bow.

"Yes. What brings you here, Dr. Matthews?" she asked. "An official or a social visit?"

"Official, I'm afraid. I stop in every day since the last attack," the doctor said.

The last attack. The phrase struck at her and she shot a glance at Carlson. The office manager shrugged uncomfortably. "Sir Mallory wanted nothing mentioned," he murmured.

"How is my father, truthfully," Rosaleen asked, turning back to the physician.

"Not at all good. Being under this constant strain is very bad, but I can't get him to go away so I stop in every day to keep a close check on him," the physician answered. "Now, if you'll excuse me." He bowed again and went into the inner office. Rosaleen glanced at the clock on the wall. She'd just make the night coach to Cornwall. She said quick good-byes and caught a cab to Charing Cross coach station. There were only two other passengers on the coach, a woman and a small boy, and Rosaleen drew a corner of the carriage around herself as it sped into the night. It was over and it hadn't been as bitter as she'd expected, she mused. A mixture of feelings swirled inside her and only time would sort them out, but one stood out above all others, shock at the shadow of the man she'd once known. Shock and a feeling she'd never thought to have again for him, care, the deep affection that had rushed back over her as though it'd never been away. The emotions were sleight-of-hand artists, shuffling themselves around to confuse and confound, she decided.

Perhaps she should never have answered his letter, Rosaleen reflected. But he had known she would. He'd known the strength of all those bonds forged through the years, those soft chains that prevent escape from the past. Or had he simply known her? Rosaleen put aside further thoughts, closed her eyes, and let the night wind cool her face. She slept to the swaying rhythm of the coach, nestled in the dark of the corner.

When she woke, the new sun was a pin line across the horizon and they were pulling into Bodwin. She picked up the Whitechapel buggy where she'd left it at Sam Tyler's stables and drove back to Raven's Wing. On the short stretch of Sopwith Road, a lone horseman overtook her. She peered at the rider, but he was not the tall, handsome man of the fog-bound night. Her half-smile was wry as she recognized both relief and disappointment in her reaction.

The morning had blossomed when she reached Raven's Wing and she stabled the carriage and the horse, tended to chores, and then went upstairs to fall onto her bed, more exhausted than she'd realized. She slept soundly until just past noon and when she woke, she realized that sleep had brought her decisions. Olivia was the first order of business. Putting it off was of no value. She brewed a pot of tea and sipped it as she looked through the papers Sir Mallory had given her, committing facts and figures to memory. When she'd finished, she put the papers into the small wall safe in the library, changed into riding clothes, a deep-blue basque jacket over a white blouse and blue tailored skirt from Redfern. She wanted to look her best for Olivia, a purely personal indulgence, she admitted.

Braemore was not more than a good ten-minute canter and when she reached the house she remembered how she'd always found it an unattractive place, unnecessarily ornate, one of those houses with a fussed-over feel to them. Olivia was on the front flagstone terrace as she rode up, watering a stone urn of lilacs and heather. There was no surprise in Olivia's face at seeing her. Word had obviously reached her sister that she had returned to Raven's Wing. Rosaleen's violet orbs narrowed ever so slightly as she came down from the saddle and surveyed her younger sister. Olivia had put on about ten pounds and it added strength to the round, little girl face but her full lips were the same, always seeming on the edge of a pout. Olivia's soft-brown hair and soft-blue eyes enabled her to convey a picture of guilelessness that was far removed from the truth. Determined not to make it a staring contest, Rosaleen spoke first.

"You're looking well, Olivia. Marriage agrees with you," she remarked.

Olivia ignored the offering. "I suppose Father asked you to go to Raven's Wing," she said, her simmering anger unconcealed.

"That's right," Rosaleen said.

"After all the years and the hating, he calls you," Olivia bit out. "I've been right here and he sends for you. I don't understand him at all." Rosaleen half-shrugged, decided silence was best. But Olivia was not to be turned aside so easily. "And I'm surprised you just picked up and came," she said with accusation on each word.

"I'm surprised, too," Rosaleen answered honestly.

"Why? I just don't understand it," Olivia flared again. She wore a low-cut dress and her high, round breasts rose in anger. "Why did he call *you*?" she flung out.

"You'll have to ask him that," Rosaleen said quietly.

"Don't worry, I intend to," Olivia snapped. "But then he always depended on you for certain things. He always turned to you."

"He always gave to you," Rosaleen said.

"And you always resented that," Olivia stabbed.

Rosaleen heard the weariness in her own voice as she said, "No, you never understood what I resented. It wasn't the giving."

"No? What then?" Olivia said.

"The taking," Rosaleen said, and there was sudden steel in her voice. Olivia gave a flounced toss of her head, a gesture so full of memories it almost made Rosaleen smile. She took the piece of paper from the pocket of the riding jacket, very glad she'd brought it now, and handed it to Olivia.

"This is the power-of-attorney he signed," she said. "I thought it best you see it for yourself. It gives me complete control of family affairs, financially and legally."

Olivia stared down at the paper for a moment. "I can't understand any of these legal things," she said impatiently, then lifting her voice, "Tony. Come out here, please."

Rosaleen's eyes went to the door of the house. It opened in a moment and the man stepped out, dark, curly hair falling casually over his forehead, brown eyes, a classic nose, a handsome face but with a soft sensuality that edged on the weakness of the sybarite. "Tony, this is Rosaleen," Olivia said. His eyes swept her with a long, undressing look.

"You needn't have told me," he said. "She's even more beautiful than I'd heard."

"Tony Darby, my husband," Olivia said with a faint hint of defensiveness. She plucked at his arm, pushed the document at him. "Read this, Tony. Rosaleen tells me Father's put her in charge of all family affairs."

Rosaleen stood quietly as Tony Darby's eyes scanned the document. When he finished, he looked up at her with a cheerful smile and then kept his eyes on her as he handed the document back to Olivia.

"That's what it seems to say, Livvie," he commented. Rosaleen kept from wincing. She always hated names pulled out of shape and made cute. It always seemed an intrusion on personal dignity. She met his frankly admiring gaze, decided he would be terribly handsome if he had less of the carpet knight in his face.

"What's it mean, precisely?" Olivia's voice cut in.

"That we deal with Rosaleen on all family matters," he explained with unruffled calm. He stepped a pace forward, his attention completely on Rosaleen. He reached out, took the document from Olivia, and gave it back. "I've wanted to meet you. I've heard a good deal about you, of course."

"I imagine," Rosaleen said blandly. Olivia interrupted again.

"I was going to see Father about Tony and I moving into Raven's Wing," she said. Rosaleen held down an instant rejection, recognizing it as an emotional, vengeance-tinted reaction. "This place is too expensive," Olivia said with a gesture to the house behind her.

"Why did you rent it in the first place?" Rosaleen asked.

Tony Darby answered and his smile was almost shy and quite disarming. "I didn't realize it would take this long to get some of my ventures moving."

"There's enough room. God, you could put ten families in Raven's Wing," Olivia said.

"Yes, I suppose there is. But I'd like to think about it more, perhaps talk to Father," Rosaleen said, deferring further discussion. Olivia's ever-ready pout slipped over her face but Tony Darby seemed unbothered. "Unless you've anything else at the moment, I'll be on my way," Rosaleen said.

"Well, there was something else...." Olivia began. Tony Darby cut her off.

"Nothing that can't wait," he said, then took Rosaleen's arm in a light grip and walked to the horse with her. "I'm very happy you're taking over things and that you're back at Raven's Wing. Olivia has told me all about what happened," he said.

"Thank you," Rosaleen murmured. He could project past the slightly lustful charm. Perhaps his rakishness was but a veneer, she mused, and wondered about the errors of first impressions.

"I know we'll be seeing a lot more of each other," Tony Darby said, and Rosaleen kept her expression still. He had a way of putting more meaning into words than they usually carried. Or was she being ridiculous, she wondered. She felt prim, school-marmish, not at all like herself. The new role, she murmured inwardly. He leaned forward, kissed her, a light kiss yet lingering perhaps a fraction longer than it might. "Take care going back," he smiled, and helped her into the saddle, one hand pressing into her waist.

Rosaleen wheeled the horse, waved at them both. Olivia managed a return gesture, Tony Darby a penetrating smile. Rosaleen sent the horse into a trot, headed for Bodwin to pick up some needed groceries. Dusk had begun to slip across the moors when she returned to Raven's Wing, the groceries stuffed into the saddle bag. She stabled and fed the horses, then fixed something for herself and ate it before the fire. Later, she sat down with the papers and the ledger of accounts she'd been given and studied them until her eyes grew tired. She went to bed, then lay in the darkness and listened to the sounds old houses make, murmurs of their own, whispers and reminders.

She'd been born here in Raven's Wing, raised here, grown up here. It had sheltered her, been a refuge and a home, protected her against all the outer elements and some of the inner, and now she'd been given the task of caring for its welfare along with the other family matters. She'd return the debt as one returns a favor to an old and dear friend. She slept finally, to the wind blowing across the moors.

She'd overslept, she realized as she opened her eyes the next day. The sun streamed across the entire room, a sign of the late-ness of the morning. She flung on work clothes, spent the rest of the morning cleaning house and stables; the noon sun had long since slid down into midday when she finished. She relaxed in a warm bath then, got out and put on a jonquil-patterned walk-ing dress with a square-necked bodice. She took the gardening shears outside with her and began to prune the rhododendron hedge that lined the side wall. She had almost completed the task when she saw the Stanhope gig enter the driveway, Tony Darby the lone occupant. He drove up to the flagstoned terrace and halted and she came forward just as, with one bound, he leapt from the wagon and thrust a magnificent bouquet of gladiolis, carnations, dragonsnaps, and roses at her, executing a sweeping bow in the grand manner.

"For the most beautiful sister-in-law a chap could hope to have," he pronounced, followed with an infectious grin as she took the flowers.

"They're beautiful," Rosaleen said. "I'll have to find a huge vase for them." She paused, met his eyes. "But really, this isn't at all necessary."

"The fun things seldom are," he said.

"True enough," Rosaleen conceded. "Thank you, Tony." She started to turn away when he reached into the Stanhope, pulled out a split of champagne.

"To complete the celebration. I feel like champagne today," he announced, took her arm, and marched into the house with her.

"Glasses are in the cabinet," she said as she found a large vase, filled it with water, and lowered the flowers into it. Tony Darby took two glasses and followed her into the living room. He worked the cork free and it popped with proper loudness.

"Where's Olivia?" Rosaleen asked as he poured the champagne.

"She had one of her headaches. She always has them when she's upset about something," Tony Darby said, raising his glass to her. "To you, Rosaleen, and to knowing you better," he said. Rosaleen sipped the drink and wondered why she kept sensing more in his words than she should. The champagne, cold and lively, felt good trickling down her throat. Tony Darby moved to the sofa, beckoned her down beside him, watched her take another long sip of her drink.

"Your first in Raven's Wing in a long time," he remarked.

"Exactly what I was thinking," Rosaleen said, looking with some surprise at him. "You're good at that sort of thing, aren't you, catching people's thoughts."

"I try to be," he grinned, leaning forward and refilling her glass. "Drink up. You deserve it, I daresay."

"Yes," Rosaleen agreed, feeling a sudden stab of triumph mixed with self-pity. She drank deeply again. "What exactly do you do, Tony?" she questioned.

"I'm a consultant in business matters. I look for people with venture capital and show them how they can make money with that capital or establish themselves in a new business. It takes a conceptual sense, a broad, overall view of what will make money. You could say it's creative business concepts," Tony Darby explained.

"Things are going slowly, though?" Rosaleen asked.

"It just takes time to put complex ventures into action," he answered. "But I'm more interested in talking about you. A woman as beautiful as you without a man is more than a waste. It's a sin."

Rosaleen finished the champagne, refused a refill. He was being complimentary, she realized, yet she felt annoyed, as she'd be annoyed to find someone peeking into her bedroom.

"You're not cut out for a life of abstinence," he commented, and her violet eyes deepened a half-shade as she focused on him.

"I'd say you were being presumptuous," she answered.

"Maybe. But right, too," he said, unperturbed, leaning toward her. "You can't keep the lid on forever, not a woman with your needs."

His rakish charm was edging toward a leer and Rosaleen felt herself growing too angry. "I'll handle my own needs, thank you. It's none of your concern," she snapped.

"But it is. Your happiness is of definite concern to me, to all of us," Tony Darby said smoothly. His hand dropped over hers. "I just want you to know that I'll help you in any way I can," he said.

Rosaleen pulled her hand away, felt unaccountably upset. "If I understand what you mean, I think you can leave now," she said.

"My, but my beauteous sister-in-law is touchy," he said.

"I'd say your implications are out of order," Rosaleen snapped. "Especially coming from my sister's husband."

"Oh, come now, Rosaleen. You've never been anything but rivals, I hear," Tony Darby scoffed at her.

"Apparently faithfulness is not part of your code," Rosaleen returned.

"You surprise me, my dear," he said unruffled. "I had expected more sophistication from a woman who lived openly with a lover. Perhaps you're reading things into what I said. Now that'd be a kind of admission of its own, wouldn't it?" He laughed as he rose and she stood up. He leaned forward, brushed her cheek with his lips, and she stood rigidly, hands clenched. "Think about that, my dear," he half-whispered and then he was off, striding smartly across the foyer and out the front door.

Rosaleen flung herself into one of the deep, stuffed wing chairs, furious with herself. She hadn't read into things. He'd been full of innuendos, she muttered silently. But he was right to have expected more sophistication. She'd handled it poorly, like a schoolgirl with her first proposition. *Damn,* she muttered. Had his presence set off emotions too long suppressed? Was she so in need? Had he touched the right places in the right ways?

He was one of those men who could do that. Ferretlike, they could unerringly uncover vulnerability, going instantly to the weak places hidden even from oneself. With their instinctive sensuality, they made connections, evoked responses. But she'd handle it better next time. There would be a next time, she was certain. Men such as Tony Darby seldom stopped at but one attempt. They really believed their sensuality could reach and eventually overwhelm any woman. In Tony Darby's case, perhaps there were added motives, an immediate attempt to establish a hold over her, a time-honored route to emotional dominance. After all, she had suddenly become important in his life, and in Olivia's, Rosaleen mused. Had his overtures been made with Olivia's knowledge? The thought hung. Olivia easily compromised pride and integrity when the end results were to her benefit. Rosaleen shook away further thoughts on Olivia's complicity. Time would reveal that, or if Tony Darby was simply a thoroughgoing bounder.

She rose, deciding that a walk would clear her mind. She took a cape from the hall closet and left Raven's Wing to saunter along the moor as the dusk began to gather, laying a soft lavender over the land. The night wind was already sending out advance messengers, puffs of breeze that caught at her cape. She let the cool, clean air chase away the unpleasantness that had wrapped itself around her and she walked farther than she'd intended, finding herself at the sharp curve of the cliffs known locally as the "point." Just around the other side of the point, a fine, old house, the Baxter-Mills place, had been closed and empty for years. It was a lovely house, with stone turrets at each corner and high, mullioned windows and atop its stone walls, a sloping hip roof with numerous dormers, giving it all the appearance of a gentle castle. As she caught sight of it in the gathering dusk, she frowned to see lights on inside.

Drawn by curiosity, she walked to the house and saw that the front terrace, long neglected, had been repaired and a lovely circle of garden flowers planted. The door of the house suddenly opened and Rosaleen looked up into the deep, intense eyes of the tall rider who'd come out of the fog-bound night. For an instant, she considered bolting away. It would be in character for a panic-stricken servant girl. His words, slowly reeled out, ended the thought.

"Good evening, Rosaleen Powell," he said. Rosaleen saw the quiet amusement in his eyes and her lips pressed together.

"How long have you known?" she asked abruptly.

"Since that night," he said blandly.

"I see," Rosaleen sniffed. "And I thought I'd done so well."

"You made a fetching servant girl, Yorkshire accent and all," he said. "But it's impossible to disguise a finely bred thorough-bred as a draft horse."

She smiled ruefully at the compliment as his deep eyes danced. "I must thank you again, then, properly this time, for your help and for keeping quiet," she said, and his nod accepted her words. "The story I told you was the truth, more or less. I did find him, but on the beach, first, and brought him to Raven's Wing. Then the others came back to find him and finish the job."

"I understand you're not wanting wagging tongues all about," he said. "Please come in, won't you? I'm Niles Brewster and we are neighbors now, of a sort."

He held the door open and she entered the house. It had been years since she'd set foot in the musty old place and her breath caught as she stepped into the living room that sparkled with richness, its former beauty restored as she had never seen it. She turned to the tall, handsome man with surprise and curiosity in her violet orbs.

"I'm an interior designer and I specialize in restorations," Niles Brewster said. "I rented the place to restore it. Of course, this is but a start."

"It's perfectly beautiful," Rosaleen said.

"Someday, I should like to see Raven's Wing. I understand it is a magnificent house," he said.

"Yes, and you may see it anytime you wish," Rosaleen said, the idea engulfing her with a rush of sudden pleasure. He would fit in Raven's Wing, this tall, strong-faced man who obviously appreciated beauty in all its forms. His accent puzzled her some, upper-class English yet with something else in it.

"Please join me for an aperitif," Niles Brewster said. "I was just about to have some Vieux Curé.

"Yes, that'd be nice," Rosaleen agreed, and sank down on the sofa done in gold brocade with blue accents. She watched him pour the two small, stemmed glasses, hand her one, and sit down across from her on a Jelliff chair whose high back echoed the arch of a cathedral.

"I wondered when I'd have the chance to meet you properly, Rosaleen Powell," Niles Brewster said. "I won't pretend I haven't heard about the family feud. You apparently caused quite a scandal once in these parts."

"Yes. I imagine tongues will never stop wagging over it," Rosaleen said, unable to avoid bitterness in her voice. "Are you from London?" she asked.

His smile was quick and warm. "The accent's been puzzling you, of course," he remarked, and Rosaleen smiled in admiration. He missed very little, but then she'd learned that in the foggy night. "I'm American, actually, but I was raised and educated in England—Eton and Cambridge. I sort of shuttle across the Atlantic."

"I've only known three Americans, two boys at school years ago, crass, pushy, and thoroughly irritating they were, and a man I've met only a half-dozen formal occasions, Frank Shields."

"The shipping magnate," Niles Brewster cut in.

"Yes, and I can't say I care much for him, either," Rosaleen commented.

"Because he's your father's chief rival?" Niles Brewster asked.

"No, because I sense a thoroughly unscrupulous man, a man totally without ethics," Rosaleen snapped back.

She saw the deep, intense eyes grow reflective a moment. "I daresay you're probably right. I've met Frank Shields, too," he said thoughtfully, and then brightening, "but I shall have to change your opinion about Americans."

He already had, Rosaleen commented inwardly. This tall man sent out a quiet charisma that circled around one, commanding yet without demand. She finished the aperitif and refused another. "It's been an upsetting day in some ways, giving me a lot to think about. I want a clear head," she said. "Some other time."

"A promise?" he asked.

"Yes, very much a promise," Rosaleen said.

"Good," he said. "It's grown dark. I'll see you back." Rosaleen started to protest, but he cut her off. "I know there's no need. You know these moors and cliffs far better than I, but it gives me a good excuse." His smile was suddenly boyish, totally disarming.

"You don't need an excuse," Rosaleen said evenly.

"A woman without pretense. Splendid," he said, and took her arm as they went outside where a half-moon hung low and the night chill had already invested the dark. His touch was comforting, remembered echoes that stirred her. "Do you prefer riding alone in the early morning?" he asked as they neared Raven's Wing.

"Yes, usually," Rosaleen said honestly. "It's a private time."

"I can understand that," he said.

"But I think I might make an exception to that," Rosaleen said, and saw his lips touched by a half-smile.

"I'm honored. But I've a better thought. You ride as you usually do, but I'll be at the point. That way you can have both, your solitude and company if you wish."

"Agreed," Rosaleen said.

"Tomorrow?" he asked as they halted outside Raven's Wing.

"Tomorrow," she said, feeling how wonderful it was just saying the word. It was an almost forgotten feeling, to look forward to tomorrow, and she held it tightly to her. Niles Brewster half-bowed, turned, and strode away without another word. Rosaleen went into the house, turned on a low lamp, and fixed something to eat. She refused to acknowledge the quiet excitement inside her, but, of course, knew that it needed no acknowledgment. She went to bed early and made herself stay away from thoughts and speculations. They led too easily to hopes and hopes too easily to tears.

But in the morning, in wine-red riding jacket and white skirt, she rode the stallion through the new mists along the beach and when she reached the point, she saw him waiting on the horse, his shirt open at the neck, his chest partially revealed, muscular and smooth. She saw his eyes survey her almost with awe.

"The rare and radiant maiden whom the angels named Rosaleen," he said.

She laughed. "With apologies to Edgar Allan Poe," and he nodded agreement, wheeling his horse beside her. They rode to a place where the cliffs opened up in a tall, rocky bower and moss-weed and starfern carpeted the flat rocks and loosestrife found a hold to grow in purple clusters. They rested and talked as the sun rose higher and swept away the morning mists. He was able to make her laugh and relax and remember how to feel young again. He told her he'd rented the Baxter-Mills house six months earlier and had begun work immediately on it. He'd also met Olivia and Tony Darby in Bodwin.

"You're quite totally different, you and she," Niles commented, eying Rosaleen. "I imagine you're a little intolerant of her," he said. Rosaleen felt her frown come at once, her lips open in protest. How absolutely incorrect, she wanted to say, but the protest died in her throat. The word had stabbed but it was the truth in it, she realized.

"I never saw it that way," Rosaleen reflected aloud, and stared at the man across from her. "You reach deep quickly," she said.

"Not so deep," he laughed. "The strong tend to be intolerant of the weak. One of the laws of human nature." He went on quickly, to other things, and the hours passed and too soon it was time to return to Raven's Wing and practical problems. But not before Rosaleen had agreed to meet the next morning and she felt his eyes on her as she rode on and he remained at the point. She returned to Raven's Wing feeling soft and warm; even the sight of the carriage drawing up later with Olivia and Tony didn't dispel the happiness that had taken root inside her.

Olivia was a shade tense, Rosaleen detected, but Tony was completely casual. "Just a welcome visit," he said. When Olivia went to the side of the house to examine the rock garden, always her special concern, he wasted no time with Rosaleen inside the living room. "Still not upset over yesterday, are you?" he asked, and his arm found her waist. "You'll believe me. I just want to be of help to you in any way I can."

"Just to me," Rosaleen said. "Not to yourself?" She slipped away from his encircling arm. "You only know one way to approach a woman, don't you, Tony?"

"It's a good way," he grinned. "Mutually rewarding."

Rosaleen resisted cutting him down, deciding to see whether he was pursuing her as a woman or a meal ticket, or both. She'd let him have time to reveal that much, she concluded silently. "Sometimes," Rosaleen allowed him, saw the satisfaction glimmer in his eyes. Olivia came back into the house and, as usual unless she were dealing with men, diplomacy deserted her.

"Have you decided about our moving into Raven's Wing?" she asked almost belligerently. Tony stepped in before Rosaleen could answer.

"Don't press Rosaleen so, Livvie, darling," he said smoothly. "I'm sure she's had enough just acquainting herself with all the things that have been dumped in her lap."

"Tony's right, there," Rosaleen agreed, according him a glance of gratitude. "I haven't thought about it, really."

Olivia's pout was instant. "I don't see it taking much thinking. There's more than enough room. It's either that or I'll need an increase in funds to stay at Braemore."

Rosaleen glanced at Tony. He shrugged. His casualness was well practiced, she thought. "It takes money to keep up appearances, you know. That's very important in my line," he said.

"I'll think about it, I promise," Rosaleen said, avoiding any reply to the double-edged proposal.

"When will you be seeing Father again?" Olivia asked.

"By next week," Rosaleen said. "Why?"

"I might go with you," Olivia said. "I'm sure he'd listen to me."

"The reason he turned family affairs over to me was precisely so he wouldn't have to listen to you," Rosaleen said, more coldly than she'd intended. Tony Darby's soft chuckle cut the moment at once and she felt a stab of honest appreciation.

"Hear, hear," he said. "Well put, sis." Rosaleen gazed at him. He was not going to be so easy to define, she decided. Olivia flounced but turned the rest of the visit to lighter things. Yet Rosaleen was glad to see them leave when dusk came. "See you soon, sis," Tony said to her in an aside, and she began to wonder if it was simply natural for him to put a leer into everything he said.

Through the window, she watched Olivia sit close against him in the carriage, holding his arm as they drove away. She was obviously completely taken with her husband. The fact was the measure of the difference between Olivia and herself, Rosaleen reflected. Tony Darby was definitely a kind of man she disliked on sight, regardless of his looks and his animal sensuality. But was simple dislike enough for Tony Darby, she wondered. Did he deserve more? Or less? She'd find out, she was certain, and she turned from the window, glad to see them leave. She took out the ledger Sir Mallory had given her and, before the evening ended, had concluded that an increase in funds for Olivia was out of the question. That left only the matter of Olivia and Tony moving into Raven's Wing, and again she pushed aside considering that. Bed, sleep, and anticipation of the morning were much more attractive than decisions about Olivia and Tony.

Dawn came with a chilly drizzle, but Rosaleen rode anyway. In the cold, gray half-light at the point, Niles Brewster was waiting. He led her to a little cottage halfway along the road to Gwyneth, a one-room stone coteen sitting mountain-goat fashion along the side of the stone slopes. A fire and a cup of hot tea made with a touch of orange rind curled around inside her like an inner scarf of warm comfort. The little coteen became a place for her and Niles to go on the chilled, rainy days when the sand and shore were unfriendly. The mornings had slipped into sweet trysts with nothing yet said, only their hands touching in a passing gesture, like songs unsung yet clearly heard. It was the way it had been with Colin, Rosaleen realized, the knowing inside that was beyond all other knowing, needing no examination, no exercise in reason, but simply there, formed and complete, pure of itself. The heart has its own wisdom, born of its own senses.

Niles Brewster's quiet strength let her talk about yesterdays without hurting and it was on the night when he first visited her at Raven's Wing that he took her hands in his and drew her close.

"You were fortunate to grow up in this great house, Rosaleen," he said. "You've had more than your share of tragedy, but from the things you've told me, you've been blessed, too." He half-smiled at her frown. "To truly love, and to be truly loved, even once, is more than many women ever experience. It is a kind of riches no one can ever take from you, and it makes you special."

"I'm hardly special," Rosaleen protested, and his hand left hers, touched her lips.

"I think you are," he said, his voice suddenly soft velvet, and then his lips were on hers, tenderly urging. She felt her mouth open, her tongue seek, eager messenger, inviting, coaxing, and she felt her skin suddenly glowing, a hurrying warmth creeping through her body. His mouth pressed harder and his hands came to touch the base of her neck, moving gently downward, caressing the swell of her breasts, and she knew one thing above all else, that she welcomed and wanted him as she had all but forgotten she could want. She heard her voice whisper words she'd thought never to say again, mean again as she had once meant them.

"Yes, Niles, yes, please, please. Take me, oh God, please." Her arms circled his neck and she pressed herself tight against his body, felt the hardness of him and gasped out in a surge of wanting. She felt him lift her, carry her from the room and into her bedroom, and only when he placed her on the bed did she pull back, take his face in her hands to stare deep into the dark, intense eyes. She asked no questions, put no words to him, but he stopped, waited, understood what she sought.

"Do you see it, Rosaleen?" he asked softly. "Do you see that I'm in love with you? I am, you know, terribly so."

She nodded, heard herself whisper, "Yes, I see it, Niles. Love me, my darling, love me, please." He came against her, lips upon lips, hands to breasts, skin cleaving skin and she felt the world open up for her again and cried in gratitude as well as ecstasy and he understood as he held her in silence. It was nearing dawn when she sat up, realized she'd been asleep in the warm circle of his arms, and saw Niles, dressed, at the edge of the bed.

"I want to be from here before dawn and prying eyes and wagging tongues are up and about," he said. "You've had enough of that."

"Indeed," she said, then a sly smile stole over her face. "I won't be riding this morning," she murmured.

"Nor I," he laughed, and bent down, pressing his lips to her face, then once quickly to each breast. "Till tomorrow, my Rosaleen of the violet eyes," he said. She lay back after he'd gone, stretched, feeling warm and thoroughly feline. Anger and love, tears and joy, they came at one from so many unexpected places, like highwaymen setting upon a victim when least expected. Each time they took getting used to all over again. But she was happy, for the first time in so long, so terribly long. It felt frighteningly good and she hugged it to herself as she slept.

The happiness was with her when she woke later in the morning and it stayed to fill each morning that followed. Her life had new wings that made the days fly, but the mornings were still a special time, the tiny stone coteen their own private place. Niles had begun work on the library of the Baxter-Mills house and twice she went to Bodwin with him to pick up things he'd ordered.

"I found a list of all the books the library originally held and I've sent letters to dealers all over. I'm going to duplicate the library just as it once was," he told her. She joined his work emotionally, sometimes actually, helping him restore a beautiful wicker chair and, as she had with Colin, becoming closer for it. The world was bright and wonderful again, time quartered by the sweet moments in Niles's arms, pressed hard against his body, sobbing with rediscovered pleasures. There were a few areas still to be improved upon. She wished for more than the few, quick visits she had time to take among her old friends in Gwyneth, and she yearned to sail again, to go out with the drifters once more. But she'd find the time, she promised herself.

Bills, taxes, and finances took more time than she'd expected and she had two interviews with applicants for caretaker, deciding against both, men with no more than earnestness to offer. Raven's Wing deserved more than that. It deserved someone who knew how to love its beauty and appreciate its strength, and she renewed the advertisement in the Plymouth journals. The days flew and she suddenly realized that the week was almost at an end and she'd not made her promised return to London. "It'll just be for a day, perhaps two," she told Niles, and realized she was reassuring herself as she clung to him.

"I'll be here, waiting and working," he told her between soft kisses. Olivia and Tony had stopped by a few times and Tony Darby still made quiet overtures, but her almost amused tolerance puzzled him. It was a reaction he obviously seldom came upon. When she left for London, she decided to take the night coach and have the fullness of the day at the Powell Line offices. Tony offered to drive her to Bodwin and she accepted, curious if he'd reveal more of his motives before she got the coach. He surprised her by saying nothing until they reached town and the coach station, where his words were an added surprise.

"You've been to Bodwin twice with that Brewster chap," he said, enjoying her flash of surprise.

"Yes," Rosaleen admitted. "I see you've your own sources of information."

"Indeed," Tony Darby said. "Been seeing him more than that, I'll wager. That could explain a lot of things."

"Such as my not responding to your charms?" Rosaleen spat at him as she carried her small overnight bag to the coach. He followed, his silence an admission.

"You might need me one of these days," he glowered.

"Not in the way you'd like," Rosaleen snapped.

"Don't be too sure. I wouldn't turn my back on those you might need one day," he persisted.

"Threats, Tony? That's a change of approach, at least," Rosaleen returned as she stepped into the waiting coach. She saw him whirl and march off with not another word. She leaned back in the coach. She'd learned nothing more about Tony Darby except that his ego was easily hurt. Perhaps, like Olivia, he was simply spoiled, acquisitive, and used to getting his own way. She was trying hard not to be intolerant, she reminded herself as the coach lurched and the journey to London began.

The trip was uneventful and she even managed a fairly long period of sleep, so she felt refreshed when she arrived at the offices on Fleet Street. Carlson greeted her and showed her into her father at once. Rosaleen hid the concern that touched her immediately as she gazed at the man. The strong face was gray, more drawn than last time, as he looked up from the sheaf of papers on his desk. His eyes sharpened when he saw her, color coming momentarily into his face. "I'd begun to think you'd forgotten," he commented.

"I almost had. Time flies," Rosaleen said, sitting on the deep leather chair across from him, avoiding mention of why time had been so fleeting and so full all at once.

"You've familiarized yourself with everything and you've questions, I take it," Sir Mallory Powell said.

"A few," Rosaleen said, and the eagle's eyes were sharp.

"Good," Sir Mallory said, tapping a finger on the top of the sheaf of papers. "These are my problems, all in one place, a list of everything that's gone wrong in the past year."

"I'd like to see that," Rosaleen said, and he lifted the top sheets, pulled out six below clipped together, pushed them at her.

"Take it with you. Read it when you want to feel depressed," he said. "Now, let's take up your questions." He leaned back, listening to each item she brought up, answering each without hesitation, the last one with grimness in his voice.

"Yes, that's the full capital trust left," he said. "I don't want to go into it again. That's another reason why I turned it all into your hands. You can say no to me if I grow desperate."

"Do you think I would?" Rosaleen asked gently.

"You should, dammit, girl," Sir Mallory thundered with sudden strength. "I'll have to fight my way out of this with the company funds." He sat back, lost in thought for a moment, then turned to her again. "You've seen Olivia by now, of course," he said.

"Yes, and Tony," Rosaleen said. Her father made a displeased grunting sound at Tony's name. "Do you know much about the business consultant thing of his, this showing venture capital how to make more money on its investments?" Rosaleen asked. Sir Mallory's displeased sound grew into a half-roar.

"He's a get-rich-quick operator, that's what he is," her father said. "He tries to find a sucker for his schemes and then sells them a bill of goods on some wild, hairy venture he's dreamed up. He's always got half a dozen things going, almost all of them unsound. The man should have been a cardsharp, probably was, for all I know."

Sir Mallory's energies suddenly depleted by the outburst, he sat back, his breathing ragged. He pressed the little desk buzzer and Carlson appeared. "Get Coops in here," Sir Mallory ordered.

"Have you thought about taking a rest?" Rosaleen said as they waited. The eagle's eyes snapped at her.

"That's all Frank Shields would want," Sir Mallory said.

The door opened and Rosaleen watched the man enter. He had thick, silver-white hair, a weathered face, an attractive man, medium height with sparkling blue eyes; he wore the navy blue jacket of a ship's master. "Captain Coops, my dear," Sir Mallory said. The man bowed graciously to Rosaleen.

"Joshua Coops at your service," he murmured.

"I told Captain Coops about the young man on the beach. Please tell him again in your words," Sir Mallory said, and Rosaleen recounted all that had happened as the captain, sinking into a chair, listened gravely. His lips were pressed tight when she finished.

"Rotten business," he muttered. "But very revealing in its own way. That young man, Reilly by name, was indeed on his way to see your father. I can only presume he felt he'd never reach London alive and tried to make it to Raven's Wing."

"Who was he, Captain?" Rosaleen frowned.

"A passing name, an able-bodied seaman who came upon some information more deadly than he realized," the captain said. "Many years ago, on the East India run, a shipment of gold bullion was to arrive in Bangkok aboard the three-masted barkentine, the *Fifeshire*. It never arrived. Somewhere along the way, it had been stolen. It was traced back as far as Chittagong where the Australian packet, the *Star of Sydney*, was to transfer it to the *Fifeshire*. But somewhere the gold bullion disappeared, a tremendous fortune stolen and hidden away. Oh, there was a great search for it, I can tell you that, but they never did find it." He paused, took a sip of water from a pitcher on the edge of the desk. "The original shippers went bankrupt over the next few years and the bullion stayed hidden and now unclaimed. The story has it that most of the original thieves died in fights over the gold and over the years many others have tried to find what has become known as the Bangkok bullion. It would belong now to whosoever finds it first."

"It's enough to finance the Powell Line and a dozen new ones twice over," Sir Mallory said.

"This Reilly lad had picked up word about it in a tavern in Perth and he came to me about it," Captain Coops went on. "He said he was going to learn more. I told him to go to your father with whatever he found out."

"Obviously, he found out too much," Rosaleen said. "Which means that the bullion still exists someplace and others are on the trail of it."

"Exactly," Sir Mallory said. "Coops, here, has another contact on it and he'll see his man next week when he goes to Tangiers. I intend to do all I can to keep after this. It'd pull the line out of the hole in one day."

"Do you know who these others are that are after the bullion?" Rosaleen asked.

Captain Coops shook his head. "It could be anyone. They'll stop at nothing, it's plain, a thoroughly ruthless lot. And they obviously know we're trying to run down any leads we can."

"Is it worth the risk to keep after this elusive bullion?" Rosaleen asked. It was Sir Mallory's voice, bitter and harsh, that answered her.

"Just study the things on the list you have in your hands. That'll answer you," he said.

"I will," Rosaleen said softly, and Captain Coops rose, excused himself with another gracious bow, and left the office. "A good man, isn't he?" Rosaleen commented.

"The best," her father answered. "A fine ship's master and a man who can see beyond the sails."

Rosaleen rose to her feet. Sir Mallory was suddenly exhausted and he put his head back against the chair. "I'll be going, now," she said. "I think you should come to Raven's Wing for a long weekend, at least."

"In time," he said. "In time."

She took a half-step forward, wanted to go to him, put her arms around him as she once would have done. But she halted, turned on her heel, and hurried from the office. The recent memories were still there, barriers, forbidding, refusing, and, angry at her own weakness, she halted in the outside office, drew a deep breath. The voice came at her from the side. "Miss Powell, how well you look." Rosaleen turned to see Harriet Woodbridge and she smiled inwardly at the greeting. Sir Mallory's secretary and Carlson's assistant had never called her anything but "Miss Powell," even as a little girl.

"Hello, Harriet. Thank you," Rosaleen said, seeing the gray hair piled atop the woman's head had been stiffened with oil and that her finely creased face was, as always, reminiscent of imprinted wax. Harriet Woodbridge was one of those women who seemed to be born formal, a closed-in person with a world that went no further than the office and her work, who had devoted a lifetime to bloodless detail. Still, Rosaleen reflected, she encapsulated her kind of faithfulness, sterile as it was.

"I'm sorry I wasn't here at your last visit, Miss Powell," Harriet Woodbridge went on. "Are you staying in London for a few days?"

"No, I'm returning to Cornwall, tonight probably," Rosaleen said, and saw Carlson appear. She beckoned to him, took him aside and urged him to get Sir Mallory to take time off for a rest. Carlson shook his head dubiously, his mousiness more apparent and more irritating than ever before.

"He won't listen to me," the man muttered.

"Just keep trying," Rosaleen snapped, and saw the surprise at her vehemence in Carlson's face. He nodded, always obedient to the sound of authority. Rosaleen left the office, hurried to Charing Cross, and caught the early stage out of London, troubled and apprehensive and wanting desperately to return to Cornwall. And to Niles.

CHAPTER FOUR

The coach reached Bodwin in the early morning and she paid Sam Tyler to drive her to Raven's Wing. A note under the door greeted her.

"Welcome back, my darling. Expect me tonight. Niles," she read aloud, and felt the warmth curl inside her. The trip had been slow, with extra stops, and she was exhausted. She went to bed, woke with the noon sun and attended to chores and had something to eat. She sat down with the papers she'd brought back from London, the list of troubles and disasters that had struck the Powell Line during the past year. She took a pencil and made notes alongside each entry. It was an upsetting document. On January 24, the clipper *Star of Madras* broke a foremast for no apparent reason and the line had to pay a shipper a £5,000 penalty. February saw the barkentine *Mary O'Malley* lose her course during the Rio to Liverpool run and then arrive four weeks late. A few days after, her master, a Captain Donaldson, resigned his position with the Powell Line. She found his name, farther down the list, as master of a Shields vessel. On February 10, the *Amenia* arrived in Boston with her entire shipment of Patras currants, St. Michaels oranges, and Egyptian wheat ruined because of incorrect packing. In March, the four-masted schooner *Argonaut* couldn't sail when her crew didn't show up. Rosaleen read on, the list a long and sorry documentation. But her curiosity grew as she read and when she finished, she went over the papers again, her frown deepening with each page.

The incidents seemed disconnected, yet there was a pattern. In almost every instance, the Frank Shields Shipping Lines had benefitted. In many of the incidents, Shields vessels were conveniently on hand to step into the breach and secure the business. Too conveniently, Rosaleen murmured to herself. In other instances, the accidents could not be explained except along one line, accidents planned and created, equipment on vessels sabotaged, cargo mishandled and purposely packed incorrectly. Crew troubles developed at just the right time to benefit Frank Shields.

The more she examined the list, the more she became convinced that the plague of troubles that had struck the Powell Line were, for the most past, engineered. She saw the pattern because she looked at the picture with fresh eyes, from a distance. Her father and the others were too close to all that had happened, too involved with the details of each disaster to step back and view it as it had met her eyes. She made further notes, then put everything in a safe place. Another trip to London was imperative, Rosaleen decided, perhaps the first of the week.

She'd just finished when she heard the horse trot to a halt outside, blow air, and stamp the ground. She rushed to the door, pulled it open to be swept up by Niles, his lips hungrily upon hers. She matched his hunger with her own, her hands pressing tight against his chest. "God, it's immoral, missing you so much in so short a time," he breathed.

"I know," she nodded, and clung tightly. He stayed the night and in the quiet moments in between, she told him of her visit to London, her concern over Sir Mallory, and then the conclusions she'd made regarding the plague of disasters. Niles listened, offered neither glib words of encouragement or condescending dissuasions but let his quiet strength help her reaffirm her own decisions.

"Maybe this time I'll meet you in London and we'll take in the theater," he said. "That new Ibsen play, *A Doll's House*, is at the Drury Lane, I understand." Rosaleen snuggled agreement and let her lips find his strong neck, travel down over the smooth pectoral muscles, down along the pulsating line of his abdomen, down upon the soft skin, nibbling, pressing, seeking as her own body grew warm with inner fires. He pulled her hard against him and the darkness closed around her, encompassing, seducing, protecting.

But as always, the dawn's first glow touched the bedroom window, a faint pink-gray smudge, and Niles rose, dressed, and left her with a last kiss and the still warm imprint of his body. Later, as the morning sun rose across the floor of the room, Rosaleen dressed and attended to chores. It was later in the day when she saw the Stanhope draw up to the house. She smiled to herself. She'd been expecting the visit since noon. Tony was his usual debonair self but Olivia's impatience and anxiety showed as they came inside. She spoke in quick bunches of words, remarking on little things about the house. It was always a sign of her nervousness, Rosaleen remembered. Olivia wore a pink crinoline and gold *jarratières* on both wrists, the outfit more fitting for an evening garden party in August. But Olivia had always worn clothes with little regard for season, time, or place. If a dress showed her to her best, she wore it anytime, anywhere.

"How was Father?" Olivia asked with unsuccessful casualness.

"Not well. I came back very bothered by the way he looked," Rosaleen said. The concern that caught hold of Olivia's round-cheeked face was real. Olivia cared, felt, loved in her way, Rosaleen knew. It was merely that her spoiled, self-centered ways obscured everything else. She watched Olivia grope for words and felt a rush of sympathy for her sister. "No, I didn't speak to him about your finances, Olivia," she said. "Or about your living in Raven's Wing. I repeat, those are my decisions now."

"Of course, and Rosaleen has a lot of other things on her mind," Tony cut in. In his eyes, Rosaleen read the private message.

"Nothing that will interfere with those decisions," she said coolly.

"Good, because we can't stay on at Braemore without a good deal more funds and I must have a proper place to entertain. I'm expecting some important people next month," Tony said.

"Increasing Olivia's draw from the trust fund is out of the question," Rosaleen said. "At least until capital has been built up again."

Tony shrugged. "Just keep in mind that if my ventures go under, Livvie might be even more dependent. She's used to a certain life-style."

"Then she'll have to get used to another," Rosaleen snapped.

"I wish you'd stop talking about me as if I weren't here," Olivia interjected.

"I'm sorry. It was rude of me," Rosaleen apologized.

"I'm going up to look for something in my room," Olivia said with an injured air. She spun away and disappeared up the wide stairway. She'd only been gone a few moments when Rosaleen felt Tony's hand on her waist, resting lightly against her hip.

"Look here, my beautiful sister-in-law. We ought not to be exchanging words. We've too many things in common for that," he said.

Rosaleen brushed his hand away. "Such as?" she asked.

"Livvie's happiness. Her well-being," he answered.

"Olivia's well-being or yours? Which do you really care about, Tony?" Rosaleen thrust. "You obviously didn't marry Olivia because you're so in love with her."

She saw his face darken. "Maybe you don't know everything there's to know about love. There's a lot you have to learn," Tony Darby glowered. She was about to snap a reply but she held back. His protest held as much injury as anger in it and there was no casual glibness in him for a moment. Olivia saved her from finding a reply as she came hurrying down the steps waving a full-bellied old bottle of Calvados.

"Found it at the bottom of my trunk," Olivia announced, linked her arm into Tony's, and looked up at him with her eyes shining. "Not all of it tonight," she giggled. "Just enough." Rosaleen caught her wink at Tony.

"Good brandy does things to me," Tony explained, his cool casualness in place again, the leer back in his voice.

"Let's go home," Olivia said to him. He cast a quick glance at Rosaleen and there was a glimmer of triumph in it. "We'll talk again soon, sis," he said to her, and Rosaleen watched him walk from Raven's Wing, Olivia hanging onto his arm. She stayed clinging to him as they drove away and Rosaleen closed the door, a small furrow digging into her brow. Tony Darby's accusation disturbed her. She wanted to throw it aside yet it clung, irritating, throwing doubt on her own certainties, and this doubly angered her. Tony Darby was the shallow one, the monument to surface trivialities. He was the one incapable of knowing the meaning of love. Without depths, without strengths, how could one really know love?

Rosaleen let the rhetoric in the question satisfy her and she sat down to peruse the financial statements, stopping only when fatigue overcame her. But it was in the morning, as she sat beside Niles in the warmth of the new sun, that Tony's accusation returned again, and she told Niles of the exchange. "The nerve of him, telling me that," Rosaleen protested. "Love is total, complete of itself. It's caring more about someone else's wants than your own, living for someone else more than yourself, and being transformed yourself by that. It's a special kind of being alive, unlike any other kind."

Niles held her close, his smile soft. "That's as it should be. But that presupposes people are as they should be," he said. "Unfortunately, they're not. Their love is as they are, made of the same strengths and weaknesses, the same compromises of the spirit, the same limitations. Your love is what you are. Someone else's is what they are. It's not the same for everyone. Ideally, it should be, but it is too much a part of each individual."

Rosaleen leaned back in the sand. "Love—the changeling spirit," she mused aloud. "I've never looked at it that way." She fell silent for a spell, then drew him to her again. "Where is my love weak, Niles?" she half-whispered. His mouth found hers in answer and he rose, lifted her with him, carried her to the small rock crevice sheltered from the eyes of the sea, and took her in the new morning. She cried out in the ecstasy of knowing only the throbbing strength of her wanting and her loving.

It was later that night, wanting Niles beside her in bed, that she felt the aloneness of the big house more than she ever had before. Or was it just wanting more than she ever had before, she asked herself with a private smile as she let sleep wrap itself around her.

The next day, after tending to the horses and trimming the hedges, she took the Whitechapel buggy into Bodwin, stopping at Harvey Ellis's Market with a list of cupboard supplies needing replenishing: Scotch oatmeal, cracked wheat cereal, a sack of potatoes and one of onions, two loaves of brown bread, a jar of red honey and two of Jacob's beans, and a list of other sundries such as soap, arrowroot, and cloves. She included a sack of good flour, toying with the idea of baking Niles a batch of honey cookies. Harvey was loading the buggy when Tony appeared in the store, having seen the Whitechapel. His face was tight with anger, she saw at once.

"One of my best prospects canceled out on a venture," he told her, his dark eyes clouded. "Got a letter from him in the morning post, damn his hide."

"I'm sorry," Rosaleen offered.

His glower didn't soften. "I stopped to tell you we won't be staying on at Braemore. It'll take time to find someone else for this deal."

"You and Olivia will have to pull in your horns a bit but you'll manage," Rosaleen said.

"Manage?" Tony Darby exploded. "You don't care at all about how your sister lives, do you? Managing won't do, not for Livvie and not for me. There's no reason why we can't live at Raven's Wing except that you're afraid it'll bother your cozy little romance with Niles Brewster. Want it all terribly private, that's what you do."

"That's nonsense," Rosaleen flung back, felt the hotness of her cheeks. "That's unfair," she added, and angrily tried to ignore the barb. But she found that, once again, she could not just push aside his words. "I think it's best we discuss this tomorrow, when you're more in command of yourself," she said.

"Or maybe when you are," he threw back with a short, grunting noise, and hurried from the store. Rosaleen paid the shopkeeper and drove back to Raven's Wing, arriving as the night slid over the cliffs. She unloaded everything, ate lightly, and then drove to the point and to Niles.

"I've decided to go to London Monday," she said. "Can you meet me there?"

"Of course. That gives me three days to finish the east wall wainscoting," Niles said. "We'll have a grand time and you'll come back refreshed and ready to tackle anything."

Words she wanted to hear and she held them to her as she lost herself in Niles's arms again, eagerly letting the pleasures of touch and sense and smell turn aside everything else until the hour sent her back to Raven's Wing. She slipped out of her clothes once again, pulled the covers tight around her. The night had turned cool the way it always did when the east wind came in low over the moors and she slept soundly. Hours later, in the deep of the night, she first thought she was simply dreaming when the pounding filtered through to her. She turned over, not more than half awake, and tried to sleep again. But the pounding continued and she opened her eyes, listened. It came again, not part of a dream but someone pounding upon the front door. Rosaleen swung long legs out of the bed, pulled on a robe, and paused in the darkness downstairs to grope her way to the cabinet where the second of the big, heavy Lefaucheux pistols rested. With her finger on the trigger, she went to the door, pulled the latch open, and stepped back. The door swung open and she saw the figure of a man there, a dark form wrapped in oilskins. A cold rain slanted down across the entranceway.

"Special delivery post, miss," the man said, thrusting an oblong, wrapped scroll-like package at her. "From London, miss. They said I was to wait for an answer."

"Take your horse to the stables. You'll find dry towels there. You can rub him down. There are oats, too," Rosaleen said.

"Very good," the man said, and Rosaleen closed the door to a hard gust of rain. She went into the library, lighted a lamp, and sat down to undo the package. The letter, wrapped tightly around a core of cardboard, was written in a hasty scrawl.

Dear Miss Rosaleen,

This night, Sir Mallory died at his club. My grief is a terrible burden but my heart goes out to you.

It is imperative that you come to London at once. I leave it to you to notify your sister and whomsoever else you deem in order. Harold Pryor, your father's solicitor, has asked me to express his urgent need to see you as soon as possible.

With a heavy heart,
Nicholas Carlson

Rosaleen put the letter down on the library table, stared silently at it. She wanted to feel shock and pain, but that would come soon enough, she knew. All she felt now was a terrible emptiness engulfing her, the world turning over and, like a giant cup, draining itself out. She sat unmoving, staring into space until the knock came at the door again and she opened to see the messenger waiting, looking drier if no less weary.

"Tell them I'll leave for London in the morning," she said.

"In the morning," the man repeated, touching the brim of his rain hood with one finger. Rosaleen closed the door as he pulled himself up onto his horse, listened to the sound of hoofbeats as they faded away. She took the letter to her room with her, put it on the bed, and lay back, her eyes staring into the darkness. But the darkness was no longer a black void. It was filled with pictures that flashed through the emptiness, moments and times flooding back to fill the night. It wasn't until the dawn that she cried, a sudden explosion of sobs for all the unsaid things and all the unfinished moments. When she finished, she rose, freshened up, and put on a gray traveling dress. She took the buggy and drove to Braemore, where she knocked at the door until Tony came down, sleepworn, curly hair disheveled, clad in a blue robe. He stared at her as she entered and she saw Olivia in the blue nightgown she'd given her years ago, standing on the bottom step of the staircase. Olivia's eyes grew round as she gazed down at Rosaleen and her hand flew to her mouth. Rosaleen nodded. "Get dressed," she said quietly. Olivia half-screamed and dissolved into shuddering sobs, then Tony was at her side at once. Rosaleen forced herself to stay cold. It was her one defense against the torrent of emotions that churned inside her, waiting to seize control.

"I'm not waiting on coach schedules. The Whitechapel buggy has room enough for bags and three people. I'll be ready to leave in an hour," she said.

Tony nodded, his full lips drawn tight. "All right. I'll have Livvie ready," he said. Rosaleen left quickly, drove in a half-circle to the point, reaching the house just as Niles was saddling his horse. He read her face at once, gathered her into his arms, held her tight. Words were unnecessary and she clung to him with a shudder coursing through her to confirm the unsaid.

"Shall I drive you to London?" Niles asked.

Rosaleen shook her raven tresses. "It won't be necessary. Tony and Olivia are going with me and we'll take turns at the reins. When I get there, I'll have so much to do we wouldn't have any time together."

"Then I'll be waiting here for you when you come back," Niles told her.

"Yes," Rosaleen breathed. "That's important, just knowing you're here, my love. It will keep me going."

She clung to him for a while more, then pushed herself away. Niles pressed his lips to her cheek. "Till you return, my Rosaleen," he whispered. She didn't dare look back as she drove away and returned to Raven's Wing. She entered the house and halted. It was still, silent as a tomb, without a creak or murmur. It knows, Rosaleen whispered inwardly, it knows. She went upstairs, packed a traveling bag with enough clothes for three or four days. She'd not be longer in London this time, but she'd be returning there soon, she was certain. She brought the stallion out and harnessed him to the buggy with the gelding in a tandem hitch, put her bags into the carriage, and drove to Braemore. Olivia, ghostly pale, was waiting outside, clinging to Tony. They got into the buggy, then Rosaleen snapped the reins and headed the team for the road to London.

It was a silent trip and they made good time, Tony sharing the driving, their only stops to rest the horses. They reached London at day's end, riding past Kensington Gardens in the gathering dusk. Tony and Olivia went directly to the Powell town house on Shaftesbury Avenue and Rosaleen drove to the Fleet Street offices. Carlson was there to meet her, looking more stooped and shriveled than ever, and Harold Pryor appeared from inside her father's office. Rosaleen met the solicitor's steady gaze without turning away. Harold Pryor was one of the finest solicitors in London, a formal man who, she'd always felt, was a little bloodless. Tall, always impeccably dressed, today in a pearl-gray frock coat with a neat diamond stickpin in his gray cravat, he said all the proper things and Rosaleen couldn't help thinking he was merely getting them out of the way. Her suspicions were confirmed when he paused, and asked: "There are other things to discuss, but perhaps you'd prefer to wait till morning, Miss Powell."

"No, let's get it done with now," Rosaleen said.

"The immediate arrangements, first. The *Times* had a fine biographical piece on Sir Mallory in today's edition. Visiting hours will be all day tomorrow at the Corrigan Chapel. I presume that you and your sister will be there throughout."

"Yes," Rosaleen said.

"Services will be the following day at Westminster Abbey. A large attendance is expected, naturally," the lawyer said. "These arrangements are, of course, in accordance with longstanding instructions Sir Mallory left with me."

"I understand. Thank you for seeing to everything so efficiently," Rosaleen offered, then noticed Harold Pryor hesitate. "Is there something else?" she asked.

"As your father's solicitor, I know the provisions of the will and the condition of his personal estate," Harold Pryor began. "The trust funds for your sister and yourself have been considerably reduced in size."

"I'm aware of that," Rosaleen told him.

"Then all that can be taken up later. But one other provision should be noted now. You have inherited his controlling shares of the Powell Line," the lawyer went on. "That may be more of a formality than anything else. There is a board of directors, you know. In fact, I'm one of them."

"Yes, I've been introduced to everyone on the board at one time or another, mostly in brief, social meetings," Rosaleen said.

"Good. A meeting of the board has been called for next week, on Thursday. It will be necessary for you to be there, I'm afraid," Pryor told her. "It won't be a lengthy meeting. The board is well aware of the problems of the Powell Line. Only Sir Mallory's presence at the helm prevented the board from voting voluntary bankruptcy. Now, without your father, there's no confidence that the tide of things will be reversed. In any case, the board will review all the options."

"I'll be there," Rosaleen said.

Harold Pryor bowed formally. "My sympathies again, Miss Powell. He was one of the greats."

Rosaleen watched the lawyer leave, then let her eyes roam slowly across the office, aware of Carlson watching her. "I'll see to everything here. I'll carry on. Don't you worry about that," he said. Rosaleen almost smiled at the reassurance, words that were helpless little bridges attempting to link yesterday and tomorrow.

"I'd like a set of keys for the office," she said, then waited as Carlson shuffled to a desk, rummaged in a drawer, and brought out a duplicate set of keys. As he handed them to her, his small eyes misted. "Thank you, Carlson. I know I can count on you," Rosaleen offered. He pushed back his stooped shoulders, found a moment of pride, and Rosaleen turned and walked from the office, suddenly a terrible and depressing place. She drove to the town house to find Tony had brought in food. She could only pick at it before going to bed in the guest room, leaving the upstairs bedroom to Tony and Olivia.

Rosaleen woke early, dressed, and was about to leave for the funeral parlor when Tony appeared to tell her that Olivia would be down later. Rosaleen nodded agreement, prepared for Olivia to stay in London but a short time. It was perhaps just as well, Rosaleen pondered on her way to Corrigan's. It would be difficult enough to hold herself together without having to cope with Olivia's emotions. Rosaleen arrived at the funeral parlor to find some people already there and a steady stream of visitors followed. The moments grew crowded and she was thankful for the need to answer questions, to greet people, to offer and receive comfort. It all helped her not to think, not to fall victim to the terrible emptiness that lay inside her. Olivia arrived in midmorning. Makeup did not hide the paleness of her skin, but with Tony beside her, she held together longer and more resolutely than Rosaleen had expected.

Faces and names, even those she knew well, soon became a blur, a procession of well-meaning platitudes. The ritual went on, ordained by fate, orchestrated by man. It was not all sound and fury, she was certain. Needs were served, and that certainty helped her stand fast.

It was but a few minutes into the evening when Rosaleen saw the stocky, broad-shouldered figure enter the funeral parlor. His eyes moved quickly across the crowd until they found her and she saw him move toward her at once. As always, Frank Shields was impeccably clothed in a dark-gray frock coat and black cravat, his brown hair combed back carefully. Rosaleen met the gray eyes that always made her think of ice floes. Frank Shields always knew the correct thing to say and the correct way to say it. In manner and word as well as attire, he presented a flawless surface. But to Rosaleen, neither clothes nor words nor manners were able to hide the gutter-ruthlessness of the man. Frank Shields, to those sensitive enough, exuded a singular predatory quality. Olivia had gone over to talk to some others as he reached her and Rosaleen let her expression fall into proper gratefulness at his words.

"What a tragic time for you, Miss Powell, and for all of us," he began. "I was so shocked and saddened when I heard."

"Thank you, Mr. Shields," Rosaleen said evenly. She'd play the game for now, she resolved inwardly.

"I'm glad I was here and able to come," Frank Shields went on. "I spend almost every other week in London. I'm a veritable cross-Atlantic commuter between London and Boston."

"It must be a strain," Rosaleen commented.

"Yes, but running a transatlantic shipping line is always a strain. I'm afraid it was too much for your father these last years. It will be up to the rest of us to carry on in his tradition," the man said.

Rosaleen allowed a small and wistful smile to touch her lips. "I imagine some people will benefit tremendously from his absence. His presence was a problem to some, I know," she said.

Frank Shields's answering smile was that of a man who could afford to be gracious. "Competition is the lifeblood of progress," he said.

"Healthy competition," Rosaleen said.

The ice-floe eyes narrowed almost imperceptibly. "Of course, healthy competition," he echoed evenly. "Again, my sympathies to you and your sister."

Rosaleen watched him walk away and was glad he had come. She welcomed the anger that rose up inside her. It filled the painful emptiness and she vowed to cling to it till the day ended. The voice at her elbow broke into her thoughts.

"Hard man, that one," it said, and she turned to see Captain Coops, a black band over the gold of his master's bars.

"Hello, Captain," Rosaleen murmured. "Yes, Frank Shields has never been one of my favorite people."

"Nor mine," Coops said. "He's a thoroughly immoral man and it's just too dammed bad to see him on top of the world, now." The man shook his silver-white hair and wandered away, immersed in his own thoughts. When the evening ended, Rosaleen returned to the town house with Olivia and Tony and went to bed at once, unwilling to think about the finality of tomorrow.

But the morning crept into existence and somehow she found herself sitting beside Olivia in the centuries-old richness of Westminster Abbey, the great windows suffused with pale colors by the lead-gray sky outside. Rosaleen watched the throng file silently into the great cathedral, finally to fill every space of every pew. She saw Sir Reginald Orms, Lord Admiral of the Royal Navy, resplendent in his dress uniform. With him were Elliot Reynall and Lord Rutherford, both Members of Parliament. Joshua Coops nodded to her as, his face heavy, he took a seat across the aisle. They were from the far corners of the globe, Australians and Indians, merchants from Lahore and businessmen from Louisiana, men her father had known in the years he built the Powell Line. Harold Pryor had furnished her with a list of those who'd sent notice of attendance. And among them all, her eyes found Franks Shields, sitting alone, the cold, gray eyes showing no expression.

The service began and the soft sound of the organ drifted through the vast reaches of the gothic walls. Rosaleen stared at her hands folded in her lap as, beside her, Olivia's muffled sobs echoed softly. She sat with hundreds, Rosaleen reflected, but she sat alone. She shared the tears of everyone, but she cried alone. She was part of a great collective grief, yet her pain was unshared. It was always so with some things, she supposed. They were beyond sharing, save with perhaps one person so close they were really but another part of oneself. She would wait for her sharing, Rosaleen promised, until she was back with Niles, in the strength of his arms.

The burial itself was private, only the loyal members of his office staff and the family and a few others—Harold Pryor, Captain Joshua Coops, and an old friend, Bennet Ryans from Dublin. The grayness had turned into a drizzle and by the time the last was over, into a typical London fog. Olivia collapsed in emotional exhaustion when they returned to the town house. Rosaleen took Captain Coops aside before he left. "I must return for a board of directors meeting next Thursday. I want you to delay any plans for sailing you might have until then," she told him.

"I'll be here," he said. "I imagine you'll be canceling most sailings anyway."

"I really can't say anything until the board meets," Rosaleen said.

"I understand," Joshua Coops said, his mouth growing tight. "Rotten business, all of it, a damn rotten shame. I've still a contact on the Bangkok bullion I wanted to pursue."

Rosaleen shrugged. "I think the board meeting will decide everything," she said.

"Yes, I'm afraid it will," he said, nodding brusquely. "Good night, Miss Powell."

Rosaleen let the silver-haired man out the front door and turned to Olivia and Tony. "I'd like to leave for Cornwall tonight," she said. "Have the Whitechapel hitched up and just go."

Olivia shook her head slowly. "No, Rosaleen. Please, I couldn't stand the trip. In the morning, first thing," she said.

"She's really not up to it," Tony added solicitously. The undisguised concern in his voice reached Rosaleen and she nodded agreement.

"All right. In the morning then, early," she said, and went to bed at once. She was first up when the day came, down at the stable seeing that the buggy was readied. She thought only of Niles during the long trip back, slowing the pace only when Tony reminded her she was pushing the horses too fast. They reached Cornwall after nightfall and she drove Tony and Olivia to Braemore, then went directly to the point. A small lamp was burning in the window of the house and Niles had the door open before the buggy came to a halt. "My darling, my darling one," she cried as he swept her from the carriage and into his arms. Her mouth opened for him, greedily, hungrily, and he carried her into the house and toward the bedroom.

"I wanted to come last night," Rosaleen breathed. His lips pressed hers into silence for a moment.

"You're here now, that's all that counts," he said, and pressed her down onto the bed. She felt her hand undoing buttons, opening snaps, heard her soft gasp at the touch of his lips upon her breast. The night was made of emotions let loose, all the grief and pain held back, contained, exploding into tears of sorrow and tears of relief and the sharing of body and soul was complete. When the first light of dawn slipped through the window, she did not rise.

"I don't care," she whispered to Niles beside her. "Let them see and think and do whatever they want." He didn't protest and it was midmorning before she finally left. The last days had not faded away but she had renewed her strength. She paused before she slipped the gown on, pressed Niles's face into her breasts, her hands holding his head tight against her. "When it grew too much, I thought of you here, waiting, and of this moment," she said.

"I'm glad for that," Niles murmured. She stepped back, pulled the gown on.

"I must go back to London in a few days. There's a board meeting on Thursday and I want to be there the day before," Rosaleen told him.

"Then every night will be ours till then," Niles said. "Will you be there long?"

"I don't think so. A few days, perhaps," Rosaleen answered, and he held her face between his hands. "Till tonight, my darling," she breathed, then quickly went outside before she changed her mind and stayed. Back at Raven's Wing, she sat down again with all the ledgers and papers, burning all the figures into her mind, alternating with the dossier on the accidents and shipping tragedies. She went over both sets of material each day until all was firm in her mind. In the nights, there was only Niles and nothing else. The day before she left for London, Olivia visited, Tony in tow as usual.

"Have you decided about our living at Raven's Wing?" Olivia asked. Rosaleen saw that her usual petulance was missing, replaced by lines of real worry. "Tony and I have been talking. There's no way we can stay on at Braemore and keep up appearances with the small sum from the trust."

Rosaleen glanced at Tony, who wore his casual blandness again. "We won't get in the way, sis," he said. "I promise." Rosaleen's violet eyes flashed for an instant at the remark.

"I'll make no decisions on anything until I get back," she said.

Tony Darby shrugged nonchalantly. "Just make the right one, love," he slid out. Rosaleen stared at him. The remark had held the faint edge of threat in it.

"Meaning exactly what?" she snapped.

The casual shrug came again. "Just that the right decision will be best for you, too," he said. "You'll be surprised how handy I can be about the house." The quick smile was touched with a leer. But the answer had been a turn-aside, the unstated threat still left hanging. Rosaleen wondered how much of Tony Darby was mere bluff, hollow words and empty gestures, but decided not to press finding out now. She turned to Olivia. Her sister looked terribly small suddenly, frightened and helpless, the way she used to look sometimes when they were little girls, before she learned the wiles of charm and pouting. With a rush of memories overwhelming her, Rosaleen clasped her arms around Olivia, pulled her close.

"We'll work something out when I come back," she said, and Olivia nodded, managing a weak smile that nonetheless held gratitude in. Rosaleen hadn't seen that smile since she promised to fix the wheel of the old donkey cart too many years ago.

"Let's be off, Livvie," Tony's voice broke in harshly, as if he resented the sudden moment which left him out completely. Rosaleen turned her eyes on him, cold violet now, and had the satisfaction of seeing him look away. She smiled silently at the small but unexpected victory, then watched Olivia go off, clinging to his arm. She went upstairs and packed then, clothes for three or four days, just in case. Niles came as darkness slipped over Raven's Wing and the world became a warm and loving place. In the morning, her body still warm from the hours beside him, he drove her to Bodwin to catch the coach.

"Hurry back," he said, and Rosaleen thought they were the most unnecessary words ever uttered.

CHAPTER FIVE

ooking back, Rosaleen could not pinpoint when the decision had been made. Perhaps in the quiet somberness of
Westminster Abbey when she sat alone among many. Or perhaps
when she faced Frank Shields again and felt the cold, overpower-
ing predatoriness of the man. Or it might have been during the
dark nights alone when the doors of the soul open in solitary
communication.

When, wasn't important anymore, only that it had been
made and she had told no one, not even Niles. There'd be ample
time for telling, explaining, asking for the understanding of
others. Many might think she'd had another course, but to her,
there was no other way, none whatever. And so she'd planned
her arrival in London on Wednesday night when the business
section of the city was tightly closed down. She went to the office
of the Powell Line, opened up with the keys Carlson had given
her, and turned on one lamp. It was sufficient, casting a quiet
glow across the silent reception room as she sank down into one
of the leather chairs.

Slowly, her eyes moved from one graceful ship model to the
next, pausing at each, circling the collection that lined the walls
of the room to return to the first. They represented more than
great vessels, more than sleek designs of smooth-wood hulls and
billows of canvas, sea-borne birds that flew across the water. They
represented an achievement, a dream come true, a heritage and
a promise. As she lingered on each vessel, she put her head back
and slowly the room dissolved and she saw the great clipper ships

racing through the seas, a great line of them, a parade of proud, eager vessels, each more beautiful than the last. They dipped and leapt, rose and fought off the seas with a shake of their smooth hulls. Her thoughts drifted, into the paneled library of Raven's Wing, and she was a young girl again, listening to her father talk with his captains. She would sit quiet as a churchmouse, most times unnoticed, as she hung on every word. It all came back, as if it were yesterday. She recalled in every detail how she listened to Captain Isaiah Cobb tell how he defeated the Australian packet in a run from Melbourne to Prawle Point. Captain Cobb had a trick of only using the royals and the topgallants when the wind was light and furling the lower sails which he felt caused more of a drag than anything else. Then there was Captain Hillary Owens, who told of the fierce storms on the run around the Cape and how he handled the ship through their fury.

Then there was Captain Abrahamson, who would regale Sir Mallory with stories of how he used the sails of his four-masted fore-and-aft schooner in shifting winds, working only the flying jib, foresail, and mizzen, playing them back and forth to catch every stray breeze. She drank in his every word and the next time she took out her own little ketch, she'd recruit Olivia and challenge the Henderson boys who lived in Newquay. She'd outsail and outrace them every time, of course, for wasn't she sailing a Powell Line clipper and they but an ordinary little ketch?

Regrettably, the images faded away and the paneled walls of the silent room took shape again before her eyes. Tomorrow, like the memories that had faded, the board of directors would dissolve what was left of the great Powell Line. Rosaleen's lips pressed hard against each other. She knew them, all those honorable men, bankers, financiers, Members of Parliament, solicitors, merchants. All were hidebound traditionalists, steeped in ledgers, clothed in rigidity, weaned on conservatism. They were heavy of purse and light of courage and they would present their facts and figures, commandeer logic and reason and decree the end of what had been built in the face of facts and logic. They'd summoned her because legal technicalities made it necessary for her to be there, an official witness to the sacrifice of a man's life, his courage and vision, on the altar of fiscal cowardice. They would call it prudence, of course.

Rosaleen rose, her face drawn tight. She reviewed the gleaming models again, then turned away to stand quietly for a moment. They had summoned her, she repeated, feeling the anger curling inside her. So be it, she commented silently. They would remember this meeting.

She turned out the light and left, pausing for a moment outside. The London fog had descended again, but not too heavily, and she decided to take the long way back to the town house. She walked the damp night streets as people appeared and vanished like so many well-dressed ghosts. The dome of St. Paul's was a fitful silhouette in the drifting fog. She turned into the Strand then down along Victoria Embankment, past where Heinrich Heine lived when he was in London. Heine's spirit of romanticism made her think of Niles at once. She pretended he walked beside her and she turned up Tottenham Court Road to Shaftesbury Avenue, hurrying to the house and the warm comfort of bed with Niles beside her, if only in her dreams.

The meeting was held in the conference room, at the long, shining-smooth table she had always regarded with admiration as a little girl. She arrived early, greeted Carlson and the rest of the staff. She watched them go about their tasks, silently, with a grim determination, the way condemned prisoners pay special attention to their daily routines because they dare not think of anything beyond. All the board members arrived within a minute of the appointed time. Punctuality was part of their being, the mark of a successful English man of affairs. Harold Pryor, always correct, left Sir Mallory's chair empty at the head of the table, and seated Rosaleen at the opposite end. She gazed down the double row of faces—austere, tight, cold faces. Emerson Ogilvy, president of the London Merchant's Bank and a precise, thin reed of a man, rose to begin the meeting. He wasted no time in preliminaries.

"I think it unnecessary for me to analyze the last financial statement of the Powell Line. You are all familiar with it and we all know the perilous condition of the Line. Whether this was due to mismanagement, rotten luck, or just the inability to compete in today's world, is of only academic importance now," he said, and Rosaleen felt the anger bristle inside her. It was of more than academic interest to her, she sniffed silently. "The only way to prevent further losses is to close the Line completely," he went on. "The sale of remaining assets will help recoup some monies. Of course, I should welcome any suggestion in this regard."

He sat down abruptly and Rosaleen watched as the portly figure of Albert Weems rose. Weems, head of Weems Financial Consultants, nodded to her with slow formality. "I must concur with the distinguished gentleman who just spoke. Sir Mallory managed to keep things afloat, in the literal as well as figurative sense. Without his hand on the helm, I'm afraid there is just no other way. Indeed, Sir Mallory may not have been able to turn things around. I suggest we do not prolong the unavoidable and take an immediate vote on a motion to close the operation of the Powell Line."

He sank back into his chair and the next to get up was Richard Lavelin, Member of Parliament. He cleared his throat in true parliamentary fashion. "It grieves me to add my voice to those just heard, but to continue on, even with hiring new and competent management, would be at best a most uncertain prospect," Richard Lavelin intoned, "The truth is that the few men capable of running the Powell Line are already involved in their own shipping enterprises. I cannot see anything but an end to operations."

Rosaleen felt the wetness coating the palms of her hands, moved them from atop the table to press them dry against her dress. She ran her tongue across her lips and swallowed, holding back the anger that seethed inside her. She had expected this and yet it infuriated her. They had the collective cowardice of small-minded men, hyenas, wealthy ones yet still hyenas, picking over the bones of the mighty. Harold Pryor got to his feet.

"I must inform the board that I received an offer for the Powell Line from Mr. Frank Shields," he said. "I'm afraid it was a totally inadequate offer."

Samuel Henderson, owner of the World Import Company, barked an answer. "Naturally. Shields has everything going his way. He doesn't need to be generous with offers."

"I'll formally turn it down," Pryor said. "We will realize more from the individual auctioning of the remaining vessels. I therefore now make the formal motion for a vote to end the operation of the Powell Shipping Line. Please announce your vote as I call your name."

He began with Weems, received a brisk yes. Ogilvy was next, his assent tinged with weariness. Henderson concurred loudly, Richard Lavelin next. Rosaleen watched as William Constable of the London Maritime Insurers voted his agreement. So it went, down one side of the long table and up the other: Sir Robert Formsby, banking interests; Allwyn Richardson, importer; Edgar Iams, Member of Parliament, each falling into place until the unanimous decision had been taken and Harold Pryor turned his eyes on her. His smile, an attempt to be gentle, was merely of deprecating tolerance.

"You have heard the disposition of the board, Miss Powell," he began. "Because Sir Mallory's stock is now in your hands, the final vote must, of necessity, be yours. We realize how difficult a task this is for you and you have our deepest sympathies. But now, if you will formally complete the considered decision of the board, this unpleasant and unhappy burden will be at an end."

He offered another smile, this time of patient urging. Rosaleen rose to her feet, let her eyes circle the table in a quick glance, knowing that they did not read the violent anger in them.

"No," she bit out, letting the single word hang in the air.

She saw the frown appear on Harold Pryor's face, to be duplicated on the brows of the others. Pryor smiled again, tolerant once more. "I'm afraid I don't understand, Miss Powell," he said. "Perhaps you'd like to be alone for a few minutes before going on?"

"There's no need for that," Rosaleen returned. "I'm not going to end the Powell Line." She felt her fists clench tightly as Harold Pryor exchanged quick glances with the others. He maintained his air of patient, cold understanding as he brought his eyes back to her.

"My dear, there is just no other way," he soothed. "The facts are what they are, I'm afraid. Everyone here has your best interests at heart, too."

"I'm touched," Rosaleen said, ice in her voice. Pryor paused for an instant, decided to ignore the remark.

"You will only ruin what little is left by prolonging the life of the Powell Line, my dear," he said, his gentle tone bloodlessly cold. "There is no other way. Face that, my dear."

"There is another way," Rosaleen threw back. "The Powell Line must go on."

"And who will run it, my dear Rosaleen?" Emerson Ogilvy cut in. "Your father was barely managing to keep it together. No one else could do it. No one else would want even to attempt it."

"I will run the Powell Line," Rosaleen said. Her glance swept the table. She almost laughed at the faces that stared back at her with shock, disbelief, even horror. Weems looked as if he had been stabbed. Her glance fastened on Harold Pryor. He was staring at her, trying to pierce into her with his eyes. The silence stayed until he cleared his throat, found tentative words, tried the tolerant smile again.

"I can't believe you are truly serious, Miss Powell," he offered.

"I mean every word of it," Rosaleen snapped. "I'm going to fight back. The Powell Line has had troubles and many were man-made."

"Have you gone mad, young woman?" Richard Lavelin said, his face flushed. "Why, the very thought is ridiculous."

"A woman running a great shipping line? Is that what bothers you?" Rosaleen flung back, her eyes now violet agates.

"It's impudent effrontery. It's unheard of," the man exploded.

"Well, the world will hear of it now," Rosaleen returned, facing his florid countenance. "I am going to run the Powell Line and make it what it was before."

"Not with me, you're not," Henderson said, leaping to his feet. "I'll not be on the board of directors of any company run by a woman, a mere slip of a young girl, at that. You can have my resignation right now."

"Accepted," Rosaleen snapped, and saw the man's mouth fall open. He glanced at the others, saw their shocked, confused stares, turned and strode from the room. "Any others?" Rosaleen asked coldly.

"You are a brazen young woman," Albert Weems said, pulling himself from the chair. "I do indeed resign my chair on this board."

"Good-bye, Mr. Weems," Rosaleen remarked. She turned to the others. Discomfort had replaced shock and horror for most of them. "If I were a young man I might be called foolish, cocksure, even stupid. But because I'm a woman I am called brazen, impudent, full of effrontery. You may think whatever you wish, but if you stay on this board you will do so under my direction. It's as simple as that, gentlemen."

"And if the board resigns completely, Miss Powell? What then?" Harold Pryor asked.

"It will make no difference," Rosaleen answered at once, allowing no hint of hesitation in her voice. "I'll find ways to get any specific advice I may need."

Pryor glanced at the others and Rosaleen listened to the uneasy shuffling of feet, caught the quick little exchanges that ran around the table like an unfelt wind. Thomas Porter, the representative of the Union Bank and Trust, rose at the far end. "I'm afraid I must resign, then," he said evenly. "I do have a reputation to consider. I shan't make myself into a laughingstock by being part of what will be a tragic farce."

"Or a company run by a woman," Rosaleen thrust.

He shrugged. "If you prefer," he muttered.

"I fear Mr. Porter's remarks pretty well fit the rest of the board members, Miss Powell," Harold Pryor said stiffly. Rosaleen saw the other heads nod, an equal number of uncomfortable and hostile glances tossed at her.

"Then, gentlemen, your association with the Powell Line and this meeting are at an end," Rosaleen said crisply. She waited, unmoving, then watched as the men got up, turned their backs on her, and filed out of the room. She remained standing until the door closed after the last of them. Then, her knees trembling, clammy with the perspiration trickling down the bodice of her dress, she sank back onto the chair. She had expected some opposition, some resignations, but not all. A wave of fright surged through her. She shook it away at once, angry at herself. She could not permit fright, doubts, misgivings. They were the termites of the soul, eating away at resolution and confidence. She made a harsh sound. Confidence was the wrong word. She had no real confidence, not yet. But she had angry determination and that would do for now. She'd make it do until the confidence came of itself. She was not alone, not so long as there was Niles. She'd draw on his strength, his comfort, his love. He would be her safe harbor in the maelstrom she was being drawn into, her place to replenish self, restore the spirit. Love would be her anchor. With that, she'd face whatever lay ahead.

Rosaleen admitted to herself that the reactions of the august members of the board might be a grim harbinger of things to come. Business and society at large would be no less aghast. She realized that now, more than she had before. But the gauntlet had been flung down, bridges burned. Others would condemn, draw back, but she would push on. She expected cancellations, and now realized that there could be more than a few. But she'd already formed plans to counter losses with more-than-compensatory gains. She'd have to expand those plans, Rosaleen told herself. She'd adjust, improvise, be flexible and quick, and above all, move forward.

Rosaleen drew a deep breath, rose, and went into the outer office. Word had already gone around. It was in Carlson's eyes, a mixture of cautious respect and uncertainty. She cut through pretenses. "I expect everyone here to carry on as usual for now," Rosaleen announced.

"Yes, indeed. It's a wonderful thing you're doing, Miss Powell," Carlson murmured. Rosaleen nodded. They were as biased in their way as the others had been in theirs.

"I'll be in Sir Mallory's office. Please send in Captain Coops," she said, then turned and moved into the inner office. She closed the door behind her and stood quietly for a moment, murmuring a small silent prayer. She was sitting behind the desk when Joshua Coops entered. He sat down in the chair opposite, his blue eyes studying her with quiet amusement.

"I'll need an operations officer, someone who knows all the practical details of running a shipping line. I'll need help, advice, and information, but I'll make all the decisions. Winning or losing will be my responsibility. Will you stay on?"

Coops studied her a moment longer. "Yes," he said softly.

"You'll be pressured, laughed at, probably," Rosaleen warned.

"Most likely," he said.

Rosaleen shot the question at him. "Why will you stay on? That's important to me."

"What if I said loyalty to your father?" the captain answered.

Rosaleen considered the answer for a moment. "I might believe you," she answered.

The silver-haired ship's master smiled. "It's part of it," he said.

"And the rest? The other part?"

"Frank Shields. I hate the man. I hate seeing him win by default. I'd be part of anything that might stop him."

"Do you think I can?" Rosaleen asked.

"No, but it'll be worth being part of the try. And who knows, you might just get lucky," Coops said.

"Then as of now, Captain Coops, you are operations manager of the Powell Line. I want a complete list of every vessel we have, large and small, and the cost of operating each," Rosaleen said. "Do you think that exists?"

"I'm sure it does. I'll have it for you," Coops said.

"Then I'll want the profits or losses for the past year accruable to each of those vessels," Rosaleen said. "And one more thing. There will be alot of talk about this, my taking over. You must know most of our major customers. Can you talk to them, keep them from canceling?"

"I can try," Captain Coops said. "And with some, I'll have a good chance of success. With others, I doubt I'd get anywhere."

"Do your best," Rosaleen said, ending the meeting. After Coops left, she summoned more detailed records from Carlson and finished the day studying them. When night came she was too tired to do more than eat lightly and fall into bed. The die had been cast. She had embarked on a course from which there was no turning back now. She pushed away second thoughts and wonderings and pressed her face into the pillow, murmuring a muffled goodnight to Niles as she fell asleep instantly.

She was in the office early the next morning and by midday Coops had assembled a good part of the information she'd requested. "I'll take it back to Raven's Wing with me tonight," she told him and saw the question in his eyes. "I'll be spending from Monday through Thursday here in London, Friday to Sunday at Raven's Wing," she said. It was a decision that had formed itself, born out of the realization of the enormity of the task she'd undertaken. She could not carry on without time for Niles and herself, without his body against hers, drawing love and strength from him as if through osmosis. Niles, Cornwall, Raven's Wing, even her old friends at Gwyneth, these would be her sanctuary, as necessary as breathing.

"I'll be on hand over weekends," Coops said. "But I will have to be at sea for some part of the time, I remind you."

"Yes, and Carlson can hold things down then," Rosaleen said. "I'm confident, Captain Coops. Optimistic, eager."

The silver-haired man patted her hand, an avuncular gesture. "Good. That'll help," he allowed.

In the afternoon, Carlson brought her the late edition of the *London Times*. The story had made the front page, she saw, then sat back to read it.

WOMAN TAKES OVER SHIPPING LINE

The business community was set astir by the announcement that Miss Rosaleen Powell, daughter of the late Sir Mallory Powell, had assumed direction of the vast Powell Shipping Line which has been plagued by troubles. The board of directors, numbering some of the leading financial and business figures, tendered their unanimous resignations. Business and financial circles could not recall a similar instance in the history of the industry. Comments on Miss Powell's action from these sources were almost unanimously negative. "Shocking" and "ridiculous" were the two most often uttered comments, though it was also termed "a new low in manners and morals." One business leader called it "Alice in Blunderland."

Miss Powell has exhibited a talent for highly independent and questionable behavior in previous family matters, it was learned. Only Mr. Robert Hedges of Merchant's Insurers Ltd. had a positive comment. "Red ink and black ink care nothing about sex. They will write the final verdict," he said.

"Good for Mr. Robert Hedges," Rosaleen muttered, making a mental note of the name before tossing the newspaper aside. She finished the day studying the material Coops had given her, then called in Carlson for last-minute instructions and caught the night coach to Cornwall. She rode with mixed feelings swirling inside her. It was an entirely new role, this directing a company. Data and figures had always bored her but she had to see them in a different light now, as symbols, the mistakes and errors of men and the fragility of events translated into addition and subtraction. It was entirely too cold and bloodless for her, but she would steel herself to it until she'd won. Sir Mallory Powell's daughter was not cut out of ordinary cloth. They had ignored that, those august gentlemen of the business community. They would not do so for long.

She dozed during the long ride home and when the coach reached Bodwin, the things she had to do were firmly set in her mind. Sam Tyler drove her to Raven's Wing where the new, bright sun flooded every room. The note, slipped under the door, made her heart quicken. "My dearest one ... Fed the horses as promised. Waiting for you to return ... Niles." Rosaleen flew out of her city gowns and into riding clothes, saddled the stallion, and galloped most of the way to the point. The mullioned windows of the house were open and Niles came out at the sound of the horse, lifted her from the saddle into his arms. She clung to him, suddenly trembling. He pulled back, frowned down at her.

"What is it, my darling?" he asked.

"Nothing. Just being here, coming back to you, a funny kind of reaction to everything that's happened," Rosaleen said. "I've so much to tell you."

"All right. Let's go inside," Niles said, but she pulled back, felt the sly little smile edge her lips.

"Afterward," she whispered, and saw his eyes understand.

"Yes, afterward," he echoed.

Later, her breasts touching the smooth muscles of his chest, she leaned on her elbows and told Niles of all the decisions she'd taken in London. She left nothing out, the board meeting, the angers, the story in the *Times*, all the things she planned to do which she had not yet told anyone else. He listened, unsmiling, his eyes probing her as she finished.

"You've taken on a tremendous task, my love," he said slowly.

Rosaleen shifted against his nakedness. "Was I wrong, Niles? Am I being a fool?" she asked, suddenly alarmed.

Niles half-shrugged, touched her face with the back of his hand. "I can't answer that. You felt you had to do this. That's all that matters," he said.

"Would you have told me not to, Niles?" she pressed.

"Probably," he said gravely, and followed with a quick and rueful smile. "But for selfish reasons," he added. "It means you'll be away from me all week."

"Friday to Sunday will be ours. We have the coteen, our own hiding-away place," Rosaleen said. His eyes held loving concern, but she sensed a holding back of something. "What else, Niles? Tell me," she asked.

"Perhaps I'm afraid. This will be a new life for you. You'll be plunged into a different world. I don't want to see you change, become someone else. I told you it was selfish. I want you just as you are, all your tender, sweet strength. My Rosaleen playing the tycoon frightens me," Niles said.

She pulled him to her. "I won't change. Besides, it won't be forever, just until the line is back in shape again and until Frank Shields realizes that all his rotten, underhanded tricks won't work," Rosaleen said. Her arms tightened around him and the words she spoke were a kind of prayer. "With you at my side, waiting to hold me when I return here, I can't lose, my love. But I can't do it without knowing you're here, always in the background, a place for me to run to and find the things only your love can give me."

"I'll be here, whenever and for whatever you need," he told her, and his lips silenced her answer and he rolled over with her and she felt the wonderful touch of his legs moving upon her, triumph upon triumph, giving upon giving.

When she finally dressed, aware of his eyes watching her with pleasure, she felt restored, aglow with that special happiness that was both exhilarating and humbling. "Till tomorrow, my darling," she said with a quick kiss and was gone. There was still time before dark to ride to Gwyneth and she took the stallion across the moors and down to the beach and along the shoreline. The coastal village materialized before her, a cluster of houses like barnacles clinging to the edge of the sea. She rode directly to Margaret Boynton's home and found Agnes Walsh there, the teapot simmering. Both women embraced her with shouts of greeting. "It's been too long," Rosaleen murmured.

"We wondered if you'd forgotten your gipper days and your friends here," Agnes said.

"Never." Rosaleen gave her a reproachful glance. "Shame on you for even thinking that. But I've come especially to see Margaret this time."

"Some tea for you, first," Margaret Boynton said, and Rosaleen sat in the straight-backed wooden chair and watched the older woman move to the simmering kettle. Margaret Boynton wore her gray hair up in a tight bun and while a little thick around the midsection, she held herself well, her ample bosom still firm and able to draw admiring glances from the men of Gwyneth. But Margaret suffered from arthritis, especially in the hands. Rosaleen had worked beside Margaret Boynton more than any of the others, drawn by her experience and motherliness. Time and again she'd taken on Margaret's work as the older woman halted to warm frost-chapped, arthritis-stiffened hands, unable to stand the salt-soaked icy water, her body aching from bending too low over the troughs. Rosaleen let Margaret pour the tea and settle herself, then spoke directly, with no coy sidling up to the matter.

"I want you to come and work for me at Raven's Wing, Margaret," she said. "You'll be housekeeper, and in charge of the kitchen as well, for I know how you love to cook." Margaret Boynton's weathered face shifted expressions, her gray eyes reflecting surprise and uncertainty. "I'll be spending most of each week in London and I'll need someone at Raven's Wing, someone capable and someone I can trust. It'd pay better than a gipper's wages, Margaret," Rosaleen said.

It was Agnes Walsh who roared an instant answer. "Take it, Maggie, or be a dammed old fool. It's what you need. The lass is offering you a wonderful chance."

The older woman smiled into space, engulfed by private thoughts for a moment. "It would be nice, working inside a fine house, warm and snug," she murmured.

"Then it's settled," Rosaleen cut in quickly. "You can move in tomorrow. You'll not regret it."

"Ah, she'll be the envy of everyone," Agnes Walsh said. Rosaleen bent forward, embraced Margaret, and saw the wetness that had come into the older woman's eyes.

"Have your tea, Rosaleen," Margaret said gruffly, then turned away. Rosaleen smiled inwardly, took a deep sip of the brew that was too strong for her tastes, half-finished it, and stood up.

"I'll have Sam Tyler pick you up with your things in the morning, Margaret," she said. The older woman nodded and

Rosaleen spoke to Agnes Walsh. "Say hello to all the other girls for me this time. I must get back," she said.

"It's a good thing you're doing for Margaret," Agnes said as she went outside to the horse with Rosaleen.

"An exchange," Rosaleen said. "Or maybe a repayment of old kindnesses. Anyway, I'm happy for it." She left then, hurried the horse back through the darkness. The fog was beginning to drift in across the moors, to lay a soft blanket along the ground. There was but one more piece of business to settle, but that would wait for the morrow. It would take no seeking out, Rosaleen reminded herself, no seeking out at all. She reached Raven's Wing, fixed something to eat for herself, and settled down with the material she'd brought back from the office. It'd be good to have Margaret at Raven's Wing. The great house was not made for loneliness, no more than she. And she was not lonely. She had Niles, and her friends at Gwyneth. Why then, she frowned, did she suddenly have a cold feeling of being alone. It had swept over her, inexplicably. Exhaustion and nerves, she told herself, the residue of all that had happened these past days. She let the explanation suffice without satisfying, and went to bed.

The morning was not half over when the carriage rolled to a halt outside and she waited as Tony and Olivia stepped down from it. Tony had a copy of the *London Times* tucked under his arm and Rosaleen half-smiled as she met his uncertain stare. "My edition just came by post," he said. "Always a day or two late, of course, but it keeps me up on things nonetheless." His lips pursed and Rosaleen saw Olivia's expectant eyes on him. Tony Darby waved the newspaper in the air in a half-circle. "I saw the story, of course. Where does that leave Livvie and me?" he asked.

"How do you mean that exactly?" Rosaleen questioned.

"Well, I mean that it seems you're going to be off and running the company, playing tycoon as it were, and where do we fit in?" Tony thrust at her.

Rosaleen's eyes darkened. "First, I'm not playing tycoon. I'm trying to save my father's company and if I do, Olivia will be the better for it, too," she threw back.

"Tony didn't mean that the way it sounded," Olivia cut in, but Rosaleen disregarded the attempt to soften Tony Darby's remarks and kept her gaze burning at the man.

"All right, I'm sorry about that one," Tony muttered, and had the grace to look uncomfortable. "But it seems to me we could play a role in all this."

"Tony's really quite good at managing things," Olivia tried.

"I have all the help I need right now," Rosaleen said. "As for your living at Raven's Wing, I suppose that's the only thing until Tony's ventures, as he calls them, take a turn for the better." She saw the instant of relief flood Olivia's face and her darting glance at her husband. "I'm having a woman, an old friend, start tomorrow as housekeeper. You can move your things into the east wing," Rosaleen went on and then, turning to Tony, met his eyes. "If you're intending to entertain or have any lavish parties, and you've suggested that's a part of your approach to prospects, I'd appreciate your letting me know beforehand."

"Of course," Tony Darby agreed, flashing a quick smile. "This is a step in the right direction, sis. You'll see it is."

"We don't have all that much to pack. We'll be moved in by Tuesday. I'll just go and have a look at the east wing rooms now," Olivia said, and bustled off at once. Alone now with Rosaleen, Tony leaned confidentially closer.

"You're not bringing that Niles Brewster in to run things with you, are you?" he asked. "I know you're right taken with him and all that."

"I hardly see what concern either of those things is to you," Rosaleen flared, but Tony Darby held his ground with dogged truculence.

"I am family, too, you know, and anything that affects family affects me, now doesn't it?" he slid out. The reply was a turn-aside one, too casual yet with a hint of goading in it. Rosaleen refused the challenge. If he were indulging in his little games she'd not give him the satisfaction of even minor success. Even with their living under the same roof, she'd not be seeing much of Olivia or Tony, and that was the way she wanted it. Olivia still took being indulged as her birthright, and Tony Darby, of course, was concerned over possibly losing a good thing. Olivia returned, full of enthusiasm for moving in, and Rosaleen was glad to see them go. She plunged into reading the reports she'd brought with her until Niles arrived after nightfall. He brought a bottle of fine Madeira and the night enfolded them in its soft arms until, with a last lingering kiss, he slipped away at dawn.

Rosaleen stayed in bed, half awake, half asleep, holding onto the embers of the night until the sun became too bright to ignore and she rose, bathed, and had just finished dressing when Margaret Boynton arrived. Rosaleen helped the woman settle into her quarters, then toured Raven's Wing with her. It was later, in the garden where Margaret had already taken to pruning away the ivy, that she told the older woman about Niles. She'd not mentioned him before to anyone in Gwyneth and the waterfront townspeople hardly ever went inland to Bodwin.

"You'll meet him tonight, Margaret," Rosaleen said. "You'll like him. He's not all gentleness like Colin, but he's a sensitive man and he laughs easily and he's so terribly handsome."

Margaret tossed her head upward as she laughed. "Oh, it's plain you're in love," she said. "I'm happy for you Rosaleen. It's time you found someone. You can't let the past be an anchor dragging behind you all the time."

Rosaleen nodded agreement. She'd given up looking backward. Indeed, with what lay ahead, there'd be no time for anything but looking to tomorrow. Once again, she felt a surge of confidence. She'd taken steps that put all the things in Cornwall into proper place, at least for the moment. Like a good chess player, she had positioned herself to do battle and she was touched with eagerness. When Niles arrived that night, she introduced him to Margaret and saw that the two of them spent time together until she drew the door to her bedroom closed on Niles and herself, the night theirs alone once again.

In the morning, as she prepared to take the early coach to London, Margaret gave her approval, which was important, for she, more than anyone else, had known Colin. "He is indeed a nice man, good for you," Margaret said. "You're alive with him, full of the stuff of happiness, and it's a good thing to see, Rosaleen, my girl, a good thing to see."

Rosaleen hugged the woman to her. "I'll be back Friday," she said. "I'm so glad you'll be here taking care of things, Margaret." The words came from the heart and when she boarded the coach, she felt relaxed. The drivers had come to know her now, and accorded her the little extra courtesies of a regular passenger, a back pillow, a robe for unexpectedly chilly nights. Rosaleen settled into a corner of the coach as the horses thundered on their way in a rhythmic cadence. A new time in her life had begun. Life was a series of plateaus, Rosaleen reflected, each one connected to yet distinct from the others. Her life had taken a turn she could not have believed possible a month ago. But tomorrows waited now and she rushed to meet them.

The weeks quickly ran one into the next. Tony and Olivia were ensconced at Raven's Wing, Olivia happy as a lark in the garden, Tony sending off letters at a great rate, trying to appear productive, and Margaret efficiently running the house. "My sister and her husband are not giving you any problems, are they?" Rosaleen asked Margaret after the first two weeks.

"None that I can't handle," the woman said with the quiet confidence that was part of her nature, and Rosaleen stayed up late telling her everything that had gone on in London that week. And there was Niles and the coteen, the world away from everything else. With Niles, she lost herself, found herself, gave and took, went over every little thing with him and in doing so renewed her strength for the next challenge. But mostly there was his love, his body against hers and her fervent response compressing the week into their three days together.

But it was in London that Rosaleen's decisions were gathering attention. Each week she gave Coops another plan to put into immediate effect, certain of her moves, not waiting to see the results of the previous one. "We're cutting off the India trade entirely. Put all the older vessels up for sale," she ordered the first week. The following week, she took four of the slower ships out of the South American runs. The week after it was three ships on the Pacific routes. Their masters were dismissed, their crews disbanded. The fourth week, she consolidated five runs of the Atlantic trade into three. There were losses incurred with each move, but the long-range picture grew brighter.

"Have you the resources to hold out and take advantage of all this? It'll take time to make itself felt," Coops asked.

Rosaleen had no answer. The figures held no promises. "I shall find a way, that's all," she replied.

But the Powell Line shares went up on the London exchange, for the first time in two years, and the financial editor of the *Times* came to her for a story. "Rosaleen Powell Talk of Shipping and Financial Circles," the headline read this time. And as society follows fame, stories of the "beautiful shipping magnate" began to appear in the social columns. An invitation came to attend the prestigious Empire Club Ball. She was going to disregard it, but Coops objected.

"Go. Let them see you. There'll be men there you will want to know," he said.

"I'm an oddity, that's all, and I won't be paraded about," Rosaleen said.

"All right, that's part of it. They're curious about you. But you must expect that. After all, you did take a step that shocked both the social and business worlds. You can't back away now," Coops said.

"Will you be my escort?" she asked.

"I'd be honored," Captain Coops said, the blue eyes twinkling. "I'm only sorry I'm not twenty years younger."

"All right," Rosaleen snapped out. "I shall go." Her eyes grew bright with quickening thoughts. She'd wear a gown that would command attention by itself. None of the Second Empire styles still favored by so many. The *ancien régime* was not for a young woman who had flown in the face of tradition. Charles Frederick Worth had opened a shop in London and she'd go there. Yes, she mused silently, a Worth gown would be appropriate, for he was an Englishman who'd broken open the traditions of French dressmaking, preparing dresses *in advance* for his clients, having gowns almost ready to wear for them. He'd gone so far as to predict that one day all women would be buying gowns already made and ready to wear. And he'd married one of his shopgirls. Charles Frederick Worth it would be, she repeated silently.

When the evening arrived, Joshua Coops wore his dress uniform and Rosaleen the ballgown she'd chosen, cut low in front, of brilliant yellow Lyon silk with a single side panel of claret. She was the focus of all eyes as she entered. Women looked at her with envy, the gentlemen with admiration tinged with uneasiness. Harold Pryor was there with his wife, a dried-up woman with a bitter face. He was politely correct, but Rosaleen laced her own politeness with disdain.

During the course of the evening, various men tried to draw her into discussions that would bring on embarrassing mistakes, but Rosaleen parried and countered, turning each attempt to her own advantage. She found herself dancing with increasing admirers and when the evening finally ended, Coops regarded her with amazement. "A bravura performance, my dear," he said. "And you enjoyed every minute of it."

"Yes," Rosaleen admitted. "It was fun to see the young ones grow more intrigued and the older ones more awed. But was it worth anything? Will it fill our holds and finance our repairs and notes?"

"In time. It will make you into a public figure and even bankers treat public figures more carefully," Coops said. "Two of our shippers were there tonight and seeing you made them agree not to pull out until we can show them what we can do."

"All right," Rosaleen decided. "I said I'd use every weapon I have to win—and I'll do it."

As with money, gossip flows in definite paths around the world. Soon the "beautiful Rosaleen Powell," the "daring young woman," was the subject of conversation in capitals all over Europe. To many, she was an amusing addition to the summer social season and to others, especially in the closed boardrooms, she was still resented, an intruder meddling in places she had no right to be. But in one place she was more than resented. In one place her name evoked cold fury.

In a building on the Boston waterfront, a man sat inside a richly paneled office designed in the style of a British landowner's study. He wore the very finest of gentlemen's clothing and the liquor cabinet in the office held the most select of gentlemen's sherries and whiskies. He had a valet and a country home in Arlington, a town house in the Beacon Hill section of Boston. He belonged to the Union League Club and the Cambridge Club. He was in every way a gentleman, except in the only way that matters, in his soul.

Frank Shields gazed at the two younger men in his office, one his general manager, Hubie Irwin, the other his chief assistant, Ed Stoker. Like many powerful men, he had the habit of hiring weaker men to surround him and then held them in contempt for their weakness. His lips drew back in a grimace, now, as he listened to Hubie Irwin's words.

"She'll fade. She's just made some lucky moves," he said.

PAMELA WINDSOR

"No, you damn fool, no luck whatever. She's made all the right moves. She's done all the things the old man couldn't see to do, was afraid to do, or just was too set in his ways to do," Shields bit out.

"Hell, she hasn't turned the Powell Line around yet," Irwin protested.

"No, not yet, but if she's left alone she'll do it," Frank Shields said, and felt his jaw tighten as he remembered what he had seen in the violet eyes of Rosaleen Powell. "That little bitch knows what's been going on," he murmured.

"She can't. She has no evidence of anything," the other man said.

"Not up here," Shields snapped, tapping one finger against his forehead. "Down here," he finished, pressing the finger to his heart. "That's all she has to know." He pulled his broad, thick figure up, went to the window that looked down on Boston Harbor and the bare masts of a thousand ships at their quays. "Goddammit, I thought I had it won. The damn little bitch," he growled.

"We'll just give her more of what we gave the old man," Ed Stoker offered.

Shields spun on the two men. "That's all you can think of? More of the same? Jesus, it's lucky I make plans in depth. It's called covering all your bets, having a couple of aces in the hole."

"No more of the same for her?" Hubie Irwin questioned.

"I didn't say that. If we have to, later. But there's more than one way to skin a cat, even a beautiful, stubborn one. When I'm finished, Miss Rosaleen Powell will be in my pocket, one way or another." The man snorted into the air. "One way or another, she'll come around."

Frank Shields turned from the window to the two men. "You get on to New York and wait for instructions, Hubie. Ed, you take the *Amandine* for Plymouth, she sails tonight. Get things ready

112

if I need you. Make your contacts again. Meanwhile, I'll be doing things my way."

The men rose and Frank Shields returned his gaze to the scene outside the window, his ice-floe eyes burning with a cold light. Rosaleen Powell, he muttered silently. An entirely unexpected turn of events. A damn fool girl. She'd learn the hard way. She'd learn.

It was Friday and Rosaleen had ridden to Gwyneth with Niles. She'd seen Agnes Walsh and told her how happy Margaret was, and spent time with Mary Orkney and Bridgit Cowand and Abraham Evans and all the other friends, and now she was in the coteen with Niles, content against the warm smoothness of his body, her lips nibbling, answering, demanding. She'd rejected the invitation for the Union Club Ball tonight, and she lay back and felt kitten-lazy now.

"It seems only a few days have passed since I began spending my weeks in London but it's been almost two months, now," Rosaleen reflected.

"Two months and I keep reading more and more about the glamorous Rosaleen Powell in the *Times*," Niles commented. "And I'm consumed with fear and jealousy, all those attractive men swarming around her at all those parties."

She put a hand over his mouth. "Not another word. When I'm with them, all I think about is you," she said.

"So far," he said, and his eyes danced. He was teasing her, but she caught something more, and pulled herself up on one elbow as his hand cupped her breast.

"I'll stop tomorrow if you say so, Niles," she told him.

His smile was love and tenderness. "No, my darling, I wouldn't ask that and you know it. You must finish what you've begun. But I do have something in my thoughts." She let her eyebrows lift a fraction and he took her face in his hands. "Marry me, my darling. I want you for always," he said.

Rosaleen felt the tightness seize her, then explode as if the sun had suddenly burst inside her, filling her with brilliance and warmth. She pressed herself into his arms, her lips whispering against his cheek. "Oh, yes, yes, Niles, my love, my darling one. Yes, oh, yes."

He held her for a long moment, then pulled back. "Not when this is all over. I want to marry you just for yourself, my love," he told her. "I want you to win, to restore the Powell Line, but that doesn't really matter to me. I just want you as my wife and nothing else. I don't care about anything else, just having you." He pressed his hands to her face again. "I may have to go back to America for a month. A letter came informing me that I've two very fine commissions waiting, but I must talk personally to the people involved. But when I return, we'll be married at once."

"Yes, yes, my darling." Rosaleen agreed, happy excitement managing to overpower the disappointment of his being away for a month. He read her thoughts, as he so often did.

"A month isn't so long," he said. "But till I return, we'll keep it our secret. That way there'll be no rumors, no insinuations, no backbiting from anywhere."

"Yes, our secret till you get back," Rosaleen echoed. She couldn't prevent her lower lip from pushing out. When will you go?" she queried.

"I don't know. I'm waiting for another letter. Meanwhile, we won't think about that but about all the tomorrows we'll have together, forever and ever," he told her, and she nestled herself happily against his chest, guardian of a very wonderful and very private glory.

When she returned to London that Monday she found Coops looking at her with curiosity. "You're unusually sparkling this morning," he remarked, and her little smile was full of happy secrets. But, she learned, the world was not unlike a bag of mixed candies, some sweet and some sour. The letter was delivered by special messenger and Coops was there as she opened it, and stared down at the single, cold paragraph.

"They can't do this," she gasped. "It's from Ogilvy, from the London Merchant's Bank. They're calling in our short-term notes. But they're not due till the end of the year." Coops gently took the letter from her hand as she echoed her words with added vehemence. "They've no right. They can't do this," she said.

"But they can, I'm afraid. I'm sure that if you read the fine print on the notes you'll see they can call them in on demand," Coops said. "It's usually no more than a protective clause they put in and it's just not done normally."

"Well, they're doing it and I'm going to find our why. Spitework, plain maliciousness on Ogilvy's part, I'll wager. It'd be like him," Rosaleen cast out, and Coops shrugged.

"Perhaps, but bankers seldom let their personal feelings interfere with business matters," Coops offered. "I daresay he could hate you, but if your account was good he'd not touch it."

"Then why?" Rosaleen flung back.

He shrugged. "I don't know. I'm only saying that I'd wager there's more than his personal pique involved."

"I'll find out," Rosaleen said, moving from the desk. "I'll find out from him face to face." She strode from the office with her violet eyes flashing dark lightning. The officers of the bank were but a few streets away and she was there in minutes, demanding to see Emerson Ogilvy and refusing to be turned aside by the somewhat timid woman at the other desk. Ogilvy consented to see Rosaleen, rose to greet her as she stormed into his office. He needed to ask no questions about the visit.

"I'm terribly sorry, Miss Powell," Ogilvy said, holding his thin form stiffly. "But I assure you there was nothing personal in it. The bank needs to increase the fluidity of its assets and the board of directors took this step."

Rosaleen let contempt blaze from her eyes. The well-turned banker's phrases rang hollowly. "I simply don't believe you," she snapped, and saw Ogilvy recoil as if she'd physically struck him. He stammered a moment before finding words. In his sterile world, one didn't just say things such as that even if one thought them.

"A most unladylike statement, Miss Powell," he said after a moment.

"In answer to a most ungentlemanly act," Rosaleen snapped.

Emerson Ogilvy looked wounded. "It was not my doing, I told you. I mean, really, I wouldn't do such a thing on a purely personal basis. I do have my own sense of the proprieties, you know," he protested.

"But it was done, proprieties or not, and you didn't halt it, did you?" Rosaleen thrust, and the man looked helpless, a frail stick of a person. "Good day," Rosaleen said, whirling and striding from his office. Outside, she paused in the weak sun that was trying to push away the mist. He had lied. Something was very wrong. An inner sense jabbed this certainty at her. Yet his denial of personal revenge had been sincere, immediate, and filled with horror. She had been about to return to the office when she turned to the left, hurried along the crowded streets until she reached the corner of Chancery Street. She hurried along it to the Public Records Office. The clerk there, a young man, was helpful in finding her the particular documents she needed. She sat down with a small tower of file folders and began to pour through them.

Halfway into the stack, her eyes already weary of the fine print of stock transfers, ownership certificates, articles of partnership, and a host of similar records, she came upon what she sought, the financial statements of the London Merchant's Bank. Major ownership in the bank, and one of the major depositors, was the Frank Shields Shipping Company. Rosaleen slammed the folder shut, sat for a moment with her fingers drumming the table in fury. She rose, hurried back to the office with the rage seething inside her. The piper calls the tune and Frank Shields was the piper for the bank. Coops listened to her frustrated rage as she pounded one small fist into the other and the violet eyes were almost purple.

"Those notes, we're finished if we default on them," Rosaleen said. "It's unfair. It's rotten. There must be some way to stop this kind of thing."

"There's a banking ethics commission, but it'll be a year before they begin to act," Coops said.

"That bastard," Rosaleen cried out. "That rotten bastard."

"Shields plays every card. He's without any sense of fair play or ethics," Coops said. "But you just may have to face defeat, Rosaleen. The man with a knife at your throat may be a thorough criminal, but he still has the knife there. Facts are facts, unhappy and unfair as they may be."

"No!" Rosaleen heard herself shout. "He won't win, not this way, not this easily." She flung herself backward into the deep leather chair, her mouth pressed into a thin line. "Sell the Pacific Coastal division, all of it. That will cover the amount of the notes," she said, noting the shock on Captain Coops's face. The Pacific Coastal division was solvent, a dozen small barks and two-masted schooners that covered the coastal routes between Australia, New Zealand, the Malays, Philipines, and Indochina.

"The Japanese wanted to buy it, didn't they, the Matu Maru people?" Rosaleen said.

"Yes, but if you keep selling off things you won't have anything left to keep," Coops countered.

"It's a matter of keeping the ship afloat, Coops," Rosaleen answered. "Afloat and alive, that comes first. Sell, Coops, I'm going to meet those notes."

Coops nodded, his lips pursed. "It's a damn shame, but you're right, my dear. There's no other way. I'll get on it immediately." He turned, halted at the door to glance back. "I've a new lead on the Bangkok bullion," he said. "I'm to be given the name and whereabouts of an able-bodied seaman who has been acting as a contact point for others."

"I've not much confidence in that," Rosaleen murmured. "But we've no right to turn away from anything, no matter how ephemeral. Tend to the sale of the division, first."

The man nodded and Rosaleen sank back, felt herself suddenly drained. She left the office early and, outside, Carlson peered at her. "You're looking drawn, Miss Rosaleen," he offered. "You can't overdo, you know."

She managed a tired smile, patted his arm. "Thank you, Carlson," she said. "I'll be all right." His concern helped take the edge from the angry bitterness that had draped itself around her and she went to the town house, managed to eat something and fell into bed exhausted. She slept fitfully and when she rose early the room suddenly swam away from her. She clutched the bedpost, her stomach quivering. She sank down onto the edge of the bed and let the intensity of the moment recede. The room stopped swimming after a few moments and she rose, steadied herself, and began to dress. She felt better, almost her normal self by the time she was dressed and at the office. The Matu Maru people had an office in London and Coops had initiated the sale proposal. There was little to do but wait, and she felt her stomach cramp with tension twice during the day. The following morning she was ill again and the tension stayed through the day but with lessening severity. But it was the third morning, still feeling ill when she reached the office, that she confessed her attack of nerves to Coops as he studied her with a frown.

"Why all of a sudden?" she complained.

"It's not all of a sudden," he answered. "It's been building inside you though you were unaware of it. Now this crisis with the notes pushed it into exploding. Strain is a terrible thing. It corrodes from inside, particularly the kind that comes at you from all sides. That's one important reason why only a few people are cut out for top positions. The rest of us just can't stand what it takes out of one."

"Are you saying I'm not up to running a shipping line?" she asked, not in anger.

Coops shrugged. "I'm saying it's possible. I'm saying it's something you have to face and be honest with yourself about. I couldn't do it. I can skipper a ship and worry about a northeaster or making a schedule, but that's a different kind of thing. You've a definite enemy to face, something you can come to grips with and win or lose all at once."

"I have to stick with it till it's over, till I've won, Coops," she said.

His hand reached out, touched her shoulder gently. "No, my dear. All you have to do is give it your best try. Nothing is worth ruining your health over. You're too young to make a nervous wreck of yourself."

"Thank you. You're a real friend, Coops," Rosaleen said. "I think I can do it, though. But I'll remember everything you've said." She reached up on tiptoe, brushed his leathered cheek with a kiss, and saw him look sheepish, suddenly a little boy as he hurried out of the office.

By midweek the Matu Maru people had agreed to the sale and furnished a cash bond. It was on Thursday that Rosaleen sent a special messenger to Ogilvy's office with the deposit to cover the notes. His lean, prim face would reflect astonishment but no more, and she thought about Frank Shields when word reached him. That was where her victory lay, in the bitter fury that would engulf Frank Shields. It was a blow struck for her father and Rosaleen felt a warm glow of satisfaction. It had been a costly victory, yet a victory nonetheless. The next evening she hurried back to Cornwall, brimming over with eagerness to tell Niles everything that had happened. The shakiness of her stomach had settled somewhat and by the next morning, cradled against Niles in the coteen, she knew calmness and peace. Later, when she told him all that had taken place, and how she'd snatched victory from defeat, she saw the touch of sternness in his face.

"That does it," he said when she finished. "It's too much all on your shoulders. We'll marry the minute I return. I want to be able to come to you whenever you need me, be with you if you need me, openly, so gossip and vicious tongues can't add to the troubles."

"Yes, yes, my darling," Rosaleen said, then pulled back. "Then you've heard? You are going?"

"The letter came today. I'll leave by midweek," Niles told her. Rosaleen's mind was instantly busy with hurried calculations.

"Taking in crossing time, you'll be away at least six weeks," she pouted.

"About that," he said. "It'll be the longest six weeks of my life, my darling."

"Promise you'll write," Rosaleen pressed.

"Every day. How about that?" Niles said, and she laughed, pulled him to her.

"That'll do fine," she whispered, and as his body pressed down against her she felt herself seem to catch fire. She pushed upward against him, flames of wanting thrusting all else aside, urged to new heights by the prospect of being alone for six weeks. "Niles, Niles, come to me, my darling, come to me," she breathed, and, as it had so often before, the little coteen became a palace of ecstasy, a tiny pleasure world complete unto itself. She spent the three days with Niles, clinging to him for a last moment before she had to return to Raven's Wing, pack her things, and catch the night coach.

"Pick a day, a time, a church, have it all ready when I return," he told her.

"Yes," she whispered. *"Bon voyage,* my love." She almost ran, not daring to look back, and later, at Raven's Wing, she closeted herself with Margaret to go over the myriad household details and finally there was only time to catch the night coach. "What's good for upset stomach, Margaret?" she asked as Sam Tyler waited to drive her to Bodwin.

"Milk and honey, my dear, nothing better," Margaret said, eying her sharply. "Unless it's more than just an upset stomach."

Rosaleen shrugged. "I've never had an ulcer," she said, and waved from the rig.

"See a doctor if it keeps up, now," Margaret called, and Rosaleen nodded, waved again. Once on the night coach, alone for most of the trip, she slept. When morning and London came together, her stomach stayed relatively calm and she felt confident as she greeted Coops at the office.

"I'm going to take out new notes and replace the vessels we sold," she said. "There's no reason why we can't go back into the coastal trade with our Japanese friends."

Coops shook his head in astonishment. "You are your father's daughter," he said. Rosaleen laughed, went out at noontime, bought a new hat, and got appointments with the Merchant's Bank and the Barclay Bank and Trust. The victory that she'd scored had reached their ears. News travels quickly in financial circles, she knew, but the victory suddenly grew sour as she was turned down by both banks. There was politeness, perhaps even a hint of admiration, but no credit. The Powell Line's financial picture had not yet improved enough, she was told. She presented facts and figures, showed them projections, and they remained adamant. The following day, she tried two more leading institutions and the answers were the same. She recalled the newspaper quotation of Mr. Robert Hedges of Merchant's Insurer's, and she went to see him. He turned out to be a portly gentleman with a brisk but nonetheless understanding manner.

"Of course they'll turn you down," he said. "Your competition has put pressure on his accounts and many of those accounts carry a lot of weight in banking circles. To overcome that, you need the kind of financial picture you don't have yet."

"And you? What about your company?" Rosaleen asked.

"I've my limits, too. I've a board of directors to answer to, also. I can let you have about half of what you're asking," he offered. "Think about it and get back to me."

Rosaleen left, not ungrateful. He had at least offered something, but she knew, as Coops pointed out when they were alone later, that half was of no use. "With only half a fleet we could never compete to regain the coastal trade," he said. "It was a bold idea but you'd best put it aside, until another day, at least."

"Yes," Rosaleen conceded. "We'll have to go on with what we have. Good night, Coops. I'm going home and sleep."

She did exactly that and in the morning, her stomach was tight as the skin of a drumhead and she fought waves of nausea. Four cups of hot tea helped and she reached the office feeling only a little better. The afternoon's news turned her stomach into knots of pain.

"Captain Masterson of the *Clydesforth* and his first mate have resigned and she's due to sail at midnight," Coops told her. "The crew won't sail with the second mate. They say they've no confidence in him."

"Do we have any other vessels in port?" Rosaleen asked.

"The *Loch Fenian*," Coops said.

"She's half the size of the *Clydesforth*."

"That's right. I contacted the shippers and asked them to let us take half the cargo on her and the other half on the *Loch Tooral* next week," Coops said. Rosaleen questioned with her stare. "They refused," Coops said grimly.

"What is her cargo?"

"Copper ore, jute, cotton, wool, and tea," Coops said.

"Why did they refuse your offer?" she asked.

"The *Lady Luck* happens to be in port, able to take on the entire cargo," Coops said.

"A Shields clipper," Rosaleen snapped. "How very clear. He simply bought off Masterson and the first mate. Can't we have them brought up before the B.O.T.?"

"The Board of Trade will want proof. Do we have it?" Coops questioned softly.

Rosaleen sank into the chair and felt fifty years older. Coops perched half on the corner of the desk. "I can take the *Clydesforth* out by midweek. The crew will sail under me. Harry Ormsby has a cargo I can get," he said.

"What kind of cargo?" Rosaleen questioned, alerted by something in the captain's tone.

"Livestock. Mostly pigs," Coops said.

"Livestock on a first-run clipper such as the *Clydesforth*?" Rosaleen protested.

Coops shrugged. "We've lost the cargo she has now and we'll have to pay the shippers a late penalty to boot. Ormsby's pigs will make up part of the loss. It's that or take the whole loss, I'm afraid, Rosaleen," Coops said with sorry patience. Rosaleen nodded after a moment, her lips tight.

"You're right, of course," she said. "Go on, do it. How long will you be gone?"

"Eight days, everything going well," he said.

"We can't win fighting a rearguard action," Rosaleen bit out angrily. "When you return we'll make plans for something more, special runs, perhaps, something to strike back."

Rosaleen went to the town house that night and slept the sleep of the emotionally exhausted. In the morning she threw up again as her stomach tightened with spasms. She lay down, stayed quiet, and finally managed some tea. The spasms subsided and she felt strong enough to go to the office. She somehow got through the rest of the week after Coops sailed on the *Clydesforth*. The mornings were always the worst, but she fought down indulging herself, arrived at the office each day, and was grateful when the week ended as she rode the coach to Cornwall. It had ended no better than it had begun. Word had come that the *Argylle Queen* had caught fire and burned to the waterline in Rio de Janeiro harbor. The harbor police believed the fire had been deliberately set and they were seeking a crewman seen leaving the ship just before the fire broke out.

She wondered if perhaps the only way to fight a man such as Frank Shields was to turn his own rotten methods back on him. But that kind of victory was really a defeat, she told herself, and thought about it all the way to Cornwall. Conscience, morality, ethics, they were burdens that saddled us from childhood, Rosaleen pondered. Once made a believer in them, we are trapped. There had to be a way to fight Frank Shields and retain one's own values, one's own sense of ethics, but she succeeded only in feeling more helpless and frustrated for the question.

Tony was in the doorway when she reached Raven's Wing in the morning. He picked up her bag, eyed her sharply. "You look tired, sis," he said, and tried a smile. "I'm glad I caught you before you get any more tired. I've caught hold of a deal that might make a jolly good investment. It'll take venture capital and Livvie suggested I ask you for it."

"Venture capital. It's out of the question," Rosaleen snapped out. "It's absolutely impossible." Tony peered at her with increased sharpness.

"I thought you had things in hand, humming along, in fact," he prodded.

"I did. I have, I will," Rosaleen heard herself sputter. Her stomach hurt and she had to fight back the sudden urge to burst into tears. She brushed past Tony Darby, to her room, flung herself onto the bed, and lay trembling, wanting the tears to explode now but feeling only the quivering inside her. She lay there until the sick feeling passed, then rose, drew a warm bath, and stayed in it until she felt better. She lay down then, managed to sleep some, and rose later in the day. Margaret was in the big kitchen as she went downstairs, the older woman's experienced eyes sweeping over her with a frown.

"Still feeling sick?" Margaret asked.

"Just emptied at the moment," Rosaleen answered as she lowered herself into one of the captain's chairs that circled the round table.

"Missing Niles, of course," Margaret commented, watching her with quick, sharp glances as she went about putting things in order in the kitchen.

"That doesn't help," Rosaleen conceded. "Let's take the afternoon off, Margaret, drive down to Gwyneth."

Margaret laughed. "Anything to get away, occupy the mind, is that it?"

"Yes, but it's always good there, full of good memories, good friends. I need that," Rosaleen said.

"Then we'll go," Margaret said. "Now, you just stay put here and I'll harness the Whitechapel." Rosaleen didn't argue and let Margaret drive. The visit to Gwyneth was everything she wanted and they returned after dark. Rosaleen had a bowl of partridge soup and went up to bed. She spent the remainder of the three days resting, keeping her own counsel except for Margaret, and the time to leave for Bodwin and the night coach came all too quickly. She was in the foyer when Tony Darby appeared in a blue lounging jacket. The usual casualness was missing from his stance and his eyes were hard.

"Margaret tells me the housekeeping funds have been cut down to the bare essentials. She claims she can't put on a formal dinner," he accused.

"That's right. It's called austerity. The living funds may be needed one of these days," Rosaleen said.

"My God, I've invited twelve people for dinner ten days from now," Tony protested.

"You'll have to cancel, or foot the bill yourself. You and Olivia do have an income," she reminded him.

"That's all earmarked by now," Tony said. "I mean, this dinner will pay off for everyone, you included, Rosaleen."

"There are no funds for extras, Tony," Rosaleen said. "You'll have to do it on your own or not at all." She lifted her traveling bag and walked to Sam Tyler's waiting buggy without looking backward but she heard Tony Darby's muttered "Damn fool girl."

Monday morning brought two cancellations by different trading companies to the office. Both protested the troubles and delays caused their shipments by late sailings, crew dissatisfaction, and change of masters aboard Powell Line vessels. Rosaleen swore silently, put the letters away for Coops to see upon his return. The following day she spent with the monthly balance sheet Higgens had prepared. The Rio run was holding its own. All the South American routes were staying together and the clippers racing around the Cape continued to make good time. But the other expenses were too much and in the final balance, expenses were outrunning profits. They could go on for a few months, perhaps six, Rosaleen estimated, unless the profit picture turned around. It was all a matter of projecting, guessing, juggling risks and uncertainties, and by the end of the day she was feeling positively ill. She went to the town house to find a letter from Harold Pryor, still acting as solicitor for the estate.

"Your father had been going to put the town house up for sale at the end of this month," the letter read. "Do you wish me to continue along those lines? It will bring a tidy profit in today's market." Rosaleen put the letter aside. It was one of the easier decisions facing her. She'd sell, put the money into the business. A small lodging somewhere nearby would cost but a fraction of maintaining the house. And Niles might not like the town house, anyway. She pulled off clothes and slept restlessly, woke in the morning with her stomach quivering. She felt gray as the skies outside and eagerly tore open the letter waiting for her at the office, the Boston address on the back of the envelope leaping up at her.

My love—

It is good renewing old acquaintances. The two new commissions sound wonderful. I look forward to doing them with you at my side. Plan that special day. Time will go quickly and soon we'll be sharing everything side by side. All my love...

Niles

The letter turned the day into sunshine until later when a special courier brought word of a crew rebellion over rations on the barkentine *Flora*, about to sail out of Marseilles. The gray drizzle returned, inside and out, and she left the office feeling drained and exhausted. Coops returned the following day and she was grateful for that but he left at once to see to the Marseilles trouble. Another letter from Niles only two days later was the sole bright spot. She decided not to return to Cornwall, largely because she felt so poorly and the daily bouts with her trembling stomach were growing worse. As she lay in bed on a Saturday she could no longer turn away from the questions that stabbed at her. She had to face the words Coops had uttered. Perhaps it was simply all more than she could cope with. Perhaps she hadn't her father's steel, after all. It would be the final irony, she grimaced, Frank Shields winning because the pressures were just too much for her. The thought made her swing from the bed, dress, and find the address and office hours for Dr. Matthews. He'd have something to help keep her stomach calm, medicines, pills, something. Rosaleen grunted, the possibility somehow reassuring. Certainly Dr. Matthews would understand her pressures and tensions better than another physician. He had helped her father fight them long enough.

She arrived at the very close of the doctor's office hours. A nurse, a tall, thin young woman with long blond hair and a valiantly reassuring smile, had her undress and wait in a plain white robe. When Dr. Matthews entered the examining room, he first sat down across from her and listened to what she had to tell him. "Yes, it could all be tension," he said thoughtfully. "Tension can kill. I've been aware, of course, of the things you've been doing."

"And you think it's all too much for me," Rosaleen said defensively.

His lips pursed. "The symptoms you describe would indicate as much."

"Then I want something to keep my stomach calm, to help me until I've seen this thing through," Rosaleen demanded. "You must have something to do that. I'm sure you helped my father in the very same way."

"Only at the very end," Dr. Matthews said sadly. "And as for you, my dear young woman, I'll prescribe nothing until I've had a thorough look at you." He rose and she followed him into the examining room. He was indeed thorough, and surprisingly gentle and patient. When he finished he'd taken blood and urine samples and she had been reduced to a series of vials and notes. Later, dressed, she sat across from him again in the outer office.

"What do you think?" she asked anxiously.

"Come in Monday morning," he said. "I'll have everything tested and analyzed by then. I won't make any diagnosis now."

She wanted to press, but his face had set itself and she saw that further prodding would avail little. She spent Sunday resting quietly. Dr. Matthews's office hours on Monday were in the late afternoon and so she was at the Powell Line offices as usual in the morning. Higgens had prepared the month's checks for her to sign and most of the morning was taken up with that. There was another letter, a short one, from Niles, and she felt better at once as she read it.

"You'll like Boston," he wrote. "You'll see it as my wife, soon, for I'll have to return, I've learned. I care more for you with each passing minute…. Niles."

She folded the letter into her purse, finished one more batch of checks, and then it was time for her to go to the physician's office. The tall, thin blond nurse showed her into the doctor's office where he sat with the rows of medical texts behind him. She sat down and felt his sharp eyes burning into her as he folded his fingertips against each other to form a small pyramid with his hands.

"I've the results of all the tests," he began. "You may be suffering from tension and worry, Miss Rosaleen. However, the reason you've been feeling so poorly is that you are going to have a baby." He paused for a moment. "Yes, you are pregnant," he said.

Rosaleen met his probing stare as his words danced inside her. He peered at her, waiting, and she almost smiled. She was astonished, totally surprised, though not in the least bit upset. It was difficult to absorb at first, but she could feel a tremendous joy surging through her. She suddenly wanted to shout, a wonderful, ringing shout, but she brought her thoughts back to the physician who continued to gaze at her expectantly.

"Did you expect tears, Dr. Matthews?" Rosaleen asked. He frowned uncomfortably. "Would that be the proper thing to do?" she pressed. "If so, I'm afraid you'll be disappointed. Or have you forgotten that I'm not a proper young woman?"

She saw his face take on a slight flush. "Defying your father, going off to live with a man in a tiny Cornish village, while scandalous enough, is not the same as being single and pregnant in London. Particularly in view of your being so newsworthy these days." He disapproved of her, Rosaleen saw, yet his words held the truth of reality. "Medical ethics will seal my lips about this but time and nature will not be sealed. I suggest you get hold of the father of this child at once and insist on, shall we say, the proper arrangements."

Rosaleen gave the doctor a small smile, her own secret curling inside it. "They will be done, I assure you, very soon and very properly," she said, watching Dr. Matthews eye her uncertainly. His professional aplomb had been jarred if not shattered by her response to his words.

"The nurse has some medicine for you," he said gruffly.

"Thank you. I shall be in touch soon," she smiled. As she left the office, the nurse handed her a small bottle of pills, which she dropped in her purse. She walked slowly through the London streets, wrapped in her own world, filled with a quietly delicious excitement. She carried Niles's child inside her. The man she loved was now a part of her in the deepest, most absolute way. She shuddered and it was a shudder of private ecstasy. There was even an added bonus. She'd not been too weak to run the Powell Line. No nervous tension at all but the small, early problem of being a mother. Rosaleen reached the town house, went inside, and pulled off her clothes. She lay down across the bed, wrapped herself in the spread, and slept wonderfully well. When she woke, she'd only a mild queasiness, which one of the pills ended almost immediately. Even the news with which Coops greeted her when she reached the office couldn't dispel her joy. A man had been caught in Hamburg trying to slash the rigging of the *Venturesome* just before she was to sail.

"He admitted he was paid to do the job but he won't say by whom. Probably because he fears for his life," Coops told her.

"No matter. We know who paid him. Will the *Venturesome* be able to sail?"

"Yes, but two days late. Let's hope a good wind helps her make up the schedule," Coops said. Carlson came in with a sheaf of letters to sign and Coops left. Later, alone, Rosaleen thought again of the plans that had already formed themselves inside her. The secret she carried was too wonderful to reduce to a letter. She'd go to Boston with her news. She wanted to be in his arms when she told him, holding him, seeing his eyes, not at a distance. Besides, Niles had roots and family in Boston, no doubt. He'd want them to meet her. She felt the excitement spiraling inside her as she thought of the moment to come with Niles. When Coops came into the office, she blurted the question at him with schoolgirl eagerness.

"When is our next clipper sailing for Boston?" she asked, and saw the questions form in his eyes at once.

"Wednesday, with the noon tide, the *Pegasus*," Coops said.

"Book passage for me on her," Rosaleen said. Coops eyes grew wider. "I'll tell you all the reasons when I get back," Rosaleen said. He half-shrugged.

"It's a happy trip. That's plain to see in the way your eyes are shining," he remarked.

Rosaleen nodded, then mused aloud: "Wednesday noon. That'll just give me time to go to Raven's Wing, pack, and get back. I shan't be gone long, less than three weeks, I imagine, counting travel time. I'm leaving everything in your hands till I return. All the regular checks have been signed and I'll sign a paper giving you use of the general emergency funds."

"Thank you for your confidence in me, Miss Rosaleen," the man said. "I'll keep everything in hand till you return."

"I know you will, Coops," Rosaleen said. "There's no one else I'd turn to for this, or for anything connected with the Powell Line. You've been a faithful friend to me and to all that my father built."

Coops smiled, then allowed himself a small frown. "I was going to go to Boston myself," he said. "But perhaps you can do something more than you intended on your visit." He paused, the frown deepening. "I don't know, though. I don't like you having to do it."

"What is it?" Rosaleen queried.

"The Bangkok bullion. I'm informed that a top contact is in Boston, an old able-bodied seaman by the name of Holderman. I was going to sail on the *Pegasus* to get to him, myself."

"Of course I'll do it," Rosaleen offered.

"It'll mean going to the seamen's places, I'm afraid," Coops said.

Rosaleen lifted her chin. "I'm not afraid," she said. "He might say more to a woman, especially the daughter of Sir Mallory."

Coops's lips pressed together. "Yes, that's a possibility. I still don't like the idea, but one of us has to stay here and you'll be in Boston anyway, so I guess it's in your hands. I'm informed he can be found in a place called the Whaler's Wharf. Remember, he'll expect to be paid for whatever he tells you and whatever you may want him to pass on." Rosaleen nodded and Coops continued. "You'll tell him that you're interested in the story of a man who never left Bangkok. He'll answer you, maybe try to put you off, but you tell him you're only interested in one special man and you'll pay good money to learn what happened to him."

"I have it," Rosaleen said.

"That's the way I was told to make contact. The rest you'll have to play as you go along," Coops said.

"I'll find out whatever there is to find out, I can assure you," Rosaleen said. "Now, let me sign the papers you'll need signed and catch the early coach to Cornwall." She called Carlson and Higgens in, informed them of plans for the next few weeks, had everything signed before the hour was over, and made the coach with but minutes to spare. She'd have twenty-four hours at Raven's Wing, just enough to pack all she'd need for the trip, she calculated as the coach rolled out of London. It was late evening when she reached Cornwall and had Sam Tylor drive her to Raven's Wing. She went to Margaret's quarters at once, and enjoyed the astonishment on the other woman's face. But she decided to let even Margaret think it was because she missed Niles so terribly, keeping her secret all to herself. She talked her excitement out with Margaret, then slept soundly the night through. In the morning she packed travel clothes, two suitcases full, and then went downstairs with the bags to find Tony and Olivia waiting in the library.

"Margaret told us," Olivia said.

"I've been wondering when you were going to get around to talk to us," Tony commented.

"There's not that much to tell. I'm just going to Boston for a few weeks," Rosaleen said, and saw Tony puff up.

"I'd say there are a number of things to go over if I'm going to be on top of things while you're gone," he said.

Rosaleen felt her forehead furrow. "I'm not sure I follow you," she remarked.

"I'm talking about running the business while you're off in Boston. I think I'd best take the coach back with you this morning," Tony said, his eyebrows deepening.

"I've taken care of that," Rosaleen said.

"What do you mean, taken care of it?" he frowned.

"Captain Coops is in charge till I get back," Rosaleen said, saw Tony's mouth become a turned-in slit across his face.

"You can't mean that. Livvie and I are family. We're the ones to leave in charge. I mean, that's the only proper thing to do," he glowered.

"I'm sorry, but I felt Captain Coops was best," Rosaleen countered. "He has a thorough knowledge of everything going on."

Tony's face had grown red with anger. "That's fine. He'd serve in the same way he does for you. But leave him in charge, that's disgraceful. What will people say, your leaving things in his hands when you've family right on hand. Why, I'll be the laughingstock of all my friends. Really, this just isn't done."

"I'm sorry, but I've done it because it's what I thought best. Perhaps some other time," Rosaleen added, the words a peace offering, but Tony couldn't accept them.

"No. Change it. I won't be insulted this way," he persisted.

"Tony could show you what he could do. You'd be really pleased, Rosaleen," Olivia tried, an almost pathetic attempt to aid her husband.

"I'm sorry. I don't see it as an insult and I'm not changing anything," Rosaleen returned stiffly.

"Well, it is, whether you want to see it that way or not. Of course, you don't care. All you want to do is run off to visit your beloved," he shouted. "Well, Niles Brewster isn't all you think he is."

Rosaleen heard herself laugh. "Your jealousy's showing, Tony," she said. "Again."

"You'll see. You'll mark my words," he threw back at her.

She dismissed him. He was simply trying to strike back, to hurt.

"Be back before you know it, Olivia," she said, pressed her sister's arm, and strode outside to where Margaret waited in the buggy.

"It's a shame to have you go off with that kind of scene," Margaret said. "But he was ready for it. I saw it in his ways when you didn't come down earlier to talk to him. He'd suspected what he learned. It wasn't such a complete shock as he made out."

"I suppose I might have handled it better," Rosaleen wondered aloud. "I just have so little regard for him I never even considered it."

"It's done. Forget it and enjoy your holiday," the older woman said. Rosaleen embraced the advice, decided to share part of her happiness with Margaret before leaving.

"We're going to get married when he returns," she said. "Perhaps he'll come back with me."

Margaret let out a small cry of joy. "How wonderful, my dear. I'm so glad for you. Now I'll have something to prepare for while you're away. Just listen to me, I'm so excited as if I were the one heading for the altar."

"It's our secret. Keep it that way till I return," Rosaleen said.

"I'll not breathe a word to anyone," Margaret promised as the buggy rolled into Bodwin and the waiting afternoon coach. Hugs and kisses were quick moments of caring and then the coach was rolling and Rosaleen managed a last wave from the window, sat back, and drew a deep breath. She was on her way, on the first steps of the long journey across the sea to Niles. Happiness engulfed her, a happiness so total it was almost frightening.

CHAPTER SIX

oston surprised her. The waterfront was everything she had expected, busy and lusty, exuding a raw energy London and Plymouth lacked. But, seen from the hansom cab she'd hired, the city proper was green and unhurried, quite the opposite of what she had imagined. She was fascinated by the lace curtains that seemed to be on almost every window of every house the carriage passed. The voyage itself had been uneventful and she'd had dinner each night with the captain, a Mr. Axelrod whom she'd never personally met though she was familiar with his name from company ledgers. She'd accepted his offer to keep her bags aboard the ship until she found a place to stay, and now Rosaleen watched eagerly as the hansom wound its way along the edge of the Commons. Flowering window boxes seemed to be as ubiquitous as the lace curtains. The Charles River wound its way along and through the city, not unlike the Thames in London, Rosaleen observed. In fact, as the hansom rolled along Beacon Street, she felt quite at home in this foreign city. She noted the women on the streets still wore a great deal of crinoline. Exaggerated skirts and tunics were also popular, as were mantelets. She saw little high fashion, but then it was midday, she reminded herself.

The hansom turned a corner and Rosaleen leaned forward as it slowed. She'd given the cabbie the address Niles had put on his letters and the carriage slowed, then halted before a modest frame house. Rosaleen was out on the sidewalk instantly, flinging the fare to the cabbie and hurrying to the door of the house. She found an iron knocker, pounded it on the door until it opened to reveal a middle-aged woman in a blue smock, a broom and dustcloth in one hand.

"Mr. Niles Brewster?" Rosaleen inquired, and the woman nodded, shifted the broom to the other hand.

"Mr. Niles Brewster?" Rosaleen inquired, and the woman nodded, shifted the broom to the other hand.

"He lives here but he's out now," she said, her voice flat, nasal. "He can be reached at his uncle's place, 10 Copley Square."

"I see. Thank you," Rosaleen said, and watched the woman close the door. She felt stupid. It had just never occurred to her that Niles wouldn't be there. Eagerness distorts reason, she sniffed inwardly as she went to the curb and hailed another hansom.

It was but a short distance to Copley Square, and she left the cab before an imposing town house, square and solid with a polished cherry-wood door and windows with deep-green shutters. This time a butler answered her knock, a tall and austere man. "I was told I could find Mr. Brewster here," Rosaleen said.

The door opened wider. "Yes, please step in," the man answered. Rosaleen moved into the house, found herself inside a spacious foyer with a floor of black-and-white, diamond-shaped tiles of striking effect. The walls were stark white and a large portrait hung upon the facing wall. It was a very fine painting, magnificently like the man it portrayed. Rosaleen stared at the ice-floe eyes that looked back at her from the canvas, heard her voice gasp out:

"Frank Shields."

"Indeed," the butler said at her shoulder. Rosaleen turned to the man as suddenly there was a triphammer pounding somewhere inside her.

"Is this a gentlemen's club?" she questioned.

"Club? No, this is Mr. Shields's residence," the butler frowned.

"Then I've made some mistake. I'm looking for another Mr. Brewster," Rosaleen said, taking a step backward, a sudden feeling of panic engulfing her.

"Mr. Niles Brewster?" the butler asked, and Rosaleen stood as if carved out of wood. "That's Mr. Shields's nephew," he continued.

The room was ice, a terrible coldness cutting into her, as if all the blood had been drawn from her in one instant. She felt dizzy. "No," she heard herself gasp out. "There's some mistake. There must be a mistake."

The butler was frowning at her now. "I beg your pardon, miss?" he ventured. Rosaleen drew a deep breath, shot a glance at the man, then swept the other end of the foyer with her eyes. Three doors led to a semicircle of rooms that opened off the spacious foyer. One was closed.

"Mr. Brewster ... *your* Mr. Brewster, is he in there?" Rosaleen asked.

"Yes, he's at a meeting," the butler said.

"Then he's not my Niles Brewster," Rosaleen heard herself say, and wondered why desperation filled her voice. "No, I'll show you," she said, starting for the closed door, knowing it was not the butler she was showing.

"You can't go in there, miss," she heard the man shout. He tried to reach for her, but she twisted away, ran, flew across the foyer, and heard small gasped sounds coming from her lips. She seized the doorknob, twisted, yanked the door open. A large conference room with a round, polished table greeted her. Two men she didn't know turned to stare at her. The third man was Frank Shields and then her eyes swept to the fourth man, hung on him as something sharp and tearing stabbed into the pit of her stomach.

"No. Oh, no," she heard herself gasp as Niles started to get to his feet, his face flooded with astonishment. She felt her lips form his name but no sound came from them. It had been no mistake, no mistake at all. Niles, her Niles, was standing before her. Niles, her Niles, Frank Shields's nephew. The world was spinning again and she heard him call her name, *Rosaleen,* but it sounded as if it came from another world. She needed no words. They were all there in the misted violet of her eyes. As she heard him call out again, she spun on her heel, raced from the doorway, almost bowling over the butler who had come up behind her. She heard the murmur of voices rise in the background, Frank Shields's hard consonants, other muffled sounds, but she had reached the front door of the house, raced through the entrance and into the bright sunlight outside. A large park loomed up across the street and she ran into it, almost a victim of a passing carriage as she darted into a leaf-laden path. But she saw no green softness, no bushes and beckoning arbors. She was racing through a strange place made of shattered glass, and she felt as if she were a shard of cracked crystal full of edges and raw places.

As she gulped in great draughts of air, she heard footsteps chasing after her, Niles's voice calling to her. She darted down a side pathway, a tiny trail, but the footsteps stayed back of her and then, in a little clearing with a flat rock at one end, she tried to swerve down another path but he was there, his hand reaching out, catching her by the wrist, pulling her back. "Rosaleen, stop. Please, listen to me," he said.

Her eyes were shooting violet flame and she tore her wrist from his grasp, half-fell back against the flat rock, straightened. "Bastard!" she spat out. "Get away from me."

"Please, you don't understand," Niles tried, and Rosaleen heard only weakness in his voice and the searing pain inside her became wreathed in burning fury.

"Oh, I understand all right. I didn't, but I do now." He reached out to touch her but she shrank away. "Don't come near me," she hissed. His hand fell to his side. "I was going to tell you," he said. "At the right time."

The puny offering shriveled in the flame of her fury. "Yes, the right time, after we were married and as my husband you'd own the Powell Line. Frank Shields plays every card in the deck, doesn't he? Nothing is too low for him ... and for his nephew," Rosaleen flung at Niles.

"Please hear me out, Rosaleen. I know how it looks, but you're wrong. Just listen to me," Niles asked.

"So you can tell me more lies?" Rosaleen screamed back. "No, thank you. I believed you once, with all my heart. I loved you and you were lying to me all along. I gave you my heart and it was all part of a scheme to you." Rosaleen heard the sob break into her words, fought it away. "Oh, you played your role well, Niles, so wonderfully well. It would have worked, too. It's just fate that it didn't, or luck, or whatever."

"Rosaleen, listen to me. I'll admit it started out that way. I am Frank Shields's nephew and he paid me to keep an eye on your father's activities in Cornwall. For my part, it was payment on a debt. But when you came along, all that changed."

"Indeed it did. Your vicious, rotten uncle saw a better way to insure his acquiring the Powell Line. Romance her, he instructed you. Marry her if you have to. It'll be well worth your while," Rosaleen shouted. "You wanted me just for myself," she mimicked. "Oh, God, how I believed you. What a stupid, lovesick little fool I was."

Niles shook his head and Rosaleen, staring into the deep eyes she'd thought held only love for her, felt the searing pain of betrayal sweep over her. "Get away from me. I hate you, do you hear me? I hate you!" she screamed. "Go back and finish reporting to your master. That's why you hurried back here, to report and make final plans."

She saw Niles's eyes turn dark, anger suddenly shining in them. "Yes, dammit, I was at a meeting, but not for that," he shouted back. "I can explain if you'll just let me."

Rosaleen felt a sudden stab of pain in the pit of her stomach. Her reason for coming to Boston flashed through her and the fury exploded beyond all bounds. "No, no more explanations from you, no more nice soothing words all rehearsed or new ones invented on the spot. Just get away from me. I don't want to see you, look at you, hear your name," she screamed.

He moved quickly, his hands lashing out to seize her by the shoulders. "You're going to listen to me," he insisted, and she shook her head furiously, her long, raven locks lashing across her face.

"No. No more lies, no more," she sobbed, and tried to twist away from him. But his grip was tight, his hands digging into her shoulders. She reached back, one hand against the flat rock. Her fingers touched something, a length of broken branch. She closed her hand around it, brought it up in a short arc as he was shouting denials at her. She felt the wood smash against his temple, the blow delivered with all the pain and rage of her betrayal in it, cutting off his angry denials. Niles staggered back, clapping one hand to his head. Rosaleen saw the trickle of red as she whirled, ran, turned down little pathways, racing along each until she saw the edge of the park. As she rushed out into the street, she hailed a hansom cab, shouted the address of the wharf where the *Pegasus* lay berthed, and sat back. Deep, racking sobs came in her as the cab rolled through the streets of Boston, this city she had liked so quickly. But then she had liked Niles immediately, too, she remembered bitterly. Inside, she was a churning, seething maelstrom, but she knew, the real pain would come later, when she was alone. The hansom reached the pier and she made herself stop sobbing, dried her face, and boarded the ship. Captain Axelrod was a gentleman, and he masked his surprise at her quick return and at her questions.

"We sail Thursday, with the midnight tide," he told her in response to one. Rosaleen's eyes narrowed in thought. Two days, not much time, but it would have to be enough, she told herself. There would be one positive thing out of this trip, she vowed with grim anger.

"A decent lodging place for a woman, not far from here, Captain," she inquired.

"The Hampton House," the ship's master said quickly. "On Salem Street."

"Thank you," Rosaleen said brusquely. "I shall be sailing back to England with you Thursday night. Meanwhile, if anyone comes searching for me, you are to tell them nothing. I should like you to contact me at the Hampton House early Thursday evening. Can you arrange to do that?"

"It's done, Miss Powell," the captain said, only the faintest touch of curiosity edging his even stare. Rosaleen nodded her appreciation and left the ship, walking along the cobbled stones of the waterfront until her eye was caught by a sign jutting from a whitewashed inn: along a winding, narrow street: THE WHALER'S WHARF. She made a note of the location and went on. The Hampton House turned out to be a neat and very modest but clean little hostelry run by two sisters who looked alike and had very different voices, one reedy, the other soft. Rosaleen took a small single room with a bath and a lone window that looked down onto the waterfront. She paid for two days' lodging, closed the door, and sank down onto the bed. She loosened her clothes, took off her dress and chemise, and lay almost naked and very, very still. She lay unmoving as night came to plunge the room into darkness, her own private shroud, for, in a very real way, she was dead. All that was precious to her had been killed...*murdered.* She repeated the word to herself. It was not too harsh a word at all, she decided. He who kills love is certainly a murderer, for he kills a living, breathing thing, as real as the body that encloses it.

The pain came with the solitary darkness, as she knew it would, a searing, shriveling force, as total as it had been when she'd lost Colin. But there was a difference. This time, a terrible, consuming anger was part of it. Once again she had loved with every fiber of her body and soul and, once again, love and happiness had been torn away from her. But this time there was the corrosive acid of betrayal to give pain and heartbreak an added edge. She felt the sob begin deep inside her, then the tears burst from her as the reason for her coming to Boston rose up to tear and slash at her.

"Oh, God, Oh, God, God," Rosaleen gasped out to the inky darkness of the little room. She had come bearing a gift, the greatest gift any woman could give, but she'd not share it with deceit. The child she carried had been conceived out of her love, her pure, honest love, neither sullied nor shadowed. She would keep her secret just that, her very own secret. He who had betrayed love did not deserve its rewards.

"Niles, oh, Niles, Niles, why did you?" she heard herself gasp in anguish, and her knees drew up in pain both physical and emotional. She turned on her side, let the pillow muffle the sobs that wracked her body. Finally, in the deep of the night, she slept.

It was almost dawn when she woke, startled, aware of being in a strange place. She sat up, then fell back down again as all that had happened flooded back over her. She felt like a discarded rag, the pain a dull ache now, a burden of the soul that would be hers forever. It was all too new, too open a wound to permit plans. But one certainty was hers with bitter clarity. She'd never let herself be hurt again. Love was a cruel joke, a glimpse into paradise torn away as soon as the heart relaxed. It offered happiness and delivered only anguish. She'd have no more of it, Rosaleen told herself. Twice she had felt its cruelty and twice was more than enough. Never again would she let herself be used, deceived, played for a fool. At once, Niles appeared before her and the anger spiraled up instantly. She was grateful for the rage inside her. It helped make her pain bearable, allowing her to strike out instead of simply shriveling up. Slowly, she let her eyes close and slept again, small, silent tremors vibrating through her while she rested, the body echoing the torment of the soul.

It was past noon when she woke next, pulled her drained form to the washbasin, and went through her ablutions as if she were a mechanical doll. Neither rest nor the new day brought any lessening of the hurt inside her, but a kind of crystallization had taken place within the cocoon of sleep. Decisions had formed themselves, become bitter flowers of pain. The seed that was inside her would stay hers alone. Of course, in time, she'd have to meet the world with her secret, but she'd not think about that now. Only that whatever she did then would be a choice made with cold determination. The heart would be tethered from this day forward. There'd not be another Niles, and at the silent mention of his name she felt the terrible pain in the pit of her stomach, as if a serrated knifeblade had been twisted inside her. Drawing a deep breath, she forced herself to open the one suitcase she'd taken with her, brought out a dark-blue street dress and slipped into it. The neckline was too low, the proud rise of her breasts pushing up from it. It would have to do, she murmured to herself. She closed the suitcase, took a small purse, and went downstairs.

The sister with the reedy voice had the teakettle on, and Rosaleen agreed to a cup. The hot brew helped her quivering stomach and she looked away as she caught the woman peering at the dark circles under her eyes. Rosaleen began to open her purse to pay for the tea. "No, no, my dear. It's part of our services," the woman said. "Is there anything else I can do for you?"

Rosaleen managed a smile as she thanked the woman for the offer and hurried outside. No, there's nothing anyone can do for me, Rosaleen murmured silently. It's all been done. She felt the rush of tears to her eyes, shook them away in anger. No tears, she ordered sternly, not now, not anymore ever. Except, perhaps, in the loneliness of her room at some distant time when the hurting would be but a dull ache. She walked briskly, hurrying her steps until she stood beneath the sign over the door of the inn. She stepped aside as two sailors emerged, holding each other upright, and peered through the dingy little window beside the door. She saw a flash of red, then a swirl of blue. There were girls inside, she saw with relief. She'd not be the only woman in the place, though hardly like the others there. Rosaleen threw back her shoulders, pushed the door in, and entered the Whaler's Wharf.

The interior was larger than she expected, tables dotting the room, a battered piano against one wall. She felt eyes turn to her, caught the quick glance of two girls, one in black-stockinged legs and a short, tight skit, the other in a dress that had almost no bodice. A man in a soiled apron shuffled toward her. Most of the tables were crowded and the inn was half-obscured by a haze of smoke. "Looking for someone, ma'am?" the man asked.

"Yes," Rosaleen said. "A Mr. Holderman."

"Alec Holderman?" the man asked.

Rosaleen hesitated a moment, nodded. "Yes, that's the gentleman," she said. The waiter made a snorting sound.

"Maybe it's him but he's no gentleman," he said. "He doesn't come in till after three o'clock." He glanced at a gray-faced clock in the one corner. "It's going on four. He'll be here soon."

"I'll wait," Rosaleen said, and followed the man to a small wooden table against the wall, still conscious of eyes turning to follow her. "Do you have any sherry?" she ventured.

"No. Brandy?" he said gruffly, and Rosaleen nodded. He returned in moments and she sipped the shot glass of brandy which turned out to be unexpectedly smooth. She let her eyes rove across the room in quick glances, avoiding eye contact with any of the others, and the half-hush that had fallen at her entrance was soon swallowed up by the usual hum of sound. The Whaler's Wharf was not a place to be upset by anything or anyone, Rosaleen decided. She had finished the brandy when she saw the waiter approaching in his shuffle, a thick-set man in a seaman's jacket behind him.

"This is the lady," the waiter said, gesturing to her as if she'd been washed ashore. The heavy man surveyed her with small, dark eyes set in a flat face made flatter by a nose that had been broken innumerable times. He eased into the chair across from her.

"What would you be wanting with Alec Holderman, a fine lady like you," he asked with a quiet sneer.

"I was told you can tell me something I very much want to know," Rosaleen said carefully as Holderman's small eyes continued boring into her. "I'm interested in the story of a man who never left Bangkok," she said.

"Holderman's eyes didn't change expression. "There's many a man that never left Bangkok," he said.

"No doubt," Rosaleen said evenly. "But I am interested in the story of one special man. I will pay a considerable amount of money to hear the truth of it."

The seaman's eyes grew smaller. "I just carry messages. But if you're really serious, it'll cost plenty, I can tell you," he said.

"I'm prepared to pay well for the right information," Rosaleen assured him.

"They won't talk to just anybody," Holderman said. "I've got to give them names."

"Rosaleen Powell," she said, and saw the man peer at her slowly, his lips parting in astonishment.

"The Powell Line?" he said.

"That's right," Rosaleen told him, then watched him lean back in his chair, study her, and close his lips.

"Meet me here tomorrow, six o'clock," he said. "I'll tell you what to do next."

Rosaleen stood up, looked down at the man's flat face. "Six o'clock," she said. "If this is a fake scheme of some kind you'll never sail on a Powell Line ship or any other," she said, putting more into the threat than she could deliver. But the glint of new respect in the man's small eyes made it clear he did not doubt her.

"There's no cock-and-bull story here," he said. "They have the goods but they want to sell to the highest bidder."

"Six o'clock," Rosaleen echoed, turned, and hurried from the tavern, making her way around small knots of sailors as the room grew more crowded. Outside, she drew in a deep breath of fresh air, walked back to the Hampton House, and arrived in time for the dinner hour. There were half-a-dozen elderly men and three ladies of determined gentility. Rosaleen nibbled at a slice of roast beef, then excused herself. She still had no stomach for food and she took a pot of tea to sip in her room as she watched the night lower over the Boston waterfront. Niles was out there someplace, seeking her. He had gone to the ship by now, of course. Perhaps he had others out combing the streets for her. She felt a smug satisfaction in knowing he'd not find her. His words returned to dance inside her. He'd been full of explanations, entreaties for her to listen to him as he tried to explain away what was beyond explaining or excusing. She hadn't dared to listen. The loving and wanting were still too much a part of her. They would have silently urged her to believe because she wanted to believe despite what her eyes had shown her. Loving was a kind of weakness, she decided. It made you vulnerable, soft, a willing victim. Betrayal and pain, they were strength, allies, they gave support. She would hold them close. She uttered a wry sound. As if she had any choice in the matter, she sniffed. They were part of her now, indelibly etched in her. She undressed slowly, and lay on the bed as she would have lain in wait for Niles, feeling the soft-hard sweetness of his touch as if he were there caressing her. Before she slept, the room was filled with her bitter sobs.

Morning came and she lay in bed till the noon hour passed. The little rented room was her refuge, her own hiding place, she reflected, and thought at once of the little coteen where she and Niles hid from the world. She swung from the bed, furious at herself. She would cease letting every little thing remind her of Niles and her time of betrayal. Dammit, she'd steel herself against the insidiousness of feeling, caring, remembering. She took her time bathing, packed the lone suitcase, and at six o'clock she was at the Whaler's Wharf again, peering through the haze of smoke. She spied the thick-set figure at the table where she'd sat yesterday. He didn't rise as she came over.

"They'll go along with you," he said, hardly glancing up.

"What does that mean?" Rosaleen asked tartly.

"It means they know who you are. It means they feel you're serious and able to pay. They won't talk to most who ask," the sailor growled back.

"Which means that they are talking to some others," Rosaleen said quickly, and saw the man's eyes flash for an instant.

"Maybe," he admitted. Rosaleen didn't pursue the matter further. There was no need. She knew there were others and from their tactics, only one man was back of them.

"What happens now?" Rosaleen asked, impatient with all the secrecy.

"Go back to England. You'll be contacted, at your offices in London. Someone will get to you there," the man said.

"No, not London. There are too many loose tongues and sharp ears in London, too many places for someone to follow and watch," Rosaleen said. "Tell them they are to come to me in Cornwall, at Raven's Wing."

The seaman nodded, half-shrugged. "All right, whatever you wish," he answered. "The man who comes to you will bring definite information and he'll tell you the price. It'll be fat, I was told to tell you."

"Tell them to make sure he has something worth saying for it," Rosaleen returned. "I'm going back to England tonight. When will I be contacted at Raven's Wing?"

"I wouldn't know that," the man said. "When they're ready and not before."

Rosaleen turned on her heel and strode from the smoky inn, omitting amenities never extended her. Outside, she hurried back to the lodging house as darkness began to sift down over the city. She'd been in her room only a few minutes when there was a knock at the door and she opened to see Captain Axelrod.

"As you ordered, Miss Powell," he said.

"Thank you, Captain. Has anyone come asking for me at the ship?" she questioned, certain of the answer.

"Indeed, a tall man, good-looking fellow. He's come every few hours and now my first mate tells me he's taken up a spot on the wharf where he's waiting and watching," the captain said.

Rosaleen felt her lips tighten. "He'll try to stop me from going aboard," Rosaleen said. "He'll want to talk to me and I don't want that."

"I can have some of my fo'c'sle boys take care of him," the captain said, and Rosaleen felt her eyes grow wide in alarm at once.

"No, please. I don't want that," she said.

"Then we'll do it another way. Be ready at ten-thirty. Two of my sailors will come for you then," the captain said. "We'll get you aboard without fuss."

"All right. Thank you very much, Captain," Rosaleen said. "Especially for not asking anything more."

The ship's master shrugged. "I was young once," he commented, and closed the door behind him. Rosaleen stared at it. I, too. I was young once, too, she murmured silently. Only the young trust.

She lay down across the bed and refused to give way to the tears that tried to erupt. Ten-thirty came quickly enough and she was waiting downstairs when the two sailors appeared to lead her to a dock some six streets north where a rowboat waited. Silently, they rowed out beyond the line of wharves, turned, and crept past the big, black shapes of the great vessels tied at dock. It smelled of oil and creosote and wet hemp and it was a smell she liked for all its acridness. The rowboat nosed gently in along the other side of the *Pegasus* and she was helped up a ship's ladder hanging down from the hull. The captain greeted her on deck as she swung over the rail.

"He's pacing back and forth along the wharf. He's seen the men making ready to sail," the captain said.

"Thank you. I'll go to my cabin now," Rosaleen said. She disappeared into the stern of the vessel, into the same cabin she'd occupied on the way over, so filled with happiness and eager hope then. The cabin would fill with cold determination, the harshness of a bitter heart on the trip back. She unpacked, had finished when she felt the ship lurch, the bowlines being cast off. She whirled, ran onto the deck and to the rail. Niles was there, on the cobbled stones of the wharf, his long, handsome face wreathed in consternation until he glanced up, saw her as the stern of the ship swung from the dock. Anguish swept over his features.

"No! Oh, no! Rosaleen, don't. Please, listen to me. Come back," he cried out. Rosaleen reached into the pocket of her skirt, closed her fingers around the change there, pulled it out and flung it over the side. The coins struck the lone figure on the wharf, bounced to land on the stones with a harsh, metallic sound.

"Your thirty pieces of silver," she cried out. "Count them."

She felt the sob tear from her throat, spun away from the rail, and raced down to the cabin, flinging herself onto the narrow bunk, unmindful of the sharp crack of her elbow against the wall. The ship gathered speed, moved out into Boston Harbor. Rosaleen stayed unmoving on the bunk until total fatigue overwhelmed her. She hardly left the cabin during the entire voyage. It took four days for her to stop hearing Niles's anguished cry, but in time she forced it from her mind. She turned to other things which now came back to her, questions that cried for answers, and she made plans for the things she'd do and request and demand when she returned. When the vessel nosed into London harbor eight days later, Rosaleen was at the rail, dry-eyed, her lovely face a magnificent carving of ice.

CHAPTER SEVEN

The report Coops had ready for her when she arrived at the office showed the same pattern, troubles for the Powell Line ships, some transparently the work of Shields's people, others somewhat more difficult to pinpoint. Delays, losses, the Powell Line ships fighting a rearguard action, always on the defensive. "This is going to change," she told Coops, and saw his eyes watching her intently. "What is it?" she half smiled.

He shook his head. "I don't know. Something about you isn't the same," the captain answered.

"A sea voyage is always a good rest," Rosaleen snapped. "It clears the mind, makes for a new person."

"I guess so. No offense meant, Miss Powell," the man offered, and Rosaleen relaxed for a moment, put her hand out to him.

"I'm sorry. I didn't mean to snap so. You're my anchor, Coops, more than ever," she said. "But I did come back with definite ideas and I'm going to implement them." She reached into her bag, took out a two-page list of questions, and handed them to the man. "I'm going to Raven's Wing for a few days. When I return I'd like all or most of these answered," Rosaleen said.

Coops ran his eyes down the paper. "I'll try. Carlson can answer the ones about the various offices and personnel. I'll do my best with the financial breakdown on running each vessel." He looked up from the paper. "What about the Boston contact on the bullion?" he asked.

"I made it. I'm supposed to be contacted by someone else here in England, one of the principals. I presume," Rosaleen said. "You can be sure that Shields is one of the others after it."

Coops nodded. "Be careful. You know the man. He stops at nothing."

Rosaleen felt the sharpness at once, invisible arrows that struck deep.

"Yes, I know," she said quietly, bitterly, and turned away as Coops left the office. She spent the rest of the day going over correspondence that needed her attention and took the late-afternoon coach to Cornwall. She sat huddled in a corner, clutching bitterness to herself. It hurt, not to be hurrying back to Cornwall to fall into Niles's embrace. She admitted that much to herself. It hurt too much to delude herself, to look the other way, but she let anger come to her aid once again. Cornwall was still a refuge for her, a place to flee from the pressures of London. It would continue to be that, but without Niles. She'd fill every weekend so there'd be not a moment for tears to fall, for memory to slip its way in. There'd be only exhaustion and falling into bed to sleep. While inside her a secret would grow, be hers alone. In time, in time, he'd hear of the child, perhaps feel certain it was his, Rosaleen realized. And perhaps one day, when it was too late for him to do anything about it, she'd tell him the truth. Maybe. She'd have to see about that, to decide at the time which would be the greater punishment for him, to know or not to know. Meanwhile, she'd force herself to wipe him from her mind. Rosaleen closed her eyes, slept fitfully until the coach reached Bodwin, and then had Sam Tylor drive her to Raven's Wing.

Margaret was still up and she saw the surprise on the older woman's face. "Back so soon?" Margaret said as Rosaleen hugged her, too tightly, for Margaret pulled back, searched her face. "It didn't go well, did it?" Margaret said, and Rosaleen knew she had no need to answer in words. "Something with Niles, wasn't it?" Margaret prodded.

"I don't want to hear his name spoken," Rosaleen said, stepping back. "Not ever." She saw Margaret waiting and the urge to pour out everything surged up inside her, but she held back. She'd vowed to take no one completely into her confidence, not now, not even Margaret.

"Sure you don't want to tell me about it?" Margaret said, and Rosaleen shook her head, fought back tears.

"Not now. Maybe in time, but not now," she said, lifting her head. "Where are Tony and Olivia?" she asked.

"Visiting in Tavistock. They ought to be getting back soon," Margaret answered.

"I'll go upstairs meanwhile," Rosaleen said, and disappeared into her room where she unpacked her lone traveling bag. She eventually heard the sound of Tony's voice and she hurried downstairs at once, her lips a thin line. Olivia was beside him, wearing a pink and light blue organdy gown which gave her face a little-girl delicacy.

"Rosaleen, you're back. That was a fast trip," Olivia remarked. Rosaleen almost ignored her sister, her eyes boring into Tony Darby. He met her stare with a forced blandness and tried to look away, but Rosaleen's stare speared into him.

"You knew all along, didn't you?" she accused. He lifted his eyebrows in a parody of surprise.

"Knew what?" he questioned.

"You know what," Rosaleen bit out, her eyes violet quartz. "Niles Brewster isn't all you think he is," she quoted. "That's what you said as I left. You knew all along." She saw a hint of smug satisfaction come into Tony Darby's face and felt her temper near the exploding point. She turned a hard glance at Olivia. "Did you know, too? Had he told you?" she demanded.

"Know what?" Olivia frowned.

"That Niles was Frank Shields's nephew," Rosaleen flung out, and saw Olivia frown uneasily.

"No, not in so many words, though Tony did let on he knew a thing or two about Niles Brewster," Olivia shuffled.

Rosaleen returned her gaze to Tony. "Why didn't you tell me?" she demanded.

"Didn't see any reason to," Tony said, hedging words.

"That's a lie," Rosaleen threw back.

He shrugged. "I figured you'd find out for yourself in time. I was right, it seems," he said. Rosaleen's fury congealed. His answers were cynical barbs and smug turn-asides.

"It was your place to tell me," she snapped out at him. He shrugged again. "As Olivia's husband, it was your position to tell me," Rosaleen continued.

"I didn't want to ruin your affair. You were having such a jolly time of it," Tony Darby returned, and the ice inside her shattered into shards of rage.

"Damn you, that's one more lie. I wouldn't agree to your demands or fall for your charms, so you wanted to get back at me," Rosaleen screamed back. "Well, now you can get out—lock, stock, and barrel. Get out of Raven's Wing, both of you."

Tony Darby's casual smugness slid away from his face. "Now, just a minute," he began, but she cut him off.

"No, I'll not wait a minute, not even a second. You've no loyalty, no sense of family, and you've forfeited any right to be here. Get out. I don't want you here."

Tony's face held something new: alarm. "Now, look here, you know we've practically no funds and nowhere to go," he protested.

"You'll find someplace. Just get out of Raven's Wing and out of my sight," Rosaleen insisted.

"Rosaleen, you can't," she heard Olivia say.

"I can and I am," Rosaleen said, ice wrapped around each word. "I'm leaving for London in the morning. I'll be back in three days and I want you gone from here by then." She turned, strode off upstairs, and slammed her bedroom door shut, refusing to wonder why righteousness didn't satisfy her.

In the morning, Margaret had eggs and rashers waiting and her face set in a noncommittal mask which, by its very carefulness, was a statement of its own. "You think I was too harsh, don't you?" Rosaleen asked.

Margaret took a moment to answer. "Maybe. I don't know. I wish I did," Margaret answered finally.

"I know," Rosaleen said. "I'll expect you to see that they're out and gone before I return." Suddenly aware of how coldly abrupt she sounded, Rosaleen put her arms around the older woman. "Bear with me, Margaret. I'll tell you all of it one day soon enough. Meanwhile, I'm going to save the Powell Line. I can't think about other people's feelings anymore. I've got to show Frank Shields that he can't get the better of me."

"Frank Shields or Niles?" Margaret remarked, and Rosaleen felt her face grow taut.

"Both, perhaps," she half-shrugged.

Margaret hugged her gently. "I'll be here for whatever you need whenever you need it, my dear," the older woman said. "Just remember, winning is no good when you've lost too much of yourself doing it. Sometimes, you can pay too big a price to win."

Rosaleen started to snap out an answer, held her tongue, and uttered a silent, wry sound. She'd paid the price already, she reflected. It was time for others to pay. She heard the sound of Sam Tylor's buggy drawing up outside, gulped down the last of the rashers, kissed Margaret on the cheek.

"Be back for the weekend as usual," she said, hurried from the kitchen. She was almost at the front door when Tony materialized from one of the side alcoves. The irritating snideness was gone from his face, she saw. He looked almost chastened, she thought in satisfaction.

"Look, we ought to talk more about all this," he began, but she cut him off.

"There's nothing more to talk about."

"I'm thinking about Livvie," he said.

"You should have thought about *Livvie* earlier. Were you thinking about Olivia when you were telling me how many of my needs you could satisfy?" Rosaleen threw at him, and saw his jaw muscles twitch.

"You might be surprised about that. Some of us have our own ways of protecting what we care about," he said.

"How touching. Doing the right thing in the wrong way, was it?" Rosaleen scoffed.

"Look, I don't expect you to believe me, but think about Livvie. Hell, I can always make do, but she's used to the best of things and in my own way I've tried to see she gets them. She's not the kind that can adjust," he said.

Rosaleen refused to hear the edge of truth in his words. "That's your problem," she snapped, then brushed past him and climbed into the waiting buggy. She looked back as the carriage rolled away, saw Tony Darby standing in the doorway. She'd expected to see anger in his eyes, but there was only sadness as he looked very small and unsure of himself. She turned away. She'd have preferred anger, damn him, she muttered inwardly, then closed off her thoughts and watched the sea birds swoop up from the edge of the cliffs. Their wild and lonely cries seemed to beckon to her as they never had before. She sat back, listened to them until the carriage rolled beyond earshot.

Coops had most of the questions she'd left with him answered when she arrived at the office. She closeted herself with the voluminous data and by the next day had made decisions. She called Carlson and Coops into the office, addressing Carlson first.

"Every office we have is to be reduced by at least one employee, the Calcutta and Sydney offices by two," she ordered. "In this office, Harriet Woodbridge will have to go." She expected the shock that pulled at Carlson's face.

"*Harriet!* Why, Harriet has served your father her entire life," Carlson said.

"I'm aware of that, but unfortunately these are extreme times that need extreme measures. She is the least important to the office now. She'll have her pension, of course," Rosaleen said.

"It's not much in these times," Carlson countered.

"I'm sorry, but my decision is final. Notify the other offices of what steps they have to take," Rosaleen said, and watched Carlson move off as if in a daze. She turned to Coops. He held his face expressionless.

"Sell all the vessels I've marked with an X," she said, handing him the list. "Take those I've checked and berth them in London and Plymouth and Yarmouth. We're going to concentrate everything on the Atlantic run."

The captain let his lips purse, voiced his musings slowly. "It'll be a gamble, a bold one. But perhaps it will pay off," he said, then walked from the office still turning thoughts in his mind. Rosaleen spent the rest of the day in her office. Outside the closed door, she knew there were tears, whispered exchanges. She wondered if Harriet Woodbridge would come in at the day's end, but only Carlson appeared with the severance voucher for her to sign.

"Harriet's left. She asked that we mail it to her," he said, disapproval on his face.

"I'm sorry she felt it was personal. It wasn't," Rosaleen said as she signed the voucher. He didn't comment, and Rosaleen stayed till everyone else had gone, unwilling to pass through a gauntlet of disapproving eyes. She'd have to develop a thicker skin, she told herself. The old Rosaleen was still clinging.

But the decisions taken required hard work to implement. Rosaleen plunged into keeping the promise to herself. London became a place of long days and exhausted nights. When she attended a ball, she stayed to the end, a new coquette, a flirt, her gowns more and more daring and her name more and more in the social columns. The weekends at Cornwall were no less enervating, spent mostly at Gwyneth where she sailed out each Saturday morning, and often Fridays, too, with Abraham Evans on his lugger. Weather made no difference, blazing heat, cold, hard rain, or a driving gale, she was there to sail out each morning. Two of Abraham's sons, Joshua and Elias, had been injured in the same accident and he welcomed her help as an experienced small-boat sailor. Sometimes, after they returned to harbor, she visited with her old friends among the gippers, staying to work alongside them until she was almost too exhausted to ride back to Raven's Wing. But the promise was kept, every moment of every hour of every week kept full. Almost. There were the warm nights, at the town house in London and at Raven's Wing, when she lay naked on the bed, both hands touching the swell of her belly which was growing with each passing week. It was still her secret, the wide gowns effectively covering any signs, but the seed was growing inside her. The nausea had long since stopped, but some mornings her breasts hurt her, one more sign of the miracle of growing things.

The first letter from Niles had come nine days after she'd returned to England. Margaret had watched her tear it up without so much as opening the envelope. The second one came but a few days later and others followed in a regular procession. Margaret gave them to her each week when she returned from London.

"Why don't you open one, at least," Margaret suggested as Rosaleen tossed the letters into the wastebasket. "He must care to keep writing so often," she went on.

"No." Rosaleen snapped the word out. "You needn't bother keeping them for me. Just throw them away as you get them."

Tony and Olivia had taken small living quarters in Alberta Rowan's house on the outskirts of Bodwin, Margaret told her one day, and Tony had made a half-dozen trips to London and Birmingham on business. Rosaleen knew Alberta Rowan's house, an old, crumbling structure. For years the woman had rented out space in it at reasonable rates. "Olivia stopped by in the carriage a few days ago," Margaret told her one Sunday. "She came to pick up the monthly trust check. She told me that Tony is genuinely sorry for not having said anything to you about Niles."

"You're too believing, Margaret. And too forgiving," Rosaleen laughed.

Margaret's eyes were unsmiling as she gazed at the younger woman. "One can become too unforgiving," she said quietly.

"Is that what I'm becoming?" Rosaleen smiled again.

"I don't know, but you've changed. You're pushing yourself too hard," Margaret said. "I've heard you are becoming known as the ruthless Rosaleen Powell."

"People always call names when they're toes are stepped on, Margaret," Rosaleen said. "I'm feeling fine and I'm going to win out in the end, you wait and see."

She left Margaret looking thoughtful and caught the London coach. The letters from Niles ceased during the next three weeks and Rosaleen grew furious with herself for even taking note of the fact. The decisions she'd taken regarding the Atlantic routes had been put into effect. New clipper ships were now available for the Powell Line runs to North and South America and once again, the financial world gave grudging admiration to her moves. But Frank Shields struck back in a matter of weeks. Coops brought her the letter from International Shippers, the largest single client of the Powell Line. She read it with anger rising up inside her, the key sentences blazing out at her:

The shipping rate offered by the Shields Lines is, as you can see, substantially lower than that we receive from your company. Therefore we feel we must take advantage of this considerable savings and cancellation of our agreements with you will be effective next month. Of course, if you are prepared to meet this rate we will naturally continue shipping our merchandise on Powell Line vessels.

Rosaleen flung the letter on the desk, glared up at Coops. "You didn't expect him not to strike back, did you?" the captain remarked.

"But no one can carry merchandise at the rate he's offering!" Rosaleen said. "He'll lose heavily on every shipment."

"That's right. But he's going to take the losses. He can afford to do so for a while, at least, long enough to drive us out of business and when he's done that, International Shippers and everyone else will see their rates go up twice what they are now."

"The rotten bastard," Rosaleen hissed. "It's one more of his stinking, unethical tactics. He doesn't know the meaning of fair competition. I think a complaint must be lodged with the Board of Trade."

"Their province is really the behavior of masters to their crews and shipping line standards for crews and passengers. Besides, they'll take far too long to hold hearings on this. It'll be a *fait accompli* by the time they get to it," Coops said.

Rosaleen stared into space, her mind seething with thoughts. "How many of our ships are making regular runs with international cargoes?" she questioned.

"Six," Coops answered.

She picked up the letter, handed it back to him. "Answer this. Tell them we'll match the Shields rate," she said. Coops stared at her, his eyebrows lowering.

"But that's impossible. We'd go bankrupt in no time," he protested.

"International Shippers cargoes will be carried on three instead of six ships," Rosaleen said. "Even with a crew bonus, the savings will let us meet the rate."

The protest in the captain's eyes took on an edge of horror. "That will mean dangerous overloading of the holds and heavy stacks of deck cargo from bow to stern," he said. "You can't do it, Miss Rosaleen. It's too dangerous."

"If cargoes are properly packed, it'll be perfectly all right. The running times may be a few days longer but we'll meet the rate and even make a profit out of it. We'll be saving the cost of three clippers and they'll be available for other work."

"The vessels will be unmaneuverable in any kind of weather. If they hit a real storm it could be disaster," Coops said.

"The captains will have to keep a sharp weather eye out and change course if they see storm signs," Rosaleen said, and saw Coops shake his head.

"A good northeaster will be on them before they can steer around it with overloaded vessels," he said.

"It will work," Rosaleen snapped. "We only have to do it for a little while, until Shields realizes this attempt has failed. He'll withdraw his rate offer and things can go back to normal. Three ships instead of six, Coops. I won't be beaten by Frank Shields and his underhanded tactics. Pay a crew bonus and there won't be any grumbling from the men. It will work out just fine."

"Your gambling with the lives of men and ships," Coops said.

"I'm keeping ourselves in business. I'm fighting to stay alive and I'm going to win," Rosaleen flared. "I've no time for timidity."

She saw Coops press his lips together, half bow to her. "I've said my piece. I'll carry out your orders," he told her, and retired from the office. She had expected no less. He was a career seafaring man. He knew there could be but one captain on a ship.

The invitation for the Queen's birthday ball came at the end of the week. Though the affair was almost two months away, invitations were sent out early to allow ample time for the custom gowns to be ordered, fitted, and made ready. It was the social event of the season and she realized that her invitation had come through Adelaide Winship. Adelaide was one of London's most indefatigable hostesses and a woman who'd come to regard the bold Rosaleen Powell as an asset to any party. Everyone of any status would be there, Rosaleen knew. Frank Shields would certainly be among the guests. Would Niles be with him, she wondered. She'd enjoy facing them both, still unconquered, still undaunted by all the crooked underhanded tactics. Her hand went to the small roundness of her body just below her waist-line, smoothed the dress down over it. Two months, she mused silently. It'd be nearing the danger point but she'd still be able to keep her secret hidden, she decided, especially in a full-skirted ball gown. She sent out the acceptance to the invitation before leaving the office for the weekend at Cornwall, dropping it in the post box with a small sniff of satisfaction.

Margaret was up when she reached Raven's Wing late that night and the older woman watched her rifle through the week's mail. "No more letters from Mr. Niles Brewster. He finally got the message," Rosaleen remarked airily.

"He was here during the week, wanting to see you," Margaret said, and Rosaleen felt herself grow pale and something approaching panic seized hold of her.

"What did you tell him?" she managed.

"That you were in London," Margaret answered. "He said he had to go to Birmingham but he left something for you." She took a letter from her apron pocket, handed it to Rosaleen. Rosaleen drew a deep breath. The panic had flown and she took the letter, hating her desire to open it, angrily tearing it in half instead and flinging it aside.

"I'm never to be in to him, Margaret. Never," she ordered, then hurried upstairs to her room, pulled off clothes, and lay across the bed. So he was back, Rosaleen murmured silently. Back to try again for his master? Or perhaps full of ordinary curiosity as to what had brought her to Boston on that terrible day that now seemed so long ago. The day blazed up in front of her again, the moment coming alive at once—Niles closeted with Frank Shields—his eyes as he saw her, full of astonishment and guilt. It was a moment when faith and happiness shattered into uncountable bits. He'd not have a second chance to hurt her, she vowed bitterly. Not ever, not here, not in London. Deceit, betrayal, they were one-time things. She pulled anger and bitterness around herself and plunged into the refuge of sleep.

In the morning, she was aboard Abraham's lugger. Within the hour, the air became hot as a furnace. A faint breeze came up when it was time for them to head in at the end of the day, carrying only a small catch. She felt ill, a headache pounding at her, and she returned to Raven's Wing and fell into bed to sleep until late the next day. She still felt heavy when she woke, though the headache was gone and Margaret drove her to Bodwin to catch the London coach.

"You look drawn. You ought to spend the next weekend just relaxing. You can't keep running forever," Margaret told her.

"I'm not running from anything," Rosaleen said, too defensively.

"Not even yourself?" Margaret asked softly, and Rosaleen snapped out a good-bye and climbed into the waiting coach, put her head back and dozed most of the trip. Her first act upon reaching the office the next morning was to issue strict orders that she was not in to a Mr. Niles Brewster if he should call.

The week began well. Merchants were taking advantage of the added Powell Line vessels on the South Atlantic run, and the reduced office expenses were reflected in the cash-flow picture. By midweek, a new customer had placed a sizable order for shipping hemp to Argentina. It was Friday and she was winding up things before leaving for Cornwall, when disaster struck. Coops appeared in the doorway, his face ashen, a cable message in his hand.

"The *Eastern Star* went down in an Atlantic gale," he said in a half-whisper. "A Brazilian merchantman picked up the only three survivors."

Rosaleen felt her hands grasp the underside of the desk. His unvoiced accusation struck at her as if it were a harpoon. The

Eastern Star was one of the ships double-loaded with a Shippers International cargo. "They said that the sea just swept over her and took her right down. With her being overloaded, she didn't have a chance to ride it out," Coops told her.

Rosaleen met his accusing eyes. "Other ships have gone down in storms, empty ones. You've no right to make that assumption," she said.

"And you've no right to refuse to see," he returned, his usually sharp eyes dulled with pain. She said nothing as he walked from the office, his words still sticking into her. Unfair, she told herself. She rejected his assumptions. Ships foundered in storms for lots of reasons. The sea did many unexpected things. She'd accept no blame and make no changes. The other ships would continue to sail with the Shippers International cargoes double-loaded. The crews were being paid extra. The world was a place of risks and pain. The matter was closed. Rosaleen turned her mind from it, a little surprised that she could do so as easily as she did. She left London within the hour and reached Cornwall feeling very tired, hurrying right to bed.

In the early dawn, the house silent and Margaret still asleep, she rose and rode to Gwyneth. It was a gray, windy dawn and she was soon aboard the lugger, standing beside Abraham Evans as he watched the wind whip along the top of the waters beyond the breakwater. "I guess I forgot to whistle last night," Abraham said. A crewman brought them mugs of hot tea with milk and honey and she sipped hers as the others began to undo the mooring lines, go below, and get into oilskins. She returned to the deck as the lugger cast off, moved out at once as the wind caught at her. By the time they cleared the breakwater, the sea was made of whitecaps and she took the tiller as Abraham went forward to help with the nets. She felt uncomfortably warm in the oilskins though the wind was chill.

The seas were building up quickly and holding onto the tiller meant hard work.

"Weight the nets," she heard Abraham order. "They'll not be near the surface with this wind blowing." Rosaleen used both hands on the tiller and felt it try to pull away from her as the sea tore at it. She felt tired, heavy, as if she'd eaten a big meal when in fact she'd had only the mug of tea and milk. She watched the men line up to shoot the nets over the side, one man fastening the lanyards to the foot line, two tossing the net over the side, while a fourth hand held the back rope, a fifth man passed the lanyards on, and a sixth watched the foot line as it went overboard to see that it didn't foul. The ship's "boy" was moving back and forth, at the ready should anyone need an extra hand.

"They're out," she heard Abraham shout back at her. "Lower the foremast. Drive with the wind, Rosaleen." She shifted the tiller, felt the lugger heel over as the wind came up behind it, plow forward like a horse given the whip. Abraham hurried back to her as he saw her having difficulty keeping the tiller pushed forward, knelt down beside her, and put a hand on the wood besides hers.

"The sea is getting bad," Rosaleen said. "I can feel the pull of it growing."

"We'll try this one run and head back," Abraham said, and the wind whipped his words away. The sea smashed over the side rail with increasing force, salt coating Rosaleen's face as she eyed the mounting green wall of water astern, swooping in to lift the little ship into the air and then down into the trough. She found herself thinking of what would happen to them if they were unable to ride the crest of the waves, and silently cursed the thoughts, pushed them aside. The wind rose with unexpected force and the skies had turned dark. The lugger shuddered with each wave that pounded into her sides, then heeled over and slowly righted herself again. The ship was sturdy enough, Rosaleen knew. She'd not come apart at the seams, but a following sea was building up that could simply wash over them and send the vessel nosing down to the bottom. She saw Abraham eying the weather, her thoughts echoed in the worry lines of his brow.

"Hold her steady," he said to Rosaleen. "I'll help pull the nets in." He went off, sliding and slipping on the angled deck. "Haul in. *Now*, dammit, haul in before we're pulled over," he shouted to the others. Rosaleen saw the men respond with anxious haste, everyone bending low against the rail, pulling at the net lines. She had to brace both feet against the lumber irons to keep hold of the tiller with both hands. The nets came in, a small catch inside them but better than nothing. It seemed to take an eternity to haul them in against the pull of wind and wave but the last of them finally rolled onto the deck. She swung the tiller around to head back to harbor. Land was out of sight now in the dark gray clouds and a hard rain had begun to fall, slanting almost sideways in the wind. Abraham was coming back toward her when the wave hit, three quarters off the aft beam. Rosaleen felt the tiller tear away from her hands and then she was hurtling across the deck. She managed to bring her arms up as she slammed into the foot of the mast. The pain in her side was sharp but she'd felt as bad before. It was the tearing pain in her lower abdomen that caused her to roll over and scream on the deck. She drew her knees up but the pain continued, a terrible drawing, pulling pain. She felt hands lifting her, carrying her down below decks, saw Abraham Evans bending over her as she was set down on a hard wooden bunk.

"What is it, girl?" he asked as she pressed both hands to her stomach and whimpered. She shook her head, turning aside answers.

"Get me back," she said. "Hurry, oh God, hurry."

Abraham Evans was hardly a novice unused to maritime emergencies. He straightened, called to Malcolm, his first mate. "Put up the foresail and the jib," he called. Through dim eyes, she saw the other man's look of protest.

"In this gale?" she heard him question.

"Put them up. Get everybody on the sheets," Abraham ordered again. He pressed a hand to Rosaleen's shoulder. "We'll have you back in no time," he said, disappearing up the short companionway ladder.

Rosaleen reached under the oilskins and pressed her hands to her belly, trying to hold herself together as the drawing, pulling ache persisted, dull now, then rising in a sharp, stabbing pain, then growing dull again. Breathing was difficult and the sea pounded the lugger and the wood bunk shook. "No, please, no," Rosaleen heard herself whispering. "Oh, please, no." A sudden, tearing pain made her scream out and she arched her back, then fell against the bunk. She held onto the edge of the bunk with one hand as the ship rolled, and then righted itself and then lay still, her breathing shallow, harsh. She saw movement at the head of the cabin entrance, glimpsed Abraham taking a quick look at her, then disappearing. The pain grew worse, not so stabbing now but a steady, tearing pain. She tried to listen to the sounds of the wind and the sea, sought the small changes that would mean they had entered the harbor. It helped keep her mind from the pain and suddenly she felt the speed of the lugger fall away, the crash of the sea against the hull diminish. They had passed the breakwater and were sailing toward the quay when Rosaleen tried to rise, then screamed in anguish as it seemed a huge knife stuck into her lower abdomen. She fell back onto the bunk and her eyes grew clouded as Abraham appeared. His form was but a dim outline to her.

She felt hands holding then lifting her, and she heard her own screams of pain and inside her, the whispered entreaty, *No, no, please God, no!* In a moment of clarity she saw she was on deck, Abraham holding her. Beyond him, the quay loomed up, ropes being flung onto mooring bitts. "Margaret. Get me Margaret," Rosaleen whispered.

"I'll send the boy on your horse," Abraham said. "But first you need a soft bed and a warm room."

"Agnes Walsh. Take me to Agnes Walsh," Rosaleen gasped as a shaft of pain shot through her pelvic region and moved down along her legs. She could feel the world growing dim as she was carried from the boat. The pain grew more intense and the dimness parted only for fleeting moments; during one of them she saw Agnes Walsh bending over her.

"Margaret, where's Margaret?" Rosaleen called out.

"They've gone for her, my poor little thing," Agnes said. The woman's hand came to rest upon her forehead. "My God, she's burning up with fever. Cold compresses, quick," Rosaleen heard the woman say. She closed her eyes and felt the tears coursing down her face as the pain seemed to cut her in two. The room swam away, darkness flooding over her, and she lay suspended, as if in a void.

Soon she lost all consciousness for hours and when she woke, it was with a sharp gasp of pain. Voices drifted to her and she felt hands half-lifting her, pulling clothes from her. A warm, sticky wetness covered the inside of her thighs and she blinked, trying to clear her vision. Slowly, Margaret Boynton's face came into focus, the older woman looking down at her as she placed another cold cloth over her forehead.

"Rosaleen, my foolish, foolish, proud Rosaleen," Margaret murmured. "Why didn't you tell me? Why?"

Rosaleen's lips moved and she tried to speak, but her throat was dry and no words came. She ran a tongue over them, swallowed, half-rose as a shaft of pain went through her. Agnes Walsh was there, hands pushing her back down on the bed, and she saw Margaret bending low over her, felt the woman's hands pushing warm cloths between her thighs. Rosaleen shuddered and the darkness came again, lowering itself over her like a great, black curtain.

This time when she woke, she felt the fire consuming her body. Her eyes sought out the dim form, forced it to take shape. Margaret looked down at her from a chair drawn up alongside the bed. The woman's face was grave and Rosaleen forced the whispered words out of her dry, parched throat. "My baby," she gasped. "My baby." Margaret moved her head slowly from side to side and the soft scream tore from Rosaleen's throat, a half-wailing cry, hoarse, weak, as weak as the cry of a newborn baby. Margaret's arms held her, half-lifted her, cradling her shuddering form.

"Why didn't you tell me? Why didn't you?" the woman crooned, a terrible lament, and Rosaleen trembled in her arms with soundless sobs, then finally lay back on the bed, shaking and cold and hot at once. Margaret put cold cloths over her head and neck while keeping the rest of her swathed in blankets. "It's you who must fight for life, now, my Rosaleen. Infection and fever have taken hold something terrible," Margaret said. There was no answer, only a trembling that made the bed shake. Rosaleen let her eyes gesture to a water pitcher on a bedside table and Margaret helped her sit up enough to sip from a cup. The water seemed to turn hot the minute it touched her throat, but at least it was liquid. By the middle of the night, Rosaleen was in a semicoma. Emma Lathrop was called. She had done midwifery for years and had a supply of pills. The fever stayed through the next day though Rosaleen became conscious enough to take the pills.

Margaret was spelled at her side by Agnes Walsh and Emma Lathrop and the days went by and still the fever remained. It broke, finally, almost five days after she'd been carried from the lugger. Rosaleen woke in midafternoon, seeing faces in focus for the first time since that first day. Margaret was the only one in the room and came to her at once, gazing down at the anguish in the violet eyes. "Yes, the fever's gone, but it can come back unless we're very careful," the woman said. "If it does, it'll be the end of you. We can't let the infection get out of hand again."

Rosaleen slowly formed words. "Which means?" she asked.

"You have to stay here, in bed, perhaps for weeks more," Margaret said. Rosaleen shook her head weakly, her words coming in a hoarse whisper.

"I can't. I must get back to London," she breathed.

"You'll go to London in a coffin, my proud Rosaleen, if you move from here now," Margaret said sternly. "They've been told you came down with pneumonia."

Rosaleen's eyes pressed shut for a moment, opened again, the corners wet. "Don't tell anyone, Margaret. Promise me. No one is to know," she said.

"Your secret is safe, my dear. Only I know, Agnes Walsh and Emma Lathrop. There wasn't time to call a doctor," Margaret said.

"Abraham?" Rosaleen questioned.

Margaret shrugged. "He well suspects but he doesn't know. In any case, he'll not speak of it, not Abraham Evans," she said. Rosaleen closed her eyes. The few moments had drained her completely. She slept, and for the first time in days it was a sleep of restoration. When she woke in the morning, she still felt utterly exhausted and it wasn't till the end of the week that strength returned to her voice. Margaret was in almost constant attendance, leaving only for a few hours each afternoon. When she returned one evening, Rosaleen pulled herself to a sitting position and held onto Margaret's arm.

"What's happened in London, Margaret. You must tell me," she pleaded.

"Your Captain Coops is handling things. He sends messages that everything is fine," Margaret said. "Now stop thinking about it. Worry can start the fever again."

Rosaleen fell back, wanting to believe the words. A few days later Rosaleen almost collapsed while moving from bed to sit in a chair. In the chair, Margaret massaged her legs, brought circulation back to them. In another day, Rosaleen managed to walk from the bed to the chair unassisted. Margaret returned at the afternoon's end and Rosaleen pried at her at once.

"Any new word from London?" she asked.

"Coops is handling everything. He says that everything is fine and you're not to think about the business till you're well," the woman said. Rosaleen pressed her lips together. Margaret was giving her soothing platitudes and nothing else. That night she lay awake wondering, worrying, and in the morning she felt flushed and weak. Margaret's eyes fixed sternly on her.

"The more you worry, the more you think about the company, the longer it will take you to get back to it," the older woman said. "Things are in hand, under control. That's enough to ask."

Rosaleen nodded, chastened. "Yes, I guess it is. I won't think about it, I promise," she said. It was a promise meant and kept and the next week saw strength flow back into her. Strangely enough, thoughts of Niles kept surging up inside her, too. She had no triumph to fling in his face, now. The child was gone, her secret and—she bit her lips together—*his* child, too. Alone with Margaret, the thought overwhelmed and she burst into a fit of sobbing.

"I did it wrong, all of it," she said to the older woman. "The baby's gone because of me. It was my fault, all my fault."

Margaret's eyes held sympathy. She was too true a friend to offer well-meaning lies. "It was your doing, Rosaleen. I don't like that word *fault*. But it was your doing, that's true enough," she said.

"And so monstrously wrong, all of it," Rosaleen cried.

"Pain, hurt, bitterness, they turn us in wrong ways," Margaret said. "You didn't bring this about on purpose."

Rosaleen recoiled as if she'd been physically struck. *"No, oh good God, no!* I wanted the baby. I was getting ready to tell you soon. Oh, Margaret, I wanted it," Rosaleen said, words breaking off in a shuddering sob.

"But the wrong reasons were first," Margaret said. "You wanted it as your own way of striking back at Niles, a secret triumph you'd use in whatever way would hurt him most." She touched Rosaleen's arm gently. "Wrong on wrong, my dear. It comes around to us, cruel payment sooner or later."

"Yes," Rosaleen said, lifting her head. Anger found its way into the violet eyes for the first time in weeks. "But it won't change how I feel about him. That's not my wrong, not my injustice."

"No, it isn't," Margaret agreed. "Now lay down and get some sleep. You're coming along fine. I think in a few days you can go home."

It was the best news Rosaleen had heard in what seemed a decade and she slept, if not happily, at least with eager anticipation. The next few days flew by and she felt almost her old self, a spasm of trembling deep inside her from time to time, but nothing more. The day came when Margaret arrived with the Whitechapel and Rosaleen embraced Agnes Walsh and Emma. "There are no words," she said. "No thanks can measure up. Somehow, someday, I'll make it up to you both."

"Just come visit us with happiness in your eyes," Agnes said, and Rosaleen nodded a promise. Margaret was unusually silent on the ride back to Raven's Wing and as the house came into sight, Rosaleen saw the field of red and purple tulips abloom in front of the main door.

"How beautiful, Margaret. How magnificent," she breathed. The carriage drew up before the front door and Margaret got out first as Rosaleen's eyes lingered for a moment on the bed of flowers.

"Gardening's never been my thing," Rosaleen heard Margaret say, then turned to the woman as she clambered down from the carriage. The door opened and Rosaleen turned to see Olivia there, a mixture of happiness and apprehension in her wide eyes.

"Rosaleen. Welcome back," Olivia said, hesitated, then rushed forward and threw her arms around her. Rosaleen responded, an automatic gesture, but her eyes were on Margaret. She glanced back at the bed of tulips.

"I should have known at once," she remarked. She was not surprised when she went into the house to see Tony there. There was apprehension in his eyes, too, but also a hint of defiance. Margaret broke the moment of uneasy silence.

"It was my doing," she announced. "I asked Olivia and Mr. Darby to come back." Rosaleen met her eyes, waited. Margaret drew a breath, plunged ahead. "Someone had to see to Raven's Wing, and speak for you in London. I was with you for the better part of twenty-four hours a day in Gwyneth, especially those first weeks. They came at once, and they did more than I could ask of anyone."

Rosaleen's eyes found Tony. "You took charge in London?" she questioned, keeping sharpness out of her voice.

"I wouldn't say that. Captain Coops is a good man, all right, but there were decisions he was reluctant to make on his own. Let's say I helped him. I did the best I could, anyway. I put off some things, delayed others, jollied along some difficult clients, and told everyone you needed a rest and had gone to southern France. Even the newspapers came mucking about," Tony said.

"Captain Coops sent a note expressing his thanks to Mr. Darby," Margaret put in. Rosaleen saw Tony half-shrug, actually looking embarrassed, and watched Olivia's hand pridefully come up to touch his arm.

"I tried to help out here, hold things together while Margaret was away. I think I did all right," Olivia offered almost shyly.

"You did splendidly," Margaret said.

Rosaleen's smile held a rueful edge to it. "The feeling is a new one for me," she began slowly. "I think it's called remorse. It's made of old mistakes and new insights and it's the thing that brings apologies. It doesn't hurt all that much."

"Here, now, apologies are a two-way street," Tony said. "I think it's time for a few truths on this side, too. I've been a ruddy bounder for too many years. When that's all you know, it's hard to be anything else. Truth is, I've always schemed my way along and I've never been terribly proud of myself. Marrying Livvie was the one honest thing I've ever done, but the habits of a lifetime are hard to change. I tried my best in London and it wasn't all that bad, but I could never sit in the top seat. I haven't got it in me, just as Livvie doesn't have your inner strength. But we aren't all that bad, either. I found that out and it's a good feeling."

Rosaleen watched the dark eyes shine like a boy wearing a new suit, a bit uncomfortably but with quiet happiness. His words had not been so much an admission as a statement of fact, the truth she'd been unable to see because of yesterday's conditioning and today's bitterness. It was so very clear now. Don't demand what can't be given. Don't expect what isn't there. Instead, find what is there and make use of it. Tony would never be a strong person, nor would Olivia, but they could fit. They could be productive. There was a place for their gifts. There was always a place for any gift, even the small ones. It was a matter of recognition and acceptance.

Rosaleen put her hand out, held it there as Tony slowly reached forward, took it in his grasp. "Thank you for everything," she said. "I won't forget it."

"I'd say none of us will. We all learned some, and that's a good thing," Tony said.

"Yes, a good thing," Rosaleen echoed.

"I'll take the carriage to the stables," Tony said, and hurried off. Rosaleen started to go to her room, halted as she saw Olivia's eyes holding on her, wide, uncertain. She paused, waited.

"He was here, twice," Olivia blurted out, and Rosaleen felt herself stiffen. "He's lost weight. He's not at the Baxter-Mills house anymore."

"Good," Rosaleen sniffed.

"He stayed a half-hour during a thunderstorm one time," Olivia said. "He said that Frank Shields is trying to capture the market for shipping around the Cape. He seemed to think you should try to prevent that."

"Did he, now? He was probably carrying out orders, another piece of trickery," Rosaleen snapped. "No, thank you. I'll not listen to any words from Niles Brewster."

She brushed past Olivia, who seemed at a loss for anything more to say, and went to her room. Margaret followed, watching after her anxiously. "You feel all right?" she asked.

Rosaleen hugged her close. "I'm perfectly fine, ready to take on the world again," Rosaleen said. "I'll get some sleep and take the morning coach for London."

Alone, Rosaleen undressed, bathed, and lay across the bed in the warmth of the night. The vow she uttered in silence was only a repetition of the one she'd made every night for the past weeks. The terrible days were over, beyond changing, beyond calling back. The battle still lay ahead, still waiting to be won. No one had mentioned any stranger trying to contact her, so the business of the Bangkok bullion still lay unresolved. In the morning she'd go to London, not without apprehension. Too many platitudes had been spoken, too much truth left unsaid. But whatever waited for her, there'd be no turning away from the battle. There'd be no turning away from anything anymore. Except Niles.

CHAPTER EIGHT

Coops was plainly annoyed with her. "I really think you ought to have told me you were going to just disappear," he growled. She'd expected the irritation, had readied answers.

"You're absolutely right," she agreed, disarming him at once. "It was the doctor's orders when he saw my attack of nerves. Immediate rest and total silence, he said. I'm sorry, but I couldn't help myself."

The man's face relaxed. "Well, I suppose that puts a different face on it," he muttered.

She gave him her best smile. "It won't happen again. Now, tell me, what is the picture here? Have we been holding against Shields?"

He took a sheaf of papers from his inner pocket. "The short-term one is in hand. The holding action, you might say, is working, but it's no more than that. Expenses will accumulate, then ease off, even if Shields gives us no more trouble. In six months, you'll be out of money," Coops told her. "You need a massive infusion of new working capital or a set of tremendous new contracts which will accomplish the same end."

Rosaleen's eyes narrowed. "Six months," she murmured.

"An estimate. More or less," Coops said.

Rosaleen's eyes stayed narrowed, her thoughts racing. "Time enough," she said quietly. She saw the puzzled expression come over the captain's face as he peered at her. "I've some thoughts. All in due time," she said. She wasn't being purposely cryptic.

The thoughts were private ones, that would need more turning over. She took the papers Coops handed her.

"You'll find it all in the figures there," he said as he left. Rosaleen put the papers into a drawer. She'd no mind for wrestling with figures. Besides, she'd find nothing he hadn't already told her. She signed some checks that Higgens had brought to her, exchanged casual pleasantries with the others in the office, and the day ended soon enough. She went to the town house, opened windows to get out the mustiness that had quickly seized hold. When night came, she bathed, undressed, and lay naked on the bed. Her words to Coops came back. The thoughts had actually formed themselves the moment Olivia had told her that Niles had been there again. He was still in England, obviously still trying to meet with her, waiting for news about her. She'd give him news of her, Rosaleen murmured in a quiet anger that came at once. The financial picture that Coops had outlined only gave added impetus to the thought. It would be a case of killing two birds with one stone.

Rosaleen rose, turned up the lamp, and stood before the full-length wall mirror, staring critically at the image before her. The proud breasts were high and firm, her abdomen flat with the softly sensuous curve it always had, the long legs unmarked, unlined, smoothly captivating. The events that had seared her left their marks only on the soul. Rosaleen turned from the mirror, shut off the lamp, and stretched out on the bed again, her mind full of dancing thoughts. She would be neither the first nor the last woman to use her beauty with calculated determination. Every beautiful woman uses her beauty. She had always done so herself, she supposed, evoking what was simply a part of her, using the gifts God and nature had bestowed upon her. The flame does not *use* its warm light. It is simply there, existence and use intertwined, one and the same.

But that was not enough, now. Her beauty was a commodity, as much an asset as a banker's real estate bonds and stock certificates, and it could be used in the same way, to attract more capital.

There would be a kind of poetic justice in it. She, not Niles, would marry coldly for gain. But there'd be no betrayal with her, no false, honeyed words. Everything would be clear and understood. She'd bargain beauty and body but not integrity. And Frank Shields would find that she had weapons she could use with as great an effect as any he had. Before she turned on her side to sleep, practical details fell into place in her mind like so many obedient soldiers. The Queen's birthday ball was only a week away. So much valuable time had been lost. Every minute would have to be measured till then. Rosaleen closed her eyes with the thought and slept.

The morning was consumed with office matters but during the noon hour she broke proper etiquette and paid a visit to Adelaide Winship without inquiring or calling for an appointment. The *grande dame* was in and, as Rosaleen had hoped, delighted to see her. "So you're back, my dear," the woman said. "I'm glad that I'm the first person you've visited. Everyone's been talking about the way you just disappeared."

"Doctor's order. The pressure was becoming too much. But I am indeed back and full of very definite plans," Rosaleen said.

"Oh?" the woman returned, all interest.

"To find a rich husband," Rosaleen said.

"That ought not to be difficult for you, my dear," the woman remarked.

Rosaleen gave a little shrug. "It could be. I'm fussy and I've definite things in mind."

"Such as handsome as well as rich?" Adelaide Winship pressed.

"That would be nice," Rosaleen said. "But rich is more important." Her answer was truthful. She had no delusions. The kind of wealth she needed would not be found in young, handsome men beginning their careers, except, possibly for an heir to a fortune and they were so often fops and insufferable dandies. What she sought—capital sufficient to run Frank Shields off the seas—would be found in an older man, hopefully not too old and not too unattractive. She'd planted the seed with Adelaide Winship. Her words would soon be all over the London social set, she knew, and after small talk and tea, she returned to the office and finished the day.

Her next visit was to the shop of Charles Frederick Worth and, luck with her again, she found him there and not at his Paris studio. But luck ended with that. She had expected protests and problems, but not the complete refusal that she got. "Impossible, absolutely impossible. Every woman in society wants a new gown for the Queen's birthday ball and I think they've all come to me. They all know I dethroned the crinoline and they want the newest of the new. I'll hardly finish those I've promised."

He waved an arm at the shop, and Rosaleen saw girls busy at the new sewing looms and machines, cutting and stitching while others pinned and pressed and an air of quiet panic prevailed. "And you, my dear Rosaleen Powell, you come to me with a description of a gown that would take a long time to conceive, much less make," he said.

"I'm desperate, Frederick," Rosaleen pleaded. "There must be someone you can send me to see, then."

She watched the designer furrow his brow in thought. "You cannot travel all over. You've no time for that," he mused aloud. "Redfern, perhaps."

"No. He'll put me in a gown that will look more like a walking suit," Rosaleen said.

The man's brow stayed wrinkled and then suddenly he half-jumped and clapped his hands together. "Doucet. Jacques Doucet, he's here in London. He delivered a gown to Madame Ashton and he stopped to see me afterward. He had a magnificent gown with him, but so daring and so beautiful that he is still keeping it in his shop. Perhaps you could prevail upon him to let you have it." The designer paused, waited.

"I'll prevail," Rosaleen said. "Where is he now?"

"At the Regency. He leaves on a channel boat tomorrow back to France," the man said.

Rosaleen was out of the shop instantly, hailing a cab. In the lobby of the Regency Hotel within fifteen minutes, she used Worth's name as a cavalryman uses a sword and finally found herself on the fifth floor, facing a slight-built, somewhat shylooking man. Once again, she wasted no time in using Worth's name.

"And he told you of my gown, eh?" Doucet said as his eyes slowly went over her from head to toe. He shook his head up and down in a slow nod. "Yes, I can see why he did so," the man said. "Your coloring, your beauty, it would be perfect. And he must know that you are not the ordinary woman."

Rosaleen allowed a modest smile. "No, I suppose I've never been that," she agreed. The designer went to a closet, opened it, and brought out a shimmering pale-lavender dream made into a gown, silk crêpe as airy and delicate as a butterfly's wings. He held it up in front of her, his eyes narrowing as he scrutinized it against her jet tresses and violet eyes.

"Go inside, put it on," he said, and Rosaleen took the dress in her arm, started into the adjoining room. His voice halted her at the door. "If you have a slip, a chemise, take it off. Petticoats, too, take them off. From the waist up, nothing is to be worn underneath. From the waist down, perhaps only a pair of thin pantaloons. Perhaps," he said.

Rosaleen nodded, disappeared behind the door with the dress. She followed his orders, undressed, and put on the gown with careful haste. It felt as if she had nothing on at all. The material crossed in front of her breasts, covering yet hardly concealing anything, so low cut that most of her full breasts were exposed. But the mirror in the room revealed a stunning gown, a work of art that vibrated against her coloring. She opened the door, stepped into the other room, and saw Doucet's eyes grow wide. *"C'est magnifique,"* he breathed. *"Formidable!* The colors are made for you. You are made for the gown." He nodded slowly as Rosaleen pirouetted, felt the soft swing of the gown with her every movement.

"I was going to give it to *Réjane,"* he said.

"The actress? The *Réjane* of *Zasa?"* Rosaleen asked.

"Yes," he nodded. "But it is yours. She could not do what you do for it. No one could. Every once in a while, a designer finds the perfect woman for his work. It has happened now." He stepped forward, took her hand, and kissed it lightly. "There is some minor fitting to do. Frederick will do it for you, and for me," he said.

"I'll have a check delivered here before you leave in the morning," Rosaleen said. "And thank you." She left with the dress over her arm, holding it tightly against her. During the week, she had it fitted at Frederick Worth's shop, and the man who was becoming the originator of ready-to-wear clothes stood back in admiration.

"There will always be a place for the one-of-a-kind gown," he said. "Especially a gown such as this for a beauty such as yours."

The week went by quickly. One of the things left to do was to inform Harold Pryor that he could put the town house up for sale. She sent him a letter to that effect. It would take time for buyers to come and to conclude a sale. By then, perhaps she'd be ready to move into even finer lodgings. When Friday night came, Rosaleen waited for Coops at the house, a dark-blue cape over the gown. She kept it pulled tight during the carriage ride and as she entered the hotel. The grand ballroom was a dazzling, glittering sight as she halted at the top step, looked down at the scene below. The great chandeliers blazed with light and sparkled as if they were fashioned of diamonds. The music floated across the hum of voices and the floor was a mass of swirling shapes and color, the center of the room cleared for the dancers and tables lining the four sides.

Rosaleen paused at the top step as the coatroom attendant came forward. She reached up to the neck of the cape, unclasped it, and handed it to the man. She heard Coops draw his breath in. Swatches of pale-lavender crêpe encased her, echoing the violet of her eyes, playing off the ebony shine of her hair. She seemed an ethereal vision as she began to move down the wide stairway and the voices below dipped to a murmur. Under the soft folds of the silk crêpe, a delicate symphony of motion, her breasts were visible yet invisible, seen then not seen, in response to each movement of the fabric. Coops caught up to her and she rested one hand lightly on his arm. When she reached the floor of the ballroom, Adelaide Winship was at her side in moments.

"I might have expected as much. The most daring and most beautiful gown at the ball. You've every tongue wagging and every head turning and you've just arrived. Magnificent!" the woman exclaimed.

Rosaleen moved into the crowd with Adelaide at her side, exchanging a few words with those she knew, nodding to others. The parade of young men who always asked her to dance began earlier than usual and she refused none of them. However, her eyes were searching the room, sweeping in every direction as she whirled and turned on the dance floor. She wanted to see Niles Brewster as his eyes found her but she saw no sign of him or his master, Frank Shields, yet. She concentrated on enjoying herself while keeping watch and it was later in the evening, when she paused by the punchbowl, that Adelaide Winship took her aside.

"Someone very special wants to meet you," Adelaide said, and Rosaleen saw the woman smile at the question in her eyes. "Yes, he very much fills the requirements you spoke to me about," she said. Rosaleen followed her to one of the tables where three men sat. All rose as she approached and one stepped forward. She saw a figure on the portly side, a round face with jowls somewhat too heavy and gray hair that retained thickness only along the sides. It was the face of a man who had never been handsome and now bore the signs of some sixty-five, perhaps even seventy years, she guessed. Yet his eyes, light brown, still held youth enough in them, and they were intent but good eyes, no mean smallness in them.

"My dear, may I present Sir Ronald Aleshire," Adelaide introduced. "And, Sir Ronald, this is the most popular Miss Rosaleen Powell."

Sir Ronald Aleshire executed a half-bow of old-world courtliness. "The most popular and most spectacular young woman in the entire ballroom," he said, and she saw his glance drop down to glimpse the slight movement of her breasts beneath the shifting transparency of the gown, then shift back to her face again. "You carry it off well," he said. "Boldness without crudeness, a difficult feat. My compliments."

Rosaleen allowed him her most dazzling smile. "You are practiced with compliments," she returned. She moved a step closer as he gestured to the other two men.

"Arthur Ellsworth, Esquire, and Mr. Ormond Baker," Sir Ronald introduced, and once again Rosaleen saw his glance drop to the flash of her breasts through the shifting silk crêpe. He saw her catch the glance, half-smiled but without embarrassment. "I offer no apologies," he said. "I am an ardent voyeur."

"I expected none," Rosaleen laughed.

"I should ask you to dance but I have had my fill of dancing this night," he said. "And as this is hardly the atmosphere for intellectual conversation, will you honor me at dinner tomorrow evening? If you have regained your strength after tonight?"

"I'll be perfectly fine. Yes, I should enjoy dinner," Rosaleen said.

"I'll send my carriage for you. Seven o'clock." He bowed again, first to her, then to Adelaide. "I must leave now. The ball can hold nothing for me now."

Rosaleen touched his arm for a moment, her breasts brushing him for a fleeting instant. "May I expect a steady diet of such compliments tomorrow night? You shall spoil me immediately," she remarked.

"We'll see," he said blandly, and moved away with the other two men. Rosaleen turned to Adelaide Winship.

"No one knows exactly how much he's worth, but it's plenty," the woman said. "He has extensive holdings in iron and coal. His wife, a wealthy woman herself, died ten years ago. He was quite taken with you, my dear."

"He sounds perfect. Thank you, Adelaide," Rosaleen said.

"I just want to be first with the news of anything that happens, or doesn't happen. My world is made of that kind of gossip," Adelaide told her.

"You shall be. I promise," Rosaleen said. Adelaide Winship's words clung for a moment after the woman left her side. The first step had been taken, Rosaleen reflected. It had actually been quite painless. But then the world, at least this world bounded by the customs of the rich and the powerful, was quite used to what was politely called a marriage of convenience. Even royalty practiced it on another level, most often for political considerations. Such marriages provided far more gossip then the ordinary ones. Young women with rich old husbands were expected to take lovers with varying discretion. Rosaleen's lips tightened. She'd not make herself part of that kind of gossip. Her marriage of convenience would have its own code. She'd not make betrayal part of it. Almost automatically, her eyes swept the ballroom, seeking Niles. Her searching glance halted at a table not too far away. Frank Shields was there, his thick figure seeming uncomfortable in evening dress. A small party of people were with him, but Niles wasn't one of them. After another hour, she decided that Niles was not at the ball at all. She felt a sharp stab of disappointment. She'd wanted so to slap him in the face with her loveliness, her confidence, her poised and contained happiness. "Damn him," she murmured angrily, and resolved to settle for another day and another way. She had Coops take her home soon after, an hour before the dawn. The night had been profitable and she slept at once, but not nearly as soundly as she'd expected.

She slept through a good part of the day but was radiant and glowing in a jonquil gown with a square neck when the carriage arrived at seven. The dinner, at one of London's most fashionable restaurants, the Savile House, was made of fine food and good conversation. To her delight, Sir Ronald was a man of erudition and real charm.

"Chose a subject to talk about," he said to her. "One you know well, and we'll see if I can hold a learned and intelligent conversation in it. Pick a difficult one. It's a game I play, a kind of test."

"Of whom?" Rosaleen asked sharply, and he threw his head and laughed hard.

"*Touché*, my dear. Very good, indeed. Let's say a test of both of us, but it really is of myself," he answered. Rosaleen, challenged, cast around for something she knew well enough, focused on a topic that was an obsession of a history professor she'd once had in upper school.

"The intervention in the Netherlands during the fifteen hundreds," she said.

"Starting with the assassination of William the Silent at Delft?" Sir Ronald said. "Or with Coligny in France and Moray in Scotland. They were all part of the same set of impending events, you know."

Rosaleen tried to shift emphasis. He seemed entirely too comfortable with the political figures. "I was thinking of the military campaigns," she suggested.

"Parma's attack on Antwerp or the Dutch error in not keeping the city open below the *Scheldt?*"

"You win that one. Let me try another," Rosaleen said.

"Please do," he agreed. She racked her brains again, drew another discipline out of her school years.

"Let's talk about the Stoics," she began.

"Ah, those early Greek practitioners of social virtues that so influenced the Romans. Who shall we start with, Zeno, Chrysippus or Cleanthes?" he answered. "Or would you prefer to discuss Laelius? You know, he was quite successful in his Hellenization of Roman society."

Rosaleen stared at him, saw the amused, almost little-boy enjoyment in his eyes. She tried another topic only to find him equally conversant in it, and then still another with the same results. "You win," she said, sitting back in admiration. "You obviously have acquired a remarkably diverse expanse of knowledge."

"Thank you for not adding, 'at my age,'" Sir Ronald laughed. Rosaleen found the evening stimulating and enjoyable. It was unnecessary to play the coquette, or any kind of games. An immediate rapport was present almost at once and she agreed to dine with him again at the end of the week. Their next evening together was just as entertaining and the evenings that followed were no less so. She became his companion at the ballet, the theater, and social events, and she kept Adelaide Winship informed of the progress of the relationship.

"I'm very fortunate," Rosaleen told the other woman. "I could have found a prospect that was a bore, a man with no sparkle whatever. I am in your debt. I see what so many others have had to settle for and I shudder."

The public press soon took notice of the companion frequently accompanying Sir Ronald Aleshire and the flames of speculation took on new fuel. Rosaleen still tried to keep at least two days a week free for Cornwall, though it was becoming increasingly difficult. She was packing to return to London after her last visit when Margaret came to her with a copy of the *London Times* in her hand.

"Rosaleen, my dear, my dear, dear girl, don't do this," Margaret said. "You're too young, too full of tomorrows to take this kind of step. It's not you, it's not the Rosaleen I know."

"Perhaps not the Rosaleen you once knew. It is the one you know today," Rosaleen answered, and saw disbelief in Margaret's troubled eyes.

"You're still trying to find a way to strike back at Niles Brewster and you think this is it," the woman said.

"Not at all," Rosaleen snapped, angering instantly. "It's got nothing to do with Niles Brewster."

"Hasn't it?" Margaret pressed.

"No, nothing," Rosaleen insisted. "It has to do with keeping the company alive, with fighting Frank Shields and winning, that's all."

"That's part of it, I'm sure, but not all," Margaret said stubbornly. Rosaleen took her bags and flounced off, glad to be returning to London. Margaret, loving person that she was, did not understand some things. It was the very next day, at the office, that Coops confronted her. In his eyes she saw the honest concern of a good friend.

"Are you sure you want to do what you're doing?" he questioned. Rosaleen, still smarting from Margaret's probing words, erupted at once. She scooped the bills and financial statements from the desk, waved them in the air.

"These make me sure. Every time I see them I become more sure," she snapped.

"Perhaps there is too high a price for winning," Coops offered.

"No," Rosaleen snapped again. "Nobody should lie, sabotage, commit every unspeakable crime, even hire killers, and be allowed to get away with it. Nobody should be able to use people as pawns, to take something beautiful and make it dirt."

She halted, saw the questions in the captain's eyes, and felt the color flood into her face. "He's just thoroughly rotten and I'll not give in to him," she said. Coops nodded, accepted the words without further comment, and left her alone. Rosaleen flung herself into the chair and refused to wonder why she trembled so.

The questions had been expressions of concern, not attempts to hurt. She drew a deep breath, forced herself to calm down. She'd a dinner and theater engagement with Sir Ronald in the evening, and she'd not go to it upset. By evening, she was in complete control of herself again and had a lovely time as usual. The following day took her to Plymouth with Coops to see a new customer who wanted extra attention. Upon her return to London, she learned that Niles had come to the office to see her. He left no message and Rosaleen found herself unaccountably annoyed at that.

But the weeks went by and finally the night came that she had known would come. She had wondered, speculated, fantasized about how it would be, how she would feel, which would be the first words to be uttered, and which the last. None of her speculations proved right. Sir Ronald had taken her to his home for a glass of sherry to end the evening, as had become their custom. A somewhat avuncular kiss often followed, or else just quiet moments when he held his arms around her. But this night was to be different. She knew it the moment he held her longer, ever so slightly tighter, and his hands passed over her breasts, in a quick, even hesitant motion. She sat on the loveseat in the living room with him, a room rich in Louis XIV pieces, soft burnished-gold drapes, and a deep blue rug. In his eyes she saw something she'd not seen before, an expression she could only call a mixture of sadness and anticipation.

"These past few months have been wonderful for many reasons and one in particular," he began. "We have needed no words. We have both understood each other without them."

"Have we?" Rosaleen asked, suddenly unsure of herself, suddenly strangely nervous.

His smile was gentle. "You know we have. There is no need to begin pretending now," he chided. "My beautiful Rosaleen, you have offered your companionship, your beauty, the pleasures of your company, and the promise of your body. You don't deny that, do you?" Rosaleen shook her head, looked down at her hands, suddenly feeling like a schoolgirl. His hand reached out, took both hers in a gentle grip, and she met his gaze. "You have not offered love and you did not have the cruelty to pretend to do so. I thank you for that, from the bottom of my heart. You could have flattered me into believing such an offer, or at least deceived me into believing it. I am not above human failings. But that would have been dishonest on your part."

Rosaleen opened her lips to protest, closed them as she saw the wisdom in his eyes. "Good, my dear. Do not start being dishonest now. You have offered an exchange, a bargain, a kind of business arrangement as it were," he said.

This time she did protest. "Now who's being crude, Ronald," she murmured.

"My apologies. I don't mean to be that. Perhaps it is I who offered the exchange, the business arrangement, trying to gild the lily with fine wine and theaters and dinners. I do not deny it. And I do not expect more, not at my age."

Rosaleen felt her sense of justice nettled. "You should, Ronald," she said. "You are a very wise and wonderful and charming man. Why shouldn't you expect love from a woman?"

"Perhaps we are talking about different kinds of love," he said softly. "Do you offer love, the kind you just meant, Rosaleen."

Rosaleen felt her lips tighten, an involuntary gesture. She almost answered yes, wanting to give what he deserved, or perhaps simply not wanting to hurt. But the moment of hesitancy spoke for itself and she saw the ruefulness in his smile. "I think I could, in time," she tried.

"Ah, in time," he said. "Yes, perhaps so, but that would be a different kind of love then, wouldn't it?"

She pressed her lips together impatiently. "I don't know. I'm not sure there are two kinds of love," she said.

"There are more than two kinds, but there is only one complete kind, one that has all the others wrapped within itself, and that is not what you offer, nor what I expect," he said.

"All right, you say I offer an exchange, a business arrangement," Rosaleen said, taking a deep breath. "It takes two to make a bargain."

Sir Ronald laughed, a low, chuckling sound. "Yes, and you shall have your bargain, Rosaleen Powell. I've much the better of it. I'll exchange coins for a goddess anytime. I shall be happy to make you my wife, happy and the envy of every man at Boodle's and White's," he said, naming two of England's most prestigious men's clubs. It was done, she heard herself murmur, his words sinking into her as if they were a slow fire. It was done, the bargain struck, the objective reached. It had happened without inner or outer struggles, and suddenly she was at a loss for words. She met his gentle eyes and heard herself whisper the two words: "Thank you."

His hand pressed her arm. "My lovely Rosaleen, so determined outside, so sweet inside. I wonder if you've really faced the price for your bargain."

"I'll keep my part of it," she said with a surge of sudden defiance.

"Will you?" he asked gently, his smile almost rueful. "Let me see you then, in all your beauty."

"Another test? Another kind of game?" she returned.

"Perhaps," was all he would say. Rosaleen held his gaze. Once again, her wonderings had been wrong. She'd known there'd be nothing so low as distaste, yet she had wondered how she'd react, how well her discipline would hold. And now there was no need of discipline, no need to act. She had a tremendous desire to please this man who had proven so erudite, charming, kind, and, most of all, understanding. She rose slowly, stood before him, and her hands moved to the little fastenings on the side of the gown. One by one, she unsnapped them. The dress dipped, fell from around her shoulders. The swaths of airy material slipped down, over her breasts. She moved her hips and the gown fell to the floor. With one quick motion, she let the chemise follow. She stood before the older man, her breasts thrust out proudly, her long, jet tresses falling loosely. She saw his lips move, his tongue come out to wet their dry surfaces.

"A goddess indeed, my proud Rosaleen," she heard him whisper. "Such breathtaking beauty. An old man's dreams come true."

Rosaleen stepped forward, closer to him. His hand reached, came to rest upon her hip. Slowly, he moved the hand across the smoothness of her abdomen, up along her rib cage, over one breast. His touch was amazingly gentle, soothing instead of inflaming. He pulled his hand away after a moment more. "We have talked enough this night. More will be a matter of time and fate. But you may make your announcement, my dear," he said. "Now let me enjoy the loveliness of watching you dress."

Rosaleen moved with simple, unhurried gracefulness, found herself enjoying his gaze. When she finished, he saw her to the carriage and she went home to the town house. She slept, but not before a strange fit of sobbing caught at her. When morning came, she told herself that she was indeed pleased with everything. Somehow, it was necessary.

Her first act was to contact Adelaide Winship and tell her the news. "Run with it, Adelaide," Rosaleen said. "Make the most of it. I'll be announcing it to the papers tomorrow."

"Don't worry, my dear. Twenty-four hours of inside news will be more than enough to keep my stock high," the woman said. When she arrived at the office, she would not let the seriousness of Coops upset her as he put the last financial statement down on her desk.

"Higgens just finished the projection," he said. "It gives us a lot less than six months at the present rate. Three, perhaps. And maybe not even that. A set of new sails I ordered for the *Glenmary* arrived torn and useless."

"More of Shields and his doings," Rosaleen said.

"Of course, but it means at least three weeks before we can get another set of sails for her. Three weeks of idleness and loss of money," Coops said.

Rosaleen's little smile was made of smugness. "We shall have all the working capital we'll need soon," she said, and Coops studied her for a long moment, then let his lips purse.

"I see," he murmured. "I should guess that congratulations are in order, then."

"Yes," Rosaleen said, and wished she felt more elation. Tony had come to London to help Higgens compile a detailed cargo manifest for three ships setting out on the South Atlantic run. He surprised her once more when she told him of her engagement to Sir Ronald.

"It'll be good for the business. It'll let you do what you want to do," he said. "But will it be good for you? How happy will you really be?"

"Happy enough," Rosaleen answered, closing the conversation. She knew about the kind of happiness he meant. It was here one moment and gone the next. She'd had enough of those mirages of the soul. That kind of happiness was not for her any longer. It was too vulnerable, too open to lies, pain, betrayal. She had made her decision and she'd live with it.

The official announcement appeared in the newspapers the following day and in the social columns over the remainder of the week. She posed for pictures with Sir Ronald and said all the proper things, but the press was, as usual, probingly accurate in its reporting. One social arbiter of the society page put it neatly:

Rumor became fact today when the world's only female shipping magnate, the daring and bold Rosaleen Powell, announced her engagement to Sir Ronald Aleshire. For a change, Miss Powell is following a time-honored custom instead of breaking tradition. It is no secret that the Powel Line has been in great difficulty.

Rosaleen flung the newspaper into the wastebasket. The mouthings of the envious were unimportant. She was only sorry she could not be present when the news reached Niles. Perhaps he would be with Frank Shields and they could both console each other in defeat.

The next three days were consumed by an unexpected trip with Sir Ronald. He took her to a château he had along the Brittany coast and she relaxed in the lovely spaciousness of the house. "Do you good to get away from the newspapers and from work for a spell," he told her. It was a quiet, replenishing time, and at night Sir Ronald watched her undress, went over her body with his soothing, gentle touch, but nothing more. She sat at his knee by a warm fire, the light glowing on the smoothness of her naked body, stretched out like a cat on the hearth. She enjoyed the total appreciation she saw mirrored in his eyes, finding it strangely satisfying, and yet she could not help waiting, wondering.

"I'm becoming an exhibitionist," she said in mild protest on the last night of their stay at the château. He drew her up to his side, stroked her neck and shoulders gently.

"Are you bothered?" he asked. "Because there hasn't been, shall we say, anything further?"

Rosaleen hesitated a moment. "No, not yet, anyway," she said honestly. "But I've wondered."

His smile was slow, quietly wry. "Everything in time," he said. "I believe very strongly in the right thing at the right time, and only then. Anything else destroys, degrades. I value memories. They should be as beautiful as the moments that created them. Unfortunately, they seldom are allowed to be that."

Rosaleen made no reply, but on the trip back she wondered about a man who had just become engaged and spoke about memories. Yet she would not dismiss his words. She had come to realize that he held a wisdom tempered with understanding that was far beyond hers. She would not challenge nor object to his words. She had come to respect him far too much. But she would continue to wonder, for now.

Upon reaching London, she closeted herself with Coops. Tony was there, too, helping to keep the machinery of the business running. Coops offered no brighter picture, yet nothing more unsettling had happened during her absence. She went to Cornwall that night and Margaret was up when she arrived. Rosaleen saw the copy of the newspaper that had carried the engagement announcement on the kitchen table, met the older woman's grave glance. She felt the tears suddenly flood her eyes, stupid, unaccountable tears that seemed to come from nowhere, and she swore under her breath.

"Dammit, I want you to be happy for me, Margaret," she cried out. "That's important to me."

Margaret gathered her close. "I want to be happy for you, my Rosaleen. But I am afraid for you," she said. "I fear what you are doing to yourself in the name of bitterness and hate."

"I'm doing what has to be done," Rosaleen said, retreating at once into herself. She heard footsteps, saw Olivia in the doorway. Olivia's round face seemed more wide-eyed and full of anxiety than ever.

"Congratulations, Ros," she said. "I hope it'll all work out for you." She paused, searched for words. "You know, you don't have to do this for us, not for Tony and me, anyway. I don't think you have to do it for Poppa, either."

"He'd approve," Rosaleen said. "He'd understand."

Olivia shrugged. "Maybe. You'd know that better than I. You understood each other in places I could never reach."

Rosaleen nodded, reached out, touched her sister's hair. Olivia was saying more than her words communicated, and Rosaleen felt grateful, deeply touched. "He's really a very fine man," she said. "Wise and kind and understanding."

It was Margaret's voice that broke in with words that struck hard. "Those are wonderful things. They're not enough, not for you, not for this time in your life."

Rosaleen whirled angrily on her. "They won't hurt me. They won't betray me and pull the world out from under me," she said.

"He was here again," Olivia's voice cut in. "The day after the engagement was announced in the paper. He looked terrible, drawn and upset."

"Did he, now?" Rosaleen said coldly.

"His anguish seemed real, Rosaleen," Olivia said.

"So did his love," Rosaleen snapped back. Olivia shrugged, turned away. "I'm going to bed," Rosaleen said. "If he comes again, tell him to keep reading the newspapers."

She stayed only one day in Cornwall but she made it a whirlwind of activity. There were checks to sign for expenses at Raven's Wing, practical matters to go over with Margaret and Olivia. The gardens outside looked beautiful and she took the time to saddle the stallion and ride along the beach, drawing in memories that suddenly became too harsh. She rode down to Gwyneth and was surrounded by the women of the tubs. "News travels fast," she laughed.

"The gippers always know what's going on," Agnes Walsh said.

"We've nothing but talk and gossip to keep us busy and you can't talk to a tub of herring," Bridgit Murphy echoed.

"You'll not be forgetting us now, will you?" someone else called out.

"Have I so far?" Rosaleen returned. "No, never. I'm not the kind for forgetting old friends."

"They say an old man is the best kind. He hasn't forgotten how to tomcat. He's just got no energy for it anymore," another voice called, and laughter drowned out anything Rosaleen might have said. References to Sir Ronald's age, even the good-natured, lusty ones, were something she'd have to learn to accept, Rosaleen decided, but she returned to London that night feeling vaguely irritated, anxious to return to the quiet gentleness of Sir Ronald.

The next weekend he gave a dinner party. The guest list included the Duke and Duchess of Montmorency, Albert Stiegel, the biologist, and three or four members of Parliament. However, it was a gentleman named Edgar Osborne he made a special effort to introduce to her.

"Edgar's paying me a visit, as he does every year or so," Sir Ronald said. "He is the largest shipper of rum, sugar, molasses, and coffee out of the West Indies and Central American market, my dear, and he has an interesting proposition for you."

Rosaleen eyed the man with renewed interest. He was a quiet man but there was steel in his eyes. "I've decided that I'm losing money shipping with too many small fleets," Edgar Osborne told her. "I'm offering a contract for all my business. Believe me when I tell you it will keep any line in the black for the next ten years. Frankly, I want to go with the line that has the fastest ships and the best skippers."

"Naturally," Rosaleen agreed. "I take it you've spoken to others about this."

"Yes, Frank Shields. I'm proposing a race from London to Boston Harbor, two clippers, both fully loaded. The winner will get the contract for all my business," he said. "The prize is a ten-year contract of unbroken profits for the winner."

"It will put the Powell Line in a position of eminence again, my dear," Sir Ronald said at her elbow.

The challenge sent her heart pounding at once, but she held back. She'd make no commitment till she spoke to Coops. "Give me till tomorrow. I'll send an answer by special messenger," she said to Osborne.

"Good enough," the man agreed, and Rosaleen felt the excitement pulling at her. But there was something else, something that irritated and disturbed. She glanced at Sir Ronald. His eyes were masked by pleasantness. Her frown stayed, at least inwardly, till the evening was over and Osborne retired to the guest room. Before leaving, she faced Ronald in the gold living room.

"Why?" she asked.

He half-smiled. "Why what, my dear?" he asked.

"Why did you have me meet him? If I take the challenge and win, I'll have no need for anything else, no finances, no capital needs. The banks will be happy to deal with me then. Are you telling me something else, Ronald? Are you looking for a way out?" she asked sharply.

"No," he said simply.

"Then why?" she repeated.

He gave her a slow, rueful smile. "Go home. Get some sleep, my dear. I shall say no more now. I've answered you." Rosaleen was unsatisfied with the answer, but left after he kissed her cheek. She drummed fingertips against her leg as the carriage took her home, irritation still with her when she crawled into bed. She was almost asleep when she sat up, felt the heat rising into her face, knew her cheeks had grown red. It was so clear now, and she so full of remorse. There'd been no telling her anything. There had been an offer, a way for her to withdraw if she wanted. "Damn," Rosaleen muttered. She was too filled with thorns for her own good. She'd done an injustice, leapt at small-minded assumptions. Not everyone betrays, she murmured inwardly, I must remember that.

She slept, woke early, and went to Ronald's home on the way to the office. He was in a maroon bathrobe and she drew him to her, held him tightly. "I'm sorry, I'm sorry, Ronald," she breathed. "Please forgive me. I should have known better."

"Now, now, my lovely one, there's nothing to forgive. If it is to be, it will be better for it. It's as simple as that," he said, and she nodded in understanding, kissed his cheeks, and hurried to the office feeling better about herself. Coops listened to her as she told him of Edgar Osborne's challenge.

"Yes, I know of Osborne. He has the entire West Indies trade cornered," Coops said.

"Can we do it? Can we beat Shields?" Rosaleen asked.

"He has some fast vessels but we have one that's faster than anything on the seas today, the *Regina Clyde*. In a fair race, we can beat him. I'd put money on it," the captain said.

"Then I'll accept the challenge," Rosaleen said. "Call in the *Regina Clyde*, have her dry-docked and made ready. We are going to get rid of Mr. Frank Shields once and for all."

Rosaleen sat down and wrote a note to Osborne, had it delivered by messenger. Within days, the Admiralty and the newspapers were informed of the race, and the date was set. Coops left London to see to the conditioning of the ship and Tony took over his office duties. Rosaleen spent what evenings she could with Sir Ronald and her excitement mounted as each day brought the race nearer. After reading in the *Times* that Frank Shields had arrived at his London office to oversee preparations for the race, she was not surprised when his letter was hand-delivered to her a few days later. Tony was in the office as she opened it, a small, grim smile touching her lips.

"He wants a meeting with me," she said. "As soon as possible, at his office or here."

"What for?" Tony questioned. "The bloody bounder isn't short on nerve, is he?"

"I'll go. I'm curious what he has to say," Rosaleen mused aloud. "At his office, tomorrow. I don't want him setting foot in here." She gave Shields's waiting messenger her answer, slept restlessly that night, annoyed at herself as she kept wondering if Niles would be at the meeting. Perhaps Shields had decided to try again at her through Niles. She vowed she'd walk out if that's what it was all about.

When she arrived at the Shields Lines offices in the morning, she wore her most fetching daytime dress but her palms kept growing damp with perspiration. She was shown into an inner office at once. Frank Shields was there alone, a decanter of coffee on his desk. She declined his offer of a cup, grew annoyed with herself for expecting Niles to pop in from one of the side doors.

"You've been a most remarkable adversary, Miss Powell," the man said, trying a wide smile.

"I'm aware of that," Rosaleen snapped. "Let's not be coy. I haven't the time nor the desire to stay here one moment more than necessary." She saw the ice-floe eyes harden, hold her gaze.

"My ship can win," he said abruptly, his tone changing at once. "But in a race there can always be the unexpected, winds failing at the wrong time, a broken spar, a fouled rudder. Too many little things can happen and there's too much at stake here for uncertainties."

"Meaning what?" Rosaleen questioned.

"Meaning that we should come to an arrangement. The pie is big enough for both of us. I'll agree, in private contract, of course, to give you half of Osborne's business if you withdraw from the race after it starts. That would automatically make me the winner and assure you of half a loaf."

"I don't want half a loaf," Rosaleen spat out. "I'm going to win everything."

"You're a fool. My ship is as fast as yours. I told you, too many things can go wrong in a race. You can't be sure," Shields growled. "I'm offering you a good deal."

"I wouldn't make any deal with you. I don't trust you or anything you say. No deals, Mr. Shields, no deals," Rosaleen said.

"You'd risk losing everything rather than take half of it? You're worse than a fool. You're blind," he shouted. "Dammit, girl, I'm offering the best deal you'll ever get. Don't be an idiot and refuse it."

"Perhaps you are, Mr. Shields, but your best isn't good enough. I'd rather lose it all than make any deals with you," Rosaleen said. She saw the man's face redden, his hands clench into fists.

"You're as stupid and stubborn as that goddamned nephew of mine," he said.

Rosaleen's eyes narrowed. "Niles?" she queried.

"Yes, Niles Brewster, the damnfool. You're two of a kind, stubborn, stupid damnfools. You're willing to give up everything because of your damned pride and he gave up everything because of you," Shields roared.

"What do you mean? Isn't he still doing your dirty work for you?" Rosaleen asked.

"No, he quit, he left me. It cost him a pretty penny but he walked out," Shields snapped.

"But that day in Boston?" Rosaleen said, feeling her breath catching at her.

"I'd sent for him to try and talk some sense into his head. But he'd refused me, even before you walked in. Good riddance, I say. I've no patience with damnfools and stupid girls. Get out of my office and be damned with you. I tried and now you'll rue the day. I'll win and see you begging on the streets," the man said.

Rosaleen heard his rantings as if from a distant place. Inside her, she felt dizzy, twisted, and sick. Niles had left him. He'd left because of her. He hadn't betrayed her, not really. She turned to Frank Shields, wanting to flee his office but holding herself together. He'd think she fled for the wrong reasons and she'd not give him that satisfaction.

"I'll beat you," she said quietly. "I'll win the race."

"Get out!" he shouted, but she was already walking from him. She went out into the street and halted, held onto a railing to wait for the dizziness to pass. She trembled and her knees felt as if they were suddenly made of water. A small park, a tiny oasis, beckoned from across the street. She moved toward it as if in a daze, sank down onto a small, wooden bench beside a thick-leafed elm tree. Shields's words had been flung hard at her and they were deep inside her, jeering, mocking, screaming, each one an accusing finger. There had been no betrayal on Niles's part,

not ever. She had been the false accuser, immersed in her own certainties. The shattering pain had been enveloping, shutting out all else, and the fear of more of the same had sealed her mind. But was her excuse really valid, she reflected. A murderer has his day in court, but she had refused to listen to even a single word, to open a letter, to entertain any emotion but bitter hate. She was the sinner, not the one sinned against. She had misjudged, condemned, wrapped herself in vengeance. She felt ill, a terrible pain in the pit of her stomach.

Only one thought rose up inside her. She had to find Niles. Nothing else mattered. Her stomach turned, twisted, stabbed at her. Perhaps he had left England, gone back to Boston after reading of her betrothal to Sir Ronald. She could not blame him. It would have been the final rejection, the last after all the others. A vision of him on the dock that night, his anguished eyes calling after her, rushed back over her with searing clarity. She had flung the thirty pieces of silver but she had been her own Judas. Rosaleen pushed herself from the bench, moved like a sleepwalker through the London crowds finally to reach the office. Coops and Tony looked up from a ledger as she entered, instant frowns on their faces. She called Coops into her office, first, told him of Shields's proposition and her rejection of it. Then she called in Tony and, with her voice trembling, told him what else she had learned from Shields.

"I must find Niles," she said. "When he left the last letter at Raven's Wing, did he say anything about where he was living?"

Tony shook his head. "Not where he was living, but I remember Olivia saying something about a design firm named Bowler and Green. It seems he had worked or was working for them."

"All right. It's a place to start," Rosaleen said. She closeted herself with the London Business Directory and found no firm named Bowler and Green. Feeling heavy as lead inside herself, she left the office early and went to the offices of the Architects and Interior Designers Association. A pleasantfaced woman there brought out a thick directory and thumbed through it with maddening slowness as Rosaleen clamped her fingers around the edge of her straight-backed chair.

"Yes, here it is," the woman said finally, and Rosaleen almost leapt to her feet. "Bowler and Green—Interiors. They're in Birmingham, 12 Arlington Street."

Shouting thanks, Rosaleen rushed from the office to the coach station, found that a late-morning coach went to Birmingham, and booked passage on it. Sleep was a fitful thing that night, a mixture of excitement and fear, elation and despair seething inside her. She lay awake hours thinking of the child that had never become a reality, her child, Niles's child, one more victim of her blind, embittered, unyielding hate. She would never let herself love again, she had promised at that time, when all the while she had never stopped loving. The hate was just the other side of the coin, the terrible, dark side of love. If vulnerability and pain were the price of loving, anguish without end was the price of hating.

She went to the office in the morning before catching the coach to Birmingham. Tony faced her, not ungently. "Your desk calendar says you've a dinner date with Sir Ronald tomorrow. Your fiancé, remember?" he remarked. Rosaleen stared at him, let herself sink back into her chair, the frown digging into her brow. She hadn't simply forgotten. The appointment had ceased to exist. Sir Ronald had ceased to exist. There'd been nothing but the need to find Niles. Tony's words had pushed realities back at her, the commitments she had so determinedly pursued for herself, all a result of the same bag of misunderstandings. She shook her head, as if shaking raindrops away. It was more than she could deal with now, more than she could begin to think about. She had to find Niles, first. Nothing else mattered. Nothing.

"I'll be back in time," she said to Tony, then went over a sheaf of things with Higgens and left for the coach to Birmingham. It was a painfully slow coach that stopped not only at the major stops such as Dunstan, Wolverton, Wellingborough, and Coventry, but at innumerable little towns in between. It was after six o'clock when it rolled into Birmingham. She caught a hansom and paid him extra to gallop to the offices on Arlington Street, arriving just in time to see a small, wizened man locking the door. He looked at her with some alarm as she rushed up to him breathlessly.

"Niles Brewster, I must see him," she gasped out. "Is he still inside?"

The man shook his head. "No, everyone's gone for the day," he said.

"Do you know where I can find him, where he lives?" Rosaleen pressed.

"He's got a room on Billing Street, number 33, I believe it is," the man told her. He hadn't finished his sentence before Rosaleen was out the door, flying down the few steps. A bobby gave her directions and she hurried down the streets of Birmingham. She found them oppressive, worn, cracked, with worn, unattractive mill-workers' houses jostling each other, the homes of the workmen of the Birmingham mills. Lunch-box streets, her father used to call them, where a cloak of determined ordinariness seemed to lie over everything. Billing Street was tucked away, a glorified alley between buildings that leaned over it and glowered. She found the building, a narrow structure of cracked concrete. Inside the vestibule she lighted a match to see the doorbell numbers, moved through a dark, narrow hallway that smelled of mustiness and peeling plaster. A closed door at the end bore the outlines of a number 4 that had once been tacked to it.

She halted, drew a deep breath. She had made but one decision. She'd say nothing of the child that never was, not now. There'd be time for that, another day, another place. This moment would be for happiness, not pain. Rosaleen knocked, suddenly aware that her heart was pounding more loudly, it seemed, than her fist. She waited, heard movement inside the room, and the door opened. Niles looked out at her, his shirt hanging loosely, open at the neck. His eyes frowned, seemed unable to believe what they saw. His face was thinner, more tightly drawn, but the sensitive handsomeness was unchanged, the quiet strength that reached out with its own magic. She saw his lips open, try to form words as the frown turned to astonishment. She flung herself at him, clasped her arms around his neck and clung there, heard her words come in quick bursts, tearing from her of themselves.

"Oh, God. My darling, my darling. Oh, Niles, Niles. I just found out. I just learned. Oh, my darling, what a fool I've been."

She heard him try to find words, but they dried in his throat before he could speak them and he pulled back to stare at her, disbelief still crowding his deep, dark eyes. She put a finger to his lips. "No, don't say anything. Just hold me, my love," she said. His face came closer, his lips opening, and then they were on hers and she felt the wetness of her face and the sweet hardness of his kiss. She pressed back, all their yesterdays flooding over her as if there had never been a breach until finally he stepped back again. His hands took her face and held it gently.

"So beautiful, so beautiful," he murmured. "My Rosaleen, the same as always. Oh, my love, my love," he said, and found her lips again. When he pulled away this time, he smiled down at her with a tenderness that speared her heart. "How much you must have loved me," he said softly. Her frown questioned the comment. "To have hated so much, to have been so consumed with bitterness," he said.

She closed her eyes for a moment, opened them slowly. "Not *have* loved, my darling, *still* love. There's so much I must tell you," she murmured. This time his hand went to her lips.

"After the things I must say to you," he told her, pulling her into the cramped dingy little room. She saw faded blue-flowered wallpaper, a worn sofa of deep green, and a small lamp over his drawing board where a sketch rested.

"There's no window," she frowned.

"No. It wasn't important. I'd no desire to see out into the world," he told her. She felt her heart twist, clasped him to her again. He drew her down on the small, worn sofa.

"It began a number of years ago when my father made a series of bad investments. He made the further mistake of borrowing money on them from my dear Uncle Shields. He may as well have gone to the Devil to borrow. Shields held the debt over the family ever since. When he suggested I go to Cornwall and keep an eye on Sir Mallory, he agreed he'd cancel half the debt. I saw the opportunity to take the Baxter-Mills house commission and a giant step at repaying my father's debt. But when I fell in love with my beautiful Rosaleen, I told him I'd have nothing further to do with him or his schemes. The prospect of the two commissions in Boston came up and I returned. Frank Shields was in a rage. He demanded I keep my agreement."

"When you refused he demanded payment of the debt," Rosaleen said.

Niles nodded agreement. "Full payment, plus all the years of accumulated interest charges and a list of other things he'd drawn up. I still refused, certain that the two commissions in Boston would let me have enough to pay him off. That day when you came to his home, he had called me in with new offers to have me continue for him, wonderfully splendid offers, I might add. I had just turned him down when you burst in."

"Oh, Niles, Niles, I wish I could undo everything," she said. "You lost the Boston commissions, didn't you, because you left to follow me back to Cornwall?"

He nodded, not without grimness. "Shields didn't stop trying to make me change my mind. When he saw that I absolutely refused, he insisted on payment. He even went to court, but the court allowed monthly payments on the debt. I had to take any job I could find in my field to send money back to meet his demands. And, of course, live as cheaply as possible. Thank God, it's all but paid back, now. The position with Bowler and Green is not doing what I do best, but it's been a lifesaver."

"My fault, all my fault," Rosaleen murmured. "If only I'd let you talk to me it would have all been so different."

"It's been hard," Niles said. "But nothing so hard as when I read of your betrothal in the newspapers." He reached out, his grip suddenly hard on her arms, dark fires flaring in his deep eyes. "You can't love him, Rosaleen. Not really," he said.

"He is a very fine man," Rosaleen said.

"Then you do love him?" Niles cut in. "And you've come here? You love him and yet you don't know, is that it?"

"No, my darling. I know. He is a very wonderful and understanding man, but I don't love him. I never offered love. To hurt him will be hard for me, but I've no choice now that I've found you again, now that I've learned how wrong I've been. Margaret was right. Most of it was striking back at you."

"Then you must tell him, at once," Niles said. "No more wrongs on top of wrongs, no more misunderstandings anywhere."

"Yes," Rosaleen agreed. "I've done enough hurting. This will be the last of it."

"Does anyone know you're here?" Niles asked.

"No," Rosaleen said, and he pulled her into his arms.

"Then stay the night. This will be our night, the night we found each other again, a night cut out of time," he said.

"Yes, yes, my love," she breathed. Her hands reached inside his shirt, moved along the smoothness of his chest. He rose, lifted and carried her into a room large enough only for the small cot it held. His hands were gentle, reminders of moments she never thought to find again. Slowly, he undid the little buttons at the side of her gown as his lips rested against the soft swell of her breasts. "Hurry, oh hurry," she breathed, and then his hands found the sweet dark places and she gasped out little sounds and the world was turned back, floodgates of fervor let loose until, finally, there was strength only to lay pressed against the smooth hardness of his body.

"Everything as I remembered, as it was, all the wonderfulness of you," she heard him whisper.

"And of you, my love, and of you," she replied. "But I want a real reunion, in the coteen. Only when I'm there with you beside me again will I be sure I'm not dreaming."

"Yes, in the coteen, our very own, first hiding place," he echoed.

She rose up on one elbow. "I must return to London in the morning. When can you come to Cornwall?" she asked.

He frowned in thought for a moment. "I'll be finished with this assignment by Thursday. I should give them a week's notice, at least. I can be in Cornwall a week from tomorrow ... that will be Friday." She nodded happily. "It'll not be till after dark. I'll have to take the coach and then rent a buggy in Devon."

"Come to Raven's Wing. I'll be there, waiting. We'll go to the coteen together," Rosaleen said, then pulled his face down to the enveloping softness of her breasts. His lips pulled on her and she cried out with renewed passion and the night grew long with their oneness and the world was a faraway place. Later, as she lay awake and the day stole over the drab little house, the truths held her in their grip. Life would never have been right with anyone else but Niles; it would have been nothing but going through the motions, an elaborate pretense, at best a put-together happiness. But that was all done with now. She was blessed beyond her wildest hopes, perhaps beyond what she deserved. She turned, clung to Niles for a last moment more as the clock brought the night of ecstasy to an end. He saw her off at the coach. "A week from Friday, my love," she said as he embraced her tightly. "I'll be waiting. I guess I've never stopped waiting."

She left with the taste of his lips on hers and a wonderful and special joy rode back to London with her. Coops was waiting for her when she arrived, brimming over with things to tell her. "The

Regina Clyde has been put back into the water. When work on the masts and sails is finished she'll be ready to go," he said. "We've guards around the pier twenty-four hours a day."

"Good. Keep her in Plymouth for now," Rosaleen said.

"Osborne has sent final race instructions. Starting line will be from mooring, side by side on the Royal Albert docks, down the Thames and out to sea," Coops said.

"A smart start will be important then," Rosaleen thought aloud. "First one down the Thames will be first into open water and good wind."

"Exactly," Coops said. "I've learned what ship Shields is going to use. It's the *Neptune*. She's fast enough but hard to handle. The *Regina Clyde* can beat her crew for crew."

"You'll skipper her, you know, Coops," Rosaleen said. "No one but you for this." The captain smiled, almost shyly, and left her alone to the papers waiting for her attention. She worked quickly, left at five, and went to the town house to change. A letter there from Harold Pryor informed her that he had found a buyer for the house and had concluded the sale. The amount had been deposited to her account and she was to vacate within the month. She put the letter into the small desk file. A month would be more than enough time. She'd be Mrs. Niles Brewster by then, living with Niles at Raven's Wing and a small, convenient room near the office during her London days.

She changed, bathed, and put on a simple, blue dress with postilian skirt. She tried to think about how she'd tell Sir Ronald what she had to tell him, but the words refused to sort themselves out. Only one thing was clear. There'd be no half-truths, no words aimed at self-protection, no sliding around her own unforgiveable wrongs. He deserved only total honesty. But when she arrived at his home she was still wondering how to begin, how to say the hurting words so that they carried the least amount of pain. It was he who dissolved her dilemma with one stab of acute observation.

"Something special has happened to you," he said. "I've never seen you look so radiant. You are actually shining."

This time it was she who assumed the slow, slightly rueful smile he so often held. "Yes, something special has happened," she said softly. Her hand reached out in an instinctive gesture, closed over his. "It's something I never dreamed would happen, never again, not ever," she said.

"But it did," he smiled, sitting back. "Tell me about it."

"Yes, every bit of it, the things I've never told anyone else and which only one or two people in this world know about," Rosaleen said, and she began at the very beginning, when she'd first met Niles. She left nothing out, colored none of her actions with a flattering veneer, and was unable to hold back tears when she spoke of the child, but finally she finished, her narrative ending with the trip to Birmingham only the day before. She sat back and her breath came from her in a long, harsh sigh. "That's all of it, the way it was, the way it is," she said.

"A remarkable tale, my dear. You were unsparing of yourself," Sir Ronald commented as his eyes studied her. She felt tears push at her again and leaned forward to him.

"I'm so sorry, Ronald. Hurting you is the last thing I wanted to do, and here I am doing just that. Please don't hate me too much. You are a wonderful man and I've come to care deeply about you," Rosaleen said.

He used a big, embroidered handkerchief to pat her face dry. "Hate you, my dear? Nonsense. You have given me so many pleasurable moments, so many memorable evenings, the kind I never expected to have again."

"But I made a bargain. It was all my planning and you went along with it, and now I'm breaking it. You're not bitter, hurt, or furious with me?" she asked.

His smile was the slow, gentle one she had come to know so well.

"When I'm at Sotheby's and I've been outbid for a magnificently beautiful work of art I wanted to be mine, to have, to enjoy, to be with at any hour of the day or night, I'm disappointed, saddened, even dejected sometimes, but not bitter, not furious. Those passions are for the young and for that total, all-embracing love that was never ours, never part of our agreement." He rose, pulled her to her feet with him, kept hold of her hands. "I'm so happy for you, Rosaleen. Things turn out the way they are meant to be, I'm convinced. In the morning you can inform the newspapers that though we have decided not to pursue our marriage plans, we are still the very best of friends."

"Yes, that we are indeed," Rosaleen said, and she clung to him for a final moment. "Someday soon I want Niles to meet you."

"I'd be most happy to do that," the older man said. He went to the door with her, kissed her tenderly on the forehead, and watched her drive away in the carriage. Rosaleen knew the sadness inside her would not quickly go away. And Niles would understand. She was, in so many ways, a most fortunate young woman, she concluded.

CHAPTER NINE

The days that followed were full ones. Coops spent most of his time in Plymouth overseeing preparations on the *Regina Clyde*, and Tony and Olivia went off on a well-earned vacation trip to the Scottish Highlands, so Rosaleen found herself swamped with office matters. She'd given Adelaide Winship first word of the breaking off of the engagement, a gesture which made Adelaide happy as a clam in mud. The announcement to the newspapers brought too many questioners and too many prying scribes and she refused to see anyone at all after the first day. In midweek, Edgar Osborne paid a visit to the office.

"Just to reassure you of my commitments to the winner," he said over tea, "and to pay a particular compliment to you, my dear. Standing alone, pioneering, breaking barriers, those things are all commendable. But you have done them and remained a desirable woman, and that is a special accomplishment." The sincerity of his words helped make the days hurry by. Despite all the details that came to her desk, Niles was in her thoughts from morning to night. The world had come alive again. Tomorrow was a wonderful word once more. When the week came to close, she took the coach to Cornwall, almost embarrassed at the schoolgirl excitement that had seized her. Upon arriving at Raven's Wing, she spent the late hours bubbling over with emotion to Margaret until finally it was time to turn in. Margaret gave her a small packet of the mail that had arrived during the previous ten days and she took it to her room.

Most of it was the usual household bills, tradesmen's notices, a few solicitations. But one small, square envelope had only her name and address, nothing else whatever. She opened it, stared down at the few words inside.

Mr. Duggan Bayles of Bangkok will be there the night of Friday the 16th.

"The bullion!" Rosaleen gasped aloud. She'd all but forgotten about it in the excitement of everything else, but the terse note was a reminder of her meeting in Boston. Tomorrow night, the night Niles was due to arrive. She grimaced. There was absolutely nothing she could do now. She'd have to stay till the man came and go to the coteen afterward. Perhaps it was a good sign, Niles and the man with word of the bullion coming at the same time. She pulled off her clothes, fell into bed, and slept late.

The house was quiet when she woke, only the sound of Margaret's voice singing in the kitchen to break the stillness. She rose, drew a hot bath and relaxed in it, then went down for a light lunch. "I'll fix a chicken casserole for you tonight," Margaret said. "If he's late you can just warm it up when you want it."

"Or take it with us," Rosaleen said.

"Yes, or take it with you," the older woman echoed. "The garden needs tending with Olivia not here to do it," Margaret remarked.

"Slave driver," Rosaleen said, rose, and took the basket of gardening tools outside. She was surprised at the chill in the wind and a grayness was seeping across the distant horizon as she looked toward the moors and the cliffs beyond. She'd lived too long at Raven's Wing not to know the weather signs of the Cornish coast. Rain, she grimaced, though perhaps not too much, and fog. You never knew about the fog until it came. It could sift across the moors like a tattered scarf, more annoying than anything else, or it could billow in thickly, impenetrably.

But it'd delay Niles, a little, at least, and she reconciled herself to the prospect.

By evening, when Margaret went up to her room, a light drizzle had begun to fall and the fog was heavy in patches. Rosaleen looked out the living-room bay window for a while, watching the fog move in and out, grow thicker, then lighten, then thicken again. It was wonderfully fitting, she reflected. It was just such a night when she'd first met Niles on Sopwith Road. The circle coming around on itself, she mused. Turning from the window, she made a small fire against the chill, seated herself in front of it, and hoped that Mr. Duggan Bayles would be the first to arrive. She wanted the matter done with and out of the way. If he brought assurances, hard fact, and the promise of proof, she'd listen and perhaps meet the demand, whatever it might be. Obviously, whoever had the bullion, or knew where it was, could not reach it or get it out of the country. Mr. Duggan Bayles had best be prepared to answer the questions in a believable way, she told herself as she settled down against a heavy cushion. The fire played its hypnotic role and she dozed off, half-woke, then dozed again. When she woke the next time, the fire was hardly burning.

She rose, poked it into life, looked at the old clock in the corner. It was nearing ten. She frowned, went to the window. The fog was thicker, rolling past the bay window like a moving blanket. Niles or Duggan Bayles or both ought to be arriving soon, she told herself, and sat down before the fire again. The heat curled around her, a soft siren song, and her eyelids grew heavy and she slept once more. This time when she woke it was to the soft sound of the hall clock striking midnight.

Frowning, she went to the window again. The fog continued to come in patches and the drizzle coated the glass with small raindrops. She felt a stab of anxiety but quickly put it down. The fog had delayed everyone. It was always worse along the cliffs of the shore road and perhaps it stretched deep inland. Maybe Niles had been moving through it for hours at a snail's pace. She made tea for herself, found a book and began to read. The words made absolutely no sense to her and her eyes constantly flicked up to the fog outside the bay window. She thought about the other man, Duggan Bayles. She'd no idea where he might be coming from and she recalled that sometimes, when the fog grew too heavy, coaches simply put into an inn and stayed the night. But Niles was driving a rented buggy. It wouldn't be his way to do that. He'd keep on and the anxiety came to stab at her again. She uttered a small prayer that he'd had no accident in the obscuring vapor of the fog. She took the book in hand and forced herself to concentrate on it.

She managed to fall into a sleep again before the warmth of the fire. She woke, finally, something making her sit bolt upright. Her eyes went to the window at once and she saw the faint, gray glow of day. The fog had become mist now and suddenly she heard it, the soft tapping at the front door. Rosaleen leapt to her feet, raced to the door, and pulled it open. The figure in the doorway was not Niles, but a short, slightly pudgy man with very wrinkled clothes and a fleshy face with small eyes that made him look faintly piggish. He seemed to be breathing hard.

"Rosaleen Powell?" he said between breaths.

"Yes," she answered. He glanced nervously over his shoulder, peered into the gray mist. She could see beyond his figure to the flatness of the moors in the distance, still covered by a low layer of mist.

"I'm Duggan Bayles. May we talk inside?" he said, again glancing over his shoulder.

"Please," Rosaleen said. "Where did you come from? You're hours and hours late."

"It was the fog, first," the man said, his small eyes blinking.

"First?" Rosaleen echoed.

He wiped his forehead with a large, damp handkerchief, and she noticed the wet, muddy stains along the side of his clothes. "I was on my way by horseback when what I thought was just rotten luck turned out to be the opposite," Duggan Bayles began. "My horse went lame, fell over a big rock. I figured I wasn't too far from here along the shore road and I turned off, found a farm fence and staked him there. Then I went back to the road and started walking. I guess I'd gone about half a mile when I spotted the first of them, waiting for me."

Rosaleen frowned. "You spotted who?"

"Frank Shields's bully boys, the bloody, murdering lot of them hired to lay in wait and stop me from getting to you," the man said. "I crouched, kept low, and found a gully right near the road to lay in. I was damn grateful for the fog, I'll tell you. They'd have seen me by day when the fog lifted enough, I knew, and I was wondering what to do when I got lucky again. They made a mistake."

Rosaleen felt a strange shiver go through her. She formed the words carefully. "What mistake? What kind of mistake did they make?" she asked.

"They thought another bloke that came along was me," the man said, almost proudly. Rosaleen felt her body grow rigid. She was suddenly made of ice.

"What do you mean, some other bloke?" she managed.

"A chap driving a buggy. He was moving slow through the fog and they had it easy jumping him. They figured nobody else but me would be driving through this night toward Raven's Wing," the man said.

Rosaleen felt herself sway, she tried to form words but they stuck in her throat. She swallowed, tried again. "This other man, did you see him? What did he look like?" she questioned.

"I couldn't see that. They just jumped him and ran the buggy right over the cliff so it'd look like an accident in the fog, the bloody bastards," the man said, his little eyes growing smaller. "I just stayed in my gully and kept down."

Rosaleen's fists were clenched so tight she could not open them. She seemed to be drained of blood and, once again, words came out of a dry, hoarse throat. "Take me there. Take me to where it happened," she said.

Duggan Bayles frowned at her. "What in hell for?" he said.

Her hand shot out as if it were made of quicksilver, fastened viselike around his jacket. "Take me there, damn you. *This instant,*" she screamed, her face contorted. The man shrank back, suddenly frightened at this young woman who seemed about to go out of control.

"Sure, sure, if that's what you want," he murmured. "They've gone. No harm now." He backed from the door, turned, half-stumbled, and started across the ground. Rosaleen followed, the mist still in layers over the earth, the chill drizzle coming down. He moved across the fields, onto the moors, walking quickly with a slight limp. He turned back to glance at her every few moments, saw her wild eyes boring into him, following as if she were suddenly some avenging angel. Her feet grew cold from the wet grass but she took no notice. Her lips were forming wordless prayers. They reached the road and the sea wind coming across the edge of the cliffs had almost cleared away the mist. The man turned on the road, led the way down for perhaps a mile, finally halted, glancing anxiously about.

"This is about it," he said. He turned to the moors. "There's the little gully back there," he said.

Rosaleen wasn't listening. She was running across the road, was almost at the very edge of the cliffs when she halted, shrank back, unable to make herself go closer. Her hands were coated with perspiration and her lips continued to make prayerful, imploring sounds as her eyes swept the still soft, wet ground at the edge of the cliff. She saw the marks the buggy made as it plunged over, clusters of heel prints dug in alongside. She swept the ground and saw it, a small, square billfold lying only inches from the edge. She fell on her knees, closed her eyes, and lifted her face to Heaven. A chill drizzle fell on it. Her arm reached out, as if by a power of its own, and she touched the billfold, clasped her fingers around it, brought it up to her. She stared down at the name card on the inside fold.

The sound that escaped Rosaleen's lips was not a scream, though Duggan Bayles half-fell backward in fright. It was the sound of the human heart tearing open, the sound of utter defeat, of happiness turning into ashes. It was the sound of Hell let loose, and now she took the final step, to the edge of the cliff to peer down at the crashing surf and the jagged rocks below. Part of the smashed buggy still hung onto the rocks, moving with each shower of spray that cascaded over it.

Rosaleen staggered back from the edge, swayed, and almost collapsed to the ground, but somehow, some way, she made her legs keep her upright. The man was watching her with his little pig eyes. She saw him only as a hazy figure, then forced her vision slowly to clear. Her eyes burnt into the man and she spoke with difficulty, each word torn from inside her. "The men, how do you know they were from Shields?" she asked slowly.

The pig eyes blinked and Mr. Duggan Bayles half-shrugged. "A guess. I figured they had to be," he said.

Rosaleen shook her head slowly, her eyes lighted with a strange, violet glow as if they were made of lapis lazuli. "No, you knew. You knew. Why?" she asked, each word distinct.

The man shrugged again. "I saw one of them with Shields once," he said. Inside herself Rosaleen felt a burning, towering rage. He was lying to her. Now, at this time when the world had come to an end, he was lying to her. The lie was visible in the little, uncomfortable pig eyes.

"You were going to go to Shields, too," she said. "You intended collecting a payment from me, a show of good faith, and then doing the same with Shields. That's how you knew they were from him. The minute you saw them you realized what he'd done. He wasn't taking the chance that you might tell me something important."

The man shrugged again. "Maybe I did mean to see him, too," he admitted.

"I want no information from you. I want no part of the bullion, if it even exists any longer. It's brought too much grief to too many good men. I want no part of it or you or anything to do with it. But you brought about what happened here tonight. I'm going to turn you in as an accessory to murder," Rosaleen accused. She saw his fleshy face pull itself into a snarl.

"You'll turn nobody in. I'm not letting you drag me into this," he muttered.

"*Murderer!*" she screamed at him. He moved with surprising quickness for the short thickness of his body, catapulting himself forward. Rosaleen froze, her back to the edge of the cliff as she stared transfixed at the figure rushing at her. He brought both arms up straight to strike full into her. An attempt to twist away wouldn't do more than deflect the blow and send her skittering off the edge. The onrushing shape loomed up before her and, with a cry of fury and helplessness, she dropped to the ground. His legs hit her shoulders and she sprawled backward, her head hitting the ground, half off the edge of the cliff. But she heard the scream of terror as the man's body shot over her to plunge down the cliff. The scream twisted and turned its way downward, ending abruptly, as if someone had closed a door on it.

Rosaleen pulled herself half up on one elbow, almost slipped from the edge herself, scooted back. Slowly, breathing in deep draughts of air, she peered downward. The tiny, broken figure lay across one of the rocks at the bottom of the cliff, but a few feet from the remains of the carriage, looking like a discarded doll. Rosaleen crawled backward, away from the cliff's edge, and finally pulled herself to her feet. Grayness still blanketed the land, and fine rain saturated everything. The world would never be anything else for her, she knew as she began to walk back across the moors to Raven's Wing. Margaret was up when she arrived. She took one glance at Rosaleen and urged her into the living room. In words that came out one by one, almost disconnectedly, Rosaleen told what had happened.

"Niles is dead. He's dead. Niles is dead," she kept repeating tonelessly, as if the words would somehow change their meaning. Margaret poured a glass of brandy for her and Rosaleen drank it down as if it were water. Finally she rose, her eyes burning with a strange, translucent light. She took two steps, half-spun around, and collapsed unconscious on the floor. Later, she learned how Margaret had dragged her to bed, then gotten Doc Traynor. He gave her strong sedatives, enough for two days, yet every few hours she would moan and thrash on the bed before falling asleep again. When the pills finally wore off, Tony and Olivia had returned and she found her sister crying at her bedside.

Rosaleen pulled herself together that evening, sat up, and had tea and toast with marmalade, brought on a silver tray by Margaret. Once again, it was Margaret who comforted her as best she could. "If you wait for answers, for some great wisdom, I cannot give it," the woman said. "We are not given the privilege to know why things happen as they do, to understand, to see logic and reason in events where there is none. We are given only the choice to accept, to suffer, and to carry on. Of all these, it is the last one that is most important. To carry on is to say that someday, somehow, we shall find the answers."

Rosaleen did not reply. Later, she gave orders that she wanted to be left alone. She did not leave her room for three days. No tears, though. They were dried up with the rest of her. And no profound meditations. Just the total aloneness in this time of inner preparation. Rosaleen thought about Margaret's words, wise and good words, but for somebody else. There'd be no acceptance, not as Margaret had meant the word. That implied a coming to terms with senseless evil. She'd carry on, but again not as Margaret had meant it, with a kind of brave obedience. She'd carry on for revenge, total and absolute revenge. The events already set in motion would go forward. She would destroy Frank

Shields or destroy herself. Nothing would stop her. Those were the dimensions of her world, now.

Rosaleen left her room on the fourth day. Packed and ready to take the coach to London, she paused in front of Tony. "I want you at the office day after tomorrow. You'll be in charge while Coops gets ready to skipper the *Regina Clyde*," she said.

"Good choice. I'll be there," Tony said. Rosaleen nodded, marched to the waiting carriage where Margaret sat with reins in hand. It was when they reached Bodwin that the older woman spoke to her, very cognizant of the hardness in her face.

"You learned what bitterness did to you, Rosaleen. Remember the lesson. Don't make the same mistake twice."

"No bitterness this time," Rosaleen said, and Margaret's eyes were questioning. "Just hate," Rosaleen finished.

"Be careful, Rosaleen, be careful," she heard Margaret call back as she climbed into the coach. Rosaleen wasn't really listening. Margaret was a rare and wonderful person, but Rosaleen vowed she'd listen to nothing now but the voice of revenge. Each day, each hour, each minute would be as one more thread added to a tapestry, all designed for but one thing, vengeance. When it was over, whatever the outcome, there'd be only the absolute emptiness left. And the memories. There'd be lots of time for the memories. She settled back in the seat and began plans for her arrival in London.

Coops was waiting with his news the next day. "I've moved the *Regina Clyde* to the starting berth, opposite the Shields vessel," he announced, his tone full of satisfaction. Rosaleen's frown was instant. "It's the safest place for her," Coops said. "Berthed across from Shields's ship, she's in the spotlight. He wouldn't dare try to touch her there. It'd be too crude, too obvious, and there'd be too many eyes watching, though I'm still keeping guards on board. He's unscrupulous but he's not stupid. Something happening to the *Regina* and not to his ship would be practically pointing the finger at himself."

"Yes, you're right," Rosaleen agreed. "A good move. Is she ready to go?"

"Except for provisions, she's all set. I'm going to start hand-picking a crew tomorrow," Coops said.

Rosaleen looked at the calendar on the desk. "Ten days," she murmured. "They'll be hectic, full of pressure."

"It's started already. The newspapers have been around wanting stories from you. The whole thing is seizing public interest," Coops said.

"No stories from me," Rosaleen said. "That's an absolute. You can tell them all that." Her eyes moved to the calendar again. "I've something to do now," she said. "Something personal." She left the office then, took a hansom to the London office of the Shields Shipping Lines.

"Frank Shields, please," she announced to the startled woman in the outer office. The woman backed away hurriedly, returned in a moment.

"Mr. Shields will see you. This way, please," she said.

Rosaleen brushed past her. "I remember the way," she said, and strode into the inside office. Shields was standing beside the desk, the cold eyes surveying her calmly.

"Well, this is an unexpected pleasure," he offered. "Have you had an attack of good sense?"

Rosaleen wasted no words on the man, her eyes violet aflame. "Your murderers didn't get Mr. Duggan Bayles," she said.

Shields's calm glance turned wary. "What did you say?" he asked.

"They made a mistake. They got the wrong man," Rosaleen said.

Shields stared at her, his eyes narrowing a fraction. "I don't know what you're talking about," he said thinly.

"Your murderers. They made a mistake," Rosaleen said, feeling her voice rising.

The man's face hardened. "You'd better leave," he growled.

Rosaleen heard the words fall from her lips almost in disarray. "It was Niles. He was on his way to me," she said, heard her voice break, let hate come to her rescue. "It was Niles they killed, Niles they flung over the cliff," she flung at him. For a fleeting instant, his face gave her all the admission she would ever need. For a fleeting instant, she saw shock strip away the careful veneer he wore, the ice-floe eyes widening, his jaw dropping. "Niles," she screamed. "Niles, your nephew, you bastard."

She watched the man pull the mask back over his face, his eyes narrow. "If Niles Brewster has been killed I wouldn't know about it," he said.

Rosaleen leaned forward, her eyes spearing into the cold, set face before her. "I'm going to pay you back, for Niles, for all the good men you've killed and ruined with your rotten, slimy tactics. I'm going to beat you and when I do there won't be a Shields ship carrying a toothpick within a year."

His eyes were narrow slits of ice now. "Get out. I've no time for damnfools," he rasped.

"Yes, I'll get out. There's just one thing more," Rosaleen said. Her hand came up, all her pain and rage behind the smashing blow she delivered to his face. He staggered back a step, his face beet red. Rosaleen turned, strode from the room, forcing herself not to run. Outside, she fairly flung herself into the waiting hansom and the wracking sobs convulsed her so that the carriage shook. They'd be her last tears, she vowed, her very last.

It was silent inside the office and Frank Shields sank into the leather chair, gingerly felt the side of his face. He stared at the door Rosaleen Powell had slammed shut as she strode away. She's dangerous, he told himself. She was the worst kind of dangerous, he mused, an implacable enemy. Moreover, she might just be lucky, as well. It was a combination he could not afford to take lightly. His fingers drummed on the desk, his mind racing with cold calculation. Her threat had been too full of the taste of prophecy. If he lost the race, the damned merchants would flock to her. She'd have it all her way and with her hatred, she'd indeed drive him off the seas. A few might stay with him but not for long. They were fickle as the wind. And the banks, they'd begin dealing with her then, supporting her. All he had done would simply vanish.

He wanted to be number one. It was an obsession, the man admitted silently. But she had a mission and that was by far more dangerous. He glanced at himself in the wall mirror. The redness had begun to go away along his cheek. He pressed the buzzer that summoned Hubie Irwin and Ed Stoker. The two men came in at once, took seats opposite him in respectful silence. Frank Shields let his thoughts gather themselves for a few moments longer. No cost could be spared. Rosaleen Powell had to be stopped, but not with direct moves that might backfire. He was still in the driver's seat. He had the upper hand. He could outbuy and outspend her a thousandfold. With his deposits in the important banks, his personal banking connections, he'd show the little bitch what he could do. He glanced at the two assistants, his voice coming out in a low growl.

"It's all out now. We have to move fast and think ahead, anticipate all the things she'll do and be there ahead of her. I'll close every door to her. I'll win this race before it starts. Osborne's conditions are clear. Each ship starts with its own crew and skipper. That's all of it. Once those conditions are met, the race is open to be won or lost. If a ship fails to start, it loses by default. Simple and clear."

He rose, began to pace the room, and barked specific orders as if from a rifle. When the conference ended, two hours later, and he was alone, Frank Shields sat back in his chair, confident that he had covered every contingency. Rosaleen Powell would learn that there were many ways to lose, but only one way to win.

CHAPTER TEN

Rosaleen received the note a few days later, immediately recognizing the classic, delicately curved penmanship:

> My dearest Rosaleen,
> I have just learned through a small report I noticed in one of the many newspapers I receive. I've no words to tell you how much I grieve for you. Such accidents always make the world seem a senseless place. Always, always remember, if you've any need for me, in any way, just ask. You deserve much better treatment at the hands of fate.
>
> Always,
> Ronald

Rosaleen held the letter in a trembling hand and she fought back the surge of tears. She'd not go to Ronald Aleshire, not now. But not because of any embarrassment, or not out of any false pride. She'd not go to him because she feared his kindness, the gentle wisdom, the understanding she'd find there. Those were weakening things. They could affect the towering hate that was her reason for living now, and nothing could be allowed to dilute that. She dropped the letter into the wastebasket. There'd be no diminution of the icy fury that was hers. She had to guard against that.

But the days brought more than Sir Ronald's note. She found Coops in her office one morning, waiting with his face grimly tight. "I can't get a crew," he flung the words at her at once. "I can't get a goddamn cabin boy."

Rosaleen frowned. "That's ridiculous. What do you mean, you can't get a crew?"

"Ridiculous but true," he returned.

"In God's name why not?" Rosaleen barked.

"Frank Shields. He's had his agents sign up every decent seaman on the docks," Coops said.

"Sign them up for what? He can't use a thousand men for his crew?" Rosaleen said.

"He's signed them up to stand by," Coops said, and Rosaleen heard her own sharp gasp of astonishment. The practice of signing up standby seamen was occasionally used when a line wanted to be sure of having a crew ready for a possible emergency. Usually it involved no more than a single crew.

"Everybody signed up as standbys?" Rosaleen frowned. "That'd cost a small fortune."

"Yes, but he's paying it. He has the money and he's using it," the captain said.

"But the *Regina Clyde* has a crew," Rosaleen protested.

"Come now, Miss Rosaleen. Crews are signed on for the voyage, or have you forgotten? A good skipper keeps his regulars, usually, but it's still a per-voyage agreement. And when a ship is dry-docked, even for a short period, seamen don't want to be dry-docked with her."

Rosaleen's lips were a tight line. "Get the usual crew. Offer them double wages for the race," she said.

Coops slowly shook his head. "He's anticipated that. He's paying double wages for standbys," Coops said. "He's even signed the drunks and the misfits."

"The bastard. The rotten bastard," Rosaleen hissed through lips that didn't move. "What about ports such as Plymouth, Yarmouth, Portsmouth, and Southampton?"

"Word travels fast. I was informed that he's had his agents do the same things at those places," Coops said. "Naturally, he'd assume you'd turn to the other major ports. He's playing every card, figured your every move."

Rosaleen's fists were clenched, her body trembled. "No, I'll find a way. He won't win, not this way," she said in tight strained tones. She saw a sadness come into the captain's eyes.

"He's done more," Coops said. "He's offered our three best masters fat contracts and good ships to skipper for the Shields Lines. He had one of his lackeys approach me with the same offer."

Rosaleen's eyes waited. "And?" she queried.

"I threw him out, of course," Coops said, his mouth tightening. "The others didn't."

"Their loyalty overwhelms me," Rosaleen clipped out.

"Self-preservation comes before loyalty with most men, I'm afraid, Miss Rosaleen. The facts of life," Coops said.

"The facts of disloyalty, you mean. Fire them. I don't want them on any of my ships again. We'll get other captains to take their ships, younger men," she said. "And we'll get a crew, somehow, somewhere. He can't have signed up all the seamen in England."

Coops shook his head again. "No, I'm sure I could find us a crew. He's only covered the major ports. But there's no time for it, Miss Rosaleen. There's but a week left before race time. Why, I'd spend the better part of it just traveling to places to sign up able-bodied seamen, to say nothing of getting them here. We've not time enough, dammit, and he's counted on that, too, you can be sure."

"He's counted on everything but one. I won't let him win," she said. "Leave me alone. I want to think by myself."

Coops nodded, slowly walked from the room. Rosaleen flung herself into the chair, her hands gripping the arms so tightly that she left fingernail marks in the wood. She seethed with rage and frustration and her head hurt from the intensity of her thoughts.

She sat alone, tried to see how she might overcome the cards Shields had dealt her. She only noticed that night had fallen when a sharp knock came at the door. More than thoughts about finding a crew had thundered through her head. Everything that had happened since she'd taken over the Powell Line had paraded by and not the least of it was Niles, always there, a party of everything she did and thought and felt. She looked up, her eyes red, her face drawn, as Coops poked his head into the room.

"It's late, Miss Rosaleen. You can sit here all night alone," he said gently. She nodded, pulling herself up, her head still pounding.

"I thought of a lot of things but each one of them fell apart as I examined it," Rosaleen said, "Time, Coops, time is against us. And money. I'd draw everything out of the family estate, all the personal funds, and we still couldn't outbid him, outmatch what he's doing."

Coops turned the lights out in the offices as he walked out with her. "Maybe something will come to me in bed," Rosaleen murmured. "I've heard it said that creative people often get their best ideas when falling asleep or just waking up," She paused in the London night, put her hand on the captain's arm. "But one thing you can count on, Coops," she said. "We won't go down by default, not if we have to sail with just you and me aboard."

Coops smiled with a wry sadness. "Good enough," he told her. "Maybe we won't get farther than the Cornish coast but we'll do our best."

Rosaleen suddenly felt a small tremor pulse through her and the captain frowned at her eyes as they took on a new fire. "What is it?" he asked.

"The Cornish coast," she said, her words almost whispered. Then she added, almost savagely, "I'll get a crew. I'll get a crew for you." Her hand dug into his arm. "Take me to Charing Cross. I can still get the night coach for Cornwall. Hurry, Coops, hurry."

The captain flagged down a passing hansom, got in, and waited as they stopped briefly at the town house, for Rosaleen to pack a small overnight bag. Coops eyes were still full of questions as the hansom reached the coach station.

"The men of the fishing fleets, Coops," Rosaleen said. "The men of the luggers and cutters, nickeys, nobbies, and fifies. The luggers aren't clipper ships but they know the sea and their way around a boat."

She saw Coops look dubious. "To beat a crack crew on the *Neptune* we'll need the best," he remarked.

"We need the best we can get now," Rosaleen countered. "And that's what I'm going to get for us."

"All right. Good luck," the captain said, and Rosaleen hurried to the waiting night coach for Cornwall. She didn't nod once during the long trip, her body tingling with excitement. Shields thought he'd covered all her moves, and he almost had, she conceded. But almost wasn't enough.

The coach reached Bodwin in time for her to get to Raven's Wing and catch a few hours' sleep. In the misty-gray dawn she was galloping the stallion along the beach, on the way to Gwyneth. She reached the fishing village in time to catch Abraham Evans before he put out to sea, told him she wanted to talk to all the men of all the boats out of Gwyneth. "Every second is important, Abraham," she said.

"About the race, is it?" Abraham said, his face stern. "We've read of it."

"Yes," Rosaleen said.

He nodded. "It makes things fit better," Abraham Evans said. He said no more when Rosaleen peered at him questioningly. "When we return from the fishing. At the church," he said, and stepped aboard the boat. Rosaleen watched the lugger until it cleared the breakwater, then turned away and drifted to the rows of long, empty tubs. She was there when the gippers began to gather and exchanged happy hugs and welcomes with Agnes

Walsh, Mary Kellen, Bridgit McCrory, and so many others. "So many new faces, so many younger girls," she remarked to Agnes as she was introduced to the newcomers.

"Many of those you knew have quit. They were young and pretty once, too, but this work ages a woman too fast. The years are hard," Agnes said. "But what brings you here now. We get the papers, here. We know about the race."

"That's why I've come," Rosaleen said. She touched quickly on the saliant facts.

"Well, you did right to come here. You'll find your help, I'm sure," Agnes said, and Rosaleen turned the talk to the problems of the women who worked the tubs. They were pretty much just as they were when she was one of them and Rosaleen knew the truth of their hardships. "One day it'll change for the better," she said.

"Maybe when it's too late," Agnes answered, then talk turned to lighter topics until the boats hove into view, began to enter the harbor. The fish would soon be dumped into the long vats and the work of the gippers would begin, fast hands and deft knife-blades moving until the barrels were filled, a fish a second tossed in according to its size and quality. After that, the fish would be tossed into the rousing tubs to be sprinkled with salt and stirred. It would be a while before the catches were dumped and Rosaleen walked to the church at the far end of the village. It was a simple wood church, a sailor's church with plain pine pews, unadorned, whitewashed wood walls, a simple structure with a thin steeple. One stained-glass window was cut in a circle over the door, a cross superimposed on a sailing ship. The altar had come from a defunct fancy clipper ship and the bell in the steeple from a great vessel that had foundered off the Cornish coast.

Rosaleen sat alone in the silent church until the men of the boats began to file in, still in their work clothes and oilskins as was their custom after coming into harbor. She let her eyes take in their faces that showed a lifetime of wind and salt spray,

weathered faces sturdy as oak. They filled the little church, most
of the men she knew in varying degrees of friendship. She spoke
to them in their own direct way.

"I'm in trouble and I need help," she began, focusing her gaze
on Abraham's lined face. "Money and deceit have combined to
put me without a crew. I must turn to you, my old friends here
in Gwyneth. I need sixty men and I'll pay well, double the usual
seaman's pay for the race and the time returning home. I know
that few of you have ever sailed aboard a square-rigged clipper
ship, but you'll get the hang of it under my captain, the best in the
business. Now, what say you? Who'll come out first?"

The men stayed motionless, then a few averted their eyes.
"You'll earn a good wage and it'll only be for ten days or so,"
Rosaleen pressed. The silence was broken only by an uneasy
shuffling of feet. "You know me, all of you. My word is good. I'll
advance half pay before we start, if you wish."

It was Abraham's voice that answered from the crowded
pews. "We know your word is good, Rosaleen Powell. That has
no part of it," he said.

"Then why do you hang back?" Rosaleen asked, more sharply
than she had intended. Abraham rose then and she saw the others turn to him. He spoke with a tired, heavy voice.

"There are few here who own our boats free and clear. You
know what a price the sea takes along these coasts. Boats are lost
with regularity and must be replaced. Most all need heavy repair
work during the year. Then there's the cost of replacing sails,
nets, lines, and anchors that are dragged loose. No man here has
the capital to lay out for all that. We go to the banks, most all of
us to the Seaman's and Merchant's Bank in Plymouth."

"Whose main office is in London," Rosaleen said, apprehension suddenly spiraling inside her. Abraham drew a piece of
paper from an inner pocket, unfolded it slowly.

"Every one of us received this letter early in the week. We
didn't know why it was sent or what to make of it, then. There

seemed no rhyme or reason for the sending of it. But your coming here today has given it that. Listen to what it says," Abraham told her. He lifted the paper closer to his face and began to read from it. "Mr. Abraham Evans: Please be advised that the outstanding loans on your boat with this bank were given you with the express understanding that you earn your livelihood in the coastal fishing trade. If you engage in any maritime activity other than that, such may be deemed a violation of the terms under which the loans were made and the bank will have the right to demand immediate payment of all outstanding monies. This applies also to all members of your family so engaged in the fishing trade with you."

Abraham lowered the letter, his eyes meeting Rosaleen's tight face. "As I said, it made little sense when we received it. But it does now," he told her, and Rosaleen swore inwardly. The letters were not a threat, couched in their banking language as they were, yet the message was plain enough. The maneuverings behind the letters carried but one signature—Frank Shields. He had anticipated even this move on her part and had closed the door beforehand, no detail overlooked, even to the exclusion of all family members, undoubtedly aware that most of the boats were family operated. Rosaleen swore at herself. She had underestimated his thoroughness, if not his duplicity. Yet perhaps he had acted quite logically in anticipating she might turn to the men of the Cornish fishing fleets. It was not a secret that she had lived, worked, developed friendships among them. Abraham was speaking again and she pulled away from her thoughts to listen.

"Rosaleen Powell, there's not a man here who doesn't want to help you. Yet there's not a man here who can risk losing his boat by having the bank call in their loans," she heard the fisherman say.

"I know, and I understand," Rosaleen interrupted. "I wouldn't ask you to risk your boats for me. I've been outsmarted and outmaneuvered. And maybe defeated." Rosaleen heard the words come from her lips and felt the acid bitterness in her mouth, yet the truth was undeniable. Her hopes had been turned to ashes and one more day gone by. She looked out at the solemn faces and managed a smile that held more bravery than confidence. "Thank you for coming to listen, and for being with me in your hearts. That helps more than you know," she told them, then stepped away from the altar rail and went out the side door of the little church. She hurried away, down through the wide street of Gwyneth to where she'd left the stallion tethered near the tubs. The afternoon was drawing to a close, the sun a half-sphere on the watery horizon. The gippers were just finishing for the day, cleaning up and hosing down the tubs. Agnes read her face instantly.

"Don't tell me they wouldn't do it," Agnes began. "Why, the bloody—"

"They had cause," Rosaleen interrupted the other woman's indignation. She explained briefly, saw sympathy come into Agnes Walsh's eyes.

"What will you do now, Rosaleen?" Agnes questioned, and Rosaleen could find only a helpless shrug in answer.

"If we'd a few years less on us, Margaret and I, we'd crew for you, you can bet on that," Agnes thundered, and Rosaleen hugged the older woman, then suddenly stiffened in the middle of her embrace and pulled away, her eyes staring. "What now, girl?" Agnes frowned.

"Why not?" Rosaleen asked.

Agnes's frown deepened. "Why not what?"

"The gippers, a crew of women," Rosaleen said, feeling the excitement pull at her. Her eyes swept the others at the tubs, and those closest half-turned to her at her words. Her glance went back to Agnes Walsh. "They all know the sea, they've all sailed on some kind of boat, and they're used to wind and weather and God know they're not afraid of hard work. Why not, Agnes?" Rosaleen said, excitement bubbling out of her like a new spring.

"Yes, why not, indeed!" Agnes echoed, turning to the others. "Certainly there are more than enough young as you," she added. "Mary Kellen. Bobbie, Florence Eamon, Kate Waleson, all of you, come here, now," she called. Rosaleen waited as the gippers left the long tubs and gathered around her.

"I've an offer," she began. "And an adventure. I want you to be my crew." She saw the instant frowns and disbelief pass over the faces before her. "Hear me out. You can do it. Maybe we won't make the best crew but we'll be in there fighting and that's the important thing now. You've no boats to lose to the banks. Frank Shields can't harm you in any way. Most important to you, it'll mean more money than you'll make in two months at the tubs."

"Hear, hear," someone called out.

Rosaleen paused for a moment of mental calculation, estimating what she could put together in cash and projecting income if she won. "If we win it'll mean as much as you'd make in six months at the tubs," she said, and heard the instant cheer go up.

Mary Kellen cut through the sound. "I'll sign up for that, but I've never crewed on a ship. I've never been on a clipper. I'd say that holds for most everyone here."

"You'll train, twenty-four hours a day for the next five days. I can sail and I'll have the finest of captains aboard and perhaps a handful of old-timers. We'll do it, somehow," Rosaleen said, her face suddenly flushed with enthusiasm.

"Count me in," someone called.

"Me, too," another voice echoed, and then another, and the chorus rose at once. Rosaleen saw Agnes beaming at her.

"It looks as if you have your crew, be as they may," Agnes said.

Rosaleen turned to the gippers crowding around her now. "I want this kept quiet. If anyone asks, you're sick or you've taken a vacation. Go home, pack, use duffel bags if you have them. We'll leave for London within the hour by carriage, wagon, anything you can fetch that will get us there," Rosaleen said, then waited beside Agnes as the others scurried away like so many leaves suddenly blown by the wind. She hugged Agnes again and rode back to Raven's Wing where Margaret listened to her as she packed.

"Do you honestly think you can win with that kind of crew? Do you really believe you can beat a ship sailed by a crew of top-notch, professional seamen?" Margaret asked.

"Maybe, for once, Shields will get all the bad breaks," Rosaleen said. "All I know is that I'm going to race. He's going to have to beat me at sea, not by his rotten tactics, and I'm going to try in every way I can to win."

"Good luck, my Rosaleen, I'm afraid you'll be needing a terrible lot of it," Margaret said. She drove the Whitechapel with the rig tied behind it and Rosaleen took the Stanhope. They were in Bodwin when the others arrived in a variety of carriages, a large group crowded into two flat-bed farm wagons. After a final embrace from Margaret, Rosaleen led the cavalcade out of Bodwin and onto the road to London. They'd reach Kensington Gardens after midnight and that was as she wanted it. Mary Kellen and four other young women rode in the Stanhope with her. Kathy Walson drove the Whitechapel with five passengers and the others followed single file. It was a strange caravan Rosaleen saw as she glanced back, and it would be an even stranger crew for a fine clipper ship. But a grim satisfaction filled her. Frank Shields was certain he had closed every avenue to her, and indeed he had. But she had opened up a new one, an avenue not only beyond his anticipation but beyond his wildest imaginings. And the surprises would keep coming. She'd see to that, she vowed as the strange parade made its slow way toward London.

She had slipped everyone into the town house, left them there with teakettles boiling, and drove to the rooming house where Coops lived. He answered her pounding in an undershirt, astonishment written over his usually imperturbable countenance.

"Get dressed and come to the town house," she said abruptly. "I have your crew and we must make use of every second." She turned, waited in the carriage for him. He reappeared in moments, his master's hat on his head. Reaching the town house, she led the way into the big living room where the young women, the gippers, lined the four walls and sat on the floor looking up at him. Rosaleen waved a hand in a sweeping gesture. "Your crew, Captain Coops," she announced.

Coops stared at the women, then at Rosaleen. "Is this some sort of joke?" he asked quietly of her.

"No joke at all, Captain," Rosaleen said. "I'll spell the details out for you later, but Shields managed to close another door before I reached it. But this time I opened a new one." She watched Coops let his eyes slowly travel around the room. "Most all of these girls and young women have sailed and they know boats and the sea," Rosaleen said.

"A square-rigged clipper ship is not a boat," Coops said coldly.

"Granted, but they know lines and sheets. It's not completely unfamiliar to most of them. A sail is a sail, even when it's on a square-rigger and a sheet is a sheet, a hawser is a hawser," Rosaleen countered.

Coops was shaking his head despairingly. "You have to know your sails. You've got to learn to climb the rigging. Men serve at least two years before the mast as apprentices."

"You have five days and five nights to give them a crash course," Rosaleen answered. "They'll sleep in shifts and learn in shifts. Didn't you say you could get hold of some men to help teach any newcomers?"

"Yes, Ezra Hoops and Willie Schiffer, old-timers with legs too far gone to stand a sea deck but they could teach," Coops said. Rosaleen watched his lips purse slowly. "I suppose we could spell each other in shifts, too."

"Of course," Rosaleen said. "We can do it, Coops. Look, you need a crew, able-bodied seamen, hands to pull ropes, feet to climb rigging, strong muscles to set sails. You have that in front of you, able-bodied seawomen."

Coops let his eyes narrow a fraction as Rosaleen's excitement flowed over him. "You're a very persuasive young woman, Miss Rosaleen," he murmured. "But a crew of inexperienced young women against a crackerjack professional crew? It's plain crazy."

"Yes, but we've nothing left but to be crazy," Rosaleen said. "We're going to race, dammit, and maybe we'll surprise the world as well as ourselves."

Coops shook his head but Rosaleen saw his lips come apart in a sudden grin. "It's crazy, but I haven't done anything crazy since I put on a master's cap. I guess it's about time," he said, and Rosaleen hugged him.

"Get hold of your two men. This will be a crash course. But not on the *Regina Clyde*. I don't want Shields to know anything about this. I don't want to give him a chance to pull something else. We have that old clipper beached in Seaford Bay," Rosaleen said.

"Yes, the *Arundel*," Coops cut in. "Out of the old South American trade. We talked of selling her off for scrap," he said, and his eyes narrowed as Rosaleen's thoughts caught at him. "Of course, she'd do fine for a training ship. She's rigged the same as the *Regina Clyde* and in Seaford Bay there's hardly anybody but the gulls to see us."

Rosaleen turned to the crew in the room. "Get yourselves into the wagons. Captain Coops will pick up his men and be back in a half-hour." She turned to Coops. "Right?" He nodded. "Then you'll head for Seaford Bay. You'll live, sleep, and train on the ship, and in five days and five nights you'll become the first all-girl crew to sail a square-rigged clipper ship," she told the others. She dropped her voice a tone. "But sailing won't be all of it. It's winning that will count. Godspeed to you all. I'll see you in five days from now," she said.

Coops left first, and the gippers stayed for last words, embraces, and excited chatter, but finally they filed out to where they'd left the assortment of carriages and wagons. Coops returned within the half-hour with two gray, grizzled, men who stared at the crew as if they were seeing creatures from beneath the sea. Coops introduced Rosaleen to them and they politely nodded, but their eyes stayed with the girls clambering into the wagons.

"I thought you were lying to us, Coops," Willie Schiffer said. "I take it back. It's true, and I'll be a one-legged carp."

"I see it but I don't believe it," Ezra Hoops said. "I don't know if I'll ever tell anybody what I'm about to do."

"You'll tell them and be proud of it when this is over," Rosaleen said. "I want you to give me back the best damn crew you can turn out."

"Yes, ma'am," the other said. "You just pray that we're good at miracles."

Rosaleen stepped back and watched the caravan move off through the silent, predawn streets of London. She went back into the house, pulled off her clothes, and collapsed across the bed. Fatigue won over the excitement still coursing through her and she slept.

CHAPTER ELEVEN

Rosaleen arrived at the office with her moves set in her mind and she put the first into effect at once, telling the staff that Coops had left over a disagreement with her about the race. The British, always a seafaring people, had been caught up by the prospect of the two great clipper ships racing each other across the Atlantic. Interest in the contest was reaching fever height and seats, she was told, had been sold along the banks of the *Thames* to watch the ships race out to sea. Journalists came in a steady parade to the office and Rosaleen refused to see most, letting Tony answer what few questions he could.

He held them off and only by a quick exchange of glances with her did he reassure himself that she was putting on a public face, so convincingly did she play her role. Finally Martin Arrowsmith, a particularly persistent reporter, caught her as she left the office.

"Is it true that you've been unable to get a crew together, Miss Powell?" he asked.

Rosaleen gave him only what she wanted the world to hear. "Yes, so far it's been impossible. It seems Mr. Shields has all the available seamen under contract to him," she said.

"Will you default if you can't get a crew?" the journalist pressed.

"I don't know," Rosaleen said softly. "I may have no choice. I don't know."

The interview was front-page news the following morning. "It's the last interview I'm giving," she told Tony. "From now on I'm going to be incommunicado, at the town house."

"What'll I say to them. They'll be here like a pack of hounds on a scent," Tony asked.

"Tell them I'm very upset at the turn of events. Give them enough to let them speculate that I'm folding," Rosaleen said. "But after midnight, I want you to come to report to me."

"I'll do my best," Tony said. Rosaleen left by a side door and returned to the town house after arranging for the newspapers and groceries to be delivered each day. It was but a little after midnight when Tony appeared, looking worn. "They're driving me mad. Everyone wants to know what you're doing, what options are left to you," he said.

"Just keep telling them that you don't know, that I'm in seclusion and not even talking to you," Rosaleen said. She let him out the back door and went to bed, slept fitfully, woke with the dawn. The best might simply not be good enough, she admitted silently, the stark fact a stabbing needle. One other decision formed itself. She could never sit in London and wait. The tension was curling her stomach now. She'd sail on the *Regina Clyde*. Win, lose, or founder on some shoal, she'd be there.

While London had become a place of mounting excitement and racing rumors, the quiet inlet of Seaford Bay seethed with another kind of fever. The arrangement of working, learning, and sleeping in shifts had worked, and day and night the old, beached ship rang with shouts and cries and seethed with swinging, pulling, climbing figures. On the aft deck, small groups, one after the other, recited the sails in unison over and over. "Mainsail...main lower topsail...main upper topsail...main upper topgallant...mizzen topmast staysail...mizzen topgallant staysail...mizzen lower topsail...mizzen upper topsail...mizzen royal." Then, on the foredeck, another group rotated learning the running rigging, the sheets and braces, buntlines, clewlines, and downhauls, while still others fought to ingest the spars, masts, and yardarms.

Little by little, the three hard-bitten, old seamen began to look with admiration at the young women who did everything they were told to do, who learned as fast as the best apprentice they ever had on their ships, and who stayed at it with aching muscles and torn skin. "God damn, you've got to hand it to them," Coops said to Willie Schiffer during a ten-minute break at the midnight hour. The old, beached ship lay bathed in the soft yellow glow of lantern light and, on the decks, clusters of young women sprawled to catch their breath.

"Aye, they've done well," the other man agreed. "But they're still just beginners."

"Beginners or not, they'll be a crew of sorts when we finish with them," Coops said, and rang the ship's bell to end the rest period. The night resounded with cries and shouts, and when the dawn's first pink crept into the inlet, another shift came topside to begin their shift.

In the London offices of Frank Shields, the shipping magnate stood tight-lipped before Hubie Irwin and Ed Stoker. The two younger men were being irritatingly optimistic and optimism always made Frank Shields uneasy.

"She's in hiding, I tell you. She's trying to find the guts to come out and back out," Irwin said.

"Or maybe she intends to sail a clipper ship by herself," Ed Stoker laughed.

Shields grunted harshly. "I wouldn't put that past her," he said.

"We've got it won. Relax," the other man said.

"You keep telling me that," Shields growled.

"You can believe us," Ed Stoker said. "The sailing drifters have been out fishing every day, we're informed. They got the message and turned her down. That was her last shot. She's had it."

"She's up to something," Shields grimaced. "I feel it in my bones. I don't trust that little bitch. She won't just give up, I tell you."

"There's nothing else for her to do. Without a crew, she's got to give up and she knows it. That's why she's in hiding," Hubie Irwin said.

"You damn well better be right," Shields growled, then watched the two men file from the room, contempt in his ice-floe eyes. There were but three days left before race time. There didn't seem anything Rosaleen Powell could do now. Still, they didn't have to be so goddamn smug, he sputtered inwardly as the two men disappeared from sight. The little bitch had a mission and people with missions were dangerous to the very last minute. He sat down, picked up the *Times,* whose front-page made him feel better:

THE SHY ROSALEEN

The shipping world is wondering what is keeping the usually tempestuous Rosaleen Powell hidden away. Some think she has simply seen the handwriting on the wall and cannot face losing by default. Though it's been said that she has been unable to assemble a crew, some people are wondering if that isn't simply an excuse for a fear of losing the race in a ship-to-ship contest.

Frank Shields laughed, a harsh, unmirthful sound, and tossed the newspaper away. The little fool should have taken his offer, he muttered inwardly. So to Hell with her. Despite his natural uneasiness, even he began to feel more optimistic as the next day passed. It was on the fourth day that one of his sources contacted him and, his face florid, he screamed for Irwin and Stoker. The two men hurried into the office and Shields flung a sheet of paper at them. "Read it," he bit out. Stoker and Irwin crowded together to look at the single sheet of neatly spaced writing. Their lips seemed to move in unison as they read it.

Water: 4 quarts daily	*Biscuits:* 1 lb. daily
Salt beef: 4 lbs. weekly	*Salt pork:* 3 lbs. weekly
Tinned meat: 1 lb. weekly	*Tinned vegs:* 4 oz. weekly
Split peas: 1 lb. weekly	*Rice:* 8 oz. weekly
Oatmeal: 8 oz. weekly	*Flour:* 1 lb. weekly
Marmalade: 8 oz. weekly	*Sugar:* 14 oz. weekly
Currants: 2 oz. weekly	*Beans:* 16 oz. weekly
Tea: 2 oz. weekly	*Coffee:* 4 oz. weekly
Mustard and curry powder: 2oz. weekly	
Pepper and salt: 8 oz. weekly	
Cocoa: 1 oz. weekly	
Barley: 1 lb. weekly	*Lime juice:* 2 quarts weekly

The two men looked up from the sheet of paper. "You know what it is, of course," Shields growled, his lips pulling back in a caricature of a smile.

"A provisions supply sheet per man for a crew," Stoker said. "Of course we know what it is."

Shields's fist smashed into the desk with the force of a hammer. "Yes, and it's the supply sheet put into Foster and Wrightson this morning by Rosaleen Powell," he thundered. "A supply sheet for a crew she doesn't have, you goddamn idiots. Now why would she order supplies for a nonexistent crew? Answer me, you blundering, stupid bastards."

The two men swallowed and shrugged and Shields kicked a nearby chair into the wall, knocking the legs from it. "I told you she was up to something, you morons," he shouted.

Stoker found his voice. "But she can't have a crew. We've closed every door to her. Maybe she just put it in to bug you," he said.

"No, no, not her. She's on to something, goddammit," the man barked, and slammed the desk again with his fist. "I want her watched every second from now on. I want that town house under constant surveillance and if she leaves it, I want her followed. Most of all, I want her stopped. Whatever she's trying, she has to be stopped. Get me Callax and his two friends. They'll know what to do."

Stoker swallowed again. "Yes, sir. Callax it is," he said, and hurried from the office. Hubie Irwin backed out as quickly and gracefully as he could while Frank Shields stared out of the window, his heavy hands clenching and unclenching, his lips muttering curses. He almost felt sorry for Rosaleen Powell.

The room in the town house was dark except for a lone candle. Rosaleen tore a page off the desk calendar; the fourth day had come to an end. She'd waited till the last moment to put in the provisions list, taking the risk that supplies might be short, but the clerk at Foster and Wrightson had assured her that everything would be delivered to the *Regina Clyde* by morning. The only thing not on the list had been the thirty bunk mattresses. She'd given him that order verbally and enjoyed the consternation in his young face. "Extra supply, I presume," he tried.

"Something like that," she had said, and hurried back to the town house and in through the cellar doorway. The mattresses were her very own idea, one of a number she had evolved during the last few days of waiting. Coops could not be expected to think as an amateur sailor, or as a woman. That was for her to do. She heard the clock downstairs in the hallway strike nine, and she took the small traveling bag from where she'd placed it on the chair. She blew the candle out and moved down the dark stairs, going out the back way. It was time. There was but one more thing left to do this night in London. She walked quickly, crossed the Strand and Fleet Street, and stopped before the dark and massive structure that was St. Paul's Cathedral.

She entered, made her way to a long, empty pew by a flickering candle. She knelt down and let her eyes go across the empty nave of the great cathedral and suddenly it was filled again with those who had come to mourn her father. She had been there, and her decisions had come out of that time. But they'd really been formed on the day she returned to Raven's Wing. So much had happened since then, so much of love, so much of happiness, so much of grief.

Had she ever really made a decision when she answered her father's summons to return? Had any of it ever been a decision? Or was it all simply meant to be, her life meant to come to this point, this moment. Where did the thread begin? When she went off with Colin, when she tried to turn her back on what could not be shut away? She half-shrugged. It didn't matter much now. The past had brought her to this moment. She had put on her father's mantle, and foolishly thought it had been a matter of choice. All he had built, struggled to make endure, the glory of a dream and a name, an inheritance of the heart. It all hung waiting now, resting in the shadow of the final struggle.

Rosaleen paused, whispered into the silence. "I'll try. I'll try or die," she said. "And for you, Niles, my beloved, for you." She shook the tears from her eyes as they came with unwanted insistence, rose, and walked from the cavernous, silent cathedral, a place to turn memories into hopes, hopes into promises. She went to the stable and got the buggy, then climbed into it and drove down Victoria Embankment, across Waterloo Bridge, avoiding the Royal Albert dock area. She headed directly south out of London, through Surrey in the dark night, a new moon half-hidden behind clouds. She drove steadily, had just passed into Sussex when she pulled up at a watering trough and let the horse drink. She'd some twenty miles to go to reach Seaford Bay and she'd be there with the dawn, she estimated. She didn't see the three horsemen until the first of them appeared in front of her, then one on either side of the buggy.

"Get down, Miss Powell," a low, rasping voice said.

"What do you want?" Rosaleen asked. "I've no money with me."

The man moved closer to the water trough and she saw a cadaverous face, long-nosed with a slit of a mouth. "Money? We're not here for money. We want information," he said. "We've been following you from the moment you left your fine town house."

Rosaleen felt the fear sweep through her. They wore only one man's mark, Frank Shields. She looked at the thin-faced man, shrugged, made as if to dismount, but at the last moment brought the whip out of its holder alongside the seat, slashed it over the horse's rump. The animal bolted forward and she saw the thin-faced man fall from the saddle as the horse all but knocked him aside. She thought she'd gotten free when the horseman came up from the side. He leapt, slammed into her, and she fell sideways. He seized the reins, brought the buggy to a halt, and then other hands were yanking her from the buggy. She felt the blow land with headsnapping force, followed by another, then another. The world spun away and she felt herself falling. Voices, faint, as if from a faraway place, drifted through the haze.

"Take the fancy Miss Rosaleen Powell into the barn," one voice said. "We can't have her screaming out here in the open."

Rosaleen tried to rise, tear away from the hands holding her. Another blow sent darkness closing over her. When her eyes opened, a candle flickered and she felt the hay beneath her fingers. She focused on the figure before her, the face cruel as it stared down at her. She lay in a stall inside a barn and her cape had been stripped from her, the dress torn down in front.

"Now, my dear Rosaleen Powell, you can do this the hard way or the easy way," the man rasped. "But either way you'll be telling us what we're here to find out. Why did you order a ship-load of crew's provisions?"

"I'll tell you nothing," Rosaleen hissed. The blow jarred her teeth. She tried to scream and was struck by another blow.

"Why?" the cold, cruel voice came. She refused to reply, and hands reached down, pulled at her clothes.

"Might as well enjoy myself," she heard the man rasp. "Get her legs." Rosaleen tried to twist away but felt other hands seize her ankles, pulling her forward, twisting. She screamed in pain and a hand was clapped over her mouth. The thin face loomed over her, came down atop her, pressed itself into her breasts. Her ankles were being firmly held, her legs pulled apart, and her own hands pressed deep into the hay at her back when her fingers touched wood, smooth, rounded. She pressed deeper, felt the smooth handle of a farm implement.

The man atop her was pulling, ripping aside the folds of her clothes, heaving and seeking and cursing softly. Rosaleen's fingers slid upward along the handle, halted at the sharp points of a rake. Her assailant's flesh was on her now, cold as his face, pressing, creeping forward. She got her palm under the back of the rake, clawing aside hay. As the man suddenly found her and rammed forward, her hand came up with the rake, smashing its sharp teeth into the thin face. She saw the half-dozen streaks of blood erupt, heard his scream, and he was rolling from her, clawing at his eyes and his face. The other two men still held her by the ankles, but stared at the third man, riveted by surprise. Rosaleen used the other end of the rake as a ramrod, thrusting it into the abdomen of the nearest man. He let out a gasping grunt of pain and doubled over, letting go of her ankle. She twisted free of the third man, swung the rake. He stepped back, stumbled, fell backward. She was on her feet, bringing the rake down in an overhead arc. It missed his head by inches as he rolled, scrambled to his feet, and bolted. The thin-faced man was sitting with one leg doubled under him, his head bent over, still pressing hands to his face and cursing. Rosaleen brought the rake handle down on his head with all her strength and he toppled forward to lay still.

She ran past the other man on the ground, still doubled over, hands clutching his abdomen.

Outside, she heard the sound of hooves galloping into the night. The buggy was there and she untied the horse from the fence post, climbed in, and sent the little carriage hurtling from the scene. She glimpsed the dark outlines of a cluster of farm buildings as she raced away. Even if the one who ran returned to Shields, he'd have no answers for him, and Rosaleen galloped the horse through the night with a cold satisfaction inside her.

Dawn streaked the sky with gray-pink clouds as she reached Seaford Bay and saw the old, beached ship wreathed in lantern light, looking somehow magical. She halted at the water's edge, called out, and a small dory rowed over to fetch her aboard. She didn't even speak of the failed attempt to detain her; it was unimportant now. Her eyes sought out Coops. She saw the other two men gather behind him, and from inside the hull the other girls emerged, greeted her excitedly.

"They've done all anyone could ask of them," Coops said.

"Are they a crew?" Rosaleen asked.

The captain's lips tightened. "They know their way around a ship now," he said.

"Have you wrought a miracle, Coops?" Rosaleen pressed.

His shoulders lifted. "Maybe, but it's a miracle without wings. There just wasn't enough time for anything else."

"It'll have to do," Rosaleen clipped out, then turned to the young women who had gathered across the deck. "It's time to take to the wagons. We'll go straight to the Royal Albert docks and the *Regina Clyde.* We'll get there in time to stow our things aboard and prepare for the starting gun. I expect there'll be a big crowd, most of them certain I won't be showing up at all."

Coops gestured to Willie Schiffer and Ezra Hoops. "They're sailing with us. Willie's a fine cook and Ezra can smell a new wind coming," the captain said. The two old salts looked as pleased as if they were starting their first voyage. The time to ferry everyone back to shore and into the wagons dragged, but soon the caravan was heading back to London. She took Mary Kellen with her in the buggy and gave her special instructions as they rode. When she finished, the girl nodded, a sly smile touching her lips.

"Why not? They've all the advantages. We'll need to use everything we can," Mary said. "I'll see to it. I know just who to use." Rosaleen drove on, the edge of quiet satisfaction upon her face.

It was nearly noon when the wagons reached the Royal Albert docks. Rosaleen had everyone get off. She lined up beside Coops, the others forming lines of two. "Let's go," she murmured and set off in a quick step along the dockside, turning into the quay where the two clipper ships were berthed opposite each other. The gasp of astonishment from the crowd reached her like a puff of sound from a huge balloon deflating. A smattering of applause followed, grew stronger as the column marched up the gangplank of the clipper and onto its decks. Rosaleen halted, glanced across the dock at the *Neptune*. She saw Frank Shields by the rail, staring, his jaw open. It was an expression duplicated by every man hanging onto the rigging and lining the rails. She moved to the lee rail and stared across at Shields. His mouth snapped shut and he began to laugh, a rolling, roaring sound. His men took it up and in seconds the air was filled with jeers, catcalls, and obscene remarks. Rosaleen's crew stored belongings below decks, returned, and took up positions on the rigging and on the deck. Coops had positioned himself at the wheel and Rosaleen went to the other rail, watched the small delegation of gentlemen in top hats and afternoon coats of charcoal gray march to the center of the dock.

One carried a large watch which he stared at without looking up, another held a starting pistol. One more figure detached itself from the onlookers and came forward, Edgar Osborne. He halted in the center of the dock, precisely between the two vessels, lifted his hat first to one, then the other.

"Gentlemen," he began. "And ladies," he added hastily. "The time is at hand. May the best ship win."

The starting gun was raised aloft, held steady, and the single shot rang out. Rosaleen's eyes swung around to the far rail to look across at the other ship. Mary Kellen and ten other girls clung to the rigging. As Coops shouted orders, they flung off blouses, baring breasts to the startled crew of the *Neptune*. As she had ordered, Mary had chosen those girls with the most generous, eye-catching breasts. The others were scrambling up the rigging, unfurling sails as Coops barked orders. But aboard the *Neptune,* the men stared in astonishment. She saw one sailor miss the hawser handed to him as, his stare fixed on the sight in front of him, he let the rope fall into the water. The stern of the *Neptune* swung around, but the men hadn't secured the lower mizzen sails and she crashed into the opposite dock. Over all the shouting, Rosaleen heard Frank Shields. "Bitch. Goddamn bitch," he roared. "Look alive, you goddamn fools."

But the damage was done. Lines were snarled and dropped into the water, sails pulled the wrong way as the men continued to stare, transfixed. The big clipper ship floundered, hung in stays, and slowly the shouts of Frank Shields and his officers penetrated. The men began to look to their ship, gather in lines, pay heed to their tasks.

And the *Regina Clyde* was off and running, in midriver, sails pulling well, on her way toward the open sea forty-two miles away. Rosaleen heard cheers coming from both shores as her crew moved smartly under the directions Coops and Ezra Hoops barked at them. Mary and the other girls slipped blouses back on, took their places on the ship. Coops gave the wheel to Bobbie Simmons and drifted to her side.

"Any more little tricks like that in your duffel?" he growled.

"Maybe. It worked, didn't it?" Rosaleen answered, and the captain's wry grin answered her. She looked astern. The *Neptune* was just getting into midriver. They'd have at least five miles on her when they reached the sea, Rosaleen noted, grunting happily. The ship moved smoothly and the whistles and shouts of other ships they passed on both sides of the river were music to her ears. When they finally reached the sea, Southend to the left, the Isle of Sheppey looming on the right, a good breeze was blowing and the clipper hoisted more sail, turned to move smartly through the Dover Straits, her prow pointing at the long swells of the Atlantic.

The *Neptune* was far back, her sails up also, but paying the price for the floundering start. It was after the dinner meal had been served, the ship going well under a steady breeze, that Coops came to Rosaleen as she stood on the aft deck. "Enjoy it while you can," he said gruffly.

She was defensive at once. "What does that mean? We've a great lead and the wind is holding. The girls are sailing the ship beautifully. I'd say we're in fine shape," she returned.

"They're doing better than we've any right to expect," Coops said evenly.

"But not beautifully," Rosaleen offered.

"Not beautifully. It's a hundred little things that add up in a race. It's how many seconds it takes to trim a sail, to climb out onto a yardarm, to correct a course. All the seconds add up. Look astern, Rosaleen," he said. She did so, saw the sails of their rival in the distance.

Rosaleen frowned, then her eyes widened. The sails of the following vessel seemed larger.

"They've gained on us," she said.

"Exactly. And they'll keep doing so. A race becomes a grueling contest made up of all those seconds—and stamina, experience, and years of seamanship," he said.

Rosaleen suddenly felt deflated and hated the captain for it. "You said we've the faster ship," she threw out accusingly.

"And we do," he answered. "That's the only thing that will help to balance out their crackerjack crew against us. If we can stay within reach of them, we'll be doing better than we've a right to expect."

"Have you given up the thought of winning, Coops? I haven't," Rosaleen snapped.

"No, but I'm a realist, my dear," he said. Rosaleen turned away, wanting to hear no more sober realism. Realists were important to have around, but they never made things happen. Only the wild dreamers did that, the ones who defied reason. She stood at the rail and watched the night move across the sea, a creeping black blanket turning the blue-green waters into ink. Before the light disappeared altogether, she looked back again for the other ship. Its sails were that of a ghost ship, faint grayness against the darkness behind. But they were closer and Rosaleen swore silently. She waited till the night watch came on, Arlene Cox and three of the newer girls. The ship moved steadily under the night wind and it seemed as if they were suspended in some black void, a place without end. She turned away and went down to her cabin, suddenly terribly tired. The events at the farmhouse suddenly rose up before her as she lay in the bunk, and she shuddered as she thought of the thin-faced man atop her, the cold touch of him against her flesh. Would she ever be able to respond to another man? she wondered. Would Niles always be with her, a silent lover of the mind, more satisfying than any flesh? She fell asleep as the thought drifted away.

The wind had freshened by morning. She felt it in the roll and plunge of the ship as she dressed. She hurried on deck, saw ten of the crew hanging onto the sheets of the top foresail, trying to bring it around, finally managing to do so. She went to the salt-sprayed rail, her eyes sweeping the surrounding waters. She gasped as she saw the sails of the other ship, a mile or two distant but in line with where she leaned on the rail. She glanced around at the deck, saw Coops directing a team unfurling the lower foresails while Ezra Hoops did the same with another crew at the mainsails.

As she watched, the ship was brought around, pointed higher into the wind, and Willie Schiffer served breakfast to all hands on deck. She took a mug of steaming coffee and a hot biscuit. For most of the morning, the two ships sailed in a direct line with each other, but by midafternoon Rosaleen saw the sails of the *Neptune* billowing out ahead as she bit her lips. They were pulling away, slowly, to be sure, yet pulling away. Coops had seen it also and she heard him bark orders, then watched a dozen of her crew, hair streaming out behind them in the wind, take hold of halyards as Willie Schiffer positioned himself by the captain and began to chant in a loud, deep baritone. He held a rolling rhythm as the crew pulled to the chant and Rosaleen heard the answering refrain they gave. She glanced at Coops and he smiled.

"We taught them everything during that crash course, including the old chanteys. They've made their own variations," he said, and Rosaleen returned her gaze to the foredeck, listened to the work chant drift back, Willie first, then the women's answer:

"This maid was neat and fair to view—"
   "A hoodah and a hooday—"
"Her hair was brown and her eyes were blue—"
   "A hoodah and a hooday
   Blow, crew, blow,
   blow my bullies, blow."
"I asked her if she'd take a trip—"
   "A hoodah and a hooday—"
"Down to the wharf to see my ship—"
   "A hoodah and a hooday
   Blow, crew, blow,
   blow my bullies, blow."

When the sails were secured, Willie gave them a few last lines with a broad-faced grin, adapting the words to fit the crew as he sang them out:

"Gypsies of the deep-sea trade,
　　Harken to the call.
One girl's song is ten girls' work
　　At winch or sheet or fall.
Take your time from the chanteyman,
　　All together, haul, now, haul."

When it came time to take in sails as the wind slacked off and dusk sifted across the sky, Rosaleen joined the others, hauling in lines, pulling at halyards. Just standing and watching had been making her feel helplessly out of it and nervous. All afternoon she had watched the other vessel creep ahead, still well in sight but steadily pulling away. Those little things, the seconds that add up, that Coops had spoken of, were lengthening the distance between them, and Rosaleen wanted to scream at the inexorableness of it. It was later, under a sky of diamonds, that Coops came to stand beside her at the rail.

"It's late. You'd best be getting some sleep," he said. "The eleven o'clock watch will be coming on in a few minutes."

She nodded and he saw the soberness in her face. "Maybe we'll get lucky," he said. "Maybe they'll run out of wind and we'll come up to them again. Lord knows, I've seen that often enough." He paused, gave her a sideways glance. "I was in the hold before. What are all the extra bunk mattresses for?" he asked.

"Bad weather," Rosaleen answered, and saw his frown deepen. "Many years ago, when my sister and I were only little girls, we were coming back from a trip to Greece with my father. A storm struck and he took our bunk mattresses, cut them in half, tied them onto us in front and in back. Our arms and legs were free but our bodies were protected. It worked. We were thrown around the cabin in the storm, into walls and furniture, but we escaped any serious injury. Without the strength, the muscle and toughness, our little bodies would surely have been badly hurt. I never forgot that. The members of this crew haven't the physical toughness of experienced seamen."

"Yes, only the years bring that, and, of course, the toughest bilge rat is in a bad way when a sea flings him across the deck and into a rail or a mast," Coops said, his lips pursing as he eyed Rosaleen again. "Let's hope we've no need to find out how your mattresses do," he said, leaving her. She went to her cabin to sleep in the cradling motion of the sea.

She worked with the foredeck crew all the next day and saw the *Neptune* become only a faint sail on the horizon ahead. The following day she was visible only through the glass from the lookout's nest and a suffocating feeling of helplessness swept over Rosaleen. Willie served plum duff for dinner, the dough tasty with raisins and a touch of brandy. She ate well but felt disconsolate.

"Why do they keep pulling away from us?" she asked Coops.

"How do your back and leg muscles feel?" he asked her.

"Sore," she admitted.

"The same goes for everyone aboard," he said.

"But they're working, doing their job," she protested.

"Yes, but each time they climb the rigging it's slower. It takes longer to go up and come down. It takes longer to pull in a sail. Nobody's sloughing off. Muscles wear down and their aches make you go slower," Coops said.

"Those seconds again," Rosaleen said, tight-lipped, and the captain nodded.

"They become minutes and the minutes become hours," Coops said. "Translated into wind and hull speed, it becomes miles."

Rosaleen fell into her bunk that night more tired in spirit than in body. It all seemed so utterly pointless suddenly, all the promises made, all the risks and work and the fighting back simply dissipated by the inexorable laws of sea, wind, and experience. *No,* she vowed fiercely, *it can't happen, not this way.* The realists couldn't simply push over the dreamers. Losing was one thing. Failing was another. She'd not have any part of either. She slept with the words clutched to her.

When she went on deck in the morning, Coops and Willie Schiffer were standing long-faced at the lee rail. Rosaleen went up to them, followed their gaze. In the distance, where the brilliant line of the morning sun drew itself across the water, a deep, dark expanse slowly moved in from the right.

"Weather. Bad, bad weather," Willie said. "The glass has been falling all night."

"Where's the *Neptune?*" Rosaleen asked.

"Headed east. The lookout caught a glimpse of her just as the sun came up," Coops said.

"She's going to outrun the storm?" Rosaleen offered.

"No, there'll be no outrunning this one, but he can stay on the edge of her until she blows out. He'll take a pounding, but nothing he can't ride out," Coops said.

Rosaleen felt a tiny stirring inside her. "He'll be driven off course. How far off?" she asked. Coops scanned the length of the bank of dark clouds starting to crowd the horizon.

"Four, maybe five hundred miles," he said.

The stirring inside her grew strong, took shape and purpose. "What's that in days?" Rosaleen questioned.

The man thought aloud. "He'll have to fight his way back through high seas even after the storm's over. Three days, I'd guess. But the same will go for us."

"No," Rosaleen bit out the word, saw Coops peer at her. "We're not changing course. We'll sail through. I want those three days," she said.

The man stared at her in disbelief. "You can't mean that. A storm this size can take you to the bottom," he said.

"And if it doesn't, we'll have three days on them. It's our one chance of winning. You know that as well as I do," Rosaleen countered.

"You might survive with no sails, no masts, or hardly anyone left to raise a sail. You've a crew of women, amateurs. It's mad," Coops protested.

"We're going through. Ships have survived storms before. It's the only chance left to win," Rosaleen said.

"You'd risk the lives of everyone aboard to win?" Coops flung at her.

"*Yes!*" Rosaleen thundered.

"This is an obsession," Coops said.

"No, a promise," Rosaleen snapped back. She turned to the rail, her eyes sweeping the distant storm clouds. She didn't blame Coops. He had been good, loyal, invaluable. But the promises were never his, the heritage not inside him, and the consuming hate not a part of his life. Her eyes watched the distant clouds continue to roll across the horizon, their leading edge glowing purple with the light of the sun behind them.

"You don't know what you're doing," she heard Coops's voice say. "You don't know the fury of the sea gone mad. You don't know what that is out there coming at us."

Rosaleen's eyes were violet fires as she stared at the distant clouds. Her lips curled in a strange half-smile. "I know what it is," she murmured. "The same enemy with a different face. It's injustice and evil. It's the last challenge and the last chance and I'm going to take it."

She turned to Coops, her violet eyes glowing as brilliantly as the flash of yellow that lighted the horizon. It was not Coops who answered, but Willie Schiffer, come up silently behind the captain, stepping out, a crooked grin on his weathered face.

"Hell, we came to win, didn't we?" the old sailor commented.

Rosaleen had to hold back from hugging him. "Start cutting up those bunk mattresses," she said.

"Good luck to us all," Coops said grimly. "I'll start taking in the topsails."

He called all hands on deck and in moments, the ship was a beehive of activity as everything loose was stored away, lines were fastened, halyards secured. Coops had all topsails reefed as Rosaleen supervised the tying of the mattresses on each girl, making sure their arms and legs had complete freedom of movement.

"They're not that heavy at all," Mary Kellen said. "And I do feel protected."

"That's the idea," Rosaleen said as she wrapped line around the cut-down portions sandwiching in Bobbie Simmons. Finally finished, she went to the foredeck and peered ahead. The sun had vanished and there was only grayness now with little edges of black-purple clouds in tall tiers. The wind was blowing up and the seas beginning to rise. Soon the wind was blowing white foam off the top of each wave and the water was a heaving expanse of dark gray-green and snarling white teeth. She felt hands pressing something against her, turned to see Coops putting two sections of mattress on her, tying them tight.

"You'll need them as much as the others," he said grimly, then hurried off to supervise taking another reef in the fore lower topsail. She walked across the foredeck, feeling like a circus fat lady when she noticed the ship shudder and her feet went out from under her. She landed on the deck, slid, halted herself, and regained her feet. Ezra Hoops was just finishing the lifelines along the port, starboard, and center of the ship, from bow to stern, and she grasped the nearest one as the ship lurched again. This time a crest of water broke over the rail and drenched her. As if from out of nowhere, the freshening wind became a gale and then a screaming, lashing whip. The storm, when it struck, seemed not a storm of wind and wave but a living thing, clawing and screaming, turning the world upside down.

Rosaleen made her way to where Mary Kellen and a dozen others clung in the lee of the rail, all eyes watching the sails. Another dozen girls clothed in their mattresses were poised along the opposite rail, with still other clusters at the fore and stem decks. Rosaleen saw Coops and Ezra Hoops at the wheel together. Her eyes grew wide as a green wall seemed to rise up over the rail, poise itself, then fling itself down. The ship seemed to shudder to a halt, then gather itself to plunge on. Water came from all directions now, seawater that pounded at her as if it were a giant fist. She saw Bobbie Simmons sent lurching forward, lose her grip on the lifeline. Her form catapulted across the wet deck to crash into the mainmast. Rosaleen watched her reach one hand up, grasp a halyard, cling to it, and right herself, half-sliding, half-crawling back. "Thank God for the mattress," she gasped. "I hurt, but my chest would have been caved in."

Rosaleen felt a moment of satisfaction when she heard the tearing, ripping sound and looked aloft. The mainsail and the mizzen upper topsail were shredding. Two more sails followed as the wind whistled like a wild creature of Hell. Coops yelled orders and she ran with the others to lower the sails. Jody and Barbara Hallmere tried to climb the ratlines. Rosaleen screamed as she saw the wave come over the side, tear them loose, and fling them across the decks. Others reached their limp forms first, and dragged them below decks. The ship was shuddering with each huge wave, now, dipping her bow deep into the sea, then coming up like a terrier shaking the water from itself. More sails were tearing and Coops had given up trying to get his crew to fight their way to the yardarms to reef in the rest. The ship seemed to heel flat on its side suddenly as a thousand tons of water pushed up from the port side. Rosaleen felt the lifeline torn from her grasp as she hurtled across the deck. She clasped arms over her head, bounced off the corner of the deckhouse, slammed into a bitt, and wound up catching hold of a loose halyard.

Her breath was ragged gasps and she was shaken but there was nothing broken, she realized. The sky grew so dark it seemed night had fallen. Tending to the sails seemed pointless. Holding onto life was an all-consuming task. She saw forms crash past

her along the deck, saved from death only by the protective mattresses. Her hands were raw and the salt caked her face and each
new wave battered a few more ounces of strength from her. She
managed a glimpse through the waves that swept over the ship
from all sides, saw three figures now clinging to the wheel, Coops,
Ezra Hoops, and big, rawboned Kate Holder. She looked again,
saw that Coops was tied to the wheel. As she watched, a gigantic
mountain of water rose up astern of the vessel, continued to grow
higher and higher till it blotted out the very sky. She screamed as
it crashed over the stern with a majestic fury, as if it were a giant
hand crushing a tiny toy. The ship seemed to nose halfway into
the sea, hang there. She tried to keep her hold on the lifeline, but
someone slammed into her and her aching, bleeding fingers tore
loose. She hurtled along the deck, downward to the bow still in
the water. As she hit the wet she felt the ship somehow bring its
prow up and less than six inches of clearance kept her from being
swept over the rail.

Her battered body still encased in the mattresses, she clung
in the shadow of the rail for a moment, shook water from her
eyes, peered along the ship to the stern. The wheel was a collection of splintered wood. Ezra and Kate Holder were gone, but
Coops lay across the smashed wheel, held there by the ropes that
bound him to it. She heard her sobs as she pulled herself along
the lifeline, each step a struggle against crashing waves, fighting
her way to the stern and the wheel. She glimpsed others moving
toward the same place, clinging to the other lifelines, then felt
someone close behind her.

She reached the smashed wheel and, with others helping,
Coops was loosened, then half-dragged, half-slid along the deck
to the companionway. Ellen Dodge was helping lower him below
decks and Rosaleen heard her gasped question: "Is he alive."

"Yes," Rosaleen managed. "I want him wrapped in blankets,
lain on the floor. Three of you stay with him and keep him from
rolling." The others disappeared below and Rosaleen turned back

to the ship. Ropes were hanging loose, whipping in the wind with deadly force, and the seas continued to batter the vessel. Somehow, the lower sails managed to stay in tact and they never lost complete headway though occasionally she wondered if the *Regina Clyde* would ever right herself. Rosaleen found a spot by a corner of the deckhouse, clung to the lifeline, and gasped up water as a wave blotted out the world. It was followed by another and still another in unending succession, and she heard the ship cry out in the crackling sound of wood against wood. She ignored the pain of her bloodied hands, pulled herself up, clung to the lifeline, lifted her head to meet the waves that slammed over the decks.

"No, damn you, no, no, no," she screamed into the sea and the wind, her voice whipped away, swallowed up by the malevolent fury of the storm. Rosaleen dropped to her knees, put her shoulder to the side of the deckhouse, and, sobbing wildly, uncontrollably, she pushed with all her might against the wall. "Don't stop," she cried out. "Keep going. Don't stop. Don't give in."

She had no idea how long she continued to rage and push, but finally, somehow, she stopped and had wedged herself into a spot between a fallen yardarm and the corner of the deckhouse. The lifeline had half-wrapped itself around her and she lay there in a semidaze. The day turned into night and the storm continued its ceaseless battering. Those who could had fled below decks, but many were still clinging for life on the deck. Yet the ship stayed afloat and, as if with a reluctant admission of defeat, the sea flung a few last crunching blows at it and suddenly grew calm. The new dawn came as the last of the wind went screaming away. The seas still ran high, but with large, rolling swells instead of the battering, pounding fury.

Rosaleen woke from her half-coma, aware of the change in the feel of the vessel under her. She sat up, pulled herself free of the lifelines, and crawled out of the spot where she'd been wedged. The sky glowed with an orange-pink light and she stared at the new sun that edged into the sky, then turned to gaze along the deck. It presented a debris-strewn picture, broken spars and yardarms that had torn loose and crashed, one half-hanging over the rail. Rope and torn pieces of sail formed a crazy-quilt pattern across the foredeck. She saw other figures coming to life, moving slowly. She tore the mattresses from her, wriggled free of the ropes, and started below decks, gasped out as every muscle in her body cried out in protest. Refusing to stop, she forced herself to the open companionway, made her way below. Two feet of water sloshed below decks and she made her legs move toward the nearest open cabin, saw one of the younger girls there. Two more of the crew were beside a bunk where Coops lay.

"We had to get him off the floor. The water was getting too high," one told her. Rosaleen halted beside the bunk, saw Coops open his eyes, grimace in pain, but manage a smile.

"We're still afloat," Rosaleen said. "The compass is still good, I'm sure. All we need is you."

"I've some ribs stove in, it feels like," Coops said. "But I'll be all right if I don't move about until we get to Boston and a doc." He paused. "I saw Willie Schiffer. His leg is hurting bad, but he's all right otherwise. So is Ezra. They're too tough to kill, those old sea birds. They'll do all I can do for you, now."

"Bandages all around his chest, tight enough to keep things from moving around," Rosaleen instructed the others, then returned to the deck to see Ezra Hoops examining the remains of the smashed ship's wheel.

"Good news," he called to her. "The shaft is all right. There's always an extra wheel in the hold. Get her topside and Willie and me, we'll fasten her into place on the shaft."

Rosaleen sent a half-dozen of her crew to bring up the spare wheel and assembled the others. Four were missing, swept overboard, Jody and Barbara Hallmere among them, and there were two broken arms and a fractured leg among the others.

Contusions, nasty cuts, and torn ligaments weren't even counted. They were endemic and the cleaning-up process was a slow and painful one. Rosaleen surveyed the remains of the sails. All the topmost sails hung in tatters and Willie Schiffer came up to stand alongside her after the spare wheel was in place. "The sail locker has canvas to replace the upper and lower topgallants, the fore royal, and the fore topmast staysail," he said. "That'll give us enough for steady headway."

"And it still leaves us with plenty of bare yardarms," Rosaleen said, eying the shredded bits of sail flapping in the wind. "How many days to Boston Harbor?" she asked.

The old sailor squinted up at the tattered sails. "With what we have, and if the wind holds, I'd guess three days," he said. "All you have to do is head due west and keep her sailing free."

"Good enough," Rosaleen said. "Because everyone is more than a little sore, I suggest three-hour watches." She saw the old seaman nod in agreement. She took the wheel at the start of her first watch, went below decks to visit Coops when it was over. Alone in the little cabin with him, she met his sober gaze.

"We have our three days," she said.

"And damn little canvas, I hear," he said.

"Enough," she returned.

He grunted. "You'd best hope so," he said. "Shields will be sailing with every piece of canvas up, you can bet on that." He moved, winced in pain, let his eyes find hers again with unsmiling seriousness. "I won't change my mind. You came through it but you were wrong. You were lucky."

"Lucky? Perhaps, but perhaps there was more. Perhaps the will to win, an absolute determination can be so powerful that, in some strange way, it embraces more than we can know or understand. The human will may have dimensions beyond our wildest comprehension," Rosaleen said.

"Luck," Coops murmured, and Rosaleen half-smiled, the exchange encapsulating the difference between the realists and the dreamers once again. But as she went on deck three hours later and watched the day begin to run itself out, her glance continued to flick astern, her eyes sweeping the rolling expanse of blue-green water, each time growing more annoyed with herself. She was glad when night came and closed out the world. At the end of another stint at the wheel, she went to her cabin and slept as soundly as aching muscles would permit.

Morning brought more than apprehension as she went on deck. The sails were hanging, but the wind was almost nonexistent, the kind of breeze sailors called "catspaw wind," as soft and silent as a cat's paw. Ezra was at the wheel, saw the worry lines on her face. "We're keeping headway," he said, words of scant comfort that vanished as headway ceased within the hour and the ship drifted in a lifeless ocean. Rosaleen scanned the horizon behind her, felt a sigh of relief escape her as nothing but the unbroken sea greeted her. The day grew hot, the sun baking the ship, and most everyone lay along the rail or under the small shade of the still sails. Rosaleen sat on the stern, leaned on the taffrail, and kept staring out along the glassy waters and hating herself for being suddenly so poor in spirit. She saw Willie Schiffer taking a compass reading, a chart rolled under his arm, and she hurried to him. He didn't need to wait for her question.

"We're still on course. If we can whistle up any kind of wind I still say we can make Boston Harbor before sundown tomorrow," he said.

"Then let's whistle," Rosaleen answered, and returned to her place on the stern rail. The day wore on in stillness, as though the ship and all aboard her had suddenly been put into a vacuum. Rosaleen fell asleep against the taffrail, roused herself angrily to see the sun slipping low in the sky. She glanced down the length of the ship to the bow. Nothing moved and she pulled herself to her feet and went below decks to where Coops sat propped up in the cabin. Sunlight still filtered in through the porthole.

"How do you feel?" she asked.

"Better than you do," he replied.

Rosaleen's rueful smile admitted the truth of his words. "I'm afraid," she said. "Suddenly I'm more afraid than I was in the middle of the storm."

Coops nodded in understanding. "A storm is something you can fight. It's a living thing, an enemy trying to kill you. You don't have time to do much but try to survive. It doesn't give you time to think and feel. But being becalmed at sea, that's when all your yesterdays come up to crowd around you. I've seen it where ships have drifted for weeks and men go mad."

"Weeks," Rosaleen gasped.

"That won't happen now," Coops assured her quickly. "We're not in midocean in the doldrums. We're in the path of the trade winds. They'll pick up in time."

"In time to win or in time to lose?" Rosaleen asked and the man's lips thinned and he made no reply. She poured a mug of fresh water for him and returned to the deck. The sun was a deep red ball dropping over the horizon and the air remained lifeless. Rosaleen sank down on the deck and stayed there till it was her time to take the wheel, the gesture academic, the big, spoked wheel unmoving, as still as the wind.

The night cooled the ship and the stars blanketed the sky with jewels. Rosaleen slept on the deck, rising just before dawn to go below to wash and freshen up. The door to Coops's cabin hung open and she heard the steady sounds of his breathing as he slept. The sky was beginning to lighten, tiny streaks of pink moving across the dark gray of dawn. Willie Schiffer sat beside the wheel and Rosaleen leaned against the rail, let her glance move up to the lower mainsail. She saw it puff out, blinked, and looked again, but it hung limply now. Her eyes went to the foremast and caught the foresail shake, billow for a moment. Rosaleen straightened, shot a glance at the mainmast again. The lower mainsail puffed out once more, stayed there this time. She felt the ship move, a sudden, quick darting slide forward.

"Wind!" she cried out, and saw Willie Schiffer snap awake. Other figures rose from the deck, Mary and Bobbie, Anne Towsand, and two of the younger girls, all eyes scanning the sails, and now the canvas pushed outward and the ship heeled to the starboard. The cheer rose, carried across the deck and, as if in answer, the ship picked up speed. It was not a strong wind but it was a wind and the only sails left, the lower ones, puffed out and pulled well. By noon, Willie Schiffer stood with the chart in one hand at the rail.

"Do you still think we'll be in Boston Harbor by the day's end?" Rosaleen questioned, and he nodded, glanced at the sails again, half-smiled. Rosaleen's little laugh of happy excitement ended in a strangled half-gasp as Caroline Rolaner's voice called out from high on the rigging.

"Sail astern," the cry whipped back in the new wind. Rosaleen spun around, her hands tightening on the taffrail. Her eyes found the small square of white just coming over the horizon. Her throat was suddenly dry and she shot a glance at Willie Schiffer at the wheel.

"Let's sail the ship," he growled. "Loosen the lower main topgallant," he ordered. "Give me more inner jib." Scrambling figures flew to the rigging to obey while others raced to the bow and the jib there. Rosaleen glanced up at the bare top masts where only the tattered strips of sail remained. The water swept past the hull, she saw. They were moving, but her eyes flicked astern. The square of white had grown larger. Within an hour it became the foresails of a full-rigged clipper. She'd no need to wonder about the pursuing ship and with each passing hour, the other ship grew larger. By midafternoon, she was clearly visible and running under full sail. With each passing minute, Rosaleen felt her stomach shrivel. Willie Schiffer gave the wheel to Bobbie for a moment, came to the stem to stand at the rail.

"She's coming like a damned express train," he muttered, then whirled away, strode to the main deck, and stared at the sails. "They're doing all they can do," he growled, and took the wheel. Rosaleen couldn't take her eyes from the onrushing vessel, now coming up to the port side. She could see every sail clearly, now, each one filled and pulling. She wrenched her eyes away, felt her throat constrict as she swallowed. Caroline Rolaner had taken up a position in the lookout's nest and suddenly her voice called out again.

"Land, ho!" she cried. Rosaleen ran to the starboard rail with most everyone else. Very low and very dim, the outline of land was visible. It seemed so terribly far off, the ship behind them so terribly near. Rosaleen heard a sound from the companionway that led below decks, saw Mary Kellen and another girl emerging with Coops between them. She rushed forward as Coops gained the deck, straightened up, moved to the starboard rail. Mary fetched him a high stool and he sank down on it, one hand holding the broad wood of the rail.

"I couldn't stay down there any longer, not now," he said, and his glance went back to the *Neptune*, then to Rosaleen. He made no comment, but his eyes said "I'm sorry." Rosaleen turned away, walked to the port rail, stared back at the ship that continued to gain on them. The New England shoreline had grown clearer, but she tried to measure distance and time and felt sick inside. Her fists pounded the top of the rail and she wanted to throw up, but she fought down the nausea.

Aboard the *Neptune* there was no frustration and no heart-rending dejection, but an astonishment that had erupted when they'd first spotted the *Regina Clyde's* stern in the distance. "God damn," Frank Shields had whispered. "I thought they were all in Davey Jones's locker by now." If it had been within him to admire anyone or anything he would have admired the ship and the crew that plowed through the waters toward Boston Harbor just ahead of him. But admiration was a luxury he'd never permitted himself and, as always, he substituted condescending resentment. "The little bitch. She damn near got away with it," he muttered.

"Goddamn gambler she is, that's what," he went on. He turned to his officers. "Keep those sails full, dammit," he growled.

Rosaleen felt as if she were being torn apart. One moment she peered ahead as the shoreline took shape, the next she stared astern as the other vessel drew closer and closer, and in between her eyes swept the tattered shreds that blew mockingly from the tops of the masts. Caroline Rolaner's voice rang out from the lookout's nest.

"The Minot Ledge Light," she called down.

Rosaleen's mouth grew tight. Minot Ledge Light was a mark which lay but twelve miles before Boston Harbor. She glanced back and saw the *Neptune* coming up hard off the port rail, her crew standing on the ratlines clearly visible now. Rosaleen turned to find Coops at the rail. He was staring down at the deck at his feet and Rosaleen went to him, fought down the half-sob in her throat.

"They'll pass us in minutes, won't they?" she said, not a question at all.

"Yes," the man answered, his voice tight. He continued to stare at the deck at his feet.

"What is it, Coops? Look at me. Look up," Rosaleen said.

He shook his head. "No. I won't watch them go by us, not now, not after all that's happened." Rosaleen looked up at the other ship, the bowsprit almost opposite their stern now. Those seconds that became minutes too fast, they had done it again, time translated into the equation of wind, sail, and sea.

"No sails, no speed," Rosaleen murmured softly.

"That's it," Coops said, his voice hardly audible. "You need sails to catch the wind, something, anything, a handkerchief, but a sailing ship must catch the wind."

Rosaleen stared at Coops. "If we had the sails now?" she asked, excitement leaping in her voice.

Coops continued to stare at the deck planks. "We could hold them off. We have hull speed on them," he muttered.

Rosaleen pushed away from the rail, began running down the deck. "You can look up, Coops. They're not going to pass us," she flung back. She ran to where Mary Kellen and a dozen of the others were clustered. Their hands lifted to beckon the rest and in seconds, the entire crew were gathered in a circle amidships. A half-shout rose and the circle came apart, some rushing below decks, others starting to clamber up the ratlines. They climbed to the very top where the yardarms held only the shredded bits of sail. There, under the brightness of the last of the sun, they tore off blouses, skirts, slips, petticoats. The garments were fastened to the yardarms, pinned to each other, brought down in long strips to form a sail of pink and rose and blue, a sail with edged lace and strange patterns. More garments were brought up from the bunks below, pinned together, made into a sail deep enough and wide enough to replace the topmast staysails, the main skysail, and the main royal. Quick hitches were taken at the corners, makeshift clewlines attached.

The ship became a beehive of scrambling figures and the sails of petticoats and skirts, slips and blouses, billowed out in the wind. Rosaleen had stripped off her blouse and skirt, then the pantaloons, strung them on the outer jib stay to replace the missing jib. The *Regina Clyde* lifted her prow high out of the water as the wind flung itself into the new sails. She darted forward and pulled away from the other vessel, which had almost come amidships of her. Rosaleen, the wind caressing her breasts and cool against her thighs, clung to the bottom of one of the ratlines and watched the last of the makeshift sails billow out. A spray of cold seawater flung itself high and half over her and she laughed, looked back at Coops. He had lifted his eyes, watched with darting glances as the ship opened a full length on the *Neptune*.

She swung from the ratlines, leapt down to the deck as the others descended from the top of the masts. At the wheel, Willie Schiffer was watching every movement of the petticoat sails, playing the wheel to catch every bit of speed he could, his weathered face wearing an ear-to-ear grin. Rosaleen ran to the port rail, the others following, watched the other vessel crash through the water on their heels. But it stayed there and she could hear Frank Shields shouting and cursing in his rasping, growling voice. The mouth of Boston Harbor lay ahead and small boats began to nose out from nearby coves, their skippers wide-eyed with astonishment as the great clipper ship plowed forward under sails made half of canvas and half of blouses and undergarments, skirts and petticoats, her crew hanging onto the rigging, more naked than not.

As the *Regina Clyde* raced into Boston Harbor, tugs and barges and small commercial craft gave room. Rosaleen's eyes swept the crowded edges of the harbor but it was Coops who called to her. "There, off the starboard," she heard him say, and her eyes followed his directions and she saw the small schooner, the banner hanging along her sides:

COMMITTEE BOAT LONDON-TO-BOSTON CLIPPER RACE

She glanced at the *Neptune.* The ship hung on their stern now but came no closer. Rosaleen felt her throat go dry. The *Regina Clyde* suddenly slowed perceptibly. "The wind's fallen off in the harbor," Coops called to her. Her eyes darted to the *Neptune* as it, too, slowed. And then, before her eyes, almost magically, they began to pull away from the other ship, head across the finish line. Her glance went aloft to the multicolored petticoat sails, saw them filled, billowing out and drawing.

"Light sails for light winds," she heard Coops call out, then glanced astern to see the heavy canvas on the other ship hardly bellied. "Light sails for light winds," she echoed. The ship moved on, the prow cutting over the finish line opposite the Committee boat and if anything further was said it was drowned out by the cacophony of whistles and bells and shouts. She barely heard the sharp report of the gun as it went off to signal victory. It was impossible to tell whether the din was for the winning, the sails of blouses and petticoats, or the mostly bare-busted and bare-legged crew hanging onto the rigging. She didn't care, and started across the deck. She felt herself spun around, arms encircling her, embraces and fervent hugs pressing her breath away as she managed a last command.

"Everyone goes shopping for new clothes tomorrow," she said. Till then, capes and old jackets and oilskins were dredged up from below decks. She slipped into a pea jacket and a pair of baggy oilskin trousers, made her way to where Coops stood by the rail, Willie Schiffer beside him.

"The human will. Maybe there is more to it than we know," the captain remarked softly.

"Or maybe there is justice, of sorts," Rosaleen said, and turned away. Suddenly she wanted to be alone. She went down to the dimness of the cabin as the others brought the ship to dock. She sank down onto the bunk, gazed through the porthole at the lights of Boston just beginning to come on in the dusk. It was over. The promises had been kept. Frank Shields was a defeated man whose path would only lead downward now, and that was certainly no more than fitting. But there was no sweet taste of victory, not even the pleasurable edge of triumph. She wanted to feel satisfied, the fulfillment of vows made and vows kept, but she felt only empty, utterly depleted. Perhaps because the promises had come out of too much pain. Or was it simply that victories shared only with memories are no victories at all.

Rosaleen lay down on the little bunk, her winning made of soft and silent tears.

CHAPTER TWELVE

Boston had gone mildly mad over Rosaleen and her crew and the story of how the race had been won in eight days of frantic sailing. There were parties and galas and she went through all of them, unwilling to interrupt the fabulous time the others were having. But finally the ship was left for repairs in Boston and everyone returned to London aboard another fast Powell clipper.

In London there was a royal homecoming. Edgar Osborne presented Rosaleen with the first material fruits of victory, the ten-year contract for all his trade, and Adelaide Winship had a hundred parties lined up for her. She turned all but the first few down. The time came for her crew to return to Gwyneth, to the life of the gippers, and they did so with heartfelt farewells and a substantial nest egg to rely upon.

Coops, his broken ribs treated and strapped, was well enough to go to the office and join Tony in accepting the deluge of new business, but Rosaleen wanted no more of it. "You're in charge, both of you," she told them. "I'm going to Cornwall. I want to rest, to be by myself." She took the morning coach, arrived in Cornwall by day's end. Olivia and Margaret were there and Rosaleen felt the warmth of home in their embraces. It was the only welcome that meant anything. The emptiness that had assaulted her the moment they'd crossed the finish line had only grown deeper. Rosaleen closed herself into the comfortableness of her room for the night and tried to sleep. It was an attempt no more successful there than it had been anywhere else.

She slept for an hour, perhaps two, then woke as she had every night since reaching Boston, Niles filling her thoughts, memories racing through her mind like pain-filled figures on a hellish carousel. The need to hate, to strike back, to make good her promises, these things had been her reason for existence. They were gone now. She had no reason to exist now. It was as simple as that. Exhausted physically, emptied emotionally, she was but a hollow shell and she had wanted to return here to Cornwall, the place where happiness had once reigned so completely, so overwhelmingly. She had come back not to exorcise Niles but to draw closer to him. Perhaps, in some way, to receive a silent spiritual message from him, a sign of knowing, a touching of souls. Promises kept had to be acknowledged in some way, didn't they? she asked of the night.

She tried to sleep again and only lay awake as she had for what seemed endless nights now. She was awake when dawn came. She had become great friends with dawn of late. But this dawn came in on a gray mist and Rosaleen rose at once, fought away exhaustion to dress, go downstairs, and slip out the side door. The mist rolled gray-white along the ground, and the air smelled of it, a thick dampness. She'd gone to meet Niles on so many mornings but the gray-mist ones were always special, shutting away the rest of the world. On those mornings they would walk the moors, the ghostly, silent moors and the cliffs where you could hear the thunder of the surf below but not see it through the milk-gray blanket.

Her footsteps moved across the grounds of Raven's Wing, on to where the moors stretched, the grayness embracing her, the air wet with a fine, fine drizzle. She walked, needing no path, and soon she could hear the thunder of the surf, a timeless sound. The ground rose, the sea wind coming across the top of the cliffs to push the heaviest mist away. Rosaleen moved forward, toward the edge of the cliffs, and suddenly a figure seemed to materialize, a few paces to the right, almost at the cliff edge. She saw the deep, intense eyes staring at her, the strong yet sensitive face she carried imprinted in her mind. She pressed her hands to her eyes, halted, trembled, heard the voice call to her.

"Rosaleen. Rosaleen, my love," it said. She pulled her hands from her eyes. The figure was still there, rising out of the gray mist. "Yes, Rosaleen. I am here. Come to me, my love," the voice said.

Rosaleen swayed, closed her eyes, opened them again. She didn't care anymore. Life without Niles was no life at all, the world a burnt-out place. Niles was calling to her. Perhaps he had been calling to her all along. Isn't this what she'd come back here for, to find a sign? Nothing else mattered now. She lived in emptiness. She flung herself forward, ran, arms outstretched, toward the mist-shrouded figure and the edge of the cliffs beyond. She ran with her eyes closed. She didn't want to see the wraith vanish in her arms as she moved to embrace it. She ran and suddenly she was not plunging over the cliffs. She was being held, arms encircling her, lips pressing on hers. Her eyes snapped open and her hands tightened on arms that were real. But the face before her was still Niles's face.

"Oh, God, God. I've gone mad," she cried out.

"No, no. It's real. I'm real. I'm here, alive," the voice said. The world swam away, her legs turning to water, and she felt herself collapse, then held up, shaken, and the lips were on hers again, remembered sweetness, remembered taste that was beyond disbelieving. She pulled back, stared, clasped her hands to the face before her, ran her fingers over it as a blind person examines an object.

"I'm not dreaming? I'm not seeing things?" she breathed.

"No, and you haven't gone mad," he said. He pulled her back from the edge of the cliffs, down to the mist-shrouded ground.

"I was thrown out of the carriage when they ran it off the cliff, my things scattered to the winds," he said.

"I found some of them," Rosaleen said. "But I don't believe any of this. It's all a mad dream," she said again, panic in her voice. His mouth pressed down on hers, his tongue seeking.

"Is that a dream?" he said. Rosaleen shook her head, still afraid to acknowledge the miracle lest it disappear.

"Somehow I missed hitting the rocks when I fell with the carriage or I'd have been killed. I landed in the water but the impact was bad enough. The tide carried me downshore where I lay wedged against some rocks for over a week, in a coma, I guess, too weak to move or call out. When they found me, I was taken to a local hospital. I'd no identification of any sort on me and my memory was completely gone, something like temporary amnesia, I suppose. I didn't know who I was and I couldn't make any connection with anything or anyone. Thank God they didn't give up on me. They kept giving me food and medicine and gave me plenty of rest."

"And slowly everything began to come back to you?" Rosaleen said.

"No, not slowly, just a few days ago, in fact. I woke up and suddenly it was all there. I knew who I was and what had happened. I'm told it often happens that way. They wouldn't let me go immediately, though, kept me for another two days, but that let me look through the newspapers in the hospital library and I read about you and the race and all of it."

He pulled her to him, and she didn't mind that he held her so tight she could hardly breathe. "Niles, Niles, oh, this is more than a dream come true. It's a kind of miracle," she whispered against his chest.

He pulled back, cupped her face in his hands. "The worst thing for me was when I snapped back and began to put things in place, and wondered whether you thought I'd just decided not to come to Cornwall that night. I wondered if maybe you'd gone through with your wedding in bitter anger. So, when they let me go last night I came here at once, not knowing if you'd even be here. It was too early to go knocking on doors, so I walked across the moors, as we used to do on the mornings like this one."

"Let's go to the coteen, Niles," Rosaleen said. "We seized the world there once. We'll do it again, this time for always." He lifted her, pressed his face against her breasts, and then they walked in the soft gray morning. The terrible emptiness inside her had been swept away, in its place a wonderful peace. There'd be no turning back clocks, no undoing wrongs, but one truth rose above all else. Passion was a tide, love a harbor. She had been unafraid to sail on the one to find the other and promises kept were answered. The little coteen rose up ahead of them and, in the distance, the great gabled roof of Raven's Wing. She was home.

www.ingramcontent.com/pod-product-compliance
Lightning Source LLC
Chambersburg PA
CBHW031339020726
47499CB00005B/1331